THE STARLIT RING

THE CHRONICLES OF LIRIDIN

BOOK ONE

CRESSIDA HAWTHORNE

Cover created by getcovers.com

Formatted with Vellum

To my loving and supportive partner

CHAPTER 1

The sun was bright over the crashing sea. Glittering waves burned my eyes and left dark patches in my vision. I leaned over the stone wall, and kept my gaze tilted downward so that I focused on the plants sprouting out the cliffside instead.

Spring was upon us, but snow still dotted the ground. Tiny green sprigs had only just emerged, peering cautiously out into the world as if afraid they might have misjudged the weather.

I drew my cloak tight against the wind, and wished I'd thought to bind my hair. Whipping mercilessly across my face, it worked in tandem with the sun to further obscure my vision.

Beside me, my sister Valeria shivered. "It's too cold. Let's go back inside."

"It's too noisy," I protested. But my voice was lost to the gale. Valeria smirked at me, point made.

I'd make the mistake of donning my new slippers, thinking that I wouldn't step outside at all, and that if I did, the snow would have already melted in the bright morning sun. I was wrong on both counts.

I followed Ria, reluctant to leave the view behind: an expanse of blue, snowcapped mountains whose peaks disappeared into gauzy clouds. Pale flowers dressed in jewel-green leaves appeared along the cliff walls seemingly overnight. I hadn't had time to fully appreciate them. Not when yesterday was overcast and frozen, and the sea beat itself into a frothy rage against the rocks. Nor the day before, when snowflakes whirled through the air, big as coins.

Castle Ackervail gleamed in the brilliant sunlight, its drab exterior glistening with melted snow. Moss worked its way into the crevices between stones, jagged and vivid, like a streak of green lightning.

Tall, arched windows revealed a glimpse of the chaos inside. Servants carried tables across marbled floors, while the florists placed bouquets of dainty roses and fragrant lilies, white as the snow crunching beneath my slipper.

The terrace was already decorated. Tables and benches everywhere, barrels of ale and wine ready to tap, potted plants strategically placed. In this wind, they'd be ripped to shreds. The servants must have realized this, because they'd already started hauling the pots back inside.

Tomorrow, banners of grey and gold would decorate the grounds. The royal crest, a stag wearing chainmail, would be displayed in every room. The castle would be even busier than it was today.

Even among the chaos, I'd still have to attend my morning lessons.

My forearm began to itch. I rubbed it absently, struggling to keep pace with Ria as she leapt deftly between the remaining piles of snow. Not that she needed to exercise such caution. Unlike me, she'd been smart enough to wear boots.

Guards stepped from our path. A few cast us irritated glances. "Sorry!" I cried, nearly colliding with one. Galar, I thought his name was, though I wasn't quite sure. He was new and rarely strayed from the gate. Given that I was almost never permitted to leave the grounds, I'd only met him once.

He grimaced at me, but I heard his frustrated hiss as I turned my back.

The terrace doors were oak, heavy and polished, carved with a banquet scene—tables laden with food, dancers and merrymakers, overflowing goblets. Tomorrow, the scene inside would be much the same. Most of our guests would arrive tonight (if they hadn't already), and the nearby inns were full to bursting.

The spring banquet was one of our most anticipated annual events. Now, with Princess Valeria's engagement broken, every noble bachelor in the surrounding lands would come to ogle her. Though she would not yet accept any proposals, our father most certainly meant to take this opportunity to evaluate potential suitors.

Which meant that our home was crawling with stuffy barons and stiff knights, extravagantly dressed nobles, and foreign dignitaries who looked as though they felt anything but dignified in the drafty stone hallways. Already, three vases were broken in a fight between viscounts, all brothers. It ended with bloody noses and shredded doublets, and I was relieved not to have run across them today.

Ria and I squeezed through the door, struggling beneath its weight and the fierce wind. The smell of baking bread and simmering berries greeted us. I inhaled deeply, relieved to be free of the biting wind.

"Thought you weren't supposed to be alone, princesses!" called a voice, high and merry. I turned to see Belinda standing behind us. Strands of hair snaked free from her famously tight bun, and her cheeks were ruddy with exertion. In one hand she carried a tray, in the other, a nearly empty sack of flour. Though stained, her apron was meticulously arranged around her wide hips, covering skirts that she would surely claim were her worst. Belinda would never sully her good clothes with labor as intensive as today's.

Ria rolled her eyes and gestured widely. "We aren't!"

"Yes, you are," scoffed Belinda, without malice. "Today, of all days, and you don't have a chaperone. What happened to Timin?"

We'd ditched her outside our rooms, craving snacks and freedom. Timin was recently hired. Too recently to know about the side door in Valeria's changing room, and certainly too recently to know where to look for us.

Ria shrugged.

Lowering her voice, as if we weren't surrounded by servants who could hear every word, Belinda said, "The viscounts. Remember the viscounts. Trust me, princesses, you don't want to end up alone with men like them. They think they can force a match." She paused to stare at each of us. Satisfied by our grimaces and apologetic winces, she directed us to an empty table along the wall. A massive portrait of our father, King Amonrew, loomed above, its gilded frame reminiscent of twisting vines. "Wait here. Don't wander the halls alone. I'm sure Timin will be along shortly."

Ria stomped over to the table in a huff. I traipsed along after her, shaking water from my slipper. Someone glared at me, and I winced in apology.

Right. Today was not a good day to make a mess. I made a mental note to try to avoid burdening the servants. I was more clumsy than messy, and most of the servants knew it, but the weight of that glare sagged my shoulders.

It didn't much matter that Father never allowed us to rely on the servants to clean our rooms. Much of my childhood was spent knelt beside a bucket of sudsy water, scrubbing floors and tubs like a proper maid. We mucked our horses' stalls and groomed them ourselves. Made our beds and dusted our own furniture. "Discipline matters," Father always claimed. "If you rely on the maids, you won't know how to do anything yourself, especially when it most matters."

When it most matters. A worst-case scenario where the castle had been sacked, and the help had fled or perished in battle.

Under such circumstances, there were worse things than a messy castle, but I never dared argue.

I dropped onto the bench beside Ria, sipping from a cup of water that Belinda brought over. It wasn't banquet material, just a servant's pewter cup, but it was clean, and I appreciated it all the same. Ria drank hers without complaint, looking as if she'd rather be anywhere else.

"I didn't think there'd be so many people here," I said. A lie. I'd been warned. For the first time in several years, a princess was eligible for marriage. Of course, the castle was in chaos.

I wasn't betrothed. Nor was I as desirable as Ria.

From the moment of my birth, whispers haunted the castle, doubting my parentage, my legitimacy. King Amonrew was dark-haired. My mother was fair, with hair the color of spun gold. My own hair was copper-colored and wavy, my eyes hazel. In turn, my siblings had straight, dark hair and blue eyes.

I must be the child of another man, people claimed. The daughter of a redheaded lover from another realm. My mother always disregarded these rumors and argued that my hair would darken as I aged, but it never did.

She died when I was very small, her cough worsening for months until she finally expired. Though Father tried his best to shield me from the murmurs of courtiers, I knew that there were calls for my death, too.

"The bastard princess. A future usurper," they'd say, and gesture to me, as though I couldn't hear them. Others insisted, "If she lives, the throne will cede to our enemies." As though they knew my parentage. As though they had any right to make such accusations. Even now, my hands clenched into fists whenever I thought about it.

"For fuck's sake!" Father had screamed at them one day. "She just takes after her mother! Leave the girl be! She's been through enough!"

The gossip was quelled. Father fined and eventually exiled

anyone who spread lies about my parentage. Over time, the worst of the accusations died away, although I was never really accepted by the public.

No one was dying to marry me. My prospects were grim; all stuffy old suitors who leered and talked down to me. Gripped by dread and revulsion, I begged Father to reconsider my matches. He reluctantly agreed to delay his efforts, but any relief (and subsequent gratitude) was short-lived. Just last week, I was informed that I must make peace with the idea of marriage, because my solitude wasn't to last much longer.

"They're all here to stare at me," said Ria, crossing her arms. Today, her dress was a pale pink, long sleeved, ruched at the waist. A necklace of crystal rested between her collarbones. Matching earrings shimmered in her lobes. Later, when the King realized she'd eschewed everything of value, everything that could mark her status, he'd be furious. Even her cloak was a tattered old thing, its fur lining in need of mending.

"You are the most interesting person here," I reminded her.

"Hardly," she scoffed. "I don't *do* anything interesting. Certainly nothing that warrants all this." She gestured around the room.

I shrugged. "You've plenty of hobbies. You're very pretty. The right person will find you."

But Ria shook her head. "Gambling and swordplay," she scoffed. "No one will be interested."

"Well, you like to read, too," I reminded her.

Ria groaned and slouched over the tabletop, delicate chin cupped in her pale hands. "Dull hobbies. Besides, I've no magic. I wasn't lucky like you."

A little surge of pride ran through me. "Well, I'm sure someone will find you fascinating."

"*Some*one," she groaned. "Nobody wants me for *me*."

This was the problem with royalty. Everyone felt this way. Especially when the marriages were arranged. Even couples who were now happily married went through a period where they felt as if their spouse would never like them. Or worse, that they'd never like their spouse back.

I dreaded the notion.

"We'll see," I said.

Before I could add anything else, a disgruntled Timin burst through the door, skirts flying, braid trailing behind her. The streak of grey hair at her temple looked somehow more robust, as if empowered by our absence. "There you are! How dare you—"

"We're very sorry," I interrupted, before Ria could say something that would only make the situation worse. "We won't do it again."

"Oh," said Timin, staggering to a halt before us. "I... Alright. See that this is the last time. There are too many strangers in the castle for me to feel comfortable with you roaming the halls alone." There was something in her expression that suggested she wasn't comfortable alone, either.

Guilt flashed through me. Maybe we shouldn't have left her behind.

We sat in the banquet hall eating the sliced bread, preserves, and hard cheese that Belinda brought us. We were done with lessons for the day. With two hours left before dinner, there wasn't much to do. Ordinarily, we might've gone on a short ride, or practiced fencing, but with the castle so full, it would be too much of a hassle. The training grounds were surely packed with sweaty, stinking knights and bravado bloated nobles. As badly as I might want to show off, I had no desire to listen to men coo at me like I was a tiny kitten flashing talons.

More importantly, Father forbade me from so much as lifting a sword while guests were about. The last time I practiced during banquet season, I nearly ruined our alliance with the kingdom of Marriwer, which would've stunted our textile industry. Marriwer provided most of the dyes and fabrics we used for our clothes and bedding, and probably lots of other things I hadn't considered.

The duke's hand had healed, but rumor had it that his pride was still raw where I'd pierced it.

Oh well. Perhaps he'd learned not to touch bosoms that didn't belong to him. Especially not when the owner of said bosom happened to be holding a blade.

Ria sulked, taking tiny bites of bread and sighing loudly every few minutes. I was afraid to say anything that might frustrate her further, and so grew bored quickly. Just as I thought to plead for a quick visit to the forge, where I spent my afternoons under the tutelage of the artificer, Cranz, Timin perked up, and said, "Let's review tomorrow's schedule, shall we?"

Ria and I groaned in unison.

"Oh, come now, it's important!"

"But we know the schedule," Ria complained. "We wake up, go to lessons, spend two hours getting ready, and then we go to the banquet."

"Yes, but you're missing the minutia," said Timin, with an enthusiasm that couldn't be faked. "Wake, dress, then breakfast, then lessons, then luncheon, then the baths, then dress for the banquet, then report to the king's side—Well, only Princess Ria," she stammered, remembering that I wasn't going to be spending the banquet at the king's side. Since I wasn't actively searching for a suitor, I'd be seated near the end of the table with my brothers, lost among the advisors and loyal barons, unclaimed as a seashell spat out by the sea.

I shouldn't complain. King Amonrew took care of me. I'd never felt like anything less than his daughter, even if many of his advisors argued that I couldn't possibly be. I had tutors, clothes, jewelry, my own rooms, my own horse. Even now, at the age of twenty-two, I was well-cared for.

"The minutia," Ria repeated dully. "Just what I wanted to hear."

"I want to go to the forge," I said, brushing crumbs from my skirts, and looking hopefully at Timin.

"You meant to say, '*May* I go to the forge?'" she reminded me. "It is unbecoming to forget your manners."

It did not escape my notice that Ria was never corrected or chastised, no matter what she said. As the eldest, she commanded more respect.

"*May* I go to the forge?" I sighed, swiping a piece of hair from my face.

"Yes," said Timin after a long pause. "We may visit the forge. You are not permitted to use it, however. We haven't the time for that."

"Thank you," I said, leaping to my feet. Cranz would be less than pleased to see me, but there was nowhere else for me to go. The library would be stuffed to the brim with judgmental lords and ladies. The same applied to the baths, to the gardens, to the tea rooms, and beyond.

The forge was located on the outskirts of castle grounds, a little stone building that shot plumes of grey smoke into the air. Voices shouted over the sound of pounding metal and the whooshing of the bellows.

My heart sang as I approached, breaking into a jog that left Ria and Timin struggling to keep up. Here, surrounded by metal and stone and magic, I felt most alive. I wove wards and tricks into jewels, setting them into the hilts of blades that could slice through flesh and stone alike.

I liked to experiment, which Cranz hated. I created blades that whispered words of encouragement, that would lead the wielder to water, or glow bright as the moon. I didn't want to imbue swords with the ability to wield lightning in a storm, or to burst into flame on the downstroke. Several dozen other artificers already did that.

Besides, I wasn't exactly good at creating weapons. I was better at enchanting hatpins to keep hair perfectly in place than I was at making weapons for war.

Worse, my creations eventually lost their power. No matter

what I did, the magic faded until I was left with a useless hat pin or button.

Cranz stared at us as we pushed through the doors. He wore an apron of heavy leather, and gloves that made his already large hands appear massive. Broad-shouldered and burly, he might've been attractive if his face weren't permanently red from the heat, and his hair plastered to his head with sweat. Beside him, Ronnie stopped the bellows. He waved a broad hand at me.

Ronnie was more cheerful than Cranz, but he wasn't an artificer, just a regular smith, so I didn't spend as much time with him. Still, he was the one who made sure I knew all the safety regulations, and guided me through my first clumsy, uneven daggers.

"What are you doing here?" Cranz grit out.

"Just paying you a little visit," I said, slipping past him to the work bench, where I'd left my notes. "I forgot something."

"I like the flower hilt," said Ronnie, looking over his shoulder to the stack of papers where I'd scribbled designs.

"I keep telling you, those are going to fly into the fire," Cranz grumbled, pointing at my pages with a gauntleted hand. "At least use a paperweight."

"He's right," agreed Ronnie reluctantly. "You need to remember to put those in a drawer."

"I know," I sighed. "I'm sorry. I forgot."

"Forgetting always ends poorly, Princess." Cranz shook his head. Sweat flew around him. Ria leapt backwards, right into Timin's chest. They nearly toppled right out the doors, but Ronnie lunged to steady them. Cranz glared. He didn't like *me* in his forge, and he definitely didn't like strangers. Even the king was only grudgingly tolerated, and that was probably because he paid the bills. "Fire hazard."

"Whoops," I said, watching as Ronnie led Timin and Ria out of the building. That was probably for the best. Ria had visited me here plenty of times, but she wasn't fond of the heat and noise, and the way Cranz hounded her about not standing too close to the fire.

"That can melt steel *and* bones, Your Highness," he'd snapped at her. Unaccustomed to being spoken to in such a manner, Ria would just stammer an apology and leave.

I suspected she might've had a crush on Cranz, but I didn't dare confront her. I couldn't exactly blame her for staring at him. He was too bulky and flushed for my liking, but he had a handsome face and green eyes and cleaned up nicely on the rare occasion I saw him outside the forge.

Besides, it didn't matter if she liked Cranz. He didn't like anybody, certainly not a skinny brunette princess who got in his way and acted as if she'd dropped her brain a few miles back without noticing every time he walked by.

More importantly, she was princess, and he was a blacksmith. A king's blacksmith, certainly. But a blacksmith nonetheless. If ever love blossomed between them, it would have no future. Our father would see to that.

Cranz would be lucky to keep his head.

"Ready for the banquet?" said Ronnie, reappearing. Soot was smeared across his brow.

"As I ever am," I told him.

"Ah, you love it. I've seen you. Will you be training with us in the morning?"

"Surely not," Cranz protested, stoking the fire.

"As always!" I chirped, clutching my notes to my chest.

Cranz groaned, and Ronnie laughed.

CHAPTER 2

Dinner passed uneventfully. The nobles danced and laughed, gorged themselves on food and drink until they vomited, or passed out along the benches. People paused to leer at Ria, who kept her gaze steady and her shoulders square. Sometimes she smiled, and sometimes she looked like she'd rather stab herself in the eye with a fork than pretend to be nice any longer.

So I smiled and waved for her. People smiled and waved back. I'd worked hard to cultivate my reputation as cheerful and pleasant, grateful, never causing problems. If everyone would scrutinize my motives and legitimacy, then I must do everything in my power to prove them wrong. I would not stir the pot, I would not act foolishly, and I would give them no reason to doubt me.

No less than six gentlemen, including a duke, a baron, and a prince of Mariwer asked Ria to dance. She obliged reluctantly, dragging her feet round the ballroom like they were made of anvils.

It would be worse tomorrow, when all the guests had arrived, stuffing the castle full as a creampuff. Tonight was only a taste of the drama and curiosity. Tomorrow, we would be on full display, and Ria would not get away with her antics.

I sat at the table and drank my wine, watching Ria move across the dance floor with the enthusiasm of a rag doll.

Sometimes, I wondered if she was upset that Father had called off her marriage to Prince Marius of Tocchia. There was a certain comfort in having known of her betrothed for her entire life, even if she'd only met him twice. The rumors Marius inspired were unremarkable at worst. Unlike most princes, he didn't embarrass himself with drink, or indulge in weeks-long hunting parties, or take mistresses, or anything scandalous. He was, if anything, terribly dull.

I had no intention of joining the dancefloor, and every intention of drinking and eavesdropping. My favorite bard would tragically *not* be joining our court this spring, so my sources of gossip were rather limited, and I was hungry for details. Luckily, nobles like to talk like no one is listening. Over the course of the evening, I learned that Madam Lira of Erimont was pregnant by a man other than her husband, that the Duke of Chara had gambled away nearly half the family fortune and had to be tied to a chair in the evenings to stop him from sneaking out and losing the rest of it, that little Halla and Ernie of Castle Ballantine were learning archery and accidentally shot a guard through the foot, that the trade routes to the east were blocked by the ongoing war in Galanta (I'd already overheard my father grumbling about that).

"Shame about the treaty," said someone I didn't recognize to a viscount from last night's brawl.

Viscount Alger of Denton grinned. "A shame indeed, to have an eligible princess again." He had a pale face, and perfectly styled blond hair, which looked as if it would not hold up to a night of exertion. I wondered if that was why he'd avoided the dance floor, even as he ogled my sister like a hound might a steak.

"Don't leap to conclusions," said the stranger. He had long legs and a dark blue coat. "Tocchia may yet retaliate."

Viscount Alger spun in a circle, gesturing around the room. "Retaliate, hmm? I don't see them here."

"They don't have to be here, idiot," said the stranger.

"Force is the only way," said Alger. "They've tried everything else. King Amonrew refuses to honor the agreement. They knew what would happen if they broke the treaty."

"I've heard they didn't," said the stranger, shrugging.

I'd heard this argument more than once. Blythewell was a border town. Neighboring Nemonia planned to attack, to expand their borders and cripple trade routes through the mountains. Tocchia claimed to have received early intelligence, said that they only sent soldiers because ours would not reach Blythewell in time to stop the impending invasion.

But if this was true, then why had they slaughtered so many villagers?

"Sixty people, dead," said Alger, ticking off five fingers.

Well. It might've been optimistic to assume he could count to sixty, but it was even more optimistic for him to assume he had enough fingers for it.

Alger's gaze caught mine. I looked down immediately, blushing, but he strode up to me as if I'd winked at him. "You are the bastard princess. Talina, isn't it?"

I nodded, pasting a smile on my face, careful to hide my distaste.

"Care for a dance? I notice you seem a little... neglected."

Coming from anyone else, it might've been a polite offer, but he smelled of mutton and wine. Bruises climbed along his jaw like flowering ivy. Still, I was in no position to refuse, so I extended my hand and allowed him to lead me to the dance floor. Ria caught my gaze and rolled her eyes all the way back into her head. At her side was a tall man who I thought might be the Duke of Prine. Before I could ascertain this, Alger spun me in a tight circle.

"You're quite good at this," he said, like he'd expected me to tumble over my own feet.

"I'm a princess, as you said. I've had plenty of dancing lessons."

"How strange to be a king's bastard. Tell me, does that make you royalty?"

"I'm not certain I'd ask questions like this in King Amonrew's court," I said, trying not to scowl. "I *am* a princess of Olmstead, or don't you remember?"

"Odd that he wants us to believe you're a real princess when we all know the truth," Alger mused. The music changed. Lutes and drums switched to a jaunty tune that would summon the drunks to the dance floor. "And yet, you're treated as something more. Tell me, Talina. Are you something more?"

His face was too close to mine. As I'd suspected, his hair had flopped loose over his forehead. Combined with the faint sheen of sweat across his face, he looked half-crazed.

"*Yes*," I said, with too much emphasis.

A grin spread across his face. Before he could say more, a voice sounded behind us. "Mind if I cut in?"

"Yes," snapped Alger, whirling us away from the stranger he'd spoken to only minutes before.

This was the worst part of dancing. Being passed around like an object, in close proximity to men who smelled funny and grabbed a little too hard, trod on my shoes, and acted like I wanted to be in their presence. Polite society left me trapped and nearly helpless.

I halfway hoped the stranger might cut in and rescue me from Alger, but that would leave him open to steal Ria away from her current dance partner. Whatever his intentions were, I doubted they were very good.

"Perhaps we should ask the lady," said the stranger glibly. "Would you like to dance, Princess Talina?"

Alger's grasp tightened around my middle. Panicked, I said, "Yes, please."

The stranger grinned. "If I may, Alger."

Alger let go of me so suddenly that I nearly lost my balance. "Fine," he snapped. "All yours. She's clumsy, anyway."

I swallowed a gasp, and the stranger took Alger's place, one hand grasping mine, another loose around my waist. "If I may ask your name, Your Grace?"

"Callum, Your Highness," said the stranger easily. "Of East Alberbrook."

"Ah!" I cried. I'd heard the name before, even if I didn't recognize the face. "The duke!"

"Yes," he said. "You'll have to forgive Alger. He's my second cousin—several times removed—and I'm glad of the distance, I can tell you that much."

I almost laughed, but feared that might be offensive, so I settled for a polite smile. "Oh my. He is… quite something, Your Grace."

"With all due respect, Your Highness, I believe the word you're looking for is 'rude,'" said Duke Callum. Up close, I realized he was much younger than I'd initially thought, perhaps only in his thirties.

I nearly laughed, but fell short when the back of my neck prickled uncomfortably. I glanced over Duke Callum's shoulder to see Alger drinking from a goblet, staring down my sister and her newest partner. The dance floor was filling up, leaving only about a foot of space between couples.

At least it will be easy to get lost in the crowd, I thought.

"Perhaps," I said, flashing my brightest smile.

He seemed taken aback, but his expression warmed into something genuine. Perhaps I'd misjudged him.

But I'd been warned, over and over again, that men would seek to take advantage me. There was always the possibility that someone might exploit my status. Any number of unpleasantries could unfold—kidnapping, blackmail, rape, coercion. If a new acquaintance seemed even slightly suspicious, I was to limit my interactions.

"No, I'm quite certain of it, Your Highness," said Callum. "I know the man well. He's always been a little too... aggressive, shall we say?"

The song changed, but we didn't switch partners. Alger was waiting to steal me back, and I'd take any reprieve I could get.

"And how is Alberbrook this time of year?" I asked, eager to chance the subject.

"Oh, quite lovely. Our tulip gardens have just bloomed. It's really quite fantastic, I'd highly recommend a visit if you can manage it." Callum ginned at me, then averted his gaze, as if suddenly fearing he'd overstepped. A single brown curl fell across his forehead. Hazel eyes held a depth I hadn't expected. A dimpled chin finished off a strong jawline.

Taken aback, I said, "Oh, that must be such a sight!" I hadn't expected him to be so pleasant, or so casual in his recommendation.

"Oh, it is. We've fine vineyards and the bluest lakes you've ever seen. Tell me, Your Highness, have you ever been?"

"Not since I was a child," I said wistfully. I remembered Alberbrook like something from a storybook, with towers and spires and red clay rooftops, brightly colored houses scattered along lazy rivers. When I imagined it now, after years spent in snowy Olmstead, it felt like a daydream rather than a memory.

"Well, perhaps you ought to return," said Callum, dipping his chin.

We parted ways shortly after that, though he remained my favorite partner of the night. He was by far the most amicable and hadn't panted in my ear or asked incessantly after Valeria.

I felt the weight of my father's gaze from his place upon the throne. Beside him, Queen Elberia glared into the night.

"ALGER," Valeria began, her voice barely above a hiss.

We were alone in her room. Everyone had retired for the evening, and we'd changed into our nightclothes. Ria sat at the vanity brushing her long, dark hair; I sat on the edge of her bed, rubbing the toe that the Baron of Neville trod upon during my second-to-last dance. "What did he say to you?"

"He asked after you," I said. I flopped backward onto the duvet, splaying out like a starfish. If Timin had seen me, she would've had something to say about my being unladylike. "And then he asked if the *bastard princess* received special treatment."

"What a terrible thing to say!" Ria cried, eyes narrowing, mouth shaping into a circle of disgust. "Honestly, I thought Father put those rumors to bed over a decade ago! And special treatment? What of it? He treats you no different than me." She let out an angry huff.

It wasn't an uncommon question. Plenty of men asked after my treatment. They wanted to ensure it would extend to them, should they marry me. "I believe he intends to become a suitor."

"Not from so far away," said Ria, scowling. "It's nearly a week's travel."

"I'm sure he feels it would be worthwhile for the fanfare. But I don't like him."

"You shouldn't," said Valeria scathingly. "He's incredibly creepy. Stay away from him."

"Luckily, the Duke of Alberbrook was kind enough to rescue me."

"Is that who that was?" Valeria began separating the hair at the back of her head into three parts. "I couldn't be certain. He didn't dance with me."

"He didn't?" I asked, surprised. "I thought everyone was here for you."

"Not officially," said Valeria, tucking one section of strands under another in the beginning of a braid. "Perhaps he has other motives." She caught my eye in the mirror, and I looked away.

"I assure you, Alger may see me as a backup plan, but the duke has no such intentions."

"Don't be so sure," said Valeria. "Father was watching you."

"He merely *suggested* I visit Alberbrook. He didn't offer to arrange anything. I'd think he might be a bit more insistent if he were truly interested. He didn't even ask me to bring *you*." I sat up, and pulled my hair free of its ribbons. I really ought to braid it for the night, but I would probably forget by the time I reached my own vanity. How could I possibly focus on things like hair when I had weapons to designs, books to pore over, a sister to comfort?

"Some men are more polite than others," said Valeria. She made a face. "And he's not even old."

"Neither is Alger," I said, shuddering. Alger was only one year older than I was, brash and overconfident in that way that so many noblemen were. Though I found him perfectly pleasant to look at, his presence filled my belly with snakes.

"Half of my potential suitors had a wife prior," moaned Valeria. "They're *old*."

"I thought Father meant to form an alliance with another kingdom," I said. "Surely he's not considering those ancient dukes."

"He isn't," said Valeria. "But he is considering Prince Grimon from Winton."

"Prince Grimon?" I said, aghast. As of last summer, Prince Grimon was in the market for his third wife. The last time I'd seen him, he was too frail to walk properly. What was left of his hair glinted silver as moonlight, and his hands shook fiercely as he reached for his goblet. And that was nearly seven years ago. The prince had been too poorly to travel of late. Father never sent us to neighboring kingdoms, so I hadn't seen him, nor had I heard any updates. I couldn't imagine his condition had improved. A perpetual bachelor, he was thrust into succession for the throne when both of his older brothers died in a duel, and his sister fell from a bridge. Only King Halda and Prince Grimon remained, both frail and in poor health. Almost one hundred years old now, the king was surely near to death.

"Yes," groaned Valeria, tying off her braid with a ribbon red as blood. "May I be perfectly frank with you?"

I sat up, suddenly intrigued. "Of course, sister dearest."

Valeria turned her chair to face me. The rage on her face destroyed my curiosity. A lance of worry replaced it. "I'm angry at Father for dissolving my betrothal."

Oh. I'd guessed that she was disappointed. But when the news came six months ago, she'd held her head high, listened to Father's long, rambling speech over the breakfast table, and retired to her rooms afterward. When I asked how she felt, she refused to answer.

I didn't ask again.

"I… wondered about that," I said slowly, knowing I must tread carefully if I wanted her to tell me more. "Whether you were upset."

Valeria slumped back in her chair. Her eyes closed. Long, dark lashes dusted her cheeks. "I was. I am."

"I think I understand," I said, folding my hands in my lap. "Even if you barely knew Prince Marius, you had some idea what to expect."

"I've spent my life preparing to become Prince Marius's wife. I've studied Tocchia's laws, trade routes, economy, environment. I read books about mountain survival and traversing the ocean, and why? For all of it to mean nothing!" she spat, blue eyes wide and furious. "Now I've got to learn about Winton. It's all pigs and plows and mud!"

I winced in sympathy, but couldn't help saying, "It could be worse. It could be war, or hurricanes, or deserts. And you won't have to rule beside Grimon long. I'm sure he… won't last."

"I'll still have to bear his child," grumbled Ria. "And you know what *that* means."

"Maybe you could get very, very drunk—" I began, regretting the words even as they spilled from my mouth.

Ria waved a hand dismissively. "If I get drunk, I'll kill him. And you know how that would go."

Right. Not well. "Perhaps Father will see sense."

"Father sees *alliances*," said Valeria, shoulders slumping. "My happiness is far from tantamount."

I frowned. Father doted upon Valeria more than me, and certainly more than my brothers, who spent most of their spare time training for battle, and not of their own volition. As a child I'd been unbearably jealous of Ria's pretty shoes and dresses, her books and toys. My own rooms were cold and drafty. My clothes were well-made but hardly marked me as a princess. I had a smaller selection of dolls and carved horses. And while Valeria initially resented having a little sister, she became my closest sibling, eager for someone her own age to sneak about the castle with.

But as we grew, I remained acutely aware of our differences. Even as a child, Valeria was a queen in the making, always perfectly dressed, wearing matching jewelry. Some of her necklaces were enchanted to magnify her beauty, or to prevent an arrow from piercing her skin, or to make her repulsive to anyone who might look upon her with poor intentions. Her lessons were more specific than mine, her tutors more insistent upon propriety and dignity. While I wasn't afraid of a little dirt, Valeria somehow managed to keep ivory dresses and matching boots clean. (A part of me still wasn't convinced that a maid hadn't slipped a charm into her pocket, but I've never been able to prove it.)

"Well," I said after a long pause. "He adores you. I'm sure he'll consider your happiness, if nothing else."

"I'm not so sure," mumbled Valeria. She stifled a yawn with her hand, flashing ringed fingers. "I suppose I ought to sleep," she said. "Tomorrow will be entirely too busy for my liking."

I bade her goodnight, and retired to my own chambers, where

I did not braid my hair, and instead laid in bed a long time, wondering if Father would really condemn her to a life of misery in exchange for better trade routes and a militia comprised of wayward pig farmers.

And if he'd do it to Valeria, would he also do it to me?

CHAPTER 3

I took breakfast in my room and attended my lessons in a haze.

The nobles were drunk by luncheon. Their laughter and guffawing became impossible to ignore. Servants darted about, sweaty-faced and anxious, hanging last minute decorations and hauling heaping platters to the banquet hall. The smells of baking bread, roasting meat and vegetables permeated the castle. I found myself far hungrier than usual, gobbling lunch with an enthusiasm earned me an elbow in the ribs from Valeria, and a horrified stare from Timin.

I forced myself to slow down, partly to keep the eyes of nosy noblemen off me. It would reflect poorly on the king if his daughter ate like she was starved.

Rarely did I miss a meal. My cheeks were plump, and there was a softness to my hips and bosom, but that wouldn't stop rumors from flying like rats from a dungeon.

My time in the forge was brief. Timin needed to stay with Valeria, so a guard accompanied me instead. I didn't recognize him, but he was pleasant enough, and seemed interested in watching the smiths work even as he fanned his face in the oppressive heat. His name was Bront, and he smirked whenever Cranz grumbled or swore, which was often.

Ronnie frantically packed orders of ceremonial armor for tonight's banquet. I helped him, sorting through pieces made for members of Olmstead's guard. Though I wanted to admire the precision, the way our crest was so skillfully engraved, I couldn't. There was simply no time. The rhythm of the hammer and anvil kept me company, kept me grounded even as the world outside grew louder and louder in anticipation of the banquet.

Carriages rolled through the streets, and horses whinnied. The castle grounds steadily filled with people. Most wore bright colors, radiant in the sunlight. Some sang or danced or juggled, earning a little extra coin for their troubles.

Even now, I heard distant singing. A part of me longed to join the throng, to dance freely like a regular girl, and not a princess, doomed to a night of boring, partnered dances.

"I was here all night packing," Ronnie said, carefully boxing a sword, silver and shining, enchanted to ensure that its user always struck true. The irony was not lost on me; the sword was ceremonial. The effort that had gone into its preparation was purely symbolic. And yet, it was expertly sharpened and polished. Gilded vines crawled up its pommel and wrapped around a large ruby like a picture frame. Cranz had sweated and agonized over it, working late into the evening until at last it was perfect. "Just packing."

"Wait!" I said, peering eagerly into the box. "Can I see it?"

Cranz snapped to attention, eyes narrowing. "Do not smear your fingerprints all over it."

"I just wanted to admire it," I said. "Someone needs to. The king knows almost nothing of smithing, after all."

Shaking his head, Cranz sighed, "Fine. You're right. Admire it. And don't imply that King Amonrew doesn't appreciate quality. I won't have rumors like that coming from my forge."

Bront examined the blade, too, wide-eyed and more than a little curious.

"Strikes true," said Ronnie proudly, as if he'd been its maker.

"Any soldier would kill for an enchantment like this," Bront said. "You mentioned that it was only ceremonial?"

"It is," said Ronnie, nodding.

"Are these difficult to make? I'd assume so. Hardly any exist." He barked a laugh. "Otherwise, the army would be stocked up!"

"Exhausting," groaned Cranz, wiping sweat from his brow. "The enchantments alone are dangerous to cast."

The guard turned to me, astonished. "And *you* help create these?"

"Well, I—"

"She has interesting ideas," said Cranz, turning his glare on the soldier. His voice was low, an undercurrent of frustration running through it. "I'm eager to see how her career unfolds."

"I didn't mean any offense," said Bront quickly, scowling at Cranz. "I only meant that I'm surprised—"

"*Don't* underestimate her," Cranz said, turning back to the fire, so that his broad shoulders were on full display. "I didn't spend the last two years training her for you to bumble in here and act shocked that she can swing a hammer."

I was more surprised by his outburst than Bront. In his years spent training me, Cranz never had a single nice thing to say. He wasn't cruel, exactly, but he was gruff, grumpy, and hated to be interrupted. Though he muttered under his breath often, he was far from talkative. To hear him defend me now was baffling.

My cheeks reddened. For once, I didn't know what to say. Ronnie caught my eye and laughed, like he knew something I didn't.

Bront looked between us, and took a step back, mouth shut.

After a quick wipe with a cloth, the sword disappeared back into its box.

I LEFT for the banquet free of sweat and soot. My hair was curled and tied back with soft pink ribbons. A verdant green with gold stitching clung tightly to my torso, but the long, flowing sleeves kept it relatively modest. The skirts were pleated, stitched to look like leaves. I was enamored of it, even as both Valeria and the tailor tried to talk me into something more practical.

The slippers were pointed and made from the same fabric as my dress. Their white, glittering tips that reminded me of mountain peaks. Peridot earrings dangled from my earlobes.

The string of pearls around my neck was enchanted to give the wearer better balance and fortitude, something I suspected I needed for a night of dancing. The trade-off was that I'd have to remember to eat and drink more than usual—additional fortitude would take its toll on my body.

Hidden in my pocket was a crystal obelisk, which I'd been working to enchant. It was supposed to light up the moment I entered a dark room, but so far worked intermittently, and only if I shouted at it. If I had a moment to sneak away tonight, I might try to adjust the enchantment. A secret project would give me a good excuse to disappear, if only for a few minutes.

"Could you *possibly* have embraced the theme more?" Valeria grumbled when she saw me. Her lavender dress cinched at the waist. Long silk skirts reached nearly to the floor, grazing the tops of her silver slippers. With her hair pulled into an updo, her eyelids painted a deep purple that brightened to silver at the edges, she was absolutely regal. Severe, elegant, pale. Like a swan gliding across a glass lake, ready to chase away anyone who dared do more than admire her. A crown atop her head would only complete the look.

"I like green," I said, spinning around so that my skirts whirled. I nearly crashed into Timin, who had just emerged from Valeria's rooms. "Whoops, sorry."

"It's quite alright, Princess Talina," said Timin, teetering on her heels, which were so high that even her voluminous, pink skirts couldn't hide them. "Though you ought to mind your manners. This banquet reflects on not only your father, but Princess Valeria. Besides," she lowered her voice, as if she were about to share a juicy piece of gossip over tea. "Rumor has it that there are suitors here. Not just for Princess Valeria," she added, grinning at me.

I squinted at her. Was she drunk already? Or actually excited?

Music and laughter echoed down the halls. Guests poured in from outside, welcomed by ushers dressed in suits of grey and gold. A sorceress passed by—tall and thin, with loose, flowing white hair. A silvery blue dress brought out the starlight hue of her eyes. Among the other guests, she was dazzling, ethereal. Beside her, the rest of us were no more than dying flowers, fluttering toward the banquet hall like a cloud of moths to a freshly lit candle.

I hadn't expected to see her in the castle. All the court wizards and other magical practitioners were supposed to be in the towers along our wall, ensuring good weather and magical defenses.

Not making the rest of us look like mere children playing dress up, I thought, watching her drift through the crowd gracefully as a rose petal among a pool of lily pads.

"King Amonrew wants to meet with you two before the banquet," Timin all but sang, leading us away from the throng and up the stairs. With some unease, I realized that I didn't recognize either of the soldiers opening the doors for us.

It seemed our guard had expanded of late, with new faces cropping up every day. Why? Was Father preparing for war? There hadn't been any battles or illnesses that would call for replacements. No crisis that would have killed or disabled anyone. Our enemies made no threats of late, though of course there were plenty of foreign nobles in our home right now.

Perhaps these were temporary safety measures taken for the banquet. Each year, it drew larger crowds.

But this year should've been different. After Father ended our alliance with Tocchia, I expected that some neighboring kingdoms might protest the banquet. And yet, every invitation was accepted, except for the ones sent to Blair, Tocchia's closest allies.

No one from Tocchia would attend, which was hardly unusual. The mountain pass was treacherous this time of year, and the kingdom often sent gifts in their absence. Crops, gold, crystal vases threaded with green and blue veins (which I begged and pleaded for as a child, thinking they'd look magnificent stuffed full of pink peonies), finely embroidered fabrics, jewelry.

It would be a lie to claim that I did not miss their annual offerings. Even if I rarely got to keep anything, it was still a joy to see the horses and carts winding their way up the mountain. With Ria and my other siblings at my side, we'd sort through the offerings.

Ria, Timin, and I continued down the hall. The guards outside my father's chambers were familiar. Hax and Larry had worked in the castle for nigh on a decade now. My shoulders relaxed at the sight of them. Good. Maybe everything was alright after all.

Besides, it wasn't like Father would tell me if it wasn't.

Our family meetings were usually held at the breakfast table, or the throne room, the war room, even the library. But today, most of these places were filled with people we didn't know or trust (aside from the war room, which was locked and guarded). Father's private chambers were some of the most secure in the castle.

While they were indeed fit for a king, Father eschewed finery as "flippant and of little import," and his rooms reflected this. The mirror on the wall had gathered cobwebs in its frame of gilded leaves and pinecones. A tapestry in the wall clung to its former glory—the maiden beneath the tree had all but faded away. Her centaur lover's legs were moth eaten. The sea of stars above them had paled into something resembling a blue sky.

A simple chest and wardrobe held all of Father's clothes. The desk was littered with candle stumps and loose papers. A fur rug lay before the fireplace, ragged and dusty.

The only sign of luxury in the room was a silver tray, holding an overturned teacup and a crust of hearty bread.

No wonder Queen Elberia preferred to keep her own chambers.

Ria and I sat in the high-backed chairs across from the tiny breakfast table while Timin stood by the door, hands behind her back. "Your Highness," she said, stiff but pleasant.

"Miss Timin," said Father, rising from his desk. "Forgive me, but I'd like for you to wait outside. I must speak to the girls alone."

Timin curtsied and departed, nearly tripping over her skirts.

"Girls," he sighed, looking toward us. "Step away from the door, please. You know how I feel about that."

"I know," I sighed, getting to my feet. "Eavesdroppers and rogues."

"Eavesdroppers and rogues," he agreed. The corners of his lips tilted into the barest hint of a smile. "You both look lovely tonight."

I spun in a quick circle to show off my dress, drawing another smile from him.

At my side, Ria nodded stiffly. "Thank you."

Father's banquet attire was militarized. His breastplate bore the family crest. His armor, though far from a full suit, covered anything vulnerable. Shoulders and knees padded, bracers on his forearms, a knife hidden on each limb, sword at both hips, he looked ready for battle. A fur lined cape was held in place by a pin in the shape of a stag. Every part of him gleamed. Even his famously unruly beard had been tamed, slicked down and tied neatly with a leather band.

"I'm sure you're already aware of the nature of this meeting," he said, voice gruff. "Valeria, after everything that happened with Tocchia, we must find you a new suitor. I've my eye on several, but I thought it best to ask if you're partial to anyone."

"No, Your Highness," said Ria coldly. "I cannot say that any are to my liking."

Father's eyes narrowed. "Then I suggest you spend tonight with an open mind, or I will be forced to choose for you."

Ria scowled at the floor. "Yes, Your Highness."

"And Talina," said Father, turning to me. "I'd advise you to do the same. At some point, you must marry. I'd like both of you to find joyful unions, if at all possible."

Ria's scowl only deepened.

I clapped my hands together, and chirped, "Of course, Father!"

Now *I* was the subject of Ria's ire, which meant that she and Father wouldn't have one of their famous arguments right before the banquet. She'd sneer and snipe at me all night, but that was fine, because she'd forgive me by morning, whereas a fight with Father would leave the entire castle tense for weeks.

"Good," said Father, his features relaxing. "I'm sure I don't need to remind you to behave yourselves tonight. Go have fun."

"Certainly," I said, curtsying. Ria followed suit with a roll of her big, blue eyes.

"I can't believe you," she muttered as soon as we were outside. "'*Yes, Father!*'" she cried, voice high and mocking. "'*Whatever you say, Father!*' As if he doesn't control every aspect of our lives already!"

I shrugged. "I must marry. I think it's kind of him to consider our wishes."

"It is the absolute *least* he can do," Ria muttered. "Honestly, it takes almost nothing to make you happy."

I winced.

At my expression, Ria pursed her lips and looked away. "I'm sorry," she said. "I'm only envious."

"It's alright," I told her, but I'd lost some of the bounce in my step.

"No," she said, lowering her voice as Timin approached.

"You're right. We must marry. I've prepared for this my entire life. I must accept it."

"That's not—" I began.

But Timin cut me off. "Princesses! There you are! I trust you had a pleasant conversation?"

"Your trust is misplaced," Ria grumbled.

"It was as we expected," I said, and shrugged. "He reminded us to behave."

"Good advice," said Timin, nodding. "Well, then. Let's head to the banquet, shall we?"

"Of course," I said, and Ria rolled her eyes.

CHAPTER 4

The opening ceremony was long and drawn out. Guests watched from their seats as a long line of soldiers lead my father to the veranda, where a podium had been placed. Small plates and thimbles of wine dotted each table, but the nobles were already restless.

I've always considered boredom an important part of any revelry. The more tedious the opening ceremony, the sweeter the celebration afterward.

"Thank you all for coming," Father began, gaze dragging over the crowd. Looking for any Tocchians in disguise, I guessed. This might make for a rather exciting game, I decided, and so I spent much of the rest of the ceremony observing the crowd, trying to decide who could be a Tocchian spy. The woman in the large yellow hat was definitely up to something, while the man spooning egg and potato mash onto his plate was merely a noble who had nothing better to do this week. But the man with his chin resting on his fist was working with the woman in the yellow hat. Watching. Waiting.

But I lost interest in the daydream as soon as one of Father's generals approached the stage, carrying a familiar box.

Father sat, and General Ullman took the podium.

"Your Highness," he began. "I'd like to present you with this token of luck and prowess. A gift from your military to you. Your fortitude, grace, and honor are unparalleled. This sword should make a fine fit," he said, opening the box to reveal the very blade I'd admired this morning. Sunlight glinted off its polished surface. In the bright daylight, the ruby looked bloody and menacing.

The sword was presented hilt-first. King Amonrew rose to take it. "Thank you," he said, bowing in each direction of the crowd. "With this blade, I pledge to honor my people. Defending them, leading them, and now," a wide grin spread across his face, "entertaining them!" The last words were all but a roar, echoing across the veranda. Guests leapt to their feet, stomping and clapping, laughing and shouting as the King waved to them, escorted inside by Larry and Hax.

The guests followed. Bracketed by guards, Ria and I were led to our seats at the royal table. Timin disappeared into the servants' quarters. Ria took her seat beside Father, while I sat next to our half-brother, Baden. By the look of it, he was already deep in his cups, propped up by his chair's high back. His hands gripped the armrests as if they were the only things stopping him from sliding to the floor.

Of late, Baden had been struggling. He, too, felt the pressure to marry, and grew steadily moodier as the months passed. We were never particularly close, as he considered me something of an abomination, but I still noticed his stress. Luckily, he never took it out on me. Hadn't since he was twelve and I was nine and he cracked my head against the back of the throne during an argument that had grown physical. I lost consciousness, but Baden thought he'd killed me. For a while, he cried every time he saw me, blubbering about how sorry he was. Even *I* felt bad for him after a little while.

Just the way I did now. It seemed he was drunk more often than not. How long until he drank himself to death?

Our half-brother, Rowan, sat on my other side, face hard. As the more seasoned fighter, he was the bulkiest of my siblings, tanned from days spent sparring and fencing in the sun; hot in the summer, blinding against snow in the winter. On good days, he let Valeria and me join him, though he was ruthless even in practice sessions, and we left with bruises and cuts that earned the king's ire.

We were supposed to practice self-defense but somehow avoid all injuries. Though I grumbled that I couldn't be expected to improve without a few scrapes, Father was firm in his convictions. Every injury earned us a lecture about maintaining our beauty.

Sometimes, I wondered what might happen if I were unlucky enough to take a blade to the face. If a scar might mar my breast or shoulder. Would I be married off to the first eligible bachelor, perhaps nothing more than a baron, never to be seen again? Was it possible that a physical flaw might remove me from Father's favor forever?

The servants arrived, carrying pitchers of sweet wine and platters of food. My stomach untwisted, grumbling now. Before us was a feast of lamb with candied almonds and fat berries; potatoes with herbs and rich gravy; carrots glazed in honey; lentils saturated in fat drippings; bread with a thick crust, soft and sweet inside; tiny, frosted cakes; a slice of rhubarb pie; cups of wine that left me giggling at the antics of nobles at the table beside us.

Their argument started as a debate about the prices of cheese in the north and devolved into a contest to see who could stuff the most into their mouth at once. So far, the baron of Elderton's youngest and drunkest son was winning, red-faced, and spraying chunks of cheese with each labored breath.

I worried that he might choke, but he worked his way through the enormous mouthful, chewing slowly, cheeks puffed like a chipmunk's, managing the occasional swallow while his friends chugged ale and cheered him on.

What was it like to be so carefree? If I choked to death on a wheel of cheese, Father would probably die of shame (Valeria certainly would), and I couldn't say that I would entirely blame him.

And yet, I was envious that I could not dive so deeply into my cups or my plates. Gluttony is unbecoming, but freedom is a relentless craving, and I would take it any way that I could. An extra spoonful of honey, five more minutes at the forge, an unattended stroll around the gardens—anything, everything.

A few of our guests excused themselves to bed early. Someone threw up on the floor and was met with excited cheers. A fight broke out and ended with the Earl of Riching's eldest son shouting obscenities and bleeding as he was escorted from the banquet by an exasperated brother and cousin.

The mingling began. The band onstage played the first of the waltzes. Nearly everyone at the royal table rose to their feet; my father, stepmother, Ria and Rowan. Even Baden downed a final goblet of wine and trudged reluctantly to the floor. I excused myself, claiming that I simply *must* finish my potatoes before engaging in the festivities, and was left blessedly alone.

Until suddenly, I wasn't. Alger dropped into the empty seat beside me and reached for Baden's abandoned goblet. He stank of ale and gravy. "Is this any different than what they served the rest of us?" he asked, tilting the liquid suspiciously.

"The very same," I assured him, though I had no idea.

"Hmm," he said, and drained the wine. Wiping the back of his mouth, he turned to me and said, "You lied."

"I did not."

"Yes, you did. You said it wasn't different. And yet, it's not nearly so sweet."

I shrugged. "Perhaps I was mistaken."

"Seems an odd thing to lie about. I'd think the king would resent his bastard telling lies."

I scowled and stood. "Forgive me, My Lord, but I'm wanted elsewhere."

Alger followed me, gesturing. "Where? Where might you be wanted? I don't see a single person who might be in want of you right now except for me, Princess, and you just walked away."

"I'm weak of stomach," I said, spotting the line for the toilets around the corner, extending down a long hallway. I started toward them. "I'm afraid you'll not want to witness this."

"Gods," he said, stopping in his tracks, a look of disgust on his face. "And you'll tell anyone that, won't you?"

"You asked!"

"You lied! You *aren't* wanted anywhere!"

"The King will want me near the toilets, rest assured." My palms began to sweat. My stomach roiled. I'd hoped Alger would give me privacy, but it seemed he had no intention of backing off. "Please, I'd be happy to talk to you later—"

"You're full of shit," he snapped, swaying on his feet.

I caught the eye of a guard and inclined my head. She approached instantly, glaring at Alger.

"He needs a little help returning to the banquet hall," I explained, smiling my prettiest smile. "I'm afraid he's a tiny bit drunk."

The guard nodded and turned to Alger. "Come with me."

"She's a liar!" Alger cried, pointing to me with a shaking finger.

"Sure," said the guard, catching his wrist, and forcibly lowering his hand. "Let's go."

"No!" snarled Alger, wrenching his arm free.

"You can't follow the princess to the toilets, sir."

I took advantage of the distraction, and scampered away, losing myself in a crowd of noblewomen and their chaperones. A hundred pairs of eyes followed me, and I fought the urge to hunch my shoulders. I didn't want Alger anywhere near me, and I certainly hadn't invited him, but I knew how it would be perceived, regardless. If he continued to force his presence upon me, I might have no choice but to marry him to retain my honor (and the king's).

And I desperately didn't want that.

I looped back to the banquet hall, skipping the toilets altogether, deciding that the dance floor would provide better security. Perhaps Duke Callum might take pity on me again.

If Alger came near me again, I'd scream. The guards would remove him despite his protests, and I'd survive the banquet without entering into a betrothal manipulated by a foul man hoping for special treatment. I wouldn't be the one to warm the cold, lonely halls of his castle for him.

Somewhere in the distance, a shout rang out.

"HAVE you told your father you are very much *not* interested in Alger?" said Duke Callum as we danced together. Twenty minutes had passed since I'd last seen Alger, and I grew hopeful that he'd slinked away to lick his wounds. In the meantime, an Earl's son had been plenty happy to dance with me until Callum cut in.

"I haven't, Your Grace," I sighed.

"You ought to. It would be most prudent. It seems like he was bothering you." Callum raised an eyebrow.

"He was," I admitted. "He is under the impression that I am the key to the king's favor."

Callum snorted a laugh at that, his hand tightening reflexively on my waist. "While I'm sure there is some truth to that, it seems he has built up an unrealistic ideal."

"I should think so," I said, taking a step back, just in time to avoid having my toe trod on. "Not to sound ungrateful."

"You don't," Callum assured me. "Merely rational."

"You are too kind," I told him, face heating.

"No," he said, grinning now. "I am simply a realist. I will tell you what I know to be true, to the best of my abilities. And I know that Alger does not share my beliefs."

"And what, exactly, are your beliefs?" I dared ask. Of the men I'd danced with last night, he was by far my favorite. A part of me wanted to know more about him, even as another feared the attention it may attract.

"What do I believe, Your Highness?" Genuine surprise crossed his face. Like so many others, it seemed as if he couldn't believe I was interested in anything outside of gardens and ballrooms and jewels. Perhaps I'd overestimated him.

Blushing, I said, "I do think perhaps I've overstepped, My Lord."

He shook his head. Brown curls bounced, soft and silky. I was drunk enough to want to touch them, but didn't dare. "No, you merely caught me off my guard. A green mistake, though I admit it's rather appropriate," he said, gesturing to my dress. "It is an intimate question, though. Are you sure you want the answer?"

I bit my lip. "I admit my curiosity is burning."

The implication was scandalous. His eyebrows raised. "I see," he said slowly. "Very well, Your Highness. I believe in truthfulness and fair trade. I hold no gods dear. I oppose cruelty, war, and sensationalism, and instead encourage rational thought. And…" His voice trailed off.

"And?" I asked. The sudden heat in his gaze sent my stomach swooping.

"I do believe my interests are misplaced," he said, just as the dance ended, and we switched partners.

What did he mean by that? That I disappointed him? That he'd considered me as an option, but had lost interest?

Or had he meant the opposite?

I didn't have long to ponder before Alger cut in. In his haste to take over, he elbowed my partner in the ribs.

"Really," he snapped, squeezing me too tightly round the waist, fingers digging into me with bruising force as my partner stumbled away from us. "That was a nasty trick. You nearly got me barred from the banquet."

"You ought to know better than to follow a lady against her will," I huffed. "I asked you to give me privacy, and you didn't. I've done nothing wrong."

"And then you ran to Callum," he complained, as if he hadn't heard me. If I thought he smelled of alcohol earlier, he positively reeked of it now. His steady feet could not conceal the slur of his words. I'd spent too much time around Baden to be easily fooled. I knew a slave to the drink when I saw one.

"I did no such thing. I happen to enjoy speaking to the duke. He is most pleasant."

A foot came down upon my toes. I gasped, more from the audacity than the pain.

Alger laughed. "And if I ask your opinion of me?"

"I'd rather keep that to myself," I said, trying frantically to catch the eye of Ria, of Callum, even of Baden.

Only my jilted dance partner noticed. When I looked to him, he turned away, as if ashamed to be caught watching us.

"You won't get away with that for long. I intend to speak to the king," Alger said, practically gloating.

Gods. My stomach flipped. I feared I might spew my dinner upon his satin waistcoat. "Why? So you can spend your life trying to tame me?"

"You won't be independent for long," he said, shaking his head. "Your kind never are."

A wave of fury cracked across my ribs like the black waves of the sea at night. I stomped on his toes with the point of my heel. Drove it down with all my might until he yelped and his grip loosened.

I took the opportunity to shove him away from me. To make it clear to anyone watching that he was a hateful, controlling man, and that he was *hurting* me.

Alger crashed into Lady Alenda, who tumbled into the arms of her startled partner.

Gasps rang out among the crowd.

"Don't touch me!" I shrieked, continuing to back away.

Guards moved toward us. Alger's expression was torn between fury and panic. The King raised bushy eyebrows and abandoned his conversation with the Duke of Cardald to stalk across the dance floor.

I held a hand to my breast, panting, ready to disappear behind the guards.

Then the screams began.

At first, Alger leapt away from me, as if afraid that he'd triggered not only my panic, but the panic of every woman in the room.

But the screams came from outside, down the hall.

The King stormed past us, checked Alger with his shoulder and muttered, "I'll deal with you later."

Alger's eyes nearly bugged from his head.

Around the room, curious glances darted from me, to Alger, to the guards racing to the doors.

Then began the mad rush to the windows and the doors, an endeavor that quickly ended when everyone outside poured back into the banquet hall, shouting and shoving their way through the crowd. Women ran with missing shoes, with hair half-fallen from elaborate updos, wild-eyed, waving their arms. Men, too, yelled over the din, their coats rumpled, hair disheveled. Someone had spots of blood along his back.

Among the confusion, I heard cries of, "Tocchia! Tocchia is here!"

My blood ran cold.

They'd had come at last.

CHAPTER 5

I would not stay in the banquet hall to be slaughtered like a goat. With sobs of, "Tocchia!" ringing in my ears, I darted through the crowd, searching desperately for Ria, Rowan, or even Callum. But I met only the hysterical eyes of strangers, streaming from the hall like frogs from a hot pot.

The doors to the terrace were barred. The heavy *thunk!* of wood echoed over the shrieking. I watched in confused horror as the guards moved to secure the main entrance, calling over the cacophony of panic to stay calm, to remain inside.

The only exit now was through the toilets, and I needed to hurry. I tore through the chaos, hoping against hope that the exit hadn't been sealed.

"I won't die here!" snarled someone to my left. Shoving his way through the soldiers, he struggled to reach the main doors. A horde of others joined him, blue and green and yellow silks and satins clashing against the guards' steel armor. Like a flock of tropical birds, they screeched and squawked, thrusting their bodies against the heavy doors, muffling the commotion from outside.

I took advantage of the madness, and raced to the toilets, utilizing my elbows to part the crowd when necessary.

My hand drifted to my skirts and pressed against the knife hidden beneath. Strapped to my thigh, it was the perfect size for stabbing through Alger's wandering hands, but too tiny to be much good in a fight. Its wooden hilt was carved with roses, painted and polished. I'd meant to enchant it, but had continuously forgotten, and now it was too late.

Still, it was better than nothing. I shot through doors attended by distracted guards. They snatched for me but did not chase me down, so I ran through the hall to the back stairwell, where a servant girl cowered. Disheveled hair fell across her heart-shaped face, and tears streaked down her cheeks.

"Get up," I said to her. "Hurry!" I added, when she only gawked at me with enormous brown eyes.

"We're being invaded," she mumbled, gaze passing through me, unseeing.

"Are you hurt?"

"They're going to kill us," she whispered.

I reached for her hand and was met with a shriek.

"I'm not going to hurt you! I'm going to bring you somewhere safe!" I cried, but she only shook her head, clutching her hand and looking at me as if I were armed with a proper sword instead of a knife so small it could be mistaken for a nail file. "We need to hide!"

Her stare moved to the wall and never left.

I left her behind, guilt pounding in my ears.

I slipped into my chambers, where I replaced my slippers with heavy boots, and tore the hem from my skirt so it wouldn't drag across the ground. I strapped a dagger to each leg, sheathed the knife and stuffed it into my corset, and grabbed my sword. I had a rucksack prepared for any and all emergencies, and I snatched it up. The bag might inhibit my movements, but I needed it to survive outside the castle.

Father would want me to hide, but I knew better. Attacks like this led to fires and raids, and I was not going to be caught alone, unarmed, and without an escape. If I had to break a window and leap into the water below, I'd do it.

A hundred times, maybe more, I'd run through similar scenarios in my mind. All of them centered around hiding, sneaking out, or concealing my identity until I found asylum.

Never had it occurred to me that Tocchia might be the enemy. That Tocchia would retaliate so quickly and brutally. I thought of Callum and Alger's conversation yesterday and felt foolish. Perhaps I should've suspected.

I tore the ribbon loose from my hair and used it to fashion a tight bun at the back of my head. Then I donned my riding cloak and headed out into the hall. I kept to the walls, pausing at each corner to listen. A great deal of commotion came from downstairs —harrowing wails that sent shivers down my spine, the sound of metal on metal, echoing shouts, the rhythmic booming of what I suspected might be a battering ram.

But there were no clanking footsteps nearby, no figures skulking about the halls of our living quarters. The doors blocking the grand stairway shuddered, but our soldiers had already barred them, and whoever attempted to enter was short on force. Dust rained down from the ceiling, and the wood groaned, but the doors held fast.

I hurried to the servants' stairs again. The girl with the heart-shaped face was gone. I hoped someone had taken her to safety, but I didn't have time to worry.

A shadow appeared at the base of the stairs.

I froze, hand on the hilt of my sword, heart pounding in my ears. A servant? One of our soldiers? Or a stranger who would run me through without regret?

I took a silent step back and drew my blade.

But I wasn't fast enough. I glimpsed a flash of steel armor, a face scowling beneath a helmet. Chainmail gleamed in the torchlight. On the breastplate was a serpent with blood dripping from its fangs.

A member of the Tocchian guard.

He glimpsed me, shook his head, and raised a finger to his lips.

I opened my mouth to scream, prepared to launch myself at him, but he turned away and departed as if he'd never seen me at all, slipping into the shadows like one of their brethren.

My hands shook. I gripped my sword and made my way slowly down. Was this a trap? Did he plan to snatch me, stab me, kill me?

Why did he want me to be quiet? Was it a warning? A gesture of goodwill?

And if it was a gesture of goodwill, then why invade in the first place? How had they gotten inside?

It would take days to move an army this size through the mountains. The pass was monitored at all times. Surely, someone would have reported it. A scout, even a bard or a villager. Someone would have told us.

Unless… had they come by sea? Raided our port, rushed inland? The castle sat on a cliff overlooking the ocean. In the cover of darkness, we could be caught off-guard. Especially if the soldiers were paid off, or distracted by their own miniature, unsanctioned celebrations. But the sea routes between Tocchia and Olmstead were treacherous, and reluctantly traversed.

Fury rose in my chest like smoke from a bonfire, overwhelming my terror. We were sold out. Someone betrayed us. Whether they arrived by land or sea didn't matter. Tocchia struck when we were distracted, but they didn't do it alone.

I thought of all the unfamiliar guards and wanted to scream. We were infiltrated weeks ago. Betrayed by our own. Blood would stain the floors of my home, the one place where I most desperately wanted to feel safe.

I reached the base of the stairs. Looked around and found the hallway empty. Most of the shouts came from the banquet hall, which I turned away from.

I'd not present myself for slaughter. No matter how my knees shook, or my heart rabbited, I would not give in. Everything with Alger felt like a fuzzy dream now.

I was unprepared for the lightning strike of pity. Not just for Alger, but for everyone trapped in the banquet hall. I imagined hundreds of people dying and bleeding, in the sort agony that I only dared imagine in my worst nightmares. My family, my friends. People who I saw on a daily basis. All of them, massacred.

My breath came in pants. I could not drop to the floor and weep as I so badly wanted to. I could not return to the ballroom for Ria, for my siblings.

No, right now I only had two choices: survival, and death.

And I'd already made up my mind.

The main hallway was filled with soldiers. Shouts echoed, steel sang. Bodies cluttered the corridor. A Tocchian soldier slipped in a puddle of blood. One of our own took the opportunity to drive a blade through a chink in his breastplate until it clashed against stone.

The Tocchian spasmed. Blood seeped from underneath his armor.

There was no making my way through this hall unnoticed. I darted back down the corridor. I could take the stairs to the servants' quarters, and escape through their private entrance. But that was assuming they weren't being held prisoner, or that their egress hadn't been discovered.

Passages tunneled between a few of the rooms, but I didn't know of any nearby enough to be of use. I'd have to go back upstairs to use them. The idea was less than appealing, anyway. It was too easy to become trapped, forgotten, in those ancient passageways.

A Tocchian soldier sliced an Olmsteadian soldier in the arm, then the knee. Sent him dropping to the floor, clanging like a fallen tray of goblets. The Tocchian held him at sword point, snarled, "Get up."

The Olmsteadian did, slowly, painfully.

"Come quietly, and we will show mercy."

The guard swayed on his feet. "No," he spat. "I won't betray my own."

The Tocchian scowled. "Fine. You'll join the others."

I braced for the squish of metal in flesh, the splattering of blood, the frantic cry of a dying man.

None came.

Instead, the Tocchian held him at sword point, and began herding him down the hall. "Come with me, and I won't kill you. Come with me, and you can see your family again."

The guard swallowed.

I never learnt his choice. Another duel came too close to me, a flurry of blades and taunts, and I faded into the shadows again.

The front doors were blown free from their hinges. Shards of wood clung to the jamb. I spotted a tree trunk in the distance, strapped to a wrought-iron cart. Soldiers swarmed. I didn't dare to try sneak past them.

My choices were limited. I could go back upstairs, and leap from a window, but I risked death or permanent damage in doing so; the sea was so very far below. I could double back, and sneak into the servants' quarters. I could break out a window downstairs, and hope not to attract attention. I could hide, and hope that there were no fires, no extensive searches for survivors.

Or I could sneak past the banquet hall, down the stairwell, and out the back garden door.

My chest heaved. The more I weighed my options, the worse they sounded. I had no hope of fighting my way out, and I didn't want to know what the Tocchians would do with me if they caught me.

Could I escape through the gardens? I knew their twisting paths and thorny hedges well. I would take this route whenever I wanted to leave the castle unnoticed. But with enemy soldiers stationed nearby, I might not be able to avoid detection.

The sound of approaching footsteps spurred me into action. I ran toward the banquet hall, darting between skirmishing soldiers. My boots slid on wet floors, but I managed to keep my balance.

I thought of my muddy slippers from yesterday, and briefly wondered if I wasn't actually clumsy, just rude.

Nobody chased after me, but bewildered stares followed in my wake. I careened down one corridor, dodging groping Tocchian gauntlets, and darted through another, where the corpses of Tocchian soldiers were stacked. I splashed through blood seeping across the stones, stomach revolting at the metallic stench. Bodies were piled three or four high, shoved off to the side like meat-stripped bones on a plate.

At first, I thought I was alone except for the cooling corpses. But as I neared the door to the toilets, someone raced after me, calling, "Princess Talina!"

I gasped and pumped my legs faster. I needed to get out of here, right fucking now. But the floor was slippery and panic had long weakened my reflexes.

The soldier tackled me to the ground. I fell with a bitten-off shriek, flailing as my face was pressed against cold stone, into blood that stank of war and death.

"What are you doing here?" the guard hissed, releasing some of the pressure on my back. I struggled, but it did no good; he was stronger and heavier than I was, and I'd never fought in real combat. If it came down to a true fight, he would win.

"I refuse to die here," I snarled, twisting this way and that, hoping to free my wrists. But his grip remained steadfast, even as his disbelieving face examined me. Olmsteadian, I realized with relief, glimpsing the stag on his armor.

"What do you know?" he demanded suddenly. "What did you have to do with this?"

I stared at him, horrified. "Have to do with what?"

"This invasion." He spat the word like a gob of snot.

"Nothing!" I insisted, appalled that he could even suggest such a thing.

The guard breathed heavily, glaring down at me. Something about the look on my face must have convinced him I was telling the truth, because he released me, and offered a hand. I didn't take it.

"We need to get you somewhere safe," he said, catching my wrist before I could flee.

"I'm not going to wait for them to kill me!" I snarled, twisting my arm. It didn't matter. The guard dragged me down the hall despite my protests.

I refused to be taken to the same room where my siblings were hidden (if indeed they were still alive). We'd be lambs for slaughter. "The banquet hall," I gasped. "Have they taken the banquet hall? What of the King?"

"King's fine," the guard snapped. "Hiding. Banquet hall is where you're going."

"So it's safe then?" The edges of my panic lost their sharpness as relief pushed its way in. I hadn't wanted to stab him. But I would, if I had reason to believe he was about to betray me.

But the guard didn't answer. Just hauled me past the toilets, where the bodies of two more Tocchian guards lay.

Why so many dead Tocchians? Why did they allow our soldiers to surrender when we took their lives without hesitation?

What the hell was going on?

The guards outside the banquet hall frowned at the sight of me. They were bloodied but whole, with dents in their armor, their faces pale but determined. "Princess Talina," one choked, shocked to see me. "How—"

"Doesn't matter," snapped the guard holding my arm. "Put her in there. Don't let her out."

"King Amonrew asked that the princess—"

"We aren't honoring requests right now," my guard said.

I couldn't help the expression on my face. Treason? Was this treason? The King would be furious if they didn't protect me. Any longstanding member of our guard knew this.

"Fine," snapped one of the soldiers, reaching for the door. It creaked open, and Ria stumbled out, eyes red, fingernails bleeding.

"Where is he?" she demanded. "Is Prince Marius here? I demand an audience. Bring him to me."

Then she spotted me, and her eyes widened. But she didn't acknowledge me, didn't ask what had happened or where I'd gone. She only squared her shoulders. Head held high, blood streaked across her face, she was more beautiful than ever.

What was her plan? Surely, she didn't intend to meet an aggressor without Father present.

"Absolutely not," one of the guards began.

"You don't give me orders," Ria said, crossing her arms. There was a stain on her dress that looked like wine, and one of her slippers was missing its buttons. "Bring him to *me*. I wish to negotiate."

The guard opened the door again, ready to shove me through.

"Leave her," Ria spat, glowering at me. "I want her here with me."

My heart sank. I remembered the guard's words even as his grip on my wrist relaxed. '*What did you have to do with this'*?

Did Ria suspect the same? Her furious glare stung.

"Fine," said my guard. "I'll see what I can do."

He dropped my arm and turned on his heel. I could practically see the steam rising from him, cooking him in his own suit of armor.

"What the hell are you doing?" Ria demanded, facing me. "Where the hell are you going? Do you want to meet the hangman?

I shook my head. "No, I—"

"You can't show up dressed to escape and assume people won't think you're involved," she hissed.

"I will not lie down and die like a good little girl," I snapped. "I won't cower in the corner while they storm my home."

Ria shook her head. "And neither will I," she said. "I'm going to fix this. Give me your sword."

I stared at her in disbelief. If she killed Prince Marius now, it would be a diplomatic nightmare.

On the other hand, murder might be the only way to stop this.

Wordlessly, I handed her my sword.

"Thank you," said Ria, exhaling slowly.

The doors creaked behind us. Shouts and cries slipped through as more guards appeared.

"I must beg you not to do this," said a guard I recognized as Hax.

Why wasn't he with the King? My blood ran cold.

But Hax was whole and hale, without blood on his armor. His sword was clean in its scabbard. Perhaps Father truly was hidden away somewhere and had sent Damon to guard the banquet hall.

It was possible, if unlikely. I doubted Hax would easily obey such an order.

"I must order you stand down," said Ria firmly. "All of you. This is the only way."

Footsteps sounded in the distance. I tried to think of something to say. Anything to talk her out of this. But I knew from the way she turned to face the oncoming danger that it wouldn't matter. Ria had made up her mind. All I could do now was stand and watch.

But as the footsteps grew nearer, something in Ria's face tensed. She looked from me to the guards and said, "Talina... I need you to wait in the banquet hall."

I shook my head. "You've got my sword."

"There are plenty of soldiers to watch out for you," said Ria.

"Cranz made that for me," I argued. *With a good deal of griping and groaning,* I didn't add. The sword was one of my most prized possessions, with a pommel the color of pink peonies.

"You'll get it back," Ria growled. "I'll make sure of it. Now go!"

I didn't get to make the choice for myself. The guard to my left grabbed me by the arm and stuffed me through the door with little ceremony.

I was shoved face-first into a crowd barely restrained by shouting soldiers. I slammed into an armored back and was thrust into the throng. "No!" I shrieked, fighting my way forward. But there were bodies all around me, crushing my arms to my sides, pushing me into a guard whose back was already pressed to the door. I tried to yell, "Stop it!" as someone slammed between my shoulder blades, but found I didn't have the air.

Gods. I was going to suffocate here.

The realization was like a strike of lightning. My nerves were electric. I could die here, in this rush.

And then there was a hand at my collar, pulling me backwards. I gasped, choked, and emerged on the other side of the chaos, stumbling against Rowan.

"Fuck!" he said, cupping my cheeks, looking me up and down. "Are you alright? Where the fuck have you been?"

"Ria's outside," I gasped. "She means to negotiate with the prince."

He groaned. His hands dropped to his sides. "Are you joking?"

"No. She took my sword."

"I thought you said she meant to negotiate!" Rowan pressed his hands to his temples, massaging. "She took your sword and shoved you in here?"

"Yes!" More or less. I supposed she hadn't really done much in the way of shoving.

"And where, um, exactly did you find a sword?"

"In my rooms," I said, looking down at the floor, unable to meet his eye. How stupid he must think me.

He followed my gaze and groaned when he saw my boots.

"You went upstairs in the middle of all this for a sword and what? A cloak? Where exactly did you think you were going?"

"Away from here," I snapped. "I'll take my chances outside, thank you."

"That's—" Rowan began, but he stopped himself, and simply said, "I'm glad you're alright."

"Where's Baden? Where's Father?"

"Baden and Father are in the cellars," said Rowan. "Hopefully not the wine cellar," he added, pinching the bridge of his nose, as if he couldn't quite believe what he'd just said. "The rest of us have to stay here. It's not safe to move."

"They're just going to leave us here to die?" I demanded. I spoke too loudly, too shrilly. Around me, voices rose in panic. Panicked guests charged the doors. The guards fought them off, but sooner or later, they'd lose momentum. The crowd was out of control, pushing forward, shoving and scratching at the doors, the walls. I noted a hole in one of our back windows. It looked like someone had shoved their fist through. The enchanted glass had performed entirely too well—no one would escape through the windows tonight.

"Damn it," said Rowan, nostrils flaring, lips pulling back into a snarl. "We've just gotten them to calm down, Talina! You can't upset them like this!"

"It's *true,*" I insisted. "Barricaded like this, what do you think will happen?"

"We've plenty of protection," said Rowan. "Please, let's just go sit—"

A great *boom!* echoed through the banquet hall, followed by shrieks as Ria shoved her way through the bodies at the door. She held my sword in her hand, knuckles white.

I gasped. Rowan and I clutched each other. He clapped a hand to his mouth. His white gloves glittered in the light of the candelabra, still shining above us.

"Stand down!" Ria screeched, voice high and furious over the cacophony of screams, the mad stampede of feet.

But she was lost in the rush. The soldiers had no hope of containing the mob. While a few nobles remained in the ballroom, holding chunks of disassembled benches, candlesticks, broken wine bottles and other makeshift weapons, most fled. Ria wailed as she fell. In the madness, I caught sight of a lavender slipper, separated from its wearer. My sword flew from her hand and clattered to the floor.

"Go inside!" commanded the guards. "Inside! Back into the banquet hall! Princess Valeria has an announcement!"

Some returned, their noses bloodied, faces white as sheets, clutching bruised limbs. Among those who had remained were Duke Callum, and regrettably, Alger, though a dark stain across his pants suggested he might've pissed himself. I felt a grim satisfaction at the sight.

Others were presumably loose among the halls of our castle, ready to flee or fight.

Nobles, I thought in disgust, watching as someone helped Ria to her feet. My sword had landed several feet away, but no one made to grab it. Someone rushed to bring Ria her shoe. Instead of accepting it, she kicked off her remaining slipper. "Do not fight!" she shouted, voice already hoarse. "Do not fight! I have an announcement! Please, you are no longer in danger!"

My stomach churned. *She's done it. She's really done it.*

"I will return to Tocchia with Prince Marius as his betrothed. We will honor the treaty," said Ria. Blood dripped from a cut on her forehead. "Tocchia has called off the invasion."

She raised her hand, revealing a raw, red slice across her palm. "I swore it."

I clutched Rowan. "She used my sword," I whispered. "She used my sword!"

"Fuck," said Rowan, struggling to detach me. "Let go, I need to speak to Ria!"

I dropped his arm like it had bitten me, and he fled as if I'd bitten *him* in return.

"What were you thinking?!" shouted Rowan, arms waving in a way that Timin would criticize as most undignified. My heart clenched. I imagined her hiding with the servants in their quarters, lip quivering in terror. I hoped she'd survived the slaughter. Annoying or not, she didn't deserve to die this way.

"It is done," said Ria with a terrible calm. "I am departing with Prince Marius to fulfill Olmstead's original treaty."

There was an outcry, voices gathering together in a flurry of protests and shocked exclamations. Everyone wanted to know if we were at war.

I took advantage of the mayhem to retrieve my sword from where Valeria had dropped it, and wiped it clean with the hem of my dress.

A strangled gasp came from behind me. I whirled around to find Callum staring at me, as if he'd just now realized that I'd stumbled into the ballroom ready to fight or flee. With blood spattered down my front, a bruise on my jaw, the hem of my dress streaked crimson, I was far from the demure little thing he'd danced with the last two nights.

Part of me felt guilty for disappointing him. Another part of me thought it was better he found out sooner rather than later. I could play the part of a good little princess, but I was so much more than that, and ready to prove it.

Swarmed with adrenaline and terror and rage, I felt like a spider, clumsily weaving my very first web. I hadn't meant to trap anyone in it, but I couldn't deny my instincts, the urge to create and experiment and defend. If anyone felt betrayed by that, so be it.

But even as I was the spider, I was also the fly, navigating through an entire castle full of others' webs, far more likely to be trapped and destroyed than to escape unscathed. All my life, I'd dodged and fought, but soon enough, I'd be caught, only to wither away, sustenance for another day's gossip among courtiers, forgotten unless my end was spectacular enough to become a cautionary tale.

A legacy as nightmare fodder for children. How *dreary*.

The doors flew open with a *bang!* King Amonrew stomped through them, hair mussed, crown askew, blood splashed across his face, furred boots soaked like he'd fallen into a barrel of wine. "Princess Valeria," he snarled, voice carrying through the room like a gale. "What have you done?"

Silence fell. With it, my stomach dropped.

The King spared me no attention. All his ire was focused on Valeria, who stood before him, pale-faced and defiant.

"I did what needed to be done to stop the slaughter."

Rage thundered across his face. "Come with me," he said. "You and I and Prince Marius have much to discuss." He scowled across the crowd, as if they were intruding on a deeply personal moment. "And the rest of you!" he shouted. "What are you waiting for? Make merry and drink deeply! It's the least you can do for me!"

Laughter and cheers exploded through the room. A few looked on, as if worried they might be ambushed, that this was a trap. But more still drank deeply of abandoned cups. After exchanging worried glances, the band started up again, a fast little jig that had the drunkest of the lot leaping onto tables and swarming the dance floor.

The ballroom dissolved into madness. The doors slammed behind Princess Valeria and King Amonrew. Rowan and I were left to the revelry.

CHAPTER 6

The ballroom still pulsed with gluttony and debauchery when the soldiers cracked the doors to reveal hallways cleared of corpses. The puddles of blood had been wiped away, but their remnants still stained the floors. The stone would remember the slaughter for weeks yet.

Rowan steered me away from a table that sheltered a fornicating couple, drunk and giggling, all skirts and silks.

It wasn't my place to judge, but I thought those skirts belonged to Lady Barrington, whose husband was currently asleep on a bench near the door. The discarded blue and gold silk pants were surely worn by the Earl of Quelling, whose wife was nowhere to be seen.

A brush with death left everyone in the room hungry and desperate. Dances were no longer organized and proper. Couples were feral, spinning and ducking and kissing as if the world was minutes from ending. Blouses dangled from the rafters. Undergarments were strewn across mostly-empty serving platters. Everything smelt of alcohol and piss and vomit.

Trapped in that drunken dream, time passed quickly. Somewhere in the devastation, a doomsday party began in earnest.

Even I guzzled several cups of strong, sweet wine, and slipped into the foray, my ankles and calves covered only by the leather of my boots. Any other day, it would've been a proper scandal. In a room strewn with lost underwear and shoes, I was nearly modest.

I stood by Rowan's side. Even when I was drunk on the dance floor, swaying to the music, he accompanied me, happy to glower at anyone who approached.

We were never close, but I appreciated him nonetheless, especially when he punched Alger in the stomach. For his troubles, Rowan received a bloody nose. A gleefully drunk bearded man I didn't know stuck a well-deserved fork in Alger's thigh. Afterward, Alger spent the rest of the night lying on a bench, moaning at anyone who stopped to check on him.

As soon as the guards released us, I waved goodbye to an exhausted and bewildered Callum, kissed Rowan on the cheek, and bolted away before anyone could stop me.

"Where is the king?" I demanded of the first guard I recognized.

He looked me up and down, snorted, and said, "I'm not telling *you* His Majesty's whereabouts."

Fair enough. Drenched in blood and sweat, I was far from my normal self. I doubted he knew me, and I lacked the energy to convince him.

But I was the pleasant princess. Ria was the assertive one, and she wasn't with me. So I nodded politely and left.

I dragged myself to my rooms, pausing to listen outside Ria's door, where I heard a faint rustling. Rats? A maid? Or Ria herself?

I threw the door open with the ceremony of a drunk stumbling her way out of the tavern.

Ria sat at the vanity, blotting away last night's makeup with a kerchief. She startled when I burst through the door.

"Talina!" she spat, leaping from her chair and holding a hand to her breast. "Don't do that."

"You're one to talk," I snapped, slamming the door behind me. "You left me locked in that ballroom for hours. What happened?"

"I—" Ria glanced nervously around the room. "I—Look, sit down, alright? I'll explain everything."

I plopped down onto the edge of the bed with such force that it squeaked and groaned beneath me. "Fine. Start explaining."

Ria returned to her chair, scooting around to face me. "I don't owe you anything," she sighed. "I did what was best."

"You *owe* me an explanation," I said, crossing my arms. Anger shivered through me. Would she try to skirt the issue? Well, I wouldn't let her. "What *happened,* Valeria?"

"Fine," scoffed Ria, frowning at me. "Fine. All right. You're right. I—Talina, you know why he's here. He wants *me.* He wants Father to honor the treaty. I had to do it, or they'd slaughter everyone. You *know* that."

"Great way to start a marriage," I huffed. "And no, I *don't* know that. The Tocchians weren't the ones doing the slaughtering."

"What are you talking about?" said Ria. All emotion disappeared from her voice. I knew that tone. She didn't want to believe me, because if she did, it meant she had acted on misinformation. Misinformation that could change the trajectory of her life, for better or for worse.

I inhaled through my nose. "I ran into a soldier on the stairs. He let me go. And the Tocchians—they were giving people a chance to surrender. And when they didn't—"

"They took the guards downstairs," finished Ria, blood draining from her face. "Fuck. Fuck! We might have had a chance."

Oh. Was that where they'd stashed our soldiers?

I gave a despondent shrug. "I think they wanted to cause the least amount of damage possible."

"While still getting the point across," Ria reminded me sullenly.

"This is Father's fault," I fumed, throwing my arms up. "Tocchia tried to negotiate with him—"

"Yes, I know," said Ria, raking the brush through her hair. "And he wouldn't hear of it. Now we're all paying the price."

I looked at Ria, her hair long and loose, a cut slashed across her forehead, bruises beneath her eyes. I hated that she was reduced to nothing more than an object for men to fight over. Like she wasn't a person with thoughts and feelings and experiences. In a royal court, this was all we were. Like the figurines in the war room, we had a name and identity assigned to us, but our birthright scrubbed us of our features, designating us to a single role.

"I'm sorry," I said, falling back onto the bed before I could think better of it. The gore splattered across my dress had long dried and felt like something from a half-remembered dream, but I shouldn't risk staining the bedspread. "So what happened?"

"I met with Prince Marius and told him I would marry him if he agreed to stop the slaughter at once and withdraw from our lands by tomorrow morning at the latest," said Valeria, too calmly. It sounded as if she were placing an order at the florist's, not describing a life-altering event that had happened only hours earlier.

"Um," I said, trying to parse out which details were the most necessary, and which ones I could draw from Valeria before she became a brick wall, as she often did when I asked too many questions. "How did you find Prince Marius?"

"Blond. Cold. Exactly as he was years and years ago," Valeria answered. "I don't like him, if that's what you're asking."

I almost laughed. Ria's preference for brunettes was notorious among our ladies-in-waiting. "Was he angry?"

"No," said Ria, setting her brush on the vanity. "He seemed... like he didn't want to be here at all. Like he wanted to go home."

"I guess it wasn't difficult to convince him, then."

"No." Ria gave a short laugh. "Father thought it was too easy. Spent *hours* negotiating with him."

"What are the terms?" I asked, sitting up and leaning forward.

"Well, for one, I have to marry the prince. Two, Father isn't allowed to retaliate, and three, we owe them a dowry."

"When do you marry?"

"I don't know," said Ria, shoulders sagging, chin dipping. "But I leave tomorrow morning."

"*Tomorrow morning?!*" I gasped. "They can't just take you—"

"Yes, they can. I agreed to it. I'm going to honor my commitments and go north with the Prince. And all of this will be but a dream."

"That's much too soon!" I said. I jumped to my feet, pushing my hands through my hair so that it finally spilled from its haphazard knot. "You can't— They can't—"

"Talina," said Ria, rising to catch me by my shoulders. "I have to go."

"But you can't just leave me here!" I burst out. Tears burned in my eyes, unshed, as Ria pulled me close and wrapped her arms around me. "You can't! Not like this..."

"I'm sorry," said Ria. Something hot and wet landed on my shoulder, and I realized that she was crying, too. "I don't want to go. But this was always going to happen, and I—I need to do the right thing. I need to do what Father wouldn't. So that you, and Rowan, and Baden, and everyone else here can be safe. I'll write to you every week, and I'll see you at the wedding, alright? It's going to be fine. You'll see. In a month, you'll forget all about me and go on forging crazy things and you'll drive Cranz insane, and it will *all be fine*."

I squeezed her tightly, burying my face in her shoulder. "I'm not ready for you to leave."

"I'm not either," said Ria. For the first time, I detected dread in her voice. "But it will be alright. I want you to make me something and bring it the wedding for me."

I drew back, confused. "What should I make?"

Ria laughed. "Whatever you want. Make me impenetrable to

the forces of darkness. Make me float. Turn me invisible. Whatever sounds most fun."

"I don't want to have fun," I grumbled. "I want to be sad."

"Fine. Be sad. Then pour your grief into something you can be proud of." She wiped her eyes, then mine with the kerchief.

I wondered what she'd ever worked on in her life. Embroidery? Fencing? Lessons? Finishing a cup of tea or a book of poetry? Once, she'd tried to bake bread with the help of one of our bakers. It had gone disastrously, with the dough expanding all over the counter until it looked as if a puffy cloud had fallen out of the sky and exploded in our kitchen.

It struck me then that for all the time we spent together, I barely knew her. She indulged my hobbies and interests with the occasional eye roll, but I didn't know what she enjoyed in her spare time. But Ria referenced work as if it were something she knew, and I believed her.

"I don't want you to go," I told her, crying again.

"Me, either," she said. "But it's going to be all right. Prince Marius isn't so bad, and we'll still visit. I promise."

I left Ria's room with reddened cheeks and burning eyes, and returned to my chambers with shaking knees.

CHAPTER 7

I packed my things in a daze. My sword, an assortment of knives, stockings and knickers, some jewelry that could be sold easily, a notebook and quill pen, a bottle of ink, and my least conspicuous clothes.

This is never going to work, mumbled the little voice in the back of my mind as I sneaked into the kitchens, raiding the pantries for dried fruit, nuts, strips of jerky, hard cheeses, and finally, a loaf of rye bread that someone had abandoned on the counter to harden overnight.

This is never going to work, said that same little voice as I slinked between transport wagons, trying to avoid the Tocchian guards stationed nearby.

This is never going to work. I hid my bag in the wagon that would be most easily accessed from the back gardens.

This is never going to work. I kissed Ria's cheek goodbye. My father's hand closed over my shoulder.

This is never going to work. I darted through the garden like a butterfly drunk on pollen, fluttering from flower to flower in a sleep-deprived haze.

This is *going to work,* I thought, almost surprised as I crammed myself into the back of the wagon, squeezing between boxes of supplies.

This is *going to work*. I slid an enchanted pin into my hair and watched as the strands turned from red to honey brown before my very eyes.

All through the city and along the steep trails into the mountains, that same thought rushed through my mind. Again and again, until I clutched my knees, buried my face in them, and wept properly.

Would the Tocchians think I was a spy? An assassin? Both crimes were punishable by death. As the day wore on, my worry compounded into something tight and crushing.

Night fell. The wagons ground to a halt. Tents were pitched, fires constructed. Voices melded with the howling wind. I held as still as I could, afraid someone might sense my presence if I dared *think* too loudly.

A rustling came from outside my wagon. The cover was pulled back. Someone grunted and dug through the supplies. I held my breath and sat as still as I could, hunching in on myself like a mouse. I pulled my hood over my head and hoped it would help me blend with the shadows.

But that wasn't enough. Eventually, the box that I was hidden behind was removed, dragged nearly to the end of the cart before I was spotted. It was difficult to see the soldier's face in the dying light, but his voice tore through me like a spear. "Stowaway! We've got a stowaway!"

Brutal hands grasped my shoulders, dragged me across the crates, threw me to the ground. A crowd gathered, soldiers and servants alike come to ogle me.

I stared back at them, panting in horror, scrambling backwards until I collided with metal-clad shins. Gauntleted hands reached beneath my armpits, hauled me to my feet.

I was right all along.

This was never going to work.

THEY BOUND my hands and hauled me to a tent. I kicked and flailed instinctively, unable to bite down panic. *I should cooperate. I should show that I mean no harm.* But they shouted, and pointed weapons at me, and Ria was nowhere in sight.

Would they kill me without bothering to ask what I was doing in their wagon? Would they throw me out into the wilderness come morn, and leave me to navigate the woods alone? (My foraging skills were lackluster at best, but I could find my way home. I'd only been gone a day. If the soldiers showed me mercy, I might survive after all.)

Would they consider stowing away some sort of treason? Had I just doomed my entire family? Would we be safer if I lied about my identity?

I wriggled and writhed as they shoved me to the ground. As I crashed to my knees, a spear angled toward my throat.

"Wait," I croaked. "I can explain—"

"And you will," hummed one of the soldiers, a mustached man. "As soon as we retrieve the captain."

The pebbled earth was rough beneath my skin. I rolled my leg very slightly, not enough to attract attention. My knives were still strapped to my thighs, though they meant nothing if I couldn't reach them.

I was too shocked to fight back. I'd assumed I'd be discovered at some point, but hadn't thought it would be so soon. If my plan (poorly conceived as it was) was perfectly executed, Ria would protect me.

But now I wondered if anyone would bring her to me. If I'd have the chance to ask.

And even if she fought for me, would anyone listen? She had no authority. After all, what was she but a prince's stolen betrothed? I thought that the Tocchians were merciful, but now I wondered if I'd made a mistake in hoping that they wouldn't kill me.

If I screamed my name, would they listen?

"The princess," I gasped. "I'm her maid. She forgot about me."

"What?" guffawed one of the guards, spinning to stare at me. His eyes were a piercing green. "I—She really expects us to believe this," he said, turning to the guard next to him, gesturing wildly toward me.

"If you find Her Highness," I squirmed, twisting my shoulders so that I faced the mustached soldier as non-threateningly as possible. "I assure you, she can—"

"Why the fuck would a maid sneak into a wagon? Are you so desperate to keep your job?" The point of a sword pressed against the pulse point of my throat. Hot tears gathered in my eyes. "Or are you a spy?"

"Please," I whispered. "Princess Valeria—"

The mustached man swore and stepped out of the tent. "I'll go fetch His Highness. Bleeding Yaarkas, of course we find a lunatic..."

Another time, the invocation might have intrigued me. I knew little of Tocchian customs, and I was surprised to hear a soldier mention Yaarkas, the sacred army of the goddess Haline, who represented fairness in war. Was the mustached man from Olmstead?

Tocchian gods were dark and haunted, and rarely overlapped with ours. Olmstead shared its southern border with Alberbrook, where the gods were gentle and serene, healers and peacekeepers that contrasted with our bloody warlords, who rode chariots through the stars, accompanied by fortune telling cats and lobster guardians.

With two weapons pointed at my throat, I couldn't afford to ponder further.

Ria was coming, I told myself. Ria would vouch for me. Ria

would get me out of here, even if it meant I was sent back home, where Father would never let me out of his sight again.

Right now, I thought that might be preferable. Stuffed into the back of a wagon, I'd crouched miserably among crates that slammed into my ankles every time we started up or downhill. The number of times I thought I'd be crushed exceeded twenty. I spent hours battling a full bladder, on the verge of regretting my decision.

But I couldn't let Ria suffer alone. Even if I respected the Tocchians for killing as few of our people as possible, they'd still attacked our spring banquet, broken down our doors, terrorized our guests, and stolen away my sister.

Whatever unknown she headed into, I wanted to be at her side.

Outside, there was a commotion. A flurry of stomping feet and cracking twigs, the rustle of skirts.

"What is the meaning of this?" snarled a familiar voice. "I have no need of a maid, I'm perfectly capable—"

The tent's entrance flap shifted, and two faces peered inside. One belonged to Ria—streaked with dirt and utterly furious. The other I didn't recognize, but I knew right away that he wasn't the captain of the guard.

Long blond hair the color of old bone was tied loosely into a ponytail that reached nearly to his waist. Wide, ice blue eyes, plush lips, a pointed chin, and a long, straight nose that accentuated already prominent cheekbones. No facial hair smoothed his sharp features. A pale blue jerkin accentuated his tapered waist and broad shoulders. Dark pants clad his long, slim legs.

He should've seemed innocuous, but I saw only raw power simmering beneath his vaguely confused expression. I didn't know why, but I was certain he could kill me if he wanted to, and I'd never see it coming.

Even bound and afraid, I couldn't help but stare. Never had I seen anyone quite like him.

"Princess Valeria," I began, wrenching my body to face her, trying not to fall flat on my face. If I fell, those blades would surely pierce my throat. The last thing I wanted to do was bleed out in front of my sister, who would probably not share the luxury of oblivion for quite some time.

"Oh gods," choked Valeria, clapping a hand to her mouth. "Wait, please! I know this maid. You can't kill her!"

"That's right!" I panted. "She can't do her own hair. It's terrible. Someone has to save her from herself—"

"It's true." Valeria glanced anxiously at the man beside her.

"We can provide you a maid, you know," he said in a low, smooth voice that sent shivers through me. While his lips pressed together in suspicion, something else danced in his eyes. Amusement? Bewilderment? "Or you could have just asked to bring her along. There was no need to go to such lengths."

"I didn't—" said Valeria, snapping her mouth shut as she thought better of it. "Well, I suggested that perhaps my favorite maid might accompany me. I didn't mean for my invitation to be interpreted this way."

"I'm sorry," I said, and meant it. "I changed my mind, and there wasn't time to find you."

Ria scowled at the man beside her. (Prince Marius, my mind supplied, though I couldn't be certain.) "Yes, there was very little time to negotiate anything. You were not the only valued servant I was forced to leave behind. Perhaps Prince Marius might be open to forgiving your intrusion, and allowing you to continue to serve me in Tocchia?" She raised an eyebrow, and the man beside her frowned.

"Are you certain she is exactly who you say she is? Merely a maid, and nothing more?" His voice was rich and smooth as the finest wine, but the note of scrutiny never faded. My cheeks colored.

"Well, she is... It is unconventional arrangement. She also serves as one of my personal guards. Hence the sword." Ria gestured to me. "Which I'm sure you'll find in the wagon, if you haven't already."

"This reeks of betrayal," said the green-eyed soldier. Again, his sword angled toward me, uncomfortably close to the soft spot between my collarbones. "She's a spy."

"I swear she is not a spy," said Ria calmly, though the tension never left her face. "She is a longtime servant of mine. If you will not allow me to keep her in my employ, then I must insist we send her back to the castle. Unharmed," she added firmly.

"This is a betrayal!" the green-eyed soldier insisted. "Kill her now and charge the princess with treason."

Prince Marius gave a long-suffering sigh. "Although I value your opinion, Klar, I can appreciate that this situation needs to be handled delicately." He stood before me. "What is your name, Miss?"

"Arina," I said, before Ria could chime in with something I couldn't possibly remember. "Arina of Malloy, Your Highness."

"This is a most unconventional method of travel, Miss Arina. I would not advise attempting this in the future." His cool gaze raked up and down my body; his lips twisted as if he saw something he didn't like. And try as I might, I couldn't fight down a wave of disappointment.

"I can assure you I've more than learned my lesson," I said, looking everywhere but his face. A froth of lace spilled from his collar, and I stared at that instead. Surely it was only the lamplight and shadows that made his sharp features so lovely. In the daylight, I would realize that he was a mere mortal, handsome but nothing special. I wouldn't blush every time I crossed his path. "I won't do it again, Your Highness."

"I am prepared to forgive this transgression once and once only," he said. "Do not give me reason to believe you are anyone other than who you say you are. I will not be so merciful if I find you are..." He raised his eyebrows. "...lying."

"Thank you," Ria said. The breath she was holding rushed out of her in a whoosh.

"Thank you, Your Highness," I managed.

"Untie her," Prince Marius addressed the mustached guard. "See that she is reunited with her things and given something to eat. In the meantime," he nodded to Ria, "you are in charge of her. If she does anything untoward, you will answer for it. Am I understood?"

"Yes, Your Highness," she said, dipping into a curtsy. The elegance of the gesture was ruined by the unbridled loathing in her eyes. Gone was last night's dull acceptance. Ria was aflame with rage. Prince Marius need not fear me, but Ria would end him in a heartbeat, and I'd help her drag his corpse out into the middle of the mountains—rocks, bears, and snow be damned.

Then that fiery gaze met mine, and I knew I was in trouble, too. Perhaps more than Prince Marius.

Considering that it had been set up only an hour ago, Ria's tent was surprisingly luxurious. A small wooden table and two chairs sat atop a patterned rug. Beside it was a cot piled high with quilts and furs. A single flickering lantern lit the space.

"Are you hurt?" Ria demanded as soon as I'd seated myself.

"No," I mumbled, though my wrists and shoulders ached. Red welts wound around my wrist where the rope had scraped against my skin.

"What were you thinking?" she exclaimed, fuming. I looked away.

A servant entered the tent carrying two steaming bowls of something that smelled like fish and beans. A second arrived with two goblets and a bottle of wine. My stomach clenched.

"I didn't have time to think!" I told her. "You were going to leave!"

"You said you wouldn't do this," she hissed as the servants departed. "I told you to stay home and stay safe, and you betrayed my trust."

"Then send me home!" I snapped. Fury whipped through me. Tears pricked at the corners of my eyes. "If you're so angry, then get rid of me."

"Calm down," said Ria, settling into her chair the same way she did at her vanity back home.

I glowered at her, unwilling to shed the tears threatening to spill.

"Look, we haven't even left Olmstead yet," said Ria, pulling her bowl closer. "If you want to go home, you can."

"Do you want me to do that?" Returning home at this point would be akin to a prison sentence, and we both knew it. King Amonrew would never let me out of his sight again. He'd marry me off to the first man who showed interest, and make me *his* problem, and that could lead to all sorts of terrible things.

She took a bite of soup. "What do *you* want to do, Arina?"

It hurt to hear a false name on her lips. She spat it like a bitter herb.

"I don't know," I answered. "I—I didn't want to let you leave alone. I didn't like the idea of you stuck in that castle all by yourself. And I—I don't want to marry Alger."

"There's always the Duke of Alberbrook," said Ria gently.

I shook my head. "He saw me covered in blood, with my ankles exposed. He'll never recover from the shock, I fear."

Her laugh was genuine, but she muffled it with her hand. "Gods forbid he's assaulted by the sight of a rogue ankle."

"I'd be the death of him," I sighed wistfully, chin on my fist, and Ria laughed properly at that.

"You might very well be. But you'd be a duchess. That's no small thing."

I thought of picturesque palaces, bustles and skirts and clicking heels, gilded paintings and marble statues, afternoon tea in rose gardens. Galas and banquets and long evenings by the bonfire, a crescent moon overhead, leering and grinning—

And Callum, polite and proper and *handsome*. The blush returned to my cheeks.

I had greater aspirations for myself: a life spent in the forge, designing weapons for men like Callum. But there was no greater achievement than marrying into nobility, was there?

Then what was the point of cultivating my skills, only to throw them out the window the moment a man showed interest in me? Surely Father meant to do more than keep me occupied when he allowed me to pursue artificing.

But he'd pitied me. Remembered my mother, remembered the way everyone around me acted as though I didn't belong, like a rat in the pantry. Was he merely indulging me? Trying to allow me a few years of peace and independence before he ferried me off to a mediocre man?

The sting of betrayal shot deep into my bones. Perhaps my skills were a selling point. A way to interest suitors. But Father would sell me to the highest bidder, no doubt about it.

He'd severed the agreement with Tocchia the moment they broke the treaty. It didn't matter if they meant to help, he'd claimed. Their army on our land was nothing more than an act of war, even if a border city was threatened by enemy forces. Nemonia denied everything, and by the time our men arrived, there was no trace of them. Tocchia lied, and Father broke the treaty to protect Ria.

Or so he claimed.

"I don't know what I want," I said. "I thought I wanted something new, but now I'm afraid I might not be able to handle it."

"I'll take you back," said Ria. "Prince Marius won't dare harm you."

I shrugged. "Do you think Father is looking for me?"

"I've no idea," admitted Ria. "Probably."

"Do you think he suspects?"

"I think he knows you ran away. I doubt he knows you followed me."

Right, because this was a terrible idea. So terrible that even my own father wouldn't expect it of me.

"What happens if they find out?"

"I guess they can't," said Ria. "We can send you away if you decide to go home. We don't have to tell anyone." She crossed her legs. "Prince Marius owes me. He knows this. I *alone* prevented a war. If I tell him he must pardon you, he will. Everything you saw just now—theatrics. All theatrics. He knows how close he came to starting a war he couldn't win. He's got no power over me."

"That might change," I reminded her.

"It won't," she said. "It will haunt him the rest of his life. I'll make sure of it. It will be the third party in our marriage. A specter no exorcist can best."

I shivered. "Prince Marius is brave to marry you."

"I'll be the heart of his regrets," said Ria, taking another bite of soup.

"A noble aspiration." But such talk was treasonous, and the walls of our tent were thin. Since it was apparent Ria would lose herself in her quest for revenge, I decided to be the one to save her, and changed the subject. "I think I'd like to stay."

"Alright," said Ria slowly. "You can stay. But you must obey me. You must be careful. And you must agree to return home if I order you to."

"Fine," I said, though I felt as if I'd just made a deal with a fae creature, tricked by pretty words and desperation. "But you have to give me a chance."

"A *chance*, Arina," said Ria firmly. "If it isn't working, I won't stand by and let you suffer. Now eat something, please."

I lifted a spoonful of soup.

CHAPTER 8

The next few days passed in a blur. There weren't many extra horses, and I wasn't to be trusted anyway, so I sat next to one of the wagon drivers. A long, grey beard hung to his belly. His irises were a deep amber, nearly orange. I tried not to make too much eye contact.

But Jerek was kindly, if a little odd, and regarded me with only some trepidation.

My arrival sent the camp into a frenzy. The first night in Ria's tent, I lay awake listening to conversations as they passed us. Everyone wondered if I was a traitor, if I was sent by King Amonrew, if Ria knew about me. I fully expected someone to try to sneak in and kill me. I was somewhat shocked when I woke in the morning, exhausted and aching, but unharmed.

There were always too many eyes upon me. My skin felt as if it might crawl from my body, and away from me. I braided my hair (luckily still brown) in an attempt to divert some gazes, but it didn't work. My long, loose waves weren't the problem, after all.

Maybe it was the sword at my hip, which I was begrudgingly allowed after I swore to multiple soldiers that I was only here to guard Ria (and do her hair). Maybe it was my skirt. I hadn't thought to bring any pants, although to be fair, I hardly owned any. Father abhorred a woman in pants, claiming that they left too little to the imagination, that he knew too much about them at first glance. The only pair I owned was for horse riding, and I didn't always wear them—Father preferred I rode sidesaddle, and I preferred not to argue with him.

Ria and I shared little resemblance, so I doubted that anyone had guessed the truth of our relationship. I was shorter and fuller-figured, where she was tall and willowy. Her hair was so dark it was nearly black, her eyes a steely blue. I was paler, with hazel eyes, and now honey blond hair, thanks to the pin. Though we had similar noses, my features were not nearly as delicate and dainty as Ria's.

My mother was fuller figured, descended from a long line of northerners, and I took after her. Strong arms, broad shoulders, thick thighs. Though I was not large, I was more robust than Ria.

Women were uncommon around camp, working primarily as servants. Few though they were, they kept the camp running—building fires, cooking food, setting up tents, tending the horses. I felt out of place as I watched them work, suddenly aware of how coddled I was.

I knew next to nothing of travel, let alone setting up a camp. I offered to help, but the servants only rolled their eyes and assured me that the process would go faster if I stayed away.

So I spent a lot of time sweeping Ria's hair into elaborate, braided updos that made her like a warrior queen, ready to ride out to battle on horseback, sword raised, breastplate gleaming in the sunrise.

This couldn't be further from the truth. She stared grumpily at me from beneath her heavy cloak, cheeks red from the cold, consternation in her eyes as I passed her the mirror. "I look like a Northerner."

"Well, that's the idea," I said, deflating. Our mother wore her hair like this sometimes, when the mood struck her. Had Ria forgotten?

"Tocchia isn't *that* far north," she said, tilting her head one way, then another. "How did you learn to do this?"

I shrugged. "Boredom, mostly." And a desire to connect with our mother, half-forgotten, more shadow than memory with each passing year.

The days dragged on. To pass the time, Jerek told me stories of Tocchia. Of princes and kings who fought knee-deep in rushing rivers, queens who crawled through broken glass to save their heirs from certain death, the merpeople who visited from the coast, of the sky islands that hovered over the forest, mist layering between treetops and floating rock. All things that sounded more fairytale than truth, but I'd heard King Amonrew mention them, too.

Olmstead didn't have mer, he'd once explained. The Halbard Sea was too cold, the rocks too sharp for them to easily come ashore.

I thought Father was just telling stories. By nature, he was not a man of whimsy. I probably should have known better, especially when Rowan once suggested trade with the mer. At the time, I thought him as drunk as Baden, and opted to politely ignore his ramblings.

"They're real," Jerek told me, laughing when my eyes widened. "They're very real. You'll probably meet them. They'll want to meet the new princess of the realm. And you'd never know it, unless you saw them crawling out of the sea like urchins. They clean up real well, they do. Not like those seaweed dragging monsters you see in all the paintings."

A tapestry in the castle library depicted the mer naked and dripping, with seaweed climbing their legs like the wrappings of elaborate sandals, starfish in their hair, conch chariots rising from the depths behind them. As a child, I'd been both fascinated and terrified by it. The mer exuded power and mystery. The stormy sky and riotous waves lent the tapestry a sinister tone. One that haunted my nightmares.

It was fire that I feared the most. The excruciating heat of flames, the choking black smoke, the voracious appetite. But the sea was not so different, I thought. Overwhelming and dark, it could drag you down, down, down into its depths. People built boats and told themselves that they were safe, but that was all up to chance, and any fool knew it.

So like any reasonable person, I chose to align myself with the forge.

Prince Marius passed by frequently, always when I was at Ria's side. Though he scrutinized me less than the soldiers, I sensed his eyes on me and tried to avoid them. I didn't like the way he looked at me—like he knew something I didn't.

Nor did I like to look at him. He hadn't gotten uglier, like I'd hoped. In daylight, he was absolutely mesmerizing. Always loosely tied back, his long hair captured the sunlight, emphasizing a berry blush of warmth in his cheeks. Those cheekbones were still prominent, his lips full and soft. Pale lashes framed glacial blue eyes. His eyebrows were too expressive for propriety, always jumping and angling and pulling together. An easy tell. I would bet good money that they nearly drove King Hergarv of Tocchia to madness. No heir to the throne should betray his emotions so easily.

This was a weakness I approved of and secretly gloated over. Prince Marius might think that he could observe me from afar without my notice, but I knew better, and did my best to either disappear from his line of sight or become unbearably boring.

He was right to be skeptical, of course. A war could be triggered if he were caught trafficking a princess—or a spy or an assassin or whatever else I might be accused of—into Tocchia.

Sometimes, I felt bad about that. Then I looked to Ria, miserable and lonely, and decided that I'd made the right choice. I couldn't abandon her now. Couldn't bear to lose her.

We would manage, somehow. Together, we always found our way.

~

MY CONFIDENCE WANED as we entered the mountains.

Snow crunched beneath my feet and dusted the branches of evergreens and the pockmarked surfaces of great, mossy boulders. Deer darted between trees and crashed through the underbrush. Once, the scouts ahead encountered a bear, massive and snarling, with scars across its muzzle and claws longer than a human finger. It disappeared into the woods, but we had no doubt that it was still out there somewhere.

At night, wolves and wind howled as one. Our tent threatened to rip free from its stakes, and I feared what might happen if it collapsed. I slept with a knife under my pillow, but what if I couldn't cut through the heavy leather in time?

The trail grew rocky and uneven. We traveled slowly, so that the horses were less likely to snap their legs.

Castle Ackervail lurked in the shadow of the mountains, in the rugged terrain along the rocky sea. Our winters were frozen, our summers mild. The mountains were great, jagged specters capped in white and grey, so lined with trees so that they appeared furred on clear days. I had little appreciation for the way the pass would swallow us whole, carrying us alongside verdant valleys dotted with brilliant, turquoise lakes and ponds. Ledges were sharp and steep. One wrong move, and I might topple into those depths—a sea of green trees, massive boulders, and swaying grasses far below. Like an open maw.

Ridges and sharp peaks stretched out before us, harsh, unforgiving, beautiful in the same way as a cougar or shark. It was easy to forget the danger until the hair stood up on the back of your neck.

As a company, we were a racket, nearly a riot, stomping

through the mountains, all clanking armor, thumping wheels, and loud voices. Sometimes, the soldiers erupted into song, and Jerek and I would join in, raising our voices high, garbling the melodies and mixing up the words. Most of the soldiers shot us dirty looks, but others conspired with us, creating parodies of the original lyrics, their laughter echoing through the trees.

This isn't to say that we weren't miserable. Winds whipped at high speed, threatening to overturn the wagons, chapping our skin, aggravating the horses. The mornings and nights were frozen. Even with the sun to warm us during the day, a cloak and boots didn't feel like enough protection from the cold.

Twice, it snowed. Fat, heavy flakes that drifted slowly to the ground, compounding the piles already there, spreading slowly across the forest floor like a pestilence. The wind was cruelly cold. It leeched the warmth from my bones and fed it to the frozen sky.

Our tent could not keep out the chill. Ria and I slept beneath a pile of heavy furs, huddled together for warmth, as we did when we were children. Except now there was no giggling. No stories were whispered, no hopes and dreams traded. Shock had stolen the words from Ria, and I feared making things worse for her by saying too much, so I kept my mouth shut, loneliness locked deep inside.

I missed my snarky, angry sister. The woman in her place was tired, lost, broken down. Sometimes I saw Prince Marius and hoped he might fall over the ledge, and land atop a bed of sharp rocks.

Why did he want Ria so badly? Vengeance? Jealousy? A sense of ownership?

For all that I wanted him dead, Prince Marius didn't seem to feel *any* of these things. So far as I could tell, he was not overtly wicked. It didn't matter what Ria did—he offered no opinion. Did not warn her away from the outskirts of camp when she went to empty her chamber pot (something I, as her new maid, had promised to do and promptly forgotten). He did not care that she never rode with him, and often preferred to walk amongst the soldiers, head held high, fine boots growing dirtier by the day.

If he were naturally cruel, he might force her to walk, or to sit beside him—whichever was worse. He might withhold food or water, or force to share his tent. But he never did any of those things.

He was far from kind, and I didn't trust him one bit, but I didn't think he posed an immediate threat.

Hypocritical though it might be, I monitored him, too. What kind of man ordered an attack on the castle of his former betrothed? It wasn't like he and Ria were in love, or he couldn't find another arrangement. If not for his hasty actions, the alliance between Tocchia and Olmstead might have one day been repaired.

I watched, and I pondered, and I waited.

CHAPTER 9

It was after midnight, and I couldn't sleep.

All night long, the wind wept and raged. Ria snored gently, one arm hanging from the edge of her cot, dead to the world.

I tossed and turned. Though I'd been exhausted when I went to bed, my energy returned as soon as my head hit the pillow. I closed my eyes and tried to think about anything other than the howling wind, and Ria's snoring.

The prince's face appeared behind my closed eyelids, angular and angry, a single brow raised as if to ask, *"Well?"*

I groaned in exasperation. Ria didn't answer.

I used the chamber pot and climbed back into bed. Still, sleep evaded me.

Finally, I threw back the blankets and donned my boots and cloak. No one told me I couldn't leave my tent at night, just that I *shouldn't*. And though I hardly wanted to be out among the soldiers at night, I didn't know what else to do. Anxiety crept through my veins like a slow-burning poison, and I couldn't stand it any longer.

Light on my feet, I slipped between tents, hardly daring to

breathe. I wasn't doing anything wrong, but it might be difficult to convince the soldiers of that.

But I needed a moment to myself. A minute or two to breathe deeply under the moonlight. No matter what I did, I'd be tired tomorrow. But I couldn't lie on that cot any longer, waiting for sleep to take me like death. Or a lover. At this point, I'd accept either.

Avoiding campfires and guards alike, I sneaked to the far reaches of camp, where the clearing turned to forest. Bare branches and trunks dripped with silvery moonlight, and I took a moment to inhale the scent of pine and birch, the sharp smell of fresh snow.

I took another step into the forest, careful to keep the camp within my line of sight. If I went missing, Ria would be devastated. Prince Marius would be somehow even more suspicious. And the soldiers would resent using any time at all to track me down. They would probably leave me to die, without even a perfunctory search. After all, I was nothing more than an unexpected addition. Another mouth to feed. Another burden to bear.

I'd never been anything else. King Amonrew treated me as part of his family, but I knew well enough what I was. A product of guilt. Father had shielded me from endless accusations, but when I looked in the mirror, I only saw a hopeless bastard, lonely and confused, playing dress-up in a princess's clothes. It didn't matter if he swore up and down that I was his child. I didn't believe him.

Leaving the tent was a mistake. I felt worse outside, standing among the trees like a woodland creature dazzled by starlight.

There was no outlet for my pent-up energy. In the darkness, I was hesitant to stray too far. The soldiers would not welcome me at their fires. I had no real friends among the Tocchians, though I strived for alliances with the servants. My new position as Ria's guardian/maid seemed to confuse them, and I couldn't blame them. It was so obviously made-up. Acceptable only because Ria vouched for me, and Prince Marius couldn't afford to anger her further.

I'd never felt more alone.

Minutes passed. Deciding there was no time like the present, I plucked the crystal obelisk from my pocket, and whispered, "Light."

Nothing happened.

I shook it vigorously. "Light," I repeated.

Only darkness.

"Work, gods damn it!" I cried, lobbing the obelisk at a tree trunk. It bounced off a boulder, and landed in the dirt, where it began to glow dully.

"Of course," I grumbled, stomping as I went to retrieve it. Nothing about this crystal had gone as planned. No number of enchantments, spells, potion baths, or anything else that usually guaranteed success worked. I had a half a mind to leave it there, glowing pitifully on the forest floor, a testament to my failure and its own triumphant stubbornness.

But I wasn't ready to go back to camp, and the dim light was better than nothing.

With the crystal illuminating my way, I slipped further into the trees, pausing to mark them with my dagger, nearly weeping as the bark blunted the blade. I told myself it didn't matter. I had nothing to do tomorrow but sit beside Jerek and sharpen my knives after supper.

This entire exercise was pointless. I already knew I wouldn't feel better. I needed to get back to camp before someone caught me and demanded an explanation. Restlessness, I'd been told time and again, was never an excuse for misbehavior.

But I so desperately needed this moment of control, where my choices were all my own, and nobody was around to criticize them.

In the distance, I heard something snuffle.

I froze, imagining a deer, or perhaps a skunk. With no desire for an altercation tonight, I started to back away.

A twig snapped behind me. I whipped around and saw nothing.

Then came the furious pounding of feet—crunching through leaves and snow, trampling the underbrush.

I fumbled for my dagger and nearly dropped the crystal.

The trees shuddered. Snow sprayed from their branches and scattered through the air. Something grunted. A pair of eyes appeared, gleaming in the moonlight.

I shrieked as the bear charged from the bushes.

Leaves clung to its matted fur. Massive paws thundered against the forest floor, talons leaving behind indentations. The stench of blood and shit was nearly overpowering.

I choked on bile.

Tiny ears twitched. The bear's mouth opened, and I glimpsed long, yellow teeth. Strings of saliva connected the top and bottom fangs.

Those fangs would soon be red with blood. Though my mind screamed at me to run, my feet were rooted to the spot.

We had bears in Olmstead. I was lucky enough to have never crossed paths with them, but even I knew that running would only make things worse. Bears rarely attacked humans, but they liked it when their snacks fought back. Fleeing would only excite it.

Eyes glinting, the beast stampeded toward me, spit flying, huffing loudly, like we'd been engaged in a game of cat and mouse for a long time now.

As if it would have to do anything more than throw itself on top of me to kill me. A single claw in the belly, and I'd bleed out.

Throw something! cried a little voice in the back of my mind that sounded a lot like my mother's. *Throw something at it!*

There was no time to stoop and pry a rock from the frozen

earth. I glanced at the crystal in my hand and made a snap decision.

I lobbed it at the bear with all my strength. Then I loosed a scream of rage and threw up my arms so that my cloak fluttered around me like a pair of massive wings.

The bear halted in its tracks, and watched me with beady eyes, head cocked as if assessing whether a puny human could harm it. Up close, I realized that it was absolutely enormous. Were it to stand, it might be well over seven feet tall. I could just barely make out the scars crisscrossing its snout, winding up its leg like vines.

Was this the bear that had been spotted a few days ago?

I didn't have time to wonder. Its mouth opened, and I ducked down, scrabbling my fingers along the ground, searching for something, anything that I could throw at it.

I wasn't exactly adept at throwing knives, and I was loath to part with my dagger, so I needed to find something else, and fast. My fingers curled around a branch, short but thick, and I stood, chucking it at the bear.

The branch bounced off its nose. A disgruntled snort. Then the bear rose onto its back legs.

And ran right at me.

I screamed again, staggering backward, groping at the air with my free hand, clutching the dagger with the other.

A shadow darted before me. A flash of silver followed.

"Run!" the shadow snarled, and I did. All of ten feet, until I found a tree with a trunk thick as a bloated corpse and sneaked behind it. I peered out into woods drenched in moonlight and watched.

The bear charged, spraying spittle as it roared.

The figure before me raised his sword. Blond hair, long and loose, draped over a dark cloak.

Shit. Prince Marius himself had come to rescue me.

There was no way he could go up against a beast of this size and live to tell the tale. Not by himself, anyway.

Bending low, I snatched up anything I could find—pebbles, twigs, chunks of bark. I stuffed branches into the crook of my arm.

"Get down!" I shouted.

Prince Marius dropped to the ground with the elegance of a potato sack. Embarrassing, but effective.

I launched the first rock at the bear and narrowly missed. Flinching, the bear took step back. I hurled another rock, and another, until it was panting, glancing around wildly.

"Are you mad?" hissed Prince Marius, grasping his sword. He remained squatted down, hands over his head, as I pelted the bear with everything in reach.

"Yell at it! Wave your arms! Flap your cloak about!" I snapped at him. Then I turned back to the bear, and screeched, "You! Begone, you massive, reeking fuckwit! No one invited you!"

The prince let out a guffaw as he stood, the corners of his cloak grasped in his hands, spread wide like a sheet as he stretched out his arms. "Yes," he rasped, nearly choking with laughter. "No one invited you!"

"Scram!" Another rock pelted its snout.

"Go away!" Marius flapped his cloak and lunged forward, not unlike an enormous bat.

The bear turned from us at last and thundered into the forest.

"I don't suppose I need to ask if you're alright," said the prince, turning to me.

"I, um, yes. I think I am. Alright, that is." My hands were badly scraped, and my knees trembled like saplings in a gale, but I didn't feel any cuts or scratches. "It didn't hurt me."

"Mm, yes, but it was about to," said Prince Marius. He sighed, as if terribly inconvenienced. "Please return to camp with me. I think we should talk, and it would be far nicer to do so in front of a nice, warm fire. Wouldn't you agree?"

Why did this feel like a trap? "Are you angry with me?"

The prince let out a huff that reminded me of the bear. "I'm *annoyed*. I'm sure I don't need to tell you how reckless it is to wander through the woods alone at night. And you should fire your artificer. That crystal is absolute shit."

Arms crossed, I scowled at him. "I happen to like that crystal."

"It only worked when you threw it," he reminded me, unimpressed. "Now please, will you let me save you from yourself?"

"I had it handled," I insisted, even as I begrudgingly made my way toward him, pausing to snatch up the crystal, which flashed weakly in my hand, and died. "But thank you anyway, Your Highness."

"Might I ask what brings a maid such as yourself into the woods alone so late at night?" Disapproval colored his voice.

I bristled. "Might I ask what brings a prince into the woods after her so late at night?"

"The screaming, mostly." His eyebrows raised, the corners of his mouth turned up into a smile that I might've found charming if he hadn't given me at least one thousand reasons to hate him. "Actually, I saw you sneaking out of my betrothed's tent, and I wondered why her guard might leave her unattended in the night."

I kicked a pebble between overgrown tree roots. "It's hardly abandonment. There are soldiers everywhere. I just couldn't sleep."

"Hmm," droned Prince Marius, so low that his voice practically vibrated. "Perhaps you went to meet someone."

"That someone would've been very lucky not to become bear food," I snapped. "There was no one out there. Just me and my thoughts."

"They looked like heavy thoughts indeed," he mused, tilting his head. "Is my camp not to your liking?"

"I'm less than pleased with the circumstances surrounding it."

His smile tightened into a grimace. "Yes, I can imagine so. What was your name again?"

"Arina, Your Highness."

"I had hoped to avoid any trouble with Olmstead, but your king refused both reason and all of my messages. This was our final option. I hope you can understand."

"You broke down the door," I said, stepping over a mossy tree root that extended far from its trunk, reaching across the forest floor like the tentacle of an octopus. "You killed our people. You took Princess Valeria."

He gave a sharp, curt nod. Official. The spark in his eye died away. "I would tell you of my regrets, but I know you won't believe me."

"You're right. I don't."

He sighed. "Regardless, I'd like to pass them on."

"I'm not in the habit of accepting other people's burdens," I snapped, skipping ahead of him. "Thank you for saving me, but I don't believe a single word from your mouth." I shook my head and turned to glower at him. "Didn't they teach you how to fight off a bear? Don't you have bears in Tocchia?"

I walked quickly, looking over my shoulder in case the great beast had returned. But we were accompanied only by silence.

"Not near the palace," said the prince slowly, tucking a strand of hair behind his ear. "But yes, I've been informed. I drew my sword because I thought you might be injured, or worse. Regardless of what you may think of me, I am not a man who rejoices in bloodshed. I don't wish to see anyone suffer, no matter how they might," his gaze lingered a beat too long on my face, "infuriate me."

"Infuriate?" I repeated, too shocked to be upset. "What have I done to infuriate you?"

"I know you're lying to me. I don't know why you're here."

"Then just kill me now!" I said, throwing my arms wide, thrusting my chest forward, so that he might drive his blade through my heart.

The implication missed him entirely. He stared at my breasts, wide-eyed and open-mouthed, until he realized what he was doing, and tore his gaze away. "I don't want to kill anyone!" he growled. "For goddess's sake, there's no need for any of this. I'm hardly going to skewer you here in the woods."

"Which goddess?" I demanded. "Plenty of them would enjoy that." Thalma, for instance, who drank the blood of lovers that betrayed her, but would accept just about any sacrifice so long as violence was involved.

"Not anyone I would make an oath to," he sighed. At my expression, his frown deepened. "We Tocchians are not barbarians, you know."

I *didn't* know, so I didn't respond.

The campsite came into view, its fires flickering orange, shadowing the peaked tents. The last of my tension faded.

"Will you speak with me?" Prince Marius asked, as we approached the first of the fires. A guard scowled at us, but Prince Marius waved him off.

"Why? What could you possibly need to know?"

"I'd hoped to make amends," said Prince Marius. "For your poor impression of me." His voice dropped. "And might I remind you that in public, you ought to use my title."

"Yes, Your Highness," I grumbled. He was right. I'd nearly given myself away.

"No experienced maid would forget something like that," he said, the ghost of a grin on his lips.

"My deepest apologies, Your Highness. I'm afraid I was quite flustered, given the situation with the bear." I kept my gaze low, away from his pale eyes.

"See that it doesn't happen again, Miss Arina. I can see you'd rather not speak further, so consider yourself excused for the evening. See that you do not abandon your post, or your charge, again." He spoke in a clipped voice, quick and professional, like he hadn't just thrown himself in front of a bear for me.

"Understood, Your Highness."

I practically ran to my tent, his penetrating gaze glued to my back as I went.

"YOU FOUGHT A BEAR?!" Ria hissed at me over a hurried breakfast of hard tack and last night's leftovers. "What is wrong with you?"

"It wasn't as though I went looking for the bear!" I whispered back, taking another bite of greasy sausage. It would sit poorly in my stomach, but I knew I'd regret skipping breakfast later, so I forced myself to eat. "And it was hardly a fight. Your betrothed saved me. Well, kind of. I think maybe I saved him. Anyway, you may want to teach him about bear safety, lest you lose him to the woods."

Ria groaned. "What happened? What are you talking about?"

My embarrassment mounted as I explained. Ria's mouth hung agape, her eyebrows angled sharply downward.

"You absolute buffoon!" she moaned when I finished, dragging her fingers down the sides of her face in exasperation.

"I know," I mumbled. "It won't happen again."

"What were you thinking? I'm going to have to vouch for you! *Again*! You cannot continue doing things like this, Arina. You're entirely too reckless, and you'll put us both in a bad position. You realize that, don't you?"

I stared down at my feet. "I'm sorry."

"Don't do it again," Ria said, stomping back to the tent.

CHAPTER 10

I heard nothing more from Prince Marius. Though he occasionally caught my eye and nodded politely, we never went within twenty feet of each other.

But the glint of his sword, the way he threw himself in front of me—it was unforgettable. An act of chivalry? Or something else?

There was no real warmth in his gaze, only idle curiosity. I didn't even like him. So why did my blood run hot whenever I saw him?

Ria barely spoke to me the rest of the journey. Whenever I made a comment, she turned her back to me, wordless, and continued whatever she was doing as if I didn't exist.

The next two weeks were miserable. Our rations ran low, and though deer and pheasant were plentiful, there wasn't always enough to go around. Snow fell at night, and the wind blew during the day. The mountains formed a cage around us, and I thought I'd never see a way out. That I could run down the trail for months, and I'd never find the end of it.

Until one morning, when we emerged at the top of a ridge. The mountains descended into brilliant green fields, punctuated by thickets of forest. Beyond them, a sapphire sea, sparkling under the rising sun.

The sight of it took my breath away. Rivers wound through a land dotted with trees, a more magnificent green than I had ever known.

At the edge of the sea, grey walls cradled a city at the top of a hill. Its roads cut through the land like the coils of a snake. Settled in the center like a tilted crown was the castle, white and gleaming, its towers capped in gold. Stained glass windows added a riot of color.

But the most shocking thing of all floated high above the hills, casting a great shadow across the land.

The floating kingdom of Liridin.

I'd seen illustrations before and thought them nothing more than flights of fancy. But now I found myself face to face with a boulder the size of an actual island, hovering perhaps a few miles away. Vines cascaded down the sides, drifting in the wind like seaweed in a current. Thick, heavy roots spiraled free from the rocky base.

Every inch of the surface was covered in trees. White clouds drifted overhead, unbothered. When I stood on tiptoe, I spotted the very tip of a tower. A flag rippled in the wind, blue and purple and white.

In my effort not to let my gaze waver, I tripped over my own feet. Ria reached to steady me. When I turned to her, I saw that her eyes were as wide as my own.

"It's real," she mumbled. "All of it."

"I know," I said, unable to look away. The floating kingdom drifted across the sky, aimless as a cloud. A veil of mist surrounded its base. The longer I looked, the higher it rose, until the trees were cloaked in clouds.

"It doesn't like outsiders," said a passing soldier. "Stop staring at it."

But I couldn't. Not yet. Not when it felt as if my entire world had cracked open, spilling free the creatures and places of myth like a rich yolk.

This place was real. And I was going to live here, at least for a time.

Would I ever want to leave? If I did, would the decision haunt me like an old scar, a half-remembered dream of awe and horror, violence and desire?

I didn't know, and that bothered me the most.

My memories of Olmstead were comparatively grey and dreary. The pops of color that I loved so much were suddenly dull and listless, no more than blobs among dirty snow and muddy roads.

Even Alberbrook couldn't compare to this magnificence. For all that I'd loved its babbling brooks and tall trees, its sun dappled streets and beautiful architecture, Tocchia's loveliness was of another tier.

Eventually, Ria and I were forced to move on, barked at by a soldier that we needed to keep up, lest His Highness be forced to intervene.

"We wouldn't want that," said Ria caustically, glaring at the solider, who lowered his visor and stared straight ahead as if he'd never spoken at all.

The next three days passed in an excited blur. No longer did I feel devoured and depleted. Spirits were high. Jerek and I sang along loudly to the marching songs, and sometimes Ria joined us. Whenever I sang the wrong words on purpose, turning the lyrics from valiant to bawdy, she was sure to elbow me in the ribs. But I caught her grinning, too.

At night, laughter and chatter echoed across the campsite. The servants flurried about like dying leaves in a gust of wind, shaking out rugs, gathering the laundry, scrubbing the pots with a fury I'd not want directed at me. But they, too, were jollier, singing and laughing as they worked.

The weather improved. The terrible, blustery wind faded to a gentle breeze. The snow on the ground lessened, then disappeared as we grew closer to sea level.

The hills were a harsh terrain, the trails wet and rocky, but none of the Tocchians seemed to notice. Occasionally, I glimpsed big eyes, fluffy cheeks, and waving tails lurking in the tall grasses. Chipmunks and weasels darted about, watching eagerly as we ate, snatching food from unattended plates.

We passed settlements where villagers waved the blue and white Tocchian flag. They ran out to greet us, eager to catch a glimpse of Prince Marius and the infamous Princess Valeria. At his side, she held her head high, kept her gaze straight ahead, unyielding and proud. Marius was more polite, making eye contact and waving, which excited everyone, especially the children. But no one dared approach him, other than an old man who spat and swore. We continued on our way with little incident.

I traipsed along after Ria, and smiled at everyone who smiled at me, because I wasn't trained in the art of resentment. Not like Ria. No, I was taught to smile and wave and act graciously, and I found it difficult to do anything else, regardless of what my new position might require.

What was wrong with a friendly bodyguard?

Probably a lot of things, but I couldn't think of any, and for now, that was justification enough.

~

We reached the city gates at midday. Though it wasn't particularly hot, the sun beat down on us, blindingly bright, a force in its own right.

Perched upon a hill, the city of Dranning overlooked the sea. The wind returned with such force that it threatened to rip my hair free from its braid. Fat, white gulls circled overhead, fighting against the gale.

A crowd gathered to watch us outside the gates, far less

generous than the peasants we'd passed earlier. The people here were just as dirty and tired, but they spat and swore with a malice that I didn't anticipate.

I stayed as close to Ria as I could without imposing on Prince Marius's guards. With one hand on my sword at all times, I felt suddenly inadequate. If someone lunged at my sister, could I fight them off?

Perhaps I should discuss my demotion with Ria later. I would make a woefully inept maid, but that would be better than allowing a situation where I couldn't defend her.

We wound through the streets, passing markets, shops, stalls selling meat and bread. My stomach clenched at the mixed aromas. I'd eaten nothing palatable in days, and I suddenly longed for fresh bread and soft, easily spread cheeses, or rich, sweet jams.

Somewhere in the distance, a hammer clanged against steel. I stopped in my tracks, transfixed by homesickness, longing for the familiar forge, and the company of Ronnie and Cranz.

I was determined not to miss Olmstead. And so far, I hadn't. I'd coasted along, careful to keep distracted so that I wouldn't be overwhelmed with trepidation and regret. Ria needed me, and she was more important than anything else.

Besides, I craved freedom from the iron gauntlet that King Amonrew had constructed around me. Every day, its grasp grew a little bit tighter, until I realized that my arms were aching, my lungs struggling to fill. There was no room to flail or fight.

Maybe in Tocchia I wouldn't have to worry about marriage, or birthright, or my perceived threat to the crown, or anything else. I could live as a normal person, and experience all that I'd coveted.

At least for a little while.

The roads carried us to the top of the hill, where a set of massive gates marked the entrance to the castle. I felt the scrutiny of guards at my back and fought the urge to shrink away.

Horse's hooves clicked against cobblestones. The wheels of our wagons grew unbearably loud.

Here, no one screamed at us. Instead, they watched our procession with curiosity and some derision, eyes locked on Ria even as they showered the prince with enthusiastic cries, sweeping bows, and dipping curtsies. We dismounted, and the wagons disappeared behind the castle, presumably to a back entrance.

The stone walls were smooth, gleaming white. They made the seagulls strutting through the streets look grey.

This was no castle, but a palace, I realized as we drew nearer. Cobblestone roads were lined with elaborately maintained hedges in the shapes of griffins, bears, albatrosses, dolphins. Flowers sprouted from carefully placed planters like clusters of jewels, pinks and blues and yellows more vibrant than I'd ever seen. An emerald lawn sprawled lazily before the palace. In its center, water sprayed from a tulip shaped fountain. Carved above the main entrance was the Tocchian crest—blood dripping from a snake's fangs. The sight of it made me uneasy.

Towers rose high into the air. Their windows were tall and rounded, the glass latticed. Vines crawled along the walls, dotted with tiny pink flowers. Balconies lined the upper floors.

The palace was at least twice the size of Castle Ackervail. Simply looking at it was overwhelming. What secrets lay within its walls? Would I get lost on the way to breakfast?

If I did, would anyone ever find me again?

How could Father paint Tocchia as weak and desperate when their royals lived in a palace such as this? Had the inside fallen to ruin? Or had I been lied to my entire life?

My heels clicked against the cobblestones. I stayed close to Ria, more intimidated than I wanted to admit.

"You'll want to see your quarters, I presume," said Prince Marius, appearing out of nowhere beside Ria, not unlike a specter. I suppressed a yelp. The last I'd seen him, he was drowning in a crowd of admirers, unfazed beneath the weight of their adoration.

Ria didn't even startle. "Yes," she said, clasping her hands before her. "I would very much appreciate some time to myself."

The prince nodded. "And her?" he said, sparing me a glance the same begrudging way one might spare a grifter a coin. "Shall I have her escorted to the servants' quarters?"

Ria shook her head. "I'll take her with me. I'll send her to her quarters after dinner."

"A word of caution: the king will be at dinner. You'll find he is an understanding man, but I'd not test him." The prince scowled. In the brilliant sunlight, he looked exhausted; his jerkin was covered in dust, his shirt stained with sweat and mud. A necklace of black stone pressed against the hollow of his throat, diamond-shaped, streaked with white veins. A silver chain held it in place.

I frowned. I'd failed to notice this before.

Then I thought of his shirts, spilling frothy lace from the collars, and realized that he'd probably been hiding it all along.

Interesting. This was no precious stone. Not onyx, sapphire, black opal, or anything else that I recognized. It had an unusual quality to it, dull and listless. An odd thing for a prince to wear, and an even stranger thing to hide. It would tempt no thief and hardly required protection.

Prince Marius followed my gaze and adjusted the clasp of his jerkin. The necklace disappeared.

It must be enchanted. For protection, anonymity, patience—any value that could be imagined.

A prince would need such baubles, after all.

And I could make them for him, if only he asked.

The I remembered that I wasn't fully trained, and my heart sank. Artificers were uncommon, but not so much that they were difficult to find. If Marius needed an artificer, he could get one without sponsoring my training.

Unless... Could I convince him? I imagined working in a Tocchian forge, finding a use for myself there. My heart raced.

But news would reach Olmstead. King Amonrew would know

that I'd slipped away with Ria. He'd use my disappearance as an excuse to attack Tocchia.

A part of me felt that Tocchia deserved retaliation, but another battle so soon would break me from cracked stone to dust.

A servant named Zellia led Ria and I through the palace, chattering nervously. Two long, neat braids hung over her shoulders. "His Highness asked me to give you the grand tour on the way to your room. So much as I can, that is!" she chirped, gesturing across the enormous entryway. "We will take the grand staircase to the third floor, where we will pass Her Majesty's Queen Tarra's quarters, Princess Odalla's quarters, and the rooms of the children. You'll be among good company."

We followed up her up a staircase of gleaming white marble, threaded with grey. A blue carpet softened our footsteps, so unbearably plush that I feared the tread of my boots might tear it. Above us, a chandelier twinkled cheerfully. The crown molding was gilded and elaborate. On the ceilings were paintings of sea monsters and winged humans, extravagant ships dripping with gold, jewels, and naked women, books whose spines were encrusted with stones and blood, a woman on a broom zipping past fluffy clouds... Everywhere I looked, a new section of ceiling depicted something else.

I tripped over my own feet, and Ria scowled at me. "Be careful," she grumbled.

"Sorry," I whispered. "Look at the ceiling!"

Ria glanced up, shook her head, and continued after Zellia as if she weren't in absolute awe.

I paused frequently throughout the tour, constantly astonished. Even the side tables were exquisitely carved, far finer than anything in Olmstead. The tapestries were few but detailed enough that I wondered if each one was the crowning glory of a different artist's career.

I stopped to admire vases, paintings and their frames, embroidered curtains, even the delicately carved tiles on the bathroom floor.

By the time we approached Ria's room, my head was spinning. How had Tocchia accumulated such opulence? How was a kingdom with a reputation as weak and small able to maintain and defend such a household?

Tocchia's subjects must be well-cared for, indeed, if they hadn't stormed the palace and smashed it to bits by now.

King Amonrew feared such retribution and spoke of it often. Was that the reason our castle was so comparatively drab? Or was it an excuse to cover up our own lack of wealth?

"You must be excited to be here," said Zellia, oblivious to Ria's total disinterest and my own distraction.

"Oh yes," said Ria, dour as ever. "I love being kidnapped."

Cheeks blossoming a brilliant red, Zellia burst out, "Oh no, Your Highness, I merely meant that you must be glad of new accommodations after so long in a tent! I can only imagine."

"If my father retaliates, you won't need to imagine," Ria hummed.

Horror and humiliation crossed Zellia's face, turning her cheeks from red to nearly purple. "I'm so sorry, Your Highness. I spoke out of turn—"

"It's very beautiful here," I interrupted, because I couldn't stand to see anyone, even a servant, so incredibly flustered. "This palace is truly breathtaking."

"Yes," Ria muttered. "Breathtaking."

I pretended that her glare wasn't directed at me and gestured to a painting on the wall. "And who is that?"

"That is but a maiden," stammered Zellia. "It is—I do not know her name."

"Oh," I said, supposing it was foolish to think that the woman sitting beneath a gnarled tree, and a sky full of shooting stars would be of significance. Long, silvery blond hair fell over her shoulders, spilling across the roots of the tree like a winding river. In one hand, she held a pitcher, in the other, the horn of a goat.

Her smile suggested that she knew something I didn't.

We paused before the royal portraits. King Hergarv clutched a sapphire-topped scepter, one eyebrow slightly raised. (I could see where Prince Marius inherited his expressive face, though he didn't share the king's features.) The crown atop his head gleamed gold; rubies and emeralds were arranged in a floral pattern across the front.

Queen Tarra's portrait depicted a serene, deeply tanned woman amid a room with pristine, gilded furniture. A pale blue dress draped to the floor. Her crown was made of gold and aquamarine, her hair tied into a braid that dangled to her hips.

We reached Ria's room, pushing through heavy doors that would surely withstand both arrow and sword, if not an ax.

The chamber wasn't as lavish as I expected. Marble pillars, paintings of a sea at storm, sweeping velvet curtains, a basin of porcelain. A blue and gold rug cushioned the floor. The balcony was large enough to host its own gathering. The sea thrashed in the distance; its horizon dotted with boats.

I was immediately enamored, but Ria pursed her lips as she approached the four-poster bed, where a decanter of wine waited for her. A tray of tiny red fruits sat beside it.

I admired the posts carved with leaves and roses, the bedspread that smelled faintly of perfume.

"It will do," said Ria at last.

"We will decorate it to your liking, my lady," said Zellia hurriedly. "His highness was not sure what you might like, so he opted to leave the room relatively unfurnished."

"He may be surprised to learn that I require very little," said Ria. "My heart will not be won with baubles and hair pins."

"Perhaps it could be softened," I said, and immediately regretted my words.

Ria whirled around to glare at me, her eyes narrowed, nostrils flared, teeth bared like a wolf's. "Do not dare suggest such things to me," she said, and whirled on her heel to bare her teeth at Zellia. "Leave us. I've been informed I must prepare for dinner, and I intend to do so *alone*."

"As you wish," said Zellia, clasping her hands and backing away as if faced with a cougar.

"Do not suggest I ought to adapt to captivity," Ria said as soon as the door closed behind us. "I don't think you understand what is going on here. I don't think you realize that I had no choice in this, that I had to cooperate or risk losing everyone and everything. I didn't want you subjected to this. I don't want to be here at all, and I don't know why you followed me, except to make my life difficult!"

I flinched. "I didn't want you to be alone. I thought you might need me."

"*Need* you?" Ria snarled. "Why would I need you? I've been training for this my entire life! Everything has revolved around becoming Prince Marius's betrothed! What could you possibly have to offer me here?" she hissed. "I wanted you safe at home, not stuck with me. Go home, Talina. I don't need you."

Tears streamed down my face, but I stood my ground, shaking my head fiercely. "No. You need somebody here with you. I don't trust Prince Marius."

"Go home," Ria said, turning her back to me. "It's what's best for both of us."

CHAPTER 11

I spent the next hour on the balcony, staring out at the sea, lost in my thoughts like a boat among the waves.

There was no way I could return home now. I'd have to hope Ria didn't banish me. As much as she might think she wanted to be alone, I knew better. This palace would become lonely fast. If I left, she would sink into melancholy.

A part of me thought perhaps she deserved to be alone. The cold ocean air was no balm for the sting of her words.

But I didn't believe in vengeance. Not in the ways of kings and courtiers, anyway.

Eventually, Ria came to join me, shamefaced. "I'm sorry," she said, joining me at the railing. "I was too harsh."

"It's alright," I said, staring out at the dark waves.

"You were wrong to follow me," she said, scuffing her toe on the white stone. "This is very, very dangerous, Talina. I'd rather you weren't here right now." She exhaled slowly through her nose. "But I'm grateful for your company. Let's go to dinner and see what we think of this place."

A real, tangible goal. Even if it was a simple one, it was a much-needed distraction.

I forced a grin. I was still upset, but there was no point in continuing this argument. "Finally!"

She rolled her eyes.

~

I STUFFED Ria into a gown of purple and silver and piled her golden hair high on her head. A necklace of silver and amethyst trembled at her throat with each breath. I painted her eyelids a deep purple, drawing out the blue of her irises.

Though this was far from the most spectacular she'd ever looked, Ria grinned at her reflection. "Perfect."

While Ria slipped into her shoes, I scrubbed down with a rag, checked that my enchanted hairpin was still in place, and prepared to follow her.

Father would never have approved of my appearance, but I was only a well-armed maid now, so I trailed after Ria, wondering where exactly we might find the dining room.

Zellia must have anticipated this problem because she met us at the end of the corridor, an anxious smile plastered to her face. "We'll be dining in the gardens tonight," she said. "A proper feast for our guest of honor."

"Thank you," grunted Ria.

I poked her in the shoulder blade, hoping to convey that a *proper* princess wouldn't be so glum.

Her spine straightened, but her frown never faded.

Whatever. I'd take what I could get.

But something niggled at the back of my mind as we wound through the long, brightly lit hallways. Would anyone here recognize me? Even with my new hair color, there was always the risk that someone might remember my face.

That was impossible, I told myself. Almost no one from Tocchia came to Olmstead. No guards had accompanied Ria. No chaperones.

I would be fine. At least for now.

We arrived outside accompanied by Zellia. Braziers blazed on either side of the door. The sun had only just begun to set, casting the sky in orange and gold.

Tables laden with food were arranged across the lawn. A fountain bubbled not with water, but with rich, red wine. Servants fluttered around us like bees at a hive, carrying trays of food and drink. Courtiers meandered about the gardens, carrying drinks or small plates with them.

My knees weakened at the smell of the impending feast. Roasted meats, sweet breads, glazed vegetables, platters of fruit, an array of desserts. I hadn't realized how hungry I was.

A band was set up around the fountain—a harp, a flute, a lute, drums, a hurdy-gurdy.

I recognized the hurdy-gurdy player at once. With his delicate red curls, and plethora of freckles, I'd know Avens anywhere.

His eyes widened at the sight of me. I was quick to brush my fingertip to my lips, and he was just as quick to dip his chin in acknowledgement.

Later, I'd have to answer his questions, but for now, I was relieved to see a friendly face. Avens wouldn't betray me, even if he *was* a terrible gossip.

A servant in coattails spotted Ria and drew toward us. "Your Highness," he said, taking her hand, kissing the back of it as he bowed deeply. "It is truly lovely to meet you. I am Herber. It falls upon me to introduce you." He took a deep breath, adjusted his hat, and cleared his throat, drawing stares from all the way across the garden. "Announcing Princess Valeria of Olmstead, betrothed to Prince Marius of Tocchia!"

Valeria raised her hand in an imitation of a wave, face forced into a pained grimace. Polite clapping followed, then faded. A hush fell over the garden. Courtiers clambered over one another for a closer look.

I recognized King Hergarv from his portrait as he stepped

forward. At his side was Prince Marius, looking less than enthusiastic. His long hair draped over his shoulders, a stark contrast to his deep blue jacket, embroidered with silver.

The color flattered him. A blush rose to my cheeks. I ignored it as best I could. So what if he was attractive? It didn't make up for the way he'd stormed our castle and taken my sister away from everything she'd ever known.

But I couldn't stop staring at his cheekbones, admiring the way his pointed chin moved as he spoke.

Gods above, he was so fucking pretty.

Prince Marius made his way toward us, the sword at his hip catching the sunlight. Ria squared her shoulders and made a face as though she'd just bitten into a salted lemon. With his jaw set and nose wrinkled in distaste, Prince Marius looked like he returned the sentiment.

They hated each other. Their animosity was unmistakable, but I'd hoped it might fade in time. Looking at their expressions now, I doubted that they would ever have a happy moment together.

What a miserable fate. I shuddered, and followed them to the banquet table, where King Hergarv and Queen Tarra waited. Beside them stood Princess Odalla, the king's eldest child. A silver circlet held her long, dark braid in place.

A man nodded to Ria. He was tall, bronze-skinned and broad shouldered, with dark, shorn hair and warm, hazel eyes. A golden jacket emblazoned with silver clung to his shoulders. This must be Queen Tarra's heir.

"Lovely to meet you," he said to Ria, bowing low. She blushed furiously. Beside her, Prince Marius looked more than a little annoyed. "I'm Prince Gavin."

"I'm delighted to meet you, Your Highness," said Ria, her voice reaching a squeak.

Prince Gavin took a step back, and King Hergarv took his place. "Princess Valeria," he said. "It's a pleasure to see you again. I hope your journey was as pleasant as possible."

"I'm sure it might have been more pleasant under other circumstances," suggested Princess Odalla gently. "I am glad to see you unharmed and well."

Ria bristled at that. "Thank you," she said. I could tell that she was burning with resentment, eager to let Princess Odalla know *exactly* how much she did not appreciate her current arrangement.

Queen Tarra barely spared Ria a glance, but her eye caught mine. I looked away and tried not to feel like a lumpy pastry scrutinized by a picky baker.

"What is this?" she demanded. "A maid? There are no maids at my High Table. Send her away."

Some of the servants puttering nearby hurried their movements. One or two spared me a concerned glance.

"This is Miss Arina," said Prince Marius, coming to stand beside me. "She has a unique role, and Princess Valeria requested her presence."

"A unique role?" Tarra repeated, pressing a hand to her forehead. "No. We don't do that in Tocchia. No maids at the table. Out with her."

"I really must insist," said Prince Marius tersely. "Princess Valeria is my future wife, and this is one of her customs. Miss Arina is both a maid and guard."

Tarra pursed her lips and stared him down for a long moment. "Fine," she snapped. "For now, she can stand behind the table with the other guards. Despite looking completely ridiculous," she added.

I didn't flinch, but it was a close call.

"A plainclothes guard has her advantages," said Ria calmly.

"It is most unconventional," said King Hergarv. He adjusted the golden circlet upon his head, and sighed. "We will discuss the propriety of this later," he added. "For now, we will abide by Princess Valeria's customs."

"Thank you, You Highness," said Ria, curtsying. It was the first time all day that she'd acted grateful for anything, and I was quietly relieved.

Dinner lasted for hours, and my stomach grumbled as each course arrived—fingerling potatoes, glazed carrots, roasted pheasant, stewed duck, sugared plums, a wine pudding that looked like congealed blood dusted in fine sugar.

By the meal's end, I was so hungry that I doubted I could easily defend Ria, let alone take down her hair.

"They usually save some food for us," mumbled one the soldier to my left, smirking at my stomach's endless, grumbling protests. "Or we eat beforehand in the barracks."

"I don't recommend these events on an empty stomach," added the soldier to my right.

How often had the servants in Olmstead starved while watching me eat? Guilt fluttered in my chest like a trapped bird. I longed to free it, but didn't know how to. Not without breaking myself open.

Conversation remained light and infrequent. The courtiers chattered endlessly at their tables, laughing and drinking, but the High Table was awkward and solemn. Ria shifted uncomfortably every few minutes, but no one paid her any heed. Queen Tarra shot me dirty looks. Prince Gavin caught my eye and gave an apologetic wince. I responded with a wince of my own. That drew a wide grin from him, and he returned to his potatoes, shoulders shaking with silent laughter.

Princess Odalla picked at her food. Prince Marius followed suit, seemingly unimpressed until the pheasant was served. Of this he ate a few bites.

Queen Tarra avoided the potatoes and ate parsnips and beets instead. Princess Odalla had room only for wine pudding and a few bites of duck. The King favored large chunks of bread dipped in leftover sauces and stews.

It seemed pertinent to know their tastes and habits. The more information I had, the more likely I was to survive this place.

With no food in my belly, the danger seemed more real than ever.

~

THE EVENING PASSED TEDIOUSLY. Ria sneaked me a few bites of bread, but they were hardly enough to sustain me as I followed her around the gardens, begrudgingly introducing herself to anyone who showed an interest. Prince Marius stood at her side, a silent statue, greeting only a chosen few.

Was he tired? Angry? I couldn't tell. Once, he caught my eye and raised a curious eyebrow, as if wondering what I thought of all this.

I didn't dare respond to him like I had Gavin, whose demeanor was pleasant and unthreatening. While I doubted Prince Marius would hurt me, he had power over Ria, and I wouldn't do anything to put her in a bad position.

We were on what felt like our millionth introduction when Prince Marius broke away, making a beeline for a table with a spread of cheese, fruits, and sausages.

Of course he was hungry. He'd practically skipped dinner. I watched him with keen desperation.

I wasn't accustomed to hunger in the way that a servant probably ought to be. This was a weakness that would rouse suspicion. One that I needed to control, and quickly.

Prince Marius thrust a plate into my hands. "Take it," he said. "I know you didn't eat. Zellia told me that you didn't report to the servants' quarters for the evening meal." An eyebrow quirked. "And I can hear your stomach."

I stared blankly down at the plate. It was a modest affair, but more substantial than anything I'd eaten in days. Berries, cheese, bread, a few slices of hard sausage that glistened with fat. "Thank you, Your Highness."

One of Marius's guards chuckled.

"Let it never be said that I don't take care of my own," Marius said, looking out over the swarming crowd.

I ate hurriedly and in silence, avoiding the suspicious glares of well-dressed nobles, and the prodding gazes of servants—some perplexed, others jealous or judgmental.

Considering the circumstances, it was the best meal I'd had in a long time.

At the end of the evening, when the members of the band had begun to sweat through their finery, Avens had all but lost his voice, and the courtiers had gone from merrily to miserably drunk, Ria bade the royal family goodnight. We returned to her rooms with Zellia at our heels, chattering away.

"You'll want to follow me to the servants' quarters," she said. "After you finish helping Her Highness, that is."

"Oh," I said, still thinking of all the food I hadn't gotten to enjoy tonight. "Is that where I'm staying?"

"Well, yes," said Zellia, looking at me in confusion. "That's where the servants live."

"Right, yes, of course," I said, flustered.

I helped Ria take her hair down and change into a night gown, then followed after Zellia, too tired to converse.

"You'll like it here," she said, leading me down one set of narrow winding stairs, then another. "Our quarters are tight, but they're clean and warm, and there's always plenty of food."

My stomach growled again, and Zellia laughed. I wondered if she'd seen Marius bring me food and wanted to flinch away.

The servants' quarters were crowded. My bed was a simple cot, separated from the others by a thin, woven divider. There was only a tiny dresser for my things, and two hooks on the wall. I stuck my sword under my bed, unsure where else to store it.

Then I slept like the dead.

CHAPTER 12

I spent the next two weeks at Zellia's side, learning my duties as a maid, and becoming acquainted with Tocchian hairstyles, clothes, and customs. Though I was constantly exhausted, and often lost, I was well-fed, and the servants proved ready to accept me. I answered constant questions about Olmstead, the battle, and the journey. It took constant effort not to give myself away. I catalogued lies the way Cranz catalogued his inventory. Unlike Cranz, I didn't have a notebook to help me keep track of everything.

My newfound popularity surprised me. I'd expected that no one would really care about me one way or another. But almost everyone wanted to know more, and few seemed to care when I fumbled with the laundry, dropped something, or tripped over my own feet.

In the mornings, I helped Ria get ready. On bathing days, I accompanied her to the royal bathhouse (which Zellia excitedly informed me that servants were allowed to use one evening a week, a highly anticipated event) and scrubbed her skin and scalp. I followed her to meals and took her laundry to the washing women outside. I cleaned her quarters, and when I was considered properly trained, I was sent to clean Princess Odalla's quarters, as well. Once inside, I understood Ria's offense at her own arrangements. Everything in Odalla's room was pristine, made of gold, silver and mother of pearl. A writing desk with a dozen different colored inks sat in the corner. Tiny, ornate daggers hung alongside the mirror. A portrait of herself and her two children took up an entire wall. Her husband, the Duke of Garick, was suspiciously absent.

Dead at war, I'd heard, although almost no one spoke of him, and there were few pictures of him in the palace. I'd have to ask Ria what she knew. Though Princess Odalla was nothing but polite, even to the servants, I doubted she would be forthcoming about the tragedy.

One evening after dinner, Avens found me. His red hair was perfectly tousled, curls draping across his forehead in the elegant way I'd expect of a noble, not the son of a farmer from Alberbrook. Though I'd enjoyed his playing over the last few days, we'd not yet had a chance to speak.

"I hear you've a new name." He grinned, attaching to my side as fluidly as he had back in Olmstead. "I think I ought to know it." A wink.

"It's Arina now," I said, keeping my voice soft so it wouldn't carry. The hallway was mostly empty, with only a few servants scuttling back to their quarters after a long day. But one could never be too careful. Even portraits of dead men have ears, after all. "Please keep my name a secret."

"Oh, my dear," he sighed, clutching his heart with a ringed hand. "I would never tell anyone. Your new role is quite clear to me." He lowered his voice. "Are you alright? What are you doing here? I heard what happened—"

"I'm fine," I whispered. "I followed Ria here."

He nodded. Today, he wore a daffodil yellow suit embroidered with flowers. Garish even by his standards. "Are you sure? Gods, I was so worried. There was no word for days, only absolute madness. I suppose you would've missed that, being in the mountains and all. I tried to reach the castle, but when I heard Ria was coming here, I changed course." He glanced around to confirm no one was watching us, and added, "I was going to write you once I knew something. Imagine my surprise when you followed Princess Valeria to the feast."

"I'm sure it was simply unbearable," I teased, hoping that it wasn't. That my arrival hadn't caused him any distress.

His eyebrows raised. "Unbearable is one way to put it. I'd say it was perhaps more dizzying. And then to have to pretend I didn't know you!"

"Thank you for that," I said, pausing beside a suit of armor, reluctant to go any closer to the servants' quarters. "No one knows—"

"And I won't say a word, believe me. I know how, um, treacherous your status is."

"Thank you," I sighed. "You're a good friend, Avens. Truly. I don't know if I've ever told you that."

"You flatter me," he said, but his smile was pleased. "Come find me if you need anything. And I do mean anything. I'll be here through the wedding. If nothing else, we ought to have a drink."

I could see the questions burning within him, but he was smart enough not to broach the subject here. "Thank you," I said, and meant it. "I'm so glad to see a friendly face."

"Come find me whenever you need me," he promised, giving my hand a squeeze. "I'm always here for you."

And then he was gone, melting into the shadows. It must be a learned skill, I mused, because no one wearing bright yellow should be able to disappear so effectively.

Especially not a person who made a living getting people's attention and keeping it.

Someone shot past me, bumping my shoulder. I stumbled but managed not to fall. My gasp rang through the corridor.

Prince Marius stalked away, shoulders tight, hair bouncing

cheerfully with every step, at odds with the fury that radiated from him like a fever.

Did he realize he'd just crashed into me? Anger coursed through me, hot as blood. "Excuse me!" I shouted after him. "Your Highness!"

People turned to stare at us. I covered my mouth, realizing I'd made a mistake. No sane servant would ever demand the Prince's attention like that.

But it worked. He stopped and acknowledged me with a glower. "Miss Arina," he rumbled, his voice husky, like he might be ill. "What seems to be the trouble?"

"You ran into me," I huffed.

"Did I?" A slow smirk transformed his face from pleasant to terrifying. There was nothing of the Prince Marius I knew in those cold, calculating eyes. A shudder ran down my spine. "I'm sorry. I don't pay attention to the *insignificant*."

He said the word as though he hadn't vouched for my very presence only a few days ago. My heart sank.

And then he was gone, as adept at disappearing as Avens.

THE NEXT WEEK PASSED QUICKLY.

Then, abruptly, the Solstice Festival arrived.

The castle was abuzz with good cheer and hurried preparations. Everywhere I looked, people were in fine spirits. Even Queen Tarra forgot to belittle the servants in her spare time, although that was largely because she was drunk on wine samples from vendors across the land.

"Representatives from Liridin are coming," Ria told me one morning in her rooms. She lay in bed, lazy as ever, while I drew the curtains and opened the balcony doors in hopes of chasing away stale, musty air. "And the sea—I mean, Plinath. I can't even imagine." A wrinkle appeared between her eyebrows. "I've been told not to try too hard. Apparently, they look very normal. No fins or anything. Very disappointing."

"You're not usually one for fairytales," I remarked. In my reluctance to speak freely, I'd grown dull and nearly silent. Not even Avens could coax any enthusiasm from me, though he certainly tried.

"No, I suppose that's more your area," said Ria. She sat up with a yawn. "You must be excited."

"I suppose so," I hummed.

Ria frowned. "What's wrong?"

"Nothing," I said quickly. If I answered the question, I'd surely break. How could I tell her that I missed Olmstead's furious sea, the slate gray mountains, the forge that boiled like dragon's breath, and most importantly, my freedom?

When I left Olmstead, I thought that I hadn't any. That I was beneath King Amonrew's thumb, nothing more than a bug caught by the leg, flailing and frantic.

And yet, I found myself more restricted in Tocchia. As a servant, I was expected to either clean or tend to Ria. I had no privacy—and no time—to work on my designs. I only just managed to refresh my hairpin's enchantment before falling asleep last night. I'd known this might be a possibility, but I kept it in the back of my mind, hidden away where I couldn't confront it.

I hadn't expected to feel so entirely despondent.

"You're lying," said Ria, finally climbing out of bed. "What's wrong?"

"When is your wedding?" I asked, eager to change the subject.

"In six weeks' time," she said, chewing her bottom lip. "Which is all the time you have to make your decision."

"What decision?" I followed Ria to her wardrobe. She stared into it as though it were a gaping maw, ready to swallow her up.

"The decision to stay or go."

"I've already made up my mind."

"I'd plead with you to consider the alternative, but I know

better," said Ria, reaching for a pale blue dress. She rubbed the fabric between her fingers and sighed.

"There's nothing for me in Olmstead," I reminded her.

"Except your friends, your forge, and everyone you've ever known," said Ria. "Isn't that right?"

"Even if I went back, I wouldn't have those things forever. You know Father would just marry me off and wash his hands of me."

"Perhaps you'd find a husband willing to entertain your vices," proposed Ria, with an enthusiasm that almost passed as genuine.

I shook my head. "That would be entirely too lucky."

"Father likes you. I don't think he'd marry you to someone who would make you miserable."

"You don't have to lie to me," I said, reluctant to discuss the subject further.

"He tried to protect me from this madness," said Ria gently, selecting a purple gown from the wardrobe. "I don't see why he wouldn't do the same for you."

Protect her? I shook my head, but didn't dare breach the subject. "Societal expectations?" I suggested. "A desire to simplify his life?"

Ria shook her head, so fiercely that her braid flew into her face. "No. You were always his favorite. You want to know how I know?"

I gaped at her like a fish on a hook. "How?" I demanded, hands on my hips.

"He always bought you the nicest things, gave you all the lessons you requested. He called tutors from South Handleton, for the goddess's sake! Anything you wanted to learn, he found a way! Do you think Cranz would let just anyone into his forge?"

"No," I mumbled. "But—I'm easier to get rid of if I'm educated."

"No!" argued Ria, tossing the dress onto the bed. "That's incorrect. An educated woman is a threat to a weak man. Father made you untamable and knew damn well it would be impossible to marry you off."

"That's not true," I said. "Not *impossible*."

Ria rolled her eyes. "*Nearly* impossible. Besides," she gestured. "It's this, or the monastery."

I winced. I very much did not enjoy organized religion, tolerating long hours in the monastery on holidays only because it was expected of us. King Amonrew firmly believed that if the peasants doubted our piety, they'd sack the castle. ("Your great-grandfather's fault," he once grumbled, half-apologetic. "Convinced them religion mattered more than anything else, now they're ready to beat even the king to death over it.")

Long minutes passed, until I tentatively admitted, "Sometimes I want to go home."

"Then go!" Ria cried. "Don't stay here! It isn't worth it."

"You'd be alone," I said, shaking my head. "Avens can only stay so long, and he's our only real ally here."

"Avens is *terrible* a gossip, and *not* an ally," Ria said. At the expression on my face, she said, "Fine. He's *your* friend. I'll never forget when he told Fanton of Hemill that I thought he was attractive. I thought I'd never hear the end of it!"

"Well, you did." After Father threatened to start chopping off heads, the rumors dulled surprisingly quickly.

"Yes, I suppose," Ria admitted. "The point is, you don't need to stay here. Not for my sake. I can send for you later if I need you."

"But the pass is impossible to navigate in winter!"

"Then I shall have to languish until spring," said Ria, as if that settled the matter. "You don't need to suffer for my sake."

I disagreed vehemently, but only nodded. One question burned at me, and I finally gave in. "And Prince Marius? How do you find him?"

"Annoying," said Ria, shucking her nightgown. "He's much too intense. Impossible to converse with. I feel like he's always in a distant realm, and I'm yelling at him from across the mountains." She shook her head. "It's unbearable."

"He's been rather abrasive of late," I said, thinking of the day he bumped into me in the hall. *Insignificant*, he'd called me. I cringed. "Not that I speak to him often."

"He doesn't want to marry me, I think," said Ria, a sullen tilt to her lips. "Which is preposterous. He went to a lot of trouble to acquire me."

"That seems far-fetched," I said. "But I'd agree. There's no other explanation. Do you think he has a lover?"

Ria shrugged. The movement accentuated her already prominent collarbones. She'd lost weight since we arrived, I realized with a guilty jolt. The stress of the move and my meddling couldn't have been more obvious. "No. If he does, she doesn't reside in the palace. And he hardly goes out."

"Maybe she comes to him."

"Seems impossible given the tight security," mused Ria. In just her underclothes, she settled at her vanity and reached for her hairbrush. "I'm sure King Hergarv would have forbidden it."

"For the time being." I shrugged. "Maybe she sneaks inside."

"Maybe." Ria glanced to me, then away. "You could find out."

"Me?"

"You're a maid. You can go almost anywhere without being noticed. I can't do that, but you can."

I considered this as I readied Ria's corset. "I'm still in training. I'm rarely alone."

"Then say you got lost."

Hmm. I *did* get lost a lot. It was plausible no one would even question it. "Maybe."

"You could trail him. He wouldn't even notice."

I very much doubted this, but Ria knew him better than I did. Maybe the prince really did have his head in the clouds. "I'll think about it."

~

I THOUGHT about it for exactly one day, then decided that Ria deserved to know if Prince Marius was being unfaithful. Not because I expected him to stop, or for Ria to care, but because it felt wrong to keep secrets without a prior arrangement. According to Ria, they'd not yet discussed the possibility of lovers, whether or not they needed to be disclosed, or were allowed at all. Plenty of royals had secret relationships, but some marriages were too high-profile, or too volatile, to allow for such risks.

If Prince Marius had a mistress, and it was discovered, the scandal would last for ages. Would probably be written into song. A ballad, most likely. But there was always the possibility that their shame would be immortalized in a bawdy drinking song—one that would linger over the course of a century or more.

It *might* even be Avens's fault.

Talk about humiliation, I thought, imagining how Ria might react to such a betrayal.

So I began taking note of Prince Marius's whereabouts during the day. Each morning began with breakfast, then a sparring session, then meetings in the war room, then a light luncheon beside my sister (they astutely ignored one another), then an afternoon in the throne room. This must have been boring, because he looked on the verge of sleep whenever I walked past. Then more sparring, a visit to the baths, and supper.

It would have been nearly impossible to steal moments with a secret lover during the day. So I trailed him quietly at night and discovered that he spent many of his evenings hidden in the library, which I had never had reason to enter.

"Are servants barred from the library?" I asked Zellia as we carried Queen Tarra's discarded clothes to the laundry.

She chewed her lip as she considered the question. "I don't think so," she said. "Some of us even work in the library. But I've never asked. I can't read, you know. Not much reason to go there." She shrugged, a self-deprecating grin on her plump lips.

"Oh," I said, startled. I'd forgotten that much of the general public had never held a real book in their hands, let alone learned to read. "I'm sorry. I didn't think—"

She laughed and patted my arm. "It's alright. You were trained as a royal companion. I expected that you could read. I just don't know the answer to your question. Ask Cook Tarion. He probably knows something about it."

I slipped into the kitchens that afternoon, claiming hunger (which was no lie—I've always been notoriously fond of food), and pleaded with Cook Tarion for a slice of crusty bread and preserves, which I eventually got.

At the kitchen table, munching happily, I asked, "So I was told you might know the answer to this: can servants use the library?"

Cook Tarion was a tall, pale man with a dark, prominent mustache. It seemed to have absorbed all the hair from his head, which was round, bare, and shiny. He regarded me with some curiosity. "Did you come here for food, or for information?" he asked, stirring the pot over the fire.

"A little of both," I admitted, slapping clotted cream on top of peach preserves with a little too much enthusiasm.

"Fine," he sighed, gently turning the spit where a slab of pork roasted. "I could use the company. Yes, you may use the library, but you must show the clerk that you have clean hands, and you cannot leave with any books. Certain sections are restricted, and of course, you cannot attend during work hours."

"Thank you!" I cried, so flooded with relief that I could collapse. "I so miss the library in Olmstead! Everything is so different here."

Flustered, Cook Tarion patted me on the shoulder, and said, "You're welcome. I didn't realize you could read."

"Of course I can," I chirped. "I was trained to follow the Princess wherever she went. King Amonrew would never allow anything else."

"That's very generous of him," said Cook Tarion.

"I suppose," I said, standing. "Thank you!"

And I was gone, needed again in Ria's rooms.

CHAPTER 13

I started carrying stones with me and enchanted them in my spare time. It was difficult to do without a workshop or forge. Most rituals involved a lot of time and materials, not to mention the repetitive spells that I wouldn't be able to cast under my current circumstances. But I enchanted little pebbles from the garden to bounce when I dropped them, or to glow dimly when shaken, or produce smoke when thrown violently. Sometimes I charmed buttons on my blouse and boots—simple little things, nothing of real consequence. A button to make my hair shinier, or to keep the soles of my shoes from falling apart.

Finding time to test them was difficult. Ria didn't appreciate it when I filled her room with smoke, so I sometimes experimented in the empty chambers as I cleaned them.

My most recent creation was a round white stone that would heat in my pocket if Prince Marius was near. Which made it easier to track him—and avoid him.

The pocket of my apron grew warmer as I neared the library. Palms sweating but thoroughly cleaned, I approached the guard at the front entrance. "I was told that servants could enter if their hands were clean?"

My voice shook. I hadn't realized how badly I wanted to use the library until I imagined being told that I couldn't.

I showed my hands, hoping they might curry the guard's favor.

He made a face at me, like I was mouse that had just darted underfoot. A long moment passed as he regarded me. "Princess with you?"

I shook my head.

"Fine," he said, standing aside. "Talk to Jorg before you touch anything. Is that clear?"

"Yes, sir."

"Good," he said. "Don't make me regret this."

"You won't," I promised him, cautiously pleased. "Thank you very much!"

I hurried through the doors before he could change his mind, the stone in my pocket burning. Prince Marius was here, as he was nearly every night. His schedule was so rigid that I might've known even without the pebble.

Tall shelves stretched from floor to ceiling, heavy with tomes. Some of the spines spanned the width my palm. Floating lanterns bobbed between shelves, following patrons like silent guardians. Heavy, mahogany tables were piled high with books.

I glanced up and saw the second and third floors high above me.

Shouldn't a library like this belong to a university, where more people could access it? No matter how well-read the staff were, there was no reason for the palace to have such an incredible hoard of books.

A tall, portly man approached me. His hair was brushed neatly to one side. His face, though severe, softened as he marched up to me and said, "Well, hello there. I have never seen you before."

"I am Arina, maid to Princess Valeria," I said, curtsying.

"I am Jorg, head librarian. What brings you here?"

I wanted to roll my eyes at his pompous tone but refrained. I couldn't risk upsetting him. I *needed* access, if only to sate my curiosity.

"I was told that the servants could read the books so long as our hands are clean?" I said, again showing my palms. The skin was dry, almost leathery, and I was nearly ashamed.

But Jorg's surprise wasn't directed at my hands. "You aren't here to retrieve something for the Princess?"

I shook my head. Valeria was never much of a reader. I liked stories and tales, while she had a better head for numbers, strategy, and fashion. "No, she didn't send me. I happen to have a free evening, and a fondness for literature."

"A fondness for literature," Jorg repeated, voice growing dreamy. "In a maid. How *unusual*."

"My upbringing was admittedly privileged," I said, glancing down at my boots, now scuffed and worn.

"I see," said Jorg slowly. "And how does a girl with such an upbringing end up as a maid?"

"My father died," I said simply. "My mother was a worker in the castle in Olmstead. That's how I got the position."

"Tragic, indeed," said Jorg with a solemn nod. "Very well. I trust you know how to hold a book and turn a page?"

"Yes," I said, confused. "I've been inside a library before."

"You might be surprised at the things some people think are acceptable behaviors. Follow me, please."

And he took me on a tour of the library, past statues of long dead royals, paintings of dragons and great battles. Figures of gargoyles looked down on us from atop the shelves. We wove between bookcases, tables, and distracted workers filing books and papers. On the third floor, hidden in the mythology section, I spotted Prince Marius sitting in an armchair, book balanced on his thigh. On the table beside him was an open notebook. The loose bun gathered at the back of his head was held in place by a pen. His jerkin was such a verdant green that it felt like something conjured in a dream.

The stone in my pocket became unbearably hot. I clenched my teeth and smiled awkwardly as Prince Marius glanced at us.

I half-expected him to demand to know what I was doing here, but he didn't seem terribly surprised, just annoyed. His eyebrows dipped downward as his lips tightened into a straight line.

Then he looked away, as if he couldn't be bothered with my presence any longer.

My stomach twisted into a knot.

Good, I told myself. *It's better this way. It was kind of him to save me, but there's no connection between us. There never was, and there never will be.*

I was accustomed to being overlooked. Looked down upon as I was for my questionable parentage, I was still afforded certain privileges. But I was never treated with the same respect as my siblings. Plenty of people disregarded me, and I rarely took offense.

So why did it bother me when Prince Marius was the one ignoring me?

I wanted to rip the pebble from my pocket and lob it at his face. Instead, I focused my attention on Jorg and passed Marius by as if he were nothing more than a throw pillow.

To my great satisfaction, the lines on his forehead deepened as he watched us go.

Fine. I don't care about you, either.

~

RIA WAS hesitant to accept my claim that there was no lover. But days passed, and I consistently found Prince Marius in the mythology section of the library, alone except for his notebook and ever-present scowl.

If there was a mistress, she met with him elsewhere. The mythology section was well-hidden on the third floor, but it was easy to watch from between the shelves on the second floor.

Conveniently, this was where the romances were located. So I read tales of grand and everlasting love while occasionally verifying that the prince was alone.

And alone he was, in the same spot every night, frustration written across his face like a script. If I'd cared about him, I might have been worried. What was he researching? Didn't he have anything better to do with his nights?

Then, most curiously, he moved to another section. The same one I always passed despite the longing in my heart—Objects and Enchantments.

What does he *want to create?* I wondered silently. Was this the time to make a move, and offer my services? But a part of me was reluctant to step forward, to say anything, insisting that now wasn't the time.

Eventually, I got lazy. I started enchanting pebbles between the shelves whenever I thought I was alone. Tested their light, their heat, their ability to track objects by changing from hot to cold depending on distance.

One evening, I was hidden away in the romance section, reading an especially steamy scene between a pirate and his recently kidnapped bride, who had fallen for his roguish charm despite their admittedly rocky start. Her blouse had just spilled open, and...

"I thought I'd find you here," rumbled a deep voice.

I squeaked and hurriedly flipped the book so that the spine was hidden. "Good evening, Your Highness."

Prince Marius loomed above me. Tonight, a cloak of midnight blue flowed over yet another frilly white shirt. Tight-fitting black pants showed off his long legs, accentuating the muscles beneath. Silver fastenings glinted on his boots; their leather was a gentle grey that reminded me of the stone floors of Castle Ackervail. Long hair draped over his shoulder like moonlight. Within the foamy collar of his shirt, the strange necklace was just barely visible.

My mouth ran dry. There was a peculiar heat in his gaze, a ravenous intensity that threatened to devour me whole. I wasn't sure if I liked it.

What if I did?

Before I could decide, Prince Marius folded elegantly into the empty chair beside me as if we were two old friends rather than a prince and a maid. "It's curious to find a maid in the library," he said, the words rolling off his tongue smooth as silk. "But I'm not surprised." He brushed a piece of hair behind his ear. "Of everything that came of our journey to Olmstead, you were by far the most unexpected."

Flustered, I began, "Well, I—"

But he continued speaking as though he hadn't heard me at all. "And yet it's even more curious that I've spotted you here several times now, bouncing glowing pebbles between the shelves. I've also noticed you change the buttons on your blouse quite frequently." His eyebrows raised. "Care to explain?"

"Well, the buttons," I sputtered, thinking of the heroine in the pirate romance, whose blouse had torn so easily beneath strong, passionate hands, buttons popping loose like seeds from a dandelion. "They weren't sewn on very well, so I—"

His scowl cut me short. "I was hoping you wouldn't lie."

"Who said anything about lying?" I demanded, shocked that he'd even noticed the changes to my blouses. I'd started charming buttons to maintain my hair color. They were harder to lose than a hairpin, and more easily replaced. Plus, I always had always a backup charm, even when I slept.

"I did, I suppose. For good reason." He sighed, and stretched out his legs, crossing them at the ankles. "I don't understand why my betrothed would lie to me about your real purpose here." He grinned, wide and foreboding. A cat taking great joy in the final, gasping moments of its prey. "Unless, of course, you've gone rogue?"

I looked around wildly, half-expecting soldiers to creep from the shadows, to shackle me and drag me down to the dungeons that I hadn't seen yet, but knew must be around here somewhere. But my gaze found only books and more books. Most of the bustle was on the first floor, where the history, strategy, war, and science tomes were contained. Up here, we were alone; two hermits whose paths occasionally crossed.

"I haven't done anything wrong," I insisted. "I don't know what you're talking about."

"You haven't done anything wrong *yet*," he purred. "I'm not stupid. I know an artificer when I see one. The question is why you're pretending to be a maid."

I sat very, very still, and did not react at all. Maybe he'd go away.

He didn't.

"That's... not true," I said after he met my eye. "If you're accusing me of what I think you're accusing me of... That simply isn't true. Your Highness," I added for good measure.

"It isn't?" His eyebrow arched. "Because I think I'm looking at a very bored artificer." A grin stretched across his face. "And I have a proposal to make. Perhaps we can come to an arrangement."

"The last time someone accepted your proposal, it didn't go very well," I snapped. The words burst out of me before I could stop myself. Horrified, I clapped my hand over my mouth.

Prince Marius only laughed. "Perhaps you'd make a better fool than artificer," he said lightly. "That might be the only way to keep you out of trouble."

"Tocchia doesn't have a fool," I reminded him. "Besides, I don't fart on command."

He snickered with genuine childish amusement. "Can't or won't?"

"Neither," I said primly, crossing my arms.

"How courtly of you," he gritted out, though it seemed he was trying very hard not to laugh.

"It isn't funny!" I snapped.

Honestly. *Men.*

"Your reaction is," he countered, still smirking.

"Tell me, do you speak to Princess Valeria in such a manner?"

The laughter in his eyes died at the mention of her name. "I hardly speak to her of anything," he said, shoulders slouching. "It is a marriage of necessity, as I'm sure you're aware, and she is hardly fond of me."

"Perhaps if you were less crass," I suggested.

"To be any less so would end me. My life is already terribly dull." He groaned, and sat up properly, planting his hands on his knees. "Back to the matter at hand. I've found myself in need of an artificer, and *I* think *you're* bored. I believe I have a solution to both of our problems."

"Believe away," I said, waving my hand. "I am no artificer."

"An amateur artificer would also be acceptable," he amended, looking at me expectantly.

"You've got the wrong maid," I told him.

"What if I assured you that I have no intention of exposing you, and that you will suffer no punishment for your deceit so long as you assist me?"

I said nothing. I couldn't risk being caught in a lie. What would Queen Tarra think if she learned an artificer posed as a maid? The deception wouldn't be tolerated—the circumstances were just too suspicious. Any sane ruler would think I was a spy or saboteur, and I couldn't blame them.

"What if I offered you an apprenticeship at our forge?"

That got my attention. An apprenticeship? At a forge?

Gods, that was endlessly appealing. No more organizing dresses and tying corsets and cleaning rooms.

But the fear of discovery lingered in the back of my mind. If word reached Olmstead, how long until Father came to collect me, likely with an army at his back?

A deal like this would decimate our already tense political relations.

"What do you want?" I asked finally, because I knew he wasn't letting up, and the idea of an apprenticeship was tempting indeed.

His shoulders relaxed. A minute motion, but one that I noticed, regardless. "I need an artificer to examine an object. It's cursed, but it isn't dangerous. Not directly, anyway."

"And the artificers in your employ won't help you because..."

An exasperated huff of air escaped him. "They have stated that I am wasting their time with utter nonsense."

That piqued my curiosity. I'd never had a court artificer turn me down. Did he seek something forbidden? Or just tedious? "I see."

"I may have become a bit... desperate," said Prince Marius, straightening his spine. "There are a number of things I'd like some help with, and yet, I seem unable to attain any."

"So this is a secret, then?"

"For now," he said, after a quick glance around. "Meet me here tomorrow. At midnight."

"That is *highly* improper," I protested.

"I cannot ensure our privacy otherwise," he said quietly. "Jorg will let you in."

"Fine," I grumbled.

Prince Marius gave a tight smile, rose to his feet, and stepped into the darkness, melding into shadow.

I remained in the library for a long time, heart in my throat, wondering how big of a mistake I'd just made.

CHAPTER 14

I didn't have long to panic, because the next day was the day before the Solstice Festival, and the palace was positively bursting with activity. I spent the morning making Ria look beautiful, then the rest of the day preparing rooms for the guests who would arrive at any moment.

Three of the guest suites had long, shallow pools built into the floor near the bed. Their size and shape reminded me of coffins. "What is that?" I asked Dalinda, the maid accompanying me.

She shook out a bedsheet with unnecessary vigor and sighed loudly. "I always forget you're from Olmstead. You wouldn't know, would you?"

I shook my head.

"Must be nice," she mused. "Your world must have been so limited."

Fine, so she wasn't going to answer me.

I frowned down at the pool. "Is it for soaking?"

"Yes," she said airily. "It's for the representatives of the sea. They can't be out of water for too long, and we can hardly lodge them in the bath house." She laid the blanket on the bed and began tucking in the corners.

"Oh," I said. The pool was hardly deep enough to submerge oneself in, but maybe that didn't matter.

"Yes," hummed Dalinda. "'*Oh.*' Honestly. Didn't they tell you anything before you came here?"

"Princess Valeria was educated in international relations. I was taught to style hair and defend her."

Dalinda wrinkled her nose. "Olmstead sounds strange."

"It would probably bore you," I admitted sullenly.

"Oh, I agree," said Dalinda, throwing the balcony doors open, so that sunlight and cool air filled the room. "I only asked to be polite."

I bit my tongue. I'd worked with Dalinda once before and found her exhausting. She was mean in the most tired, exasperated way possible. Despite my best efforts, her comments got under my skin. The worst part was that I wasn't even sure if she meant to upset me.

She probably did, but I couldn't prove it, and she would never admit it.

Even partnered with Dalinda, the afternoon passed quickly. My shoulders and lower back ached from all the beds I'd prepared, the floors I'd mopped, surfaces I'd dusted—an endless litany of chores. I was so exhausted that I barely managed to shovel down tonight's pottage before rushing upstairs to watch Ria eat in the great hall.

Usually, the servants' dinners were heartier. Tonight was pottage because it was easy to make, allowing the cooks to focus their energy on their preparations for the festival tomorrow, but I was still disappointed. Plenty of people throughout the world subsisted on pottage and pottage alone for their entire lives, but my expectations were admittedly higher. Perhaps too high, considering my current circumstances.

Worse, the High Table always had the most delectable of dishes—seasoned meats, honeyed vegetables, beautiful desserts. Weeks had passed since I'd taken a bite of cake, or a sip of wine. I knew I should be grateful I got to eat at all, but I was resentful of these royals and their delectable meals.

Guilt roiled in my stomach as I recalled everything I'd taken for granted in my previous life. Guaranteed shelter, extravagant food, security, the king's favor. Things that only gained significance when I had to live as a servant. It didn't matter that Father forced us to do our own chores as children; until now, I had no real appreciation of my privilege.

I tried not to stare at tonight's spread—braised beef, seasoned parsnips, buttery carrots, crusty bread, tiny cakes. By the way his lip twisted, I knew Prince Marius had caught me. I was quick to look away, but I didn't dare hope I'd fooled him.

There were plenty of people I didn't recognize, including two men with massive wings on their backs, shiny and chitinous like an insect's, folded against their spines, not unlike a moth at rest. When they moved, their wings shimmered.

I could not help but ogle them. At first glance, they seemed nothing other than human, wearing dark leather pants, and tight black shirts whose backs scooped down like some of Ria's more scandalous dresses. Making room for the wings, I supposed.

"Sky Kingdom," mumbled one of the guards to my right. Hanson. I liked him well enough. He always seemed to know whenever I needed an explanation and was happy to offer one. "The dark-haired one is Toral. The blond is Halin."

Toral and Halin. I tried to commit the names to memory. "Thank you," I whispered.

"Toral is acting as regent while they wait for the heir to reappear," Hanson added. "Remember that."

Wait for the heir to reappear? Had I heard that correctly?

But now wasn't the time. Too much chatter would be seen as disrespectful, and I didn't want to deal with Queen Tarra's fury today. "And Halin?"

"Halin is a trusted advisor. Respect him, and you'll be fine."

I swallowed hard. "Right."

Neither representative from Liridin dressed to reflect their status. Both looked like they were ready for a day of sparring, not dinner at a royal palace.

No one cared. Toral and Halin sat across from King Hergarv, beside three extravagantly dressed individuals. Jewels were sewn into their jackets. Rings glittered on their fingers. One had tiny starfish pinned to his braid, while another wore a necklace of seashells. A woman with pale hair wore earrings that might've been tiny sea urchins.

These must be the representatives from the sea. They were terribly human, with no signs of fins or scales. Ria was right—they were indiscernible from the rest of us, at least while they were on land. I wondered if they changed when they reached the sea, or if they navigated the depths in human bodies. That seemed ineffective, but then again, I wasn't a very experienced swimmer.

I wanted to ask Hanson, but before I could, King Hergarv climbed to his feet and clapped his hands. The room fell silent. Even the servants ceased their bustling and stood at attention.

"I'd like to thank you for all for being here," he began, smiling broadly. He wore a robe of pale blue, so long that it draped over his heavy leather boots. The Tocchian crest was emblazoned on his breast, grim and fierce as ever. "I know the journey is not always easy, so I appreciate your presence even more."

A few people clapped. Others smiled and nodded, a humble acknowledgement of their efforts.

"This is a very special celebration, as many of you are aware. Princess Valeria of Olmstead has agreed to marry my firstborn son, Prince Marius. She is here with us today, and I'd like to introduce her."

At his beckoning, Ria rose. The expression on her face told me all I needed to know: she was fighting down panic.

Personally, I'd rather get it over with and stand before a crowd for a brief moment before returning to the safety of my seat, but

Ria was in agony. Her grimace was tight and forced, her wave weak.

She would prefer *a million* personal introductions over *one* in front of a crowd, I thought, fighting the urge to roll my eyes.

The crowd, for its part, was very polite. Applause rang out, and Ria's cheeks colored.

"Now that the introductions are over, I'd like to welcome you all to my court. Please enjoy yourselves! Tomorrow, we celebrate!" King Hergarv returned to his seat. Ria sat, nearly boneless with relief. Prince Marius spared her no concern and began buttering a roll.

And with that, the wine flowed, the food was devoured, and guests spilled out into the gardens, drunk and chatting amongst themselves.

Why did Prince Marius think I could possibly meet him at midnight? It was already evening, and this party wasn't winding down any time soon. I could not escape my duties any more than he could his.

What a terrible plan. Why had I agreed to it?

I followed Ria for the much of the night, which meant that I was at Marius's side, too. Not that he paid me any attention.

"Toral," cried Marius, pausing as we passed one of the winged men from Liridin. "It has been too long! How are you?"

Toral embraced Prince Marius as one might a brother, grinning and slapping him on the back. "Lovely, as always," said Toral. His gaze fluttered to Ria, and back again. "And this is your betrothed, yes? I apologize; we barely spoke over dinner. I've heard much about you over the years."

"Oh?" Ria raised a skeptical brow. "What of me?"

"Your wit and beauty, primarily," said Toral. "Which I can see now is absolutely true."

Ria turned to me. "You can thank my maid. She's responsible for this." She gestured to her hair, braided into an elaborate bun.

I curtsied and tried to keep my face neutral. "I can take no credit for her wit."

"But you can be proud of your work," said Toral, beaming when I broke into a reluctant giggle.

"It's a *lot* of work, Your Highness," I said, only a little guilty about joking at Ria's expense.

"Oh." He shook his head, expression changing rapidly to something full of sorrow and regret. "No, I'm not... Please don't address me as royalty. I'm merely a stand-in."

"The heir of the Sky Realm has been absent for twenty-five years," explained Prince Marius hurriedly.

"We have faith that he will return," said Toral, though he didn't sound especially convinced.

"Oh," I said, twisting my hands and thinking how hopeless it all sounded. "Twenty-five years is a long time."

"It is," said Toral, smiling sadly at me. "A very, very long time. What is your name, Miss?"

"Arina," I said.

"Miss Arina, it has been nice to meet you."

"I hope I haven't overstepped."

"You haven't, I assure you," said Toral. "Speaking to you has been most refreshing. I find these royals quite stuffy."

Marius gasped and clutched his heart, mocking offense.

I stared at him, dumbfounded. Was he drunk? I'd never seen him make a joke before.

"I jest, I jest," said Toral, bumping his shoulder against Prince Marius's. "You know I'm never bored."

"That isn't quite a compliment," Prince Marius pointed out, but the corners of his mouth lifted into a crooked grin.

"Well, it isn't quite an insult, either," said Toral, rolling his eyes. He sighed. "But alas, I must return to making the rounds. I look forward to seeing you all tomorrow at the solstice." He nodded at me. "You will be there, and not behind the scenes styling hair?"

I glanced at Ria and Marius sheepishly. "I plan on it—"

"She will be," said Ria firmly. "I'd hardly ask her to miss out."

"Good," said Toral, and he was gone, wings bouncing as he walked.

"Are those... do his wings really work?" I said, unable to stop staring.

It might have been my imagination, but I thought Prince Marius pursed his lips in disapproval. "Yes," he said. "They really work, but you won't see them used here. Centuries ago, our people would shoot his from the sky for sport. Though we've reached an agreement, they're reluctant to fly anywhere near the surface. Only messengers and scouts will get within one hundred feet of the ground."

"That's horrible," said Ria, and I could see the rant building in her. Later, she'd tell me exactly what she thought about this. For now, we were wise enough to keep our mouths shut.

"It is," said Marius. "I cannot answer for my ancestors, but I can assure you that I will not allow anything like that to ever happen again."

"How altruistic," said Ria, eyes flashing.

I looked away. People could be both good and bad, I reminded myself. At least Prince Marius was *trying* to do what was best for his kingdom and the surrounding ones, even if he attacked Olmstead over a broken treaty.

I still worried that war would break out. King Amonrew was probably stewing in his war room right now, moving figures across a map and swearing. He'd agreed to let Ria go, but a part of me wondered if the wedding would ever happen. As the days passed, reality settled in. Father wouldn't tolerate this arrangement. Tocchia hadn't just exercised poor judgment—they'd also humiliated him. He'd been given a choice: submit, or admit that he could've prevented the slaughter at the Spring Banquet, and didn't.

I wouldn't be terribly surprised if Father tried to retaliate tomorrow. A festival for a banquet.

And he would have no mercy.

But Tocchia was not so easily caught off guard. Ships might come in the night, but the sea was notoriously treacherous between our realms. The flatlands before the mountains would not long conceal an army, and the scouts would've warned us long ago if soldiers from Olmstead were in the area.

"I *would* beg your pardon," said Prince Marius to Ria, interrupting my musing. "But I know you're not the generous sort."

Ria's jaw dropped. "A bold insinuation," she said.

"Not even if I *begged*," continued Marius. The frozen wrath in his glare was unlike anything I'd ever seen. Ria scowled. All around us, people stopped and stared at the prince and his betrothed, who looked ready to come to blows.

My gaze flickered to Ria. What was Marius talking about? *Had* he begged her already? And for what?

I could've told him that such behavior would earn him no favors with my sister, but of course, he hadn't asked.

"I'm afraid the desserts are calling me," said Ria, spinning on her heel. "I will reunite with you later, *future husband*." She spat the words with vitriol. I almost felt sorry for the prince as I darted after her, desperately hoping that we might actually stop at a dessert table, and knowing already that I would be disappointed. Servants didn't get cake, and my sister wasn't fond of sweets to begin with.

"We're supposed to put up a united front," Prince Marius hissed after us, but Ria ignored him.

We passed a table absolutely buckling beneath an assortment pastries, cakes, cookies, and puddings. Ria didn't spare it a glance, but I was halfway to salivating at the sight.

Several people attempted to greet Ria, but she tore through the crowd like an arrow from a crossbow, and didn't stop until we reached the gardens outside.

"That foul, foul man," she snarled, when we were finally alone. "How dare he say such things! In public, too," she fumed, fanning at her face with her hand. We found an empty bench, and Ria all but collapsed onto it, like her legs had given out.

I didn't know what to say. Any attempt to reassure her would be received poorly, so I just sat beside her and patted her on the shoulder.

"It's like he thinks he deserves forgiveness," she snarled. Furious tears spilled over her long lashes. "As if I owe him anything after what he did!"

I bit my lip. While it would probably be easiest to forgive Prince Marius and carry on as though nothing had ever transpired, I understood why Ria couldn't do it. Couldn't ignore the violent loss of her autonomy, the disappointment she must've felt when she realized she couldn't marry someone new and more compatible, the terror and fear as she left the castle more or less a hostage.

"You don't," I said. "Just be careful, alright?"

"I make no promises," said Ria, wiping her eyes. The kohl around them smeared. When I went to fix it, she slumped back against the bench, and said, "Leave it. I'm not perfect, and my makeup doesn't have to be, either."

The rest of the evening was tense. We were eventually joined by a sheepish Prince Marius, who gave no apologies. But when he offered his arm, Ria took it, and I supposed that was good enough.

CHAPTER 15

By nightfall, things were winding down. The remaining guests had retreated to the great hall for cards and wine. The band played on; Avens continuously wiped his sweaty brow. I tried to make eye contact, but he was busy putting on a show and barely noticed me.

Fine. I wouldn't let my neediness distract him.

The king and queen went to bed shortly before midnight, and Ria excused herself almost immediately after, claiming a headache. I followed her up to her chambers, my feet aching. I'd nearly forgotten about the meeting in the library and groaned aloud when I realized I still had *that* to look forward to.

I dragged myself to the library with the enthusiasm of a prisoner on the way to the gallows. So late at night, I didn't want to be alone in the palace. Though laughter and chatter echoed from the great hall, the corridors were eerie and silent, and I hurried along, shoulders hunched against the chill.

The torches in their sconces gave off no warmth, and the shadows had depths I'd never noticed before. I pulled a pebble from my bodice and shook it until a soft glow enveloped me.

I was incandescent as a ghost for the rest of the journey.

~

"THERE YOU ARE," said Prince Marius as I approached, weaving between shelves to his preferred seating area, a little nook that overlooked the rest of the library. Two overstuffed armchairs rested on either side of a tiny, scuffed table, already stacked high with books from the alchemy section. As always, he wore his midnight blue cloak. Underneath, tonight's finery still clung to his slim form. Silver fastenings and lace adorned a maroon jacket and matching pants. His shoes were so polished as to be nearly blinding. I noted with muted satisfaction that blades of wet grass clung to his heels.

"Here I am," I huffed, rubbing the exhaustion from my eyes.

"Thank you for coming," he said. "And thank you for your patience tonight. It was not my intent for you to bear witness to our disagreement."

That foul bastard. I gave a hollow laugh. "I don't have a choice, do I?"

His answering grimace was tight, strained. For the first time, I realized he looked as tired as I felt. Beneath his eyes were the beginnings of bruises. "I suppose not." He sighed. "I apologize. That was not one of my finest moments.

"Do you react this way every time someone fails to praise you?"

"No," he said, settling into a chair. "I don't. But I've grown weary of endless insults and rude comebacks. I understand that it's all my fault, but I—I let myself grow frustrated, and I shouldn't have."

"You won't get anywhere with her if you aren't polite," I warned. "Let her walk all over you for a while. She'll warm up eventually."

"People have certain expectations of me as a prince, you know," he said glumly. "I can't exactly let her walk all over me, even if I wanted to. At a certain point, I have to defend my honor."

"Do you want a happy marriage or a good reputation?" I crossed my arms. "I'd do whatever I could to keep both, personally."

"Words of wisdom," he chuckled. "If only it were so simple." He leaned forward, his icy gaze catching mine. "And I mean no offense. I really have no idea how to achieve both."

I probably could've given him some advice, but that wasn't why we were here. "What did you want to show me?" I tucked a loose strand of hair behind my ear and fought the urge to rub my eyes.

He rubbed a hand over his forehead, smoothing the lines there. "You must first swear you'll keep it a secret. On pain of, erm, exile," he said finally.

I tried to keep the shock and fear from my face. *Death.* He was going to say *death. Fuck.*

I schooled my features and smiled solemnly. "I promise, Your Highness."

After a moment of scrutiny, he said, "Good enough," and reached into a satchel concealed beneath his cloak. From it, he produced a small black box, sleek and smooth. "Please don't touch."

"I might not be able to tell you very much if I can't touch it." I crossed my arms and examined the shelf beside me, scanning over the titles, looking for anything interesting. Trying to pretend I didn't care about Marius's mysteries.

"That's fine. Do your best." He placed the box carefully on the stack of books and opened it.

Inside was a band of stone, so pale that it resembled bone. The longer I looked, the more certain I became that it was, in fact, bone.

Its prongs were set to hold a substantial stone, which might have improved the appearance of the ring, except that the stone was missing. The empty prongs reminded me of the open claws of a great beast, ready to strike.

It didn't appear expensive, just *cursed*. No longer did I worry about observing the ring from a distance. Prince Marius couldn't pay me to go any nearer. Just looking at it made the space between my eyes pulse painfully.

"What is it?" I asked, massaging my temples, trying to keep my gaze on the ring, and failing.

"It's a family heirloom," said the prince gravely. "One that I'm afraid I've been stuck with."

"The stone is missing."

"Yes," Prince Marius said, his gaze glued to me. "It was removed some time ago and still needs to be replaced."

"Lost or stolen?"

He hesitated. "I'm not certain."

How unhelpful. "What kind of stone did it hold?"

The question caught him off guard. He frowned as he considered. "A ruby," he said at last, but I didn't believe him.

I bent closer to the ring, careful not to touch. A horrible buzzing filled my ears. A drone so loud that I felt like I'd been trapped inside a wasps' nest. I recoiled as if I'd been slapped.

Prince Marius gave a sympathetic wince. "Sorry," he said.

"Is it *supposed* to hurt?" I asked.

He shrugged. "I've been told that it doesn't do this when it's in use."

"So why aren't you wearing it?"

"The stone is *missing*," he said slowly, as if I might be daft. "What else can you tell me?"

I closed my eyes and tried to focus. Sometimes, without even looking, I could sense an enchanted object's purpose. By feel, I knew which pebbles were for conjuring light, loud noise, or tracking Prince Marius. When I had enchanted blades in my possession, I knew without touching which ones struck true, which inflicted an instantly fatal wound, which were meant to cause incredible pain but not death. The vibrations were slightly different, the energy sinister or gentle. Some were cool and cleansing, others ranged from warm to uncomfortably hot.

This ring absolutely pulsed with a putrid, burning energy. It writhed between my eyes, slithered beneath my skin, groped for my bones.

The sensation was familiar, drawing me back to the time when Cranz produced a sword from the locked shed. The blade was cursed to incapacitate its victims, making it so that even the tiniest cut would render them lame for the rest of their lives. The wound would deepen and spread until it was a foul, gaping thing that no healer could close.

I dared not pull it from its sheath, too overwhelmed by the rippling hatred and agony to do anything other than step away, as though its energy could infiltrate me without the faintest physical touch.

Now, with Prince Marius at my side instead of Cranz, I stared down at the ring. *Focus,* I told myself. *Do not flee. Focus.*

But my feet were too light, ready to carry me right out of the library and all the way down to the servants' quarters, where I could lie in my cot and pretend none of this happened. I inhaled deeply, forcing myself to stay calm.

When I concentrated on the ring, all I sensed was chaos and destruction, an urge to wriggle into tiny cracks and expand until everything around it exploded. With this came a distinct sensation of *lack*. Poverty? Famine? Something else?

"Chaos," I mumbled at last. "And breaking things. And... poverty?"

The prince gave terse nod. "Any idea how to neutralize it?"

I shook my head. "I'm not a sorceress."

"Yes, I know," he grumbled bitterly. "They are too busy to waste time on cursed rings. Even for a high price."

I frowned down at the ring. Where was the energy coming from? There was no stone, no adornment. Just a simple band. "Whose bone is this?"

Prince Marius let out a long-suffering sigh. "No one knows."

"That might help," I said, though of course I had no real idea if it would or not.

"I've scoured books and death records," he snapped. "I've examined graves. I'm uncertain whose bone this is. Or if it's even human."

"It's definitely human," I murmured, thinking back to all the books Cranz forced me to read before he let me attempt a single spell. "Animal bones won't hold contempt like this."

"Interesting," murmured Prince Marius, his gaze suddenly far away. "Anything else?"

I shook my head.

The box snapped shut, and my headache dulled to a throb.

"Thank you," said Prince Marius. "That's all I needed. Are you alright?"

"I think so," I said. I felt like someone had taken a hammer to my temples, and cracked my skull in two, but I didn't want to show weakness in front of him. "It's… difficult to get too close to. I doubt I could've touched it if I'd wanted to."

"That's probably for the best," said Prince Marius, placing the box back inside his satchel. "If—for any reason—you happen upon it, do not touch it. Do not even lift the box. Call for me, and I will retrieve it."

"Why would it be—"

"It's got a mind of its own. And thieves have targeted it more than once. Most aren't capable of taking it very far, but that hasn't stopped them from trying."

"Oh," I said, unable to imagine anyone going to the trouble of stealing a ring made of bone. It was objectively ugly, cheap, and fragile. What was the point of crafting something like it, if not for sinister reasons? "If people are willing to steal it—"

"Then they know more than I do," said Prince Marius gravely. He rubbed the back of his neck, frowning into the distance. "Not a single thief has given me a satisfactory answer. Despite our efforts to... motivate them."

"Not one?" I echoed in disbelief. King Amonrew claimed that torture was ineffective, but his advisors said otherwise, urging him to send captured spies into the chambers constructed by my great-grandfather. I suspected Tocchia enforced similar methods of interrogation.

Regardless of what my father said, I couldn't imagine keeping secrets after being placed upon the rack.

Prince Marius shook his head. His hair bounced with the motion. "One is still in the dungeon and has yet to tell me anything more than his name and origin. The rest, as you may have guessed, are dead or exiled."

"How do you decide their punishments?" I asked, choking on my own voice. I'd just interacted with something that people were willing to risk everything to acquire. Was this information I should even have?

"It depends on my mood," said the prince flippantly. His laugh echoed through the library, reverberating between shelves.

I tried not to flinch, but a muscle must've twinged in my face, because he rushed to correct himself.

"That isn't true," he said quickly, angling his body toward me. "We have protocol for this sort of thing. Our laws dictate punishments. Someone whose only crime is sneaking inside the palace will be exiled. Someone who kills multiple guards and servants to do so will likely be hanged. And someone who steals... Well, the punishment depends on the value of the object, and whether or not the theft was successful." He watched me carefully as he spoke, eager to quell my fear, or perhaps temper my opinion of him.

I knew, logically, that I was in danger. That no matter what I did, I was still working for people who were powerful and vengeful. That I'd hidden my identity in a way that could probably get me killed or at least imprisoned.

"I see," I said, afraid to appear too sympathetic to the thieves.

In many ways, I'd grown up outside of the typical royal experience. So many people despised my very existence. When I was young, I spent a lot of time looking out my window, at the cities in the distance, wondering what my life might be if I were born outside the castle walls. For a time, I was obsessed with the lives of peasants. Father declared they were terrible in all ways—filled with filth, starvation, and rot—I glamorized them into something else: people with freedom and choice. As the years passed, my tutors began to indulge me, sharing their perspectives; a glance into the mind of someone who had seen the rest of the world.

Thanks to them, I had a basic understanding of the ways the world worked. The poor weren't lazy or incompetent. They were poor because wealth seemed to accumulate in cities and castles, piled at the feet of kings. I knew better than fall into the trap of believing that only the wealthy deserved to keep their money.

But it was impossible to convince a king—even my doting father—the error of his ways. I had no doubt that Prince Marius was equally set in tradition.

His gaze burned into mine, molten like steel, and then he bid me goodnight, dissolving into the darkness like he, too, was made of shadow.

CHAPTER 16

The next day was so chaotic that I completely forgot about Prince Marius and his cursed ring. I spent the morning making Ria look like a goddess, stuffing her into a pink and green gown, braiding ribbons into her hair, coloring her eyelids. By the end of it, no one would ever guess that we'd had three arguments, done her hair twice over (my first attempt was off-center) and that she'd accidentally launched a shoe across the room in her attempt to dress quickly.

I was near to tears by the end, furious at both Ria and myself. I dared not tell her anything about my meeting with Prince Marius, but my exhaustion was visible, and she kept asking if I'd slept at all the night before.

He hadn't even mentioned the position with the forge. Fury burrowed into my breast like a wild, clawing animal. Even though I knew I didn't want to explain myself, that it was better if I never saw the position, I couldn't help but feel betrayed. I sneaked out and I stayed up late, all to help him stare at a piece of carved bone that made my insides crawl.

Ria was upset about her lopsided braid (which I'd already

corrected), and my hands were shaking, my stomach was growling, and everything was dreadful.

At last, Ria was more than presentable, and I followed her to breakfast, where I had to watch her eat all the things I'd once loved. I'd skipped breakfast because I overslept and found myself deeply regretting every decision I'd made to end up here.

The festival would not start until afternoon. Already, everything was set up outside. Tables, flowers, a maypole, statues carved from ice and charmed to withstand the heat of the sun. *Like something from a dream*, I thought, glancing out the window as I ran loads of laundry up and down the stairs.

With only an hour to go before the festival's official start, I lost my footing and tumbled down the stairs. The stack of folded sheets I carried spilled from my arms. I made a noise not unlike the squeal of a startled pig and rolled down the steps. When I reached the landing, I slammed against the stone floor. Pain darted up my spine. My head cracked against the wall. Though it didn't hurt especially badly, I started to weep, more from humiliation than anything else.

The palace was nearly empty, with everyone outside or in the kitchens. I sat uselessly on the stairs—tailbone throbbing, wrists aching, skin scraped raw on my hands and knees—sniveling like a child. I climbed to my feet unsteadily.

A worried voice rang out behind me. "Miss Arina? Are you alright?"

I nearly groaned. Of course Prince Marius had witnessed my fall. *Of course* I couldn't just suffer in silence for five minutes, until I felt well enough to carry on with my day.

No, he was merely the decorative garnish on an already shitty morning. "Your Highness," I stammered, turning round to spy not only Prince Marius, but Prince Gavin as well. "I am perfectly fine."

Gavin stared at me, startled by my splotchy face.

I stooped to reach for the sheets, but Marius beat me to it, jogging down the stairs and snatching them up with such ferocity that I thought he might be angry with me. My stomach clenched.

"I'm sorry, Your Highness," I said. Gavin's presence reminded me of my manners. Prince Marius might tolerate some familiarity, but I wouldn't assume the same of the rest of his family, even mild-mannered Gavin. "I slipped."

"Are you sure you're alright?" Marius asked, looking me up and down.

My cheeks flooded with heat. I looked terrible. My braid was disheveled, I wore no makeup, and my dress was in dire need of laundering. I hadn't yet changed for the banquet.

I nodded and hid my scraped palms behind my back. "I'm fine. It was just a little tumble."

"You're crying," he pointed out.

"I'm just having a bad day," I mumbled. I'd checked the phase of the moon, and strongly suspected my monthly bleeding was about to start, but I wasn't about to admit that to anyone. Especially not Prince Marius, of all people. "Thank you for your concern, Your Highness, but I really should return to my duties."

"Maybe you should go lie down," said Prince Gavin. He gestured at his own eyebrow. "You've got a bit of blood here."

"Oh," I said, wiping my face. When I looked down, blood was smeared across my palm. "I'm sorry."

They stared at me like I'd sprouted a third eyeball. I wanted to sob again, but forced myself not to. I just had to get through tonight and then I'd find somewhere quiet and lonely to cry in private.

"It's alright," said Prince Gavin gently. He was far burlier than Marius, with thick thighs and a torso that I'd glimpsed once or twice, so muscled that it reminded me of the statues I'd seen of Balligor, god of war. His biceps alone were bigger than my thighs.

He'd never been anything but polite, yet I found myself startled by the concern in his expression.

Nobody knew I was Ria's sister, but it must've been apparent that we meant something to each other, because the royal family was far kinder to me than they ought to be. Kinder than I would have been. I knew better than to assume royalty would be nice for the sake of it.

"I'll go with you to the laundress," said Marius abruptly. There was no hint of amusement in his gaze. None of the flippant charm I'd grown accustomed to, only a strange intensity, overlaid with alarm.

I must have looked worse than I thought.

"Oh," I said, caught off-guard. I badly wanted to be left alone, but I couldn't very well tell him so. "That's very kind, but there's no need—"

"I insist," he said, and I couldn't argue with that.

Gavin smirked as we departed, and I fought the urge to fold in on myself. There would be rumors. And with them, danger.

I'd be lucky to survive Queen Tarra's scrutiny.

GOOD AS HIS WORD, Prince Marius followed me to the laundress's, the stack of sheets piled high in his arms.

"Isn't this below your station?" I pleaded. We'd already received a number of odd looks and crossed more than one servant who would surely report everything she'd witnessed to the others. By late afternoon, everyone would know that Prince Marius had done my job for me.

"You *fell*," he replied. "*Hard*. I saw it. Honestly, I'm surprised you're able to walk right now."

My tailbone all but screamed with every step, but Marius didn't need to know that. "I fought a bear, didn't I? It takes more than a fall to incapacitate me." Absolute lies. I would've laid on the floor and wept if the embarrassment wouldn't have haunted me for the rest of my life. "I'm really alright—"

"At least let me do this, if you're going to insist on being stubborn," he huffed, clutching the sheets closer to his chest. "I've fallen down the stairs before, too, you know. It isn't the same as surviving a battle, but it's grueling all the same."

"I don't understand," I began.

The prince cut me off again. "Falling down hurts," he said, emphasizing each word. His severe blue gaze softened as he let out a humorless laugh. "Really, I'm beginning to wonder if you scrambled your brains."

"*People will talk,*" I hissed, because clearly my fall had scrambled his brains, too. "I could get into trouble for this." I rubbed at my sore wrist. "You're engaged to my… employer, and I shouldn't be alone with you."

"You are a staff member, and we are not alone in a locked room. It's perfectly fine," Prince Marius scoffed. "I've no idea what things are like in Olmstead, but in Tocchia, this is hardly a death sentence."

"I think you've no idea what it's like to be a servant," I snapped, then clapped a hand over my mouth.

Prince Marius stared at me. His eyebrows raised. "I have some idea," he said. One hand reached for the pendant between his collarbones, just barely visible over the frothing waterfall of lace at his neck. "I'm certainly less privileged than my siblings. I've… problems," he finished, slightly crestfallen.

This was too personal a reveal. I didn't want to know more. Whatever Prince Marius's problems were, I preferred he kept them to himself. The less I knew, the safer I was.

Besides, the downward tilt to his plush lips, the set of those broad shoulders told me all I needed to know; I'd upset him. Guilt rippled like a current under my skin. I wanted to squirm away from it.

"I've overstepped," I said, looking away from the perfect column of his throat. "I'm sorry."

"Don't be," he said, though he wouldn't meet my eye. "You are right. I'm sure it seems I'm playing games with your life and livelihood. I promise that isn't my intent."

"I'm sure it isn't, Your Highness."

For a long moment, he was quiet, contemplative. "How long will you stay?" he asked, so abruptly that I realized the question must've burned at him.

"In Tocchia?" I said, confused. Why would he assume I was going to leave?

Then I realized. He must've overheard me speaking to Ria or Avens. If he overheard that, what else did he know? My blood ran cold.

"Yes."

"I suppose for as long as Princess Valeria wishes me to," I said. "I've never worked for anyone else."

"I see," hummed Prince Marius. He didn't say anything more.

We exited the palace, and made our way around back, where the washing lines stretched from one pole to another, laundry waving in the wind. Most of it had already been collected for the day, but a few leftover sheets twisted in the breeze.

The laundresses stopped in their tracks, staring at the spectacle before them: Prince Marius carrying a heap of rumpled sheets, and a red-cheeked maid beside him, empty-handed. He waved at them as though there was nothing out of the ordinary about this. "Where should I put these?"

Three laundresses ran up to him, reaching hesitantly for the sheets. They looked from Prince Marius to me—curious, but afraid to ask.

"I fell and dropped everything," I explained, face burning with embarrassment. "His Highness was kind enough to accompany me here."

"You have a bruise," one laundress whispered to me. The sunlight caught her bright red hair, illuminating strands of honey gold and auburn. Worry shined in her eyes.

"And the next stop is the infirmary," said Prince Marius,

moving to stand beside me. There was a polite eagerness about him. It might've been endearing if I'd actually liked him.

I hardly required an escort, but only nodded pitifully.

"Those sheets were Princess Odalla's," I told the laundress. "I'm so sorry—"

"Don't be," the laundress whispered. "You're limping. Did he—" Her gaze flitted to Prince Marius. The question hung in the air like a noxious smell.

"No," I said quickly. "I fell all on my own. Down the stairs. He just witnessed it."

The laundress winced. "Take care of yourself," she said, and she was gone amongst the whipping sheets.

I followed Prince Marius to the infirmary with great reluctance, and only because I had no idea where to find it. My teeth grit together with each step. The laundress was right; I *was* limping. My head pounded. And somehow, I had to survive the banquet.

Maybe I needed a visit after all.

We passed through the west wing, where most of the guests were staying, and then traversed two flights of stairs, and a long hallway until we came to the infirmary. It was smaller than I expected, with only twenty or so beds, but then, I supposed that battles didn't typically take place at the Palace, so extra beds weren't needed.

An oversight, in my opinion. Goddess knew we didn't have enough in Olmstead.

A middle-aged woman in a tunic and pants spotted Prince Marius and bustled over to us. "Good afternoon! What seems to be the problem, Your Highness?"

He gestured to me. The rings on his slender fingers caught the sunlight streaming through the windows and glittered. His fingernails were impeccably clean. I fought the urge to hide my hands behind my back. "Hello, Iana. Miss Arina here fell down the stairs."

"Oh," said the healer, clapping her hands. "And you escorted her here? How kind!" She led me to the bed nearest to the door and prompted me to sit. I did, trying not to wince.

"After witnessing it, I could do nothing else," said the prince, crossing his arms, and coming to stand at my bedside.

I'd think he was downright noble if I didn't know better.

"How *chivalrous*! Well, if you've places to be, I'm sure we're fine here," Iana chirped, already pawing through the cabinet beside my bed. Bottles of potions, blocks of powders, and tiny vials were neatly arranged on the shelves, like lines of soldiers before battle.

"I can wait," said Marius, smiling his most dashing smile. "This is my betrothed's personal guard. I'd like to ensure she's fit for service tonight."

"Oh," said Iana, her voice culminating in a squeak. "Well, we'd best get on with things then." She turned to me. "Tell me, what hurts?"

"My tailbone," I said after a long pause, reluctant to admit that my ass hurt in front of a prince. He'd already settled himself into a chair on the other side of the bed, and set about examining his nails, the lacy ruffles of his sleeves. It was as if he hadn't heard me at all. "And my head."

"Yes," she said, trailing her fingers past the cut on my forehead. "I can see that. Well, we'll get you fixed up!"

And fix me up she did, first by handing me a tonic that smelled like bog water and tasted worse, then asking me to lie down while she ran her fingers over my forehead, chanting something in a language I didn't recognize.

I'd always hated healers and their chants. Their gifts were acquired through alliances with the gods, and while I understood that the gods had their requirements, that didn't change the fact that the chants were incredibly creepy. The more theatrical the healer, the more horrifying the overall experience. Iana had a flair for the dramatics. Her words ground against my eardrums, faster and more overwhelming as they went on, until there was nothing but me and the healer, and an endless stream of babble, oppressive and demanding.

I wanted to vomit, but refused to do so in front of Prince Marius, so I just gritted my teeth and rolled onto my belly when instructed, eyes squeezed shut so that tears couldn't leak out.

Healing hurts. It's not just the chanting that makes the whole experience so terrible. Healing magic is an uncomfortable squeeze beneath the skin, like something has slithered between the layers and taken up residence there. And then there's the actual pain. A bone knitting back together isn't a quick process. Everything that one might've felt during the natural healing process is squeezed into the duration of the spell, making every second unbearable.

I whimpered when the healer's focus turned to my tailbone, which probably wasn't broken. But the pain was already at the edge of what I could reasonably bear. Now, it compounded into two long minutes, where dozens of pins stabbed straight into my bones.

At the end of it, I was still sore.

Prince Marius spared me only a single concerned glance, which I was eternally grateful for. I didn't want him gawking at me in my time of agony. I would've very much preferred if he had left the room, but I knew better than to hope for so much.

"Come back if anything hurts!" called the healer, waving merrily after us.

I absolutely would not.

"Better?" asked Prince Marius as we turned a corner.

I gave an exhausted nod. "As I'll ever be."

"Good enough," he answered. If his smug grin was any indication, he was quite pleased with himself.

CHAPTER 17

"Your missing heir," said Gavin to the representatives of Liridin hours later, after the wine flowed, and everyone danced in its river, drunk and laughing. A bright moon hovered overhead. The band played loudly, and the gardens overflowed with guests, drunk and giggling, unsteady on their feet as they made their way to the dance floor. "I'm still shocked he hasn't appeared."

I was at Ria's side, too exhausted to do my job properly, hoping that my presence alone would deter any potential problems. My backside ached fiercely, and my temple still stung. Though the healer had dulled the pain, she hadn't repaired me.

That wasn't the point of a healer, of course. I didn't expect every wound to fully close. That would take a tremendous amount of energy. Not something likely to be wasted on a maid, even one escorted by Prince Marius.

I perked up at the mention of the missing heir. This was *not* a scenario that would be entertained by the royals in Olmstead, or any neighboring kingdoms. If an heir went missing, there would be a manhunt. If it was unsuccessful, the throne would then pass to whoever was next in line.

Unless there was no one to pass the throne to. I shivered at the implication.

"Yes," said Fallamor, one of representatives of the Sea. Tonight, he wore his hair in a long, loose braid. Tiny, spiral shells were pinned to it. He was stunningly handsome, and I repeatedly found my gaze drawn to him. If he noticed, he never let on. I was grateful for his discretion; certain I couldn't stomach the embarrassment if he'd chosen to say something. "Do tell us more about that. I can assure you that in Plinath we would never wait so long."

"There's a prophecy," pointed out Toral. Like yesterday, he wore black, but tonight, his clothes were far more appropriate for a banquet. Hundreds of tiny, shining scales were sewn into his shirt and pants, so that he shimmered everywhere he went, not unlike a dragon. His massive, black wings outshined his outfit, and caught the light from the chandelier. I couldn't stop looking at them, amazed by their sheen. "It says he will return. So we wait."

"A prophecy?" asked Ria, brow furrowing. She swilled the wine in her goblet, but did not take a sip. Already, she was slurring her words. "And that has merit?"

"Liridin is known for the accuracy of its prophecies," said Prince Marius, draining the dregs of his wine. A new goblet appeared in his hand almost instantly, replaced by a servant who disappeared as quickly as she arrived. He must've been rather tipsy, because he seemed confused as to how it got there. "You can ignore a prophecy from the mainland without much consequence, but it would be unwise to do so in Liridin."

"I see," said Ria, setting her nearly empty goblet on the table.

No servant came to give her a new one.

"That's true," said Halin, nodding. He plucked a slice of cheese from his plate and rolled it around a tiny sausage. "Our prophecies have earned a reputation among the continent. And this one is no different from the others. Would you like to hear it?"

Ria frowned. "Is it relevant?"

The table burst into whooping laughter and guffaws. The sound echoed across the lawn, drawing the attention of Queen Tarra, who glared at us. Toral laughed so hard that he looked halfway to tears, while Marius and Gavin dissolved into sniggers that would've been more befitting of schoolchildren. Even Fallamor joined in.

"Yes?" Halin ventured. "I think it is very relevant."

Ria's cheeks were red as apples, from both wine and humiliation. "I-I didn't mean any offense," she stammered.

Prince Marius took a massive gulp of wine and sprayed it all over the table when Halin climbed on top of the bench, mug in hand. He wavered about, sloshing ale as he began, "It goes as such: The first and only heir of the Ice King will vanish in a torrent of wind and frost, only to reappear on the wings of a moth, fleeing the fires of war." He had to shout to be heard over Prince Marius's gasping laughter and Ria's sputtering. I hung onto every word, eager to hear more.

Fallamor turned to me, his brilliant, sea foam green eyes meting mine. "There you have it," he said. "The infamous prophecy."

"Is Liridin on the brink of war?" I asked, watching as Halin wobbled on the bench. Toral was quick to help him down, a disapproving scowl on his face.

"No," snorted Fallamor. He observed as Halin fumbled to his seat, grin a little too sharp, on the verge of mocking. Then his gaze flitted to me, hard and critical. "But hope springs eternal."

I thought there might be a second implication there, so I looked away before my embarrassment could flare. Of course I'd never pursue a prince of the sea, but Fallamor was impossibly beautiful, his face carved from the finest marble, his jawline strong enough to cut diamond, perceptive eyes constantly scanning the room.

"'*The first and only heir*,'" I mused, eager to change the subject. "It's a miracle the Sky Kingdom hasn't been attacked."

Fallamor shrugged. "They've protection from Plinath and from Tocchia. And hardly anyone believes they exist, which is certainly helpful. Few kings will waste resources attacking a mythical kingdom."

"Don't underestimate their greed," I said, watching as Prince Marius frantically mopped up the spilled wine, contrite under Tarra's chilling stare.

"Tocchia is difficult to reach. Most realms are content to allow Tocchian representatives to come to them. It makes things easier for Liridin." Fallamor yawned, revealing pointed teeth.

I'd noticed them before, of course; it wasn't as if the prince never spoke or opened his mouth. But I hadn't realized just how sharp they were, or how many fit into his mouth, which was suddenly impossibly wide, stretching like a snake's. I could see all the way past his tongue, and down the back of his throat.

Fallamor's jaw snapped shut, and he batted his eyelashes innocently at me. "Stick to Marius," he murmured, so that only I could hear him. "I bite. He doesn't."

His laughter echoed in my ears as I recoiled, shame and anger flaring in my chest.

Prince Marius caught sight of my expression, and his eyes narrowed. Before I could move, he plopped down on the bench between Fallamor and I.

"Educating the Olmsteadians, are we?" said Marius to Fallamor, practically purring.

Ria frowned between Marius and I, clearly wondering if she'd missed something.

I shrugged. I wondered the same.

"Someone has to," said Fallamor innocently. "I don't think your new wife's bodyguard knew I was of the serpents."

"Ah," said Marius, not bothering to mention that he wasn't married yet. "In that case, I can't blame you."

A pointed tongue poked between Fallamor's pointed teeth as he smirked. "I don't condone their ignorance. Nor can I accept it."

"Naturally," agreed Prince Marius, sipping more wine. "I imagine this is a rather miserable affair. Forced to educate the ignorant when you could be riding the waves and hunting sharks."

My face heated.

"It is a nice change of pace," said Fallamor, shrugging. "Even the sea grows dull sometimes."

"I am well aware," groaned Prince Marius, feigning a swoon, dipping backward so that his coattails brushed against the cobblestone pavement. "I seem to be forced to entertain you whenever you're bored."

Fallamor beamed smugly.

"You are a very dramatic drunk," I complained, scooting away from Marius, until my hips were flush against Ria's.

"I am dramatic most days," he informed me, lifting his goblet in imitation of a toast. Wine sloshed. "Drunk or not."

What lovely, stable rulers Tocchia would one day have. I wished Queen Tarra and King Hergarv longevity. If not for their sakes, then for the sakes of their people. I couldn't imagine the nonsense Marius and Ria would condemn the kingdom to.

But maybe that was unfair. Yes, my sister was moody and grumpy more often than not, but she understood diplomacy, at least in theory. Prince Marius's understanding of the subject remained to be seen.

"You're the most dramatic person I've ever met," Gavin scoffed. He sipped from his mug of ale, and wiped foam from his lips. "Don't even try to deny it."

"I didn't," Prince Marius huffed. "Which you would know if you were paying attention. Besides, Miss Arina is not so easily fooled."

"I guess that's true," said Gavin, though there was something dissatisfied in his expression. Suspicion? Doubt?

"Is she the maid or the guard?" asked Halin, his strange blue gaze landing on mine.

"Both," I said, straightening my shoulders.

"It's a unique position," said Ria with a practiced air.

I nodded, trying to project a confidence I didn't feel.

Gavin watched Ria from across the table. The way she sipped her wine. The way her delicate fingers, bare of rings and adornments, tapped against the table when she was restless.

He'd had just enough ale to have forgotten himself. I kicked his shin under the table. When he startled, I shot him a warning glare.

He gave a slow, careful nod that only Fallamor and I saw. I'd not spill his secrets, but it wouldn't do to lust after my sister so openly.

Or was it lust? They spoke often, quick jibes and brief greetings, nothing particularly notable. But sometimes I caught Ria grinning to herself long after Gavin waved to her in the hallway, and I wondered.

A servant replaced Ria's goblet, slipping behind me so silently that I almost didn't notice. I glimpsed a pale hand with a dark mole, and then it was gone.

How long would it take me to reach that level of expertise? Where I could glide between people like nothing more than a breeze?

Ria stared down at the wine with reluctant acceptance. She'd have a headache tomorrow, but had apparently already decided anything was better than sitting through this banquet sober. All morning, I'd listened to her express reluctance to attend at all and thought to myself that this was going to be the rest of her life. Banquets and meetings and galas and ceremonies. If she didn't learn to enjoy or at least tolerate events, she'd be miserable.

She hadn't appreciated me telling her that.

Fallamor popped a grape into his mouth, crunching loudly.

Prince Marius was saying something, but I couldn't understand the words. My ears rang. My vision blurred. Courtiers and dancers blended together like subjects in an oil painting.

Something was horribly, terribly wrong.

The sensation faded, and I was left clutching the hilt of my sword, glancing around wildly.

I'd forgotten about the buttons on my boots. One for a warning. The other for good luck. I'd sewn them after my first month in the palace, an experiment. They were new designs that I'd never tested and quickly moved on from.

Prince Marius might've observed my ever-changing buttons, but I was so accustomed to them that I barely even remembered swapping them out.

One for a warning.

Beside me, Prince Marius was saying something to Fallamor, eyes crinkled in mirth. Across from me, Gavin tugged at a loose thread on his jacket, his face a mask of concentration. Toral and Halin plucked at an already picked-over plate of sweating meats and cheeses. A dancer and her partner whirled past. Her blue gown shimmered in the candlelight. Voices echoed around me. Laughter filtered through the air.

Ria reached for her goblet.

I glimpsed the strange film along the top, the tiniest speck of white powder. Before I knew what I was doing, I'd smacked the goblet from her hand. It clattered to the ground and rolled beneath the table.

Wine sloshed over Ria's breast, across the cobblestones. Everyone at the table gasped.

"Talina," Ria hissed, forgetting herself.

"That's poisoned," I choked out, shocked by the realization. "Did you drink any?"

"No!" snapped Ria, staring at me in disbelief. "How could I? It's all over my dress."

"There was powder on the rim," I managed to say, my voice thin and reedy.

Prince Marius leapt to his feet, and crouched down, peering curiously at the goblet, which had rolled to a stop against Gavin's shoe.

"Careful," warned Fallamor. He procured a crisp linen napkin and passed it to the prince.

"Bring me a torch!" called Marius. One appeared in his hand almost instantly, passed from a wide-eyed, trembling servant.

By now, we'd attracted quite a bit of attention. Even some of the dancers stood off to the side, watching. Avens shot me a questioning look from the stage, and I pressed my finger to my lips. That satisfied him, and he went back to his hurdy-gurdy as though nothing had happened.

Servants gathered around us. Nobles forced their way through the crowd, gawking openly at the scene before them, accusations spilling from their lips like the wine from Ria's goblet.

"Is that blood?"

"It's wine, you bloody idiot!"

"The maid must've been jealous."

"Which maid? The pretty one?" A courtier's finger jabbed at me. I flinched away like it was a knife.

"Silence!" Gavin boomed, coming to stand beside Ria and me, his brawny figure shielding us from frantic nobles.

"There *is* a strange sheen," Prince Marius confirmed, rising to his feet in one fluid motion.

Ria's jaw dropped.

Queen Tarra stomped her way over to us, holding her skirts around her ankles. "What happened here?" she demanded, voice shrill.

Marius turned to her, chiseled jaw set, eyes narrowed. "Someone tried to poison my betrothed."

The uproar was instantaneous. Servants shot each other worried glances and hurried into place. Nobles stampeded around us, shoving and arguing amongst each other, eager for a look at the spilled wine. Others reached for the swords at their hips or the knives in their boots. The royal guard leapt to attention, drawing weapons and fanning out to investigate. Ria was whisked away by Zellia. I tried to follow, but a hand on my shoulder stopped me.

"You!" spat Queen Tarra, her nails digging into my skin. "You wait right here."

Prince Marius stood gesturing with his hands, trying to explain the situation to King Hergarv. Gavin stood beside him, occasionally chiming in.

"The goblet—"

"Miss Arina spotted—"

Fallamor and Toral appeared, flanking me on either side. Queen Tarra glowered at them. "Tell me what happened here," she growled.

"Someone replaced Princess Valeria's wine," I explained, grateful for the representatives' presence. They'd seen everything. I hoped they meant to defend me, though a sharp of pang of dread in my chest warned me otherwise. Such assumptions were dangerous in a royal court. "I spotted a trace of powder on the rim as she went to sip from it."

"Show me," said Queen Tarra, her voice deathly calm.

By now, there was silence all around. Stunned faces waited for the truth. Crickets chirped.

I gestured to the red stain spreading across the stone. "Here, Your Highness."

Frowning, Queen Tarra squatted down.

"My queen!" cried a servant. "Your skirts!"

"Hush," said Queen Tarra. "There are more important things in life than skirts. Pass me a torch," she commanded.

A servant appeared, handed over the torch, and scampered away like he'd been burned.

This time, I stooped to examine the evidence. I stared down at the stain, heart in my throat. This wine was too dull, too sticky not to have been spiked with something.

"Hmm," said Queen Tarra, swiping her finger through the puddle. Horrified cries followed as she examined the tip of her finger. "Poison." She paused, tilting her head. "A golden sheen. Billianberry root."

King Hergarv sighed, his shoulders sagging. Gavin and Marius shared the crowd's shock—King Hergarv seemed only resigned.

Queen Tarra stood, meeting startled faces. "What?" she demanded. "Did you think I would be so easily fooled? That I wouldn't have taken steps to protect myself? That I would move to a foreign kingdom and assume everyone was my friend? Of course I can identify poisons!"

"Good idea. Maybe we ought to start doing that, too," whispered someone to my left.

"Someone tried to kill her?" squealed someone to my right. A noblewoman in a pink dress, whose skirts draped like elegant flower petals.

"Good riddance," mumbled someone else.

"Enough," said King Hergarv, clapping his hands together "The festivities have ended."

The band faltered to a stop.

"An investigation must be carried out," the king continued, scratching at his beard, staring out over the gardens, where tables were still piled with platters of food. Wine flowed from the fountain. Avens wasn't even sweating yet.

"It was just one poisoning!" argued a noble in red, crossing his arms.

"A single poisoning!"

"*Singular*!" emphasized a drunk, holding up one finger, and waving it about.

Uproar. A king, no matter how powerful, was no match for a bunch of drunken, riotous noblemen and their ilk. Some returned to dancing. Others shouted at the band to start up. And still others resumed drinking, though most were smart enough to choose ale over wine.

Marius whispered something to Hergarv, who scowled.

I scanned the attendees, searching for a familiar face. Or, more importantly, a familiar mole. But I was too far away to be of any help. "I saw the hand of the person who brought the wine, Your Highness," I told Queen Tarra, who remained beside me. "I could probably identify—"

"My dear," sighed Queen Tarra, adjusting her crown. "They are certainly gone by now."

Prince Marius was at my side in an instant. "That isn't necessarily true. If Miss Arina saw—"

"I think Miss Arina has had a busy day, and needs to spend less time with you, and more time with her charge," said Queen Tarra firmly. She waved him off with a gloved hand.

I blinked. Did she know that I'd seen Marius outside of my designated working hours? Did she disapprove of the way he sat beside me today, and not Ria?

It was unconventional for a princess to have female guards. In part, this was to prevent the sort of situation Queen Tarra probably imagined—a husband more interested in the guards than his wife.

But it meant that queens and princesses were sometimes put into bad situations by the very people meant to protect them. Seduction was often blamed, but I knew better. A little force, a little too much wine, and some time alone in a room... Not all guards were loyal. Not all princesses could fight.

"I'm not sure if you've noticed," said Marius to Tarra, a glower on his face. "But Miss Arina's charge is my betrothed, which means that we're often together. Am I not to speak to her?"

King Hergarv wore an odd expression—strained, even angry. "You'd do well to watch your tongue," he suggested. "A castle can quickly become a prison for a prince."

Prince Marius closed his mouth slowly, indignant scowl spreading across his perfect face.

"You ought to leave," said the Queen to me. "Go find your charge."

I stumbled out of the gardens, toward the main door. Fallamor followed me. "Out of curiosity," he murmured, just loudly enough that I could hear him over the chaos. "What did the hand look like?"

"There was a mole on the right ring finger," I said, relieved that *someone* cared, even if it was only the man who was apparently half-snake. "Bigger than usual."

"Excellent," said Fallamor, nodding. "And good work. You saved the Princess, regardless of what Queen Tarra thinks."

"Thank you," I managed. "That might've been catastrophic."

The word felt insufficient. Losing my sister would be soul-destroying. Earth-shattering. War-initiating.

"Billianberry root may not have killed her," said Fallamor, stroking his long braid thoughtfully. "Just incapacitated her."

We stopped just short of the doors.

"What would be the point of that?" I demanded, too stressed, tired, and hungry to deal with anymore cryptic comments.

"I've no idea," said Fallamor with a shrug of his elegant shoulders. "Why poison her at all? Why not poison Marius, or Gavin, or one of the royal family?"

A terrible thought occurred to me. "Was Prince Marius poisoned? What about you? You all drank the wine, didn't you?"

Fallamor chuckled. "I think we would know by now if we'd been poisoned. Billianberry is fast-acting."

I leaned back against a table stacked high with cakes and pastries. My fingers itched to grab one, to scarf it down in front of Fallamor, and dare him to say something. "Does it kill, or merely incapacitate?"

"It's hard to say." Fallamor's sea foam green eyes darkened. "Billianberry root is difficult to acquire. It only grows in West Alberbrook. I can't say I'm terribly familiar with it, just that I know it isn't always deadly."

Alberbrook. I thought of Duke Callum, and his handsome face, and felt a pang of longing for home and familiar company.

"Why would someone want to incapacitate her?" I mused.

Fallamor shook his head. “I’ve no idea. To sow discord?”

I pursed my lips. “That can’t be right.”

“No,” Fallamor agreed. “I’m sure they wanted her dead.” His gaze was gentle, pitying. For the first time, I feared that he’d caught onto me. But his expression shifted to something more serious. “I’ll pass your information along,” he said, drifting past me with the elegance of a flower petal in a breeze. “Thank you. Take care.”

And he disappeared back into the crowd like a fish into the sea.

CHAPTER 18

"I'm *fine*," said Ria the moment I entered her chambers. "The healer already checked me over."

I raised my hands and feigned innocence. "Oh, yes, of course, Your Majesty. You *weren't* nearly poisoned, so I *won't* ask how you're feeling."

Ria groaned. She'd shucked her outer layers but remained stuck in her wine-stained corset. Sitting in her vanity chair, pearl-lined hairbrush in hand, she reminded so much of home that I nearly choked. Was it really only weeks ago that we'd sat in her bedroom in Olmstead, while she brushed her hair, and I laid spread out on her bedspread like a starfish?

"Fine," she said. "It's a reasonable question. I just don't want to answer it anymore." Her face softened. "Thank you. As angry and humiliated as I am, I'm glad you noticed."

"You're welcome," I said. I lowered onto the edge of the bed with an exhausted grunt. Adrenaline coursed through my body, but I detected the underlying weakness in my limbs, the haziness of my mind. I'd hardly slept and barely eaten. I could fall asleep like this, fully clothed on top of a scratchy, embroidered bedspread, and barely notice. "Sorry I spilled it all over you."

"Better all over my dress than in my veins," sighed Ria. She slouched against the back of the chair, hairbrush dangling from her fingertips.

"Agreed," I said, fluttering over to her. "I'm so glad you're safe."

But safety felt fragile and intangible now, a concept so foreign that it became more myth than reality. Dread spiked in my belly.

DAYS PASSED, and the would-be assassin was not discovered. Though King Hergarv threatened to start cutting off hands, no one came forward with information. I was the only person who had witnessed anything of value, and even my claims were called into question. I was "interviewed" three times in the throne room, with Ria peering over my shoulder as if our roles had been reversed.

Prince Marius was never far behind, watching with intensity as King Hergarv asked question after question, ready to intervene at the first sign of trouble.

Why did he care? Ria's continued contentment was in his best interest, but I refused to believe this was his motivation.

All this couldn't be for my sake, could it?

Maybe he needed more help than I'd anticipated. Especially if it was true that no one else was willing to look at his cursed ring.

"You're sure there was a mole?" said King Hergarv, leaning forward in his throne during my third interrogation. "We've found not a single mole on a single ring finger, regardless of the hand."

"I remember it distinctly," I said, trying not to fidget. "It was a large mole near the first knuckle of the ring finger on the right hand."

Prince Marius chewed the inside of his cheek and said nothing. So far he'd stayed silent, a looming presence in the background. With each passing interview, he seemed more concerned.

Today, he constantly shifted his feet, as though prepared to step between us.

He made me nervous. The guards showed no interest in me, but I suspected that Marius knew something I didn't.

"I see," said King Hergarv with a sigh. "This is the best you've got?"

"I'm afraid so." I clasped my hands and lowered my head, hoping I seemed earnest. So earnest, in fact, that he'd absolve me of all suspicion, and never mention this again.

"You see, it's beginning to sound like a *story* to me. Like something you made up to take the attention off yourself," King Hergarv continued, looking me dead in the eye. "I've been told you poisoned the glass. That you hoped we might keep you here in Tocchia if you proved your worth." He turned toward the window, his voice pondering. But there was an edge to it, fine as a razor. Dread filled my belly. "Now why would you be so desperate to stay? Not because you planned to report back to King Amonrew in the spring, hmm?"

Shit. I forced myself to take a deep, slow breath. If I answered this incorrectly, I'd probably be executed. "That isn't true, Your Highness. My loyalty lies with the Princess, and your court. I've no knowledge of poisons, and would never—"

"Enough of this," snarled Prince Marius, coming to stand between us, long blond hair flying out behind him. He smelled of pine and sword oil, of the lemon and mint soaps at the baths. "Miss Arina has provided the information three times over, as per your request. This is getting ridiculous. Your accusations hold no ground."

Ria's simmering anger turned to astonishment. Marius had come to my defense more than once, but there was a fervor to him now, an unfamiliar wildness not unlike that of a bobcat. I half-expected him to bite.

Guilt churned in my stomach. I'd put myself in this position. Marius chose to raid the castle, but I chose to sneak into the back of the wagon, and complicate Ria's life. I'd never live down the regret.

"You know as well as I do that the help likes to lie," said King Hergarv, with the exasperation of someone forced to explain something for the twentieth time.

"I was beside her the *entire* time. I would've noticed if she poisoned the wine," said Marius. His hands balled into fists at his sides. "There's no point in poisoning the glass just to orchestrate a rescue. And Fallamor—"

"Fallamor will do anything for a pretty face," snapped King Hergarv. He drew back as soon as he spoke, unruly beard trembling.

"I think the people of Plinath might not like to hear that," said Prince Marius, eyebrow raising high.

King Hergarv released a long, whistling sigh. "You're right. They wouldn't. The fact remains that I don't trust your judgment."

I focused on breathing slowly and staying still. Any squirming might be taken as a sign of guilt. My heart was in my throat, threatening to hammer free. Every passing second was torturous. Would they kill me? Or would the king see reason?

"You've never trusted me," said Prince Marius, gesticulating wildly, fury written plainly across his face. "Not once in my life! Not a single thing I've ever said has been enough for you! I'm sick of it! Miss Arina is important to my betrothed—"

The king sucked in a furious breath through flared nostrils. His lip curled to bare yellowing teeth. "*You* are prone to flights of fancy, and your *betrothed* would do well to learn that!"

Ria took a step back, mouth open, clutching the fabric of her skirt so tightly that it would surely wrinkle. She looked to me, then to Marius, whose face had turned to a snarl. A blue vein bulged in his forehead. A muscle spasmed in his jaw. "You would never say such things to Gavin."

"No!" spat King Hergarv, leaning forward like he might leap

from his throne. "*You* are not Gavin. *He* does not need to be reminded of such things!"

"You think I'm weak," Marius challenged, stepping closer.

I thought I was about to witness a regicide. Prince Marius breathed heavily, muscles cording in his neck. He was always armed and today was no exception—there was a sword on his hip, a knife visible in his boot, and probably more blades hidden in other places.

I shivered at the thought of hunting them down, plucking them from beneath his clothes, feeling taut, shivering muscle beneath my hands as I sought blade after blade…

Then I stopped myself, appalled. Where had *that* come from?

"You *are* weak!" King Hergarv growled. "You've been sick since you were born! Do not challenge me now!" His chest heaved. "I know you're itching for a fight, but you don't want to find it in me, boy. I could destroy you without a second thought!"

Prince Marius's astonished expression deepened into something thunderous. "You wouldn't *dare*."

"I'd do a lot worse than dare," King Hergarv bellowed. Droplets of his saliva landed on Prince Marius's face, his collar. "You foppish rat! You dare challenge me, after everything I've done for you? I'll kill the maid, then. See if I care what kind of a start your marriage gets off to. After everything I've done—"

"No!" Ria screamed, shoving her way between Marius and the King.

Hands landed on my shoulders. One belonged to King Hergarv's knight, the other to Prince Marius.

"No, no, no!" Ria shrieked. Her foot stamped down, dangerously close to the toes of King Hergarv's boots. "If you do this, I will ensure that Olmstead has no future cooperation with you! I will break the betrothal, I will set our armies on you—"

I felt faint. Too stunned to fight off the heavy, gauntleted hands wrapping around my wrists like frozen talons. What buttons were sewn into my blouse today? One for maintaining my hair color, another for tracking down Prince Marius, which burned like a brand against my breast. And what was the third one...?

"Release her," Prince Marius demanded, voice frantic in a way I'd never heard before. "Release her, you must release her—"

"Little princes would do well to learn their place," said one of the knights, hands tightening painfully on my wrists. "I can't take your orders over the king's, Your Highness."

Ria still screeched in the background. I glimpsed King Hergarv's face. Equal parts enraged and bewildered as this quiet, skinny princess screamed in his face, arms waving, hair coming loose from its bun. A guard approached to intervene, and King Hergarv waved him off.

Then it happened. "Silence!" he roared, saliva spraying across the room.

Everyone fell quiet.

King Hergarv's gaze fell upon my disheveled figure. One shaking finger raised to point at me. "Who the *fuck* is she?"

Ria shrank back.

Prince Marius froze in his tracks, and wiped a bead of moisture from his cheek, making a face of disgust. "Am I in a fucking rainstorm right now?"

I started to laugh, and couldn't stop.

CHAPTER 19

The dungeons were located to the west, facing the sea, and accessed through a back stairwell that I'd never noticed before. Down, down, down into a darkness so heavy that even the torches struggled to pierce it.

The guards were rough, despite Prince Marius's commands. I bowed my head and tried to cooperate, but it was difficult when the guard on my right dragged me at a slower pace than the one on my left. In the hallway outside the throne room, I tripped over my own feet and was given no time to right myself. A hand fisted in my hair, yanked me upright. When I looked up, an audience had gathered. The servants I'd spent so much time with over the last few months stood watching, awestruck. Zellia pressed the palm of her hand over her mouth, her eyes bulging.

I wanted to beg for help, but I knew better. Even if the servants believed me, I'd done nothing to earn their loyalty. The soldiers were stronger, better armed, and acting on the king's orders. Going against them would be a death sentence. I avoided eye contact and tried to not to sob as I was hauled down the stairs.

How was it that the Tocchian soldiers ensured minimal bloodshed during the attack in Olmstead, and yet took such delight in wrenching my wrists and grasping at my hair until my scalp screamed?

I wasn't yet in chains, but I had no hope of fighting them off. If I survived this, I'd have bruises all over my body.

If they didn't kill me as soon as I reached the dungeons.

Not every ruler enjoyed a spectacle. While Father believed it was best not to rob the people of an execution and the accompanying fanfare, I'd heard stories of other monarchs who had their enemies put to death quietly and quickly.

A guard squeezed my shoulder until I thought it might pop.

I should identify myself. I should make sure the guards knew that I was Princess Talina. They would at least hesitate before throwing me in a cell, or worse. But the only thing that escaped my mouth was a pained gasp.

Knees aching, scalp burning, wrists bruising, I could only succumb to the guards' whims as I was dragged down one long, dark, winding hallway, and into another. Torches lined the walls, barely illuminating heavy doors with metal grates. I tried to memorize our path, but it was difficult when the hand in my hair kept tugging my head back and forth, as if trying to prevent me from doing that very thing.

By the time they threw me into a cell, my mouth tasted of iron and salt.

~

HOURS PASSED. In the distance, I heard singing—a scratchy voice, an offkey tune, indeterminate words. Metal armor clanked. A door slammed. A high laugh echoed through the hallway. Waves crashed against the rocks outside.

I'd never set foot in a prison before, let alone a proper dungeon. Though I'd heard plenty of stories, I was unprepared for the chill that wrapped itself around me and seeped into my bones. Everything ached. There was a leak in my cell, a continuous dripping of water that could quickly grow maddening. When I attempted to look through the grate on my door, the tip of a spear appeared, mere inches from my eye.

No passing soldiers would stop to talk to me. My voice echoed across the cell, reverberating off the stone walls.

There was nowhere to sit but the floor. Damp seeped into my skirts. I tried to squat rather than sit, to keep from growing any colder, but eventually the strain in my legs became too much, and I was forced to stand again. I paced back and forth like a kenneled dog, salivating at the thought of freedom.

I'd always pitied Father's hounds, but never fully understood the hell they lived in—nights crammed into a cage, days spent running across rough terrain in exchange for scraps of meat and the chance to hunt vermin. Skinny and scrawny, they begged for affection, for food. Designed to hunt, kept desperate enough to comply.

If I'd felt sorry for myself on the day of the Spring Banquet, it was nothing compared to the way I felt now. For hours, I'd had no food, no water, no human interaction. My legs were beginning to ache from pacing, but I'd freeze if I sat on the stone floor.

This was where they put criminals. Was I a criminal now?

Following Ria here was stupid. I'd entered the kingdom under false pretenses, which might've been forgivable on its own, but I'd moved right into the palace and served as the princess's maid. My lies would be punished based on my proximity to the royal family. If King Hergarv thought I was a spy, then I was well and truly doomed.

I should've seen this coming. I knew better than to get caught. Ria had tried to send me home at least a dozen times.

I should've listened.

If they came for me, I would confess. I would scream until I was blue in the face that I was Princess Talina of Olmstead, under the protection of King Amonrew. I'd repeat myself until they either listened or killed me, whichever came first.

No one would kill a princess, I told myself, squeezing my eyes shut so tears couldn't escape. There would be an investigation. My execution would be a diplomatic scandal. After so much effort to acquire Ria, Tocchia wouldn't leap straight into war.

A thought struck me. Did King Hergarv throw me in here to force a confession? Did he hope I'd admit to whatever nefarious deeds he suspected of me?

Eventually, my shock turned to exhaustion. Pressing my forehead to the rough, cold stone, I closed my eyes and tried to rest.

I'd never fallen asleep standing up before. Avens used to claim that it happened to him sometimes, when a king forced him to play on throughout the night without breaks. That he didn't collapse, didn't faint—just fell asleep, so that the hurdy-gurdy slipped from his fingers, and crashed to the floor. One of his favorite things about Olmstead, he'd claimed, was King Amonrew's willingness to provide breaks, drinks, and food. Even when he played through an illness, he never worried about actually collapsing.

I couldn't imagine the exhaustion he must've felt. For all the times I'd been punished by my father, forced to scrub floors or muck stables until my back ached, I'd never fallen asleep on the job.

I thought of my mother, her long blond hair, her tense features, her hand carding through my hair as one person after another accused her of betraying her husband. How had that felt? Was she as frightened and lonely then as I was now?

In the loneliness of my cell, I gave way to my grief. Grief for my mother, who died before I really had a chance to know her. Grief for Avens, who never knew if he was going to allowed a break, if he was going to be propositioned by courtiers he couldn't say no to. Grief for everyone who'd died during the attack in Olmstead. Grief for the family I'd lied to and abandoned.

Grief for myself, trapped in this dark cell, waiting for death.

It was not death who arrived at my door some hours later, but

Queen Tarra, flanked by guards and torches. Her crown was askew, her skirts wrinkled. She looked every bit the inconvenienced royal until she saw me, and something in her gaze shifted. "Come with me," she said.

On stiff, sore legs, I followed. If I tried to curtsy, I'd crack in half, I was sure of it. Too stunned to say anything, I followed her down the hallway and up the stairs, trembling all the way. Faces appeared at the grates. Some simply observed, hollow and haunted, skeletal in the shadows. Others shouted for help, for mercy. Queen Tarra stared straight ahead, as if she hadn't heard them. But I met their eyes, and watched their lips move, and heard their words, and ached. What were they here for? Were they servants? Merchants who had tried to cheat the king? Would-be assassins and thieves?

How long had they languished here, pleading for help?

Did they deserve it?

Did it matter?

We emerged in the daylight. A long hall greeted us. The guards walked close to me, ready to intervene if I tried to flee. But I was too exhausted for that.

Sunlight streamed through the windows, blinding me. I blinked furiously as I struggled to keep up.

I assumed we were going to the throne room, but the Queen took us up another flight of stairs, and round the corner to a cozy little room set up for tea.

Surely this wasn't for me. This was a test. Or some kind of torture. Only time would tell.

Queen Tarra swept elegantly toward the carved chair at the head of the table. She gestured to the seat nearest her. "Sit."

Afraid to do anything other than obey, I sat. Fragrant teas steamed in tiny, pale cups with gilded rims. The pink roses painted on the sides seemed to dance and sway, but maybe that was because I was exhausted. I blinked, but the details never cleared.

Stacks of cakes and sandwiches rested on ornate platters. My stomach gave a rumble of agony.

The queen gestured to the table. "Please, help yourself. You must be hungry."

What could I do but oblige? I spooned some preserves onto a plate, added a couple of thin cookies and a miniature sandwich.

Queen Tarra reached for a frosted pastry and took a delicate sip from her cup. "Needs cream," she grumbled, and a servant rushed to present her a pitcher.

After adding cream and sugar to her tea, the queen raised her gaze to me. "Eat," she said. "I'm sure that was no easy night."

I took a hesitant bite of the sandwich. I wanted to gulp it down the same way I imagined Fallamor might, jaw unhinged and all, but I forced myself to take small bites. "Thank you, Your Highness."

The queen took a sip of tea, sighed, and returned the cup to its saucer with a soft clink. "I'm sure you're wondering why you're here." Her gaze fixed on something behind me. I fought the urge to turn and see what it was.

"I am… curious, Your Highness," I admitted, stirring cream into my tea. Never one to deny myself simple pleasures, I admired the way it bloomed and swirled, contrasting with the murky water.

"It will come as no surprise to you that my husband is an idiot," said Queen Tarra, sounding very, very tired. "Whenever I suggest keeping information to yourself, it is for a reason." She met my eye, and I blanched.

"I'm sorry. I thought—"

"You did the right thing, technically speaking. It just wasn't the best thing for *you*. There is a difference, and it would serve you well to learn quickly." She stirred her tea, silver spoon clicking against the golden rim. "In any case, we found the perpetrator hiding in a nearby village. The staff were able to identify her as having been in the palace on the day of the festival."

I took a quick bite of a cookie and tried not to groan as sweetness flooded my tongue.

They'd caught someone? Did that mean that I was absolved of guilt?

Worry churned in my gut. What if they got the wrong person? What I only *thought* I saw the mole?

"I see no need for further bloodshed," said Queen Tarra with a wave of her manicured hand. "I'm not convinced you're capable of spying, and I would advise you not to try. You're free to return to your duties."

Gratitude washed through me. All my worries about a possible wrong victim disappeared. "I—Thank you, Your Highness."

Her eyes narrowed. "Don't be so quick to thank me. I've one more subject to broach."

Oh. My smile faded.

"Prince Marius said that you'd assisted him with his... inheritance. A ring."

Shit. Should I admit to everything? Or hope that she wouldn't press?

Surely, she hadn't freed me only to throw me back into the dungeons.

"I... Yes, Your Highness. I've some experience as an artificer. He asked me to look at it."

"Never mention that to anyone again," said Queen Tarra. Her shoulders firmed. "People will talk. But you have my permission to continue assisting him. I don't approve of his interest in you, but he... has been ill most of his life, and he needs something to keep him occupied." A scowl. She put her head in her hands. "I do hope the Princess can keep him from causing further trouble."

"What sort of trouble? If I may ask, Your Highness," I added. Marius was ill? King Hergarv had said something along those lines, but I couldn't imagine vibrant, energetic Prince Marius as anything other than healthy.

"He is stubborn," groused the queen. "Troublesome. When he

wants something, he chases it. So much so that we all agreed that he ought to be the one to go fetch his bride."

My jaw dropped. I couldn't believe she would share this information with me.

Queen Tarra must have noticed my expression, because she spoke her next words coldly. "King Amonrew was not open to negotiation. We were left with little choice."

"May I ask a question?" I said. Muscles tensed, I waited for her reaction.

Her gaze swept over my face. A moment passed. "I'll allow it."

"Thank you, Your Highness." I took a deep breath. "Was another bride not a possibility?"

Queen Tarra studied me, then returned to her tea. If my question bothered her, she didn't show it. "No," she said. "Not when we believed the treaty had been honored, and King Amonrew refused to negotiate. *That* is an insult, and it leaves only war."

I took a bite of cookie, hoping to cover my frown.

"We acted according to the terms of the treaty when we sent soldiers across the border to clear the Nemonians from Blythewell," the queen continued. "Our soldiers were closest, and we acted as allies."

This was the third time I'd heard such a story. There must be some truth to it.

I nodded. "Thank you for explaining, Your Majesty."

"Well, we can't allow this misconception to continue unchecked," said Queen Tarra. A stray curl fell in front of her face, and she tucked it delicately behind her ear. "Anything else?"

I shook my head.

"Then feel free to leave. The servants anticipate your return, as does Princess Valeria."

"Thank you, You Highness," I said again. With a mournful glance at the spread of cakes and sandwiches before me, I rose, and left the room.

In a trance, I made my way back to the servants' quarters,

where I changed into clean clothes. Someone had leaned my sword and scabbard against the wall, in the same place that I always left it. I felt a little more like myself when I belted it to my waist.

Then I sought out Ria. My legs were shaky, and I was certain I stank, but I didn't know what else to do. Queen Tarra had not given me permission to sleep the day away like I really wanted to, so it only made sense to return to my duties.

Ria was not in her rooms, as I half-expected her to be. A worried Zellia spotted me in the hallway.

"You must be looking for the princess!" she said, voice loaded with false cheer.

I winced and wished she'd lower her voice. My head hurt, and I couldn't bear to confront the other servants yet. If they heard Zellia's shouts, they'd surely come to ogle me. "Do you know where she is?"

"I do. She's out riding with the prince."

"Oh," I said. Ria hated anything to do with riding. I suspected she and Prince Marius were having a less than lovely time together.

"Are you alright?" Zellia whispered, glancing around to ensure no one was nearby. But it was just the two of us, and our long, stretching shadows in the marble hallway.

"I'm fine," I answered. I was well aware of how I must look—hair falling out of its bun, dirt smeared across my face, mud on my boots, dark circles under my eyes. "Just tired."

"I thought we'd seen the last of you," she admitted, ducking her chin as she avoided my eye. "What happened?"

"They suspected that I may have been the culprit," I said, careful to keep my voice low. "Please don't tell anyone."

Zellia's expression grew sympathetic. "Oh, no, they found the culprit last night. Hiding in the ale house. Nemonian, they said. Bought a room and didn't leave for days." She shook her head. "Must've been her first time. No idea why she stuck around."

How odd, I thought. Why *would* she stick around? Unless she was afraid of being caught on her way outside the city gates. A very real possibility, given how quickly the information was provided, and passed on. All exits were blocked, every guest examined for a mole on their ring finger. Maybe she hadn't escaped soon enough. Maybe she thought it was better to wait for the danger to pass.

Had the would-be assassin already been killed? Were we down in the dungeons at the same time? How long was I left there after the real culprit was discovered?

"Did she say why she did it?" I asked, hoping against hope that Zellia knew something.

She laughed. Actually laughed, loud and merry. "Isn't it obvious?"

"No," I said, almost pleading. "Tell me."

"Somebody doesn't want the Princess to marry Prince Marius," said Zellia, with a self-assured nod.

Even *I'd* already assumed as much. I'd hoped for deeper insight.

"Of course," I said, trying not let my face fall. "I wonder why."

"Loyalty to Tocchia, probably," said Zellia, shrugging. "I've heard plenty say the Prince ought to have just found somebody from a kingdom that actually *wants* to unite with us."

"Why kill the Princess, though?"

"Frees him up to choose someone else, I'd think."

I chewed my lip. "Interesting."

"I know things are different in Olmstead," said Zellia. "Tell me: were the dungeons cold? I always heard they were cold, but they don't send us maids down there, so I don't actually know."

"Dreadfully cold." I shuddered, and Zellia clucked sympathetically.

Some of the chill around my heart began to melt as I followed her from room to room, collecting linens, and dusting wardrobes.

For a while, things felt normal again.

CHAPTER 20

"There you are!" said Avens, appearing behind me as I made my way upstairs from the laundress'. "I was so worried about you! I heard they threw you in the dungeons!"

"Hello, Avens," I said, pausing so that he could catch up to me. Today, he wore an outfit of emerald green silk that flattered his slim body and enhanced the brilliance of his eyes. No instrument case bounced off his thigh today. His hair was mussed, his face frantic as he stopped beside me.

"Are you alright?" he asked. Firm fingers touched my arm. I yelped as he brushed over bruises, and he recoiled. "Shit, I'm so sorry—"

"It's alright," I tried to assure him. "I'm sorry, I'm sorry! It's just bruised. I'm fine, I think—"

We embraced there and I cried against his green shoulder, trying and failing to keep my tears from staining the fabric. He patted me on the back and made soothing noises, held me tight until I said I wanted to sit down, right there on the stairs. He sat beside me, and listened while I told him everything of the dungeons, that I now knew what it was like to fall asleep standing up, that I had no idea what would happen to me next.

"You could always go home," he reminded me, wiping a stray tear from my cheek. A worried smile strained his face.

Faint lines formed at the corners of his eyes, his mouth. When had they appeared? When had the energetic young bard who graced my summers aged?

Avens was only two or three years older than me, barely past his mid-twenties. We'd spent so much of the last seven years traipsing around court together, getting into all kinds trouble. That he'd lost his youthful essence over a single winter shocked me.

He was thinner, with bags under his eyes, a new tightness to his mouth. Only his full head of fiery hair and dashing grin hadn't changed.

I'd been so wrapped up in my own problems that I hadn't realized I wasn't the only one struggling.

"I can't leave Ria," I mumbled.

"I know it feels that way," he said, his smooth voice like a cool river, rushing over my raw wounds. "But you can. I'll be returning to Olmstead for the summer, as per usual. You could come with me."

I shook my head. "Father would have your head."

"Not if we make something up," he said, a little too cheerfully. He knew it was a bad plan but played along for my sake.

"No," I insisted, hiccupping a little.

"Fine. You're probably right. You know him better than I do. Alright, then, if you won't return, do you think you'll be safe here?"

I mulled over my response, tasting the options like flavors. Finally, I said, "I think so. I just need to keep my head down."

"Don't you miss being a princess?" he asked, keeping his voice low even though we were alone. "I'd think the arrangements are a little better, personally."

"I didn't want to marry an absolute oaf," I said. "And I have… a sense of purpose here."

"But you had the forge back in Olmstead. And plenty of friends and family. Doesn't that mean anything?"

A part of me wanted to be offended that he dared question my choices, but the reality was that he cared for me, and I valued his perspective. "It does," I answered. "But this was the first real decision I made for myself."

He nodded sagely. "I understand that. I remember my first time at court. I chose to spend a winter in Luminden, despite everyone else's advice, because the pay was good and I thought I'd have an easy time getting there." He chuckled, a tiny bit morose.

"I didn't know you ever went to Luminden."

"Only once," he said. "The journey was horrific. No one warned me that the mountains were impassable in autumn. I was wildly unprepared. Nearly died on the way there. Then discovered that King Paulin, *who had invited me,* liked neither my music nor my *kind,*" he spat. "Like he wasn't fucking his jester. So I spent much of that winter hiding from him, unpaid. I was extremely lucky that I was able to bargain a ride back to the plains come spring. Honestly, I thought I would die there." He sighed, shoulder brushing against mine. "But I didn't regret it. It was my choice to go, and I learned a lot about what I needed to avoid in the future. Tocchia doesn't seem half so bad."

"It isn't," I said. "Not so far, anyway."

"Just be certain," said Avens softly. "When the pass closes, you'll be trapped here."

"I'll think about it," I told him, rising slowly. "Thanks, Avens."

"Anytime, Miss Arina," he said, bowing to me, grinning. "I'll be around."

With that, he jogged down the stairs, wavering like a blade of grass in the wind.

I watched him go and turned to go upstairs.

Something shifted in the shadows. I froze, blinking furiously, as Prince Marius emerged, icy blue eyes gleaming.

"Nice to see you're alive," he said, arms crossed, coattails swishing.

His expression was unusually cold. It made him look crystalline, statuesque—soulless and calculating.

A chill flared down my spine, racing to my still aching tailbone. "Yes, I believe I must thank—"

"Don't worry about it," he said, waving his hand lazily as if batting a wayward wasp from his drink, as I'd seen him do so many times before in the garden. "Anything for Princess Valeria."

Why was he acting like this?

But then, he'd grown cold and distant the first time he saw me with Avens, too. Was he *jealous*?

The corners of his lips quirked into something halfway to deranged.

My instincts screamed at me to leave, but I could not stop staring at him—spine ramrod straight, his gaze piercing, pink lips parted to reveal white teeth, cheekbones high and proud, jaw tight, coattails trailing behind him like the proud wings of a moth. At his throat, the strange stone rose and fell with each breath, on full display today thanks to his shirt, for once devoid of lace.

He was heartbreakingly, achingly beautiful even in fury and he would never, ever be mine.

A pang of loneliness and loss coursed through me. My stomach twisted into a sailor's knot. Heat burst into my cheeks, and tears burned at the corners of my eyes.

"I think—I think I ought to return to work," I mumbled, looking down at the marble floor. "Good day, Your Highness."

And I fled, ignoring the way that he watched me with something that *couldn't* be disappointment.

RIA WAS silent and sullen at dinner. When I tried to ask her what happened, she snapped at me, then apologized, citing a long day.

She didn't ask about the dungeons. I didn't volunteer any information, but I was hurt. Didn't she want to know what happened?

But all I got from her was a clipped, "I'm glad you're all right," as I left that first night.

The next two days were quiet and dull. Fallamor and Toral both offered their condolences to me over breakfast, easing some of my resentment. At least someone cared. Even if their words were purely diplomatic, I appreciated them, anyway.

Prince Marius ignored me with the fervor of a scholar driven mad by research, swirling dramatically past me at every opportunity, nose high in the air, every bit the distinguished and snobby royal.

My dismay grew. Marius and I were never friends, but I thought we got along well enough considering the circumstances. What had changed?

I'd made sure to bathe since my night in the dungeons. And while my face was a little sallow, my eyes a little sunken, I looked and smelled fine. I did my job with the same diligence as before.

Marius had fought the King over my sentence, arguing that there was no need to throw me in the dungeons, that there was no proof I'd done anything wrong. He'd spoken with passion, even rage.

If I was worth that kind of effort only a few days ago, why wasn't I now?

Prince Marius was less attentive to Valeria, eschewing her gaze, responding only in clips and monosyllables. Ria wasn't the least bit perturbed by this, and carried on as usual, but his mood grated on me.

On the fourth day, I could stand it no longer. While readying Ria in her chambers, I gave in to my curiosity.

"What happened between you and Prince Marius?" I asked, twisting a lock of her hair, and pinning it in place.

"What do you mean?" she asked, giving me an exaggerated pout in the mirror.

I laughed at that and pinned a piece of hair into place. "He's been so quiet and angry lately."

"Oh." She shrugged her delicate shoulders. "I don't know. I… We had a fight. After they took you away."

A chill wrapped around my throat like a cold hand. "What happened?"

"King Hergarv threatened to have Marius thrown in the dungeons for aiding and abetting. I tried to calm him, but he was… uncontrollable. Angry like I've never seen him." She sighed. "But it's not as if I know him. He's always been a bit of a mystery."

Oh. I'd assumed that he must have opened up to Ria. If anything, he claimed he wanted a pleasant marriage and seemed willing to put forth the effort. I was surprised that he hadn't said anything.

"I'm sorry," I said, and adjusted a wayward curl. The updo was coming along nicely, Ria's dark hair piled elegantly atop her head.

"Anyway, I thought he seemed…" She chewed her lower lip, gaze flickering to me. "I think he might… prefer you over me. And I confronted him."

"*What*?!" I squeaked, shrill enough to crack glass.

Ria winced and covered her ears. "Goddess, Talina! Are you trying to deafen me?"

"Sorry," I said, lowering my arms. My hands were numb. Blood thundered in my ears. "But isn't that preposterous? How could he possibly prefer—"

"He's hardly blind, Talina. And unlike me, he isn't deaf, either," she grumbled, rubbing at the lobe of her ear.

"That's not— that's impossible."

"I think there's more truth to it than any of us would like to admit," said Ria bitterly. "I think you like him back." Her lips thinned into a line. "I know you met with him a few times."

"I—" My face flushed. There was no denying it. "He said he needed an artificer."

"Damn it, Talina!" Ria cried, leaping to her feet, spinning to face me. With her hair half up on only one side, she looked positively crazed. "Why did you tell him that?"

"I didn't!" I cried, taking a step back from her bared teeth and wild eyes. "I didn't admit to anything! He deduced it!"

"From what?" Ria demanded, hands on her hips.

"That night back at camp—in the woods, I mean—I had a-a glowing obelisk. And he realized later that I'd probably created it. And he said that—that my buttons changed too often, and—I don't know, he just knew! I didn't admit to anything, but I agreed to look at something for him, and—"

"He noticed your *buttons*?" Ria exclaimed, throwing her hands in the air. "Your fucking *buttons*?!"

"I, well, that's what he said. I, um, I rotate them—"

"Why the fuck is he looking at your buttons?!" Ria roared. The muscles on her neck corded out, and I stumbled back into the bed, terrified, as she came closer and closer, chest heaving, hands clenched.

"I—I—"

"What the fuck is going on?" she screamed.

The force of her voice blew the hair back from my forehead. "Ria, please!"

She startled back to herself, inhaled sharply. Jaw clenched, fists tight, she sat on the edge of the bed. I remained at the vanity, feet rooted to the floor. "You're right," she choked. "You're right. It's not your fault."

"I'm sorry," I whispered. Legs shaking, I joined her on the bed, careful to keep distance between us. "I—I'm not trying to take him away from you. He asked for help, and I—I finally gave in."

"Why didn't you tell me?" she demanded.

I felt like a mouse under the eyes of a hawk. "I don't know. He asked me not to say anything to anyone."

Ria snorted. “Of course he did. What else did he do?”

“Nothing,” I insisted. “Please, he didn’t do anything. He’s never done anything. He’s never even touched me.”

Ria watched me carefully for some indication that I was lying.

And I was, I realized. Marius had helped me up all of twice. But those were chivalrous gestures, only done for the sake of politeness.

They barely counted.

Then, of course, there was the time he’d bumped into my shoulder, and nearly knocked me down.

Alright, so he’d touched me exactly three times, and one of those was on accident. I hoped it was an accident, anyway.

“Never?” she said, brow raising.

“He helped up once or twice when I fell,” I huffed. “That’s it. Nothing to be jealous of. He was even wearing gloves.”

“Fine,” Ria groaned, slumping back against one of the posts supporting the canopy over her bed. “Fine. Alright. I’m sorry. It’s just… He seems to like you quite a bit.”

I shrugged. “Isn’t that a good thing? It would be nice to get along with your husband. Besides,” I reminded her. “It’s not as if he can change his mind about you.”

She chewed her lip as she considered this. “You’re right. That… might present a challenge.”

“I didn’t realize you liked him so much.”

Her eyes flashed.

Uh-oh. Wrong thing to say.

“It’s not a matter of liking,” said Ria. “It’s a matter of wondering what I’ve done wrong. I was worth going to war for, but he doesn’t want to get to know me?”

When she put it like that, I could understand her pain. “You spend a lot of time with him. Maybe he thinks he knows you already.”

She tugged at a loose curl. “Maybe. But he hasn’t… made the sort of effort I would expect after everything, honestly.”

"Have *you* made an effort?" I asked, half-expecting to be slapped.

The back of Ria's head thunked against the bedpost. "No. Not particularly. We've exchanged a few stories and discussed our likes and dislikes pertaining to food and entertainment, but that's all."

"Well," I said, cheering greatly at the prospect of finally *being* helpful. "What if I helped you think of some things to discuss with him? Maybe you'd feel more connected."

"I suppose," Ria after a long moment. Her finger tapped against her chin. "If anything, I might dread my wedding night less."

Heat flooded my cheeks. Ria would spend her wedding night with Prince Marius. I'd avoided thinking about it until now, afraid all my feelings would come to the surface; jealousy, lust, longing. I was unprepared for the way I wanted him. Especially because I typically regarded men with passive interest. Once in a while, one would strike my fancy, and I'd be hopelessly besotted. Then, my passion would wane, and I'd be glad that nothing came of it. Even my most vulnerable self was fickle, and I knew it.

This newfound lust would fade. In a few weeks, I would barely even notice Prince Marius.

"I knew it," said Ria, studying my face. Her voice was resigned. "I knew you liked him."

My fingernails carved half-moons into the meat of my palm. "I —he's very dashing," I admitted at last.

"He's *dashing*?" She shook her head. "He's got the complexion of a corpse."

So did Ria, but I didn't dare tell her that. "I… I've eyes, alright? I think he's very nice looking."

Her nose scrunched. "Ugh. Next, you'll tell me he's charming."

"Sometimes," I admitted begrudgingly.

"I thought you meant to reassure me," she said, arms crossed.

"I am! I have no intention of causing any problems! Prince

Marius hasn't touched me! If he speaks to me again, I'll tell you. I promise."

I thought of my conversation with Queen Tarra and realized I *couldn't* promise Ria anything. I'd already said I would help him again if he asked.

"Good," said Ria sullenly. "You should. Tell me when my future husband is flirting with you, and I'll stop him."

I nodded. "I—I will. I promise."

"Thank you," said Ria, exhaling slowly.

CHAPTER 21

We arrived late to breakfast, pink-cheeked and fuming.

Ria needled me about Marius the entire walk to breakfast. It didn't matter what I said—nothing could reassure her that I wasn't out to steal her betrothed. Admittedly, a part of me couldn't stop thinking about him, but the suspicion hurt.

Prince Marius didn't even like me. He might make me blush, but he had no interest in me beyond my skills as an artificer. Ria could be offended all she wanted; it didn't change the fact that I was no one to him. She was engaged to him. Poised to one day rule over these glorious, mystical lands; lands that I would likely never see again. Now a servant, I'd be lucky to leave the palace more than once or twice a year. Ria would be expected to tour the realm after their marriage. She would get to see the embassy of the sea, the long, winding bridge to Liridin, all the strange and wondrous things that crept through verdant forests and drifted through a spectacular, turquoise sea. And I would fold laundry and scrub chamber pots and long for something else. Something I would never get.

As a princess, my movements were limited. I might be very

lucky one day and marry a man of high standing. Probably not a prince, given the doubts surrounding my parentage, but someone of repute, nonetheless. Perhaps he would take me on a tour of his lands. We'd visit the mountains, or the sea, or the cliffs, or whatever spectacle was closest. He might dote upon me, enjoy my company as we traveled.

Perhaps, perhaps, perhaps. And that was only if I returned to Olmstead and faced Father's wrath.

But what if... What if I simply *didn't* marry? What if I worked in a forge? What if I just designed swords and buttons and trinkets, and imbued them all with their own special powers? So what if my spells didn't hold as long as they should? I could learn. And if I couldn't, then I'd just charge a reduced rate.

The thought nearly dumbfounded me.

There was no way King Amonrew would allow that.

But... What if I didn't return home? What if I left the palace, stayed in Tocchia, and just... did as I pleased?

Princesses didn't get to become artificers. It was too much to hope for. But as the morning wore on, my hands tingled in excitement. Something like hope blossomed in the depths of my heart, pushing away the fears that festered there.

I was startled from my thoughts when the eastern door flew open with a bang, and two winged men I'd never seen before marched in, their faces tight. Barely contained fury glinted in their eyes.

They stalked through the palace and into the great hall, stopping at the Royal table, where Toral and Halin sat. Guards trailed behind them, hands on the hilts of their weapons.

A hush fell across the room as Toral and Halin rose, their expressions grim. Those massive, shiny wings moved gracefully even in a crowded space.

"There's an urgent matter," said one of the messengers. Only now did I notice the tear in his trousers, the slight discoloration of the black fabric. Blood? Or something else? "In Rylerian."

"I assumed so," said Toral. A line of worry creased his forehead. "Speak."

"Three messengers were shot from the sky just this morning," said one of the strangers. "No messages. No bodies. They fell, and disappeared."

"Fuck," said Toral.

"Eloquent," commented an already drunk noble, leftover from the festival.

Toral shot him a dirty look.

I frowned. Liridin should be nearly impervious to attack. I was no strategist, but the only way for a regular human to access the island was to traverse the narrow, winding bridge that appeared and disappeared seemingly on a whim. It would be awfully difficult to storm.

No, the Sky Kingdom would be most vulnerable to attacks from within. I'd never visited, but Zellia told me that it was terribly hard to gain access. The bridge, though beautiful, was steep and seemingly endless. Plenty who crossed it felt as if they were journeying into the mouth of hell itself, maddened by thirst and the sunlight, blinding against glittering white stone.

Outsiders weren't banned, but the journey was discouraged. Most everyone from Liridin had wings. Foreigners forced to rely on the bridge.

"I can assure you all that this action was not sanctioned by Tocchia," said King Amonrew, climbing to his feet. "Liridin is our ally, and we will rise to your defense."

"Thank you," said Toral, bowing deeply. But his eyes were narrowed in consideration. "Your aid is most appreciated."

"And Plinath," said the dark-haired man to Fallamor's left. I'd only been briefly introduced, but I thought his name was Girrar. He was tall, elegant, and serious, entirely devoid of social niceties. The exact opposite of Fallamor.

"Thank you," said Toral, dipping into another low bow.

Was it customary for an acting regent to bow to an advisor? I wasn't sure.

For the next two hours, the palace was in a flurry. Royal advisors flocked to the war room, flanked by the king, queen, representatives, and even the princes. Only Princess Odalla stayed behind, herding her children upstairs, away from the ruckus.

Though most of the nobles who attended the festival had left by now, a few still remained. They fretted about the dining hall like distraught peacocks, drinking wine even at the early hour, and speculating loudly about what might've happened.

Prince Marius among the last to depart. His eyes held a haunted trepidation, and he spent a good deal of time at the great hall's massive window, staring out into the sky as if expecting to witness another execution. It was Gavin who dragged him off to the war room, quite literally by the collar of his embroidered jacket.

Ria and I were allowed onto the veranda but asked not to roam the grounds. I only just concealed my contempt. Did they think us too fragile to face the truth? Did they think we might get in the way of any messengers or scouts? I hardly thought that roaming the gardens would affect anyone, but clearly, the royal guard disagreed. So we spent much of the morning on the veranda, watching as people came and went.

From our vantage point, we could not see Liridin, which loomed on the other side of the palace.

Goblet in hand, a worried frown on her pretty face, blue skirts trailing behind her, Princess Odalla joined us at the railing.

"The omens have been less than favorable lately," she said, taking a sip of wine. Wide eyes drifted to the fluffy clouds in the sky. "I'd hoped that nothing would come of it."

"Are you a Seer?" asked Ria, turning slowly.

Odalla's answering smile was pained, quick. "No. That would be your betrothed." She sighed, stretched her arms behind her back. Wine splashed in her goblet. "No, I'm merely attuned to symbols, signs."

"Wait," said Ria, confused. "Prince Marius is a Seer?"

With a nod, Odalla said, "Of sorts. He… is reluctant to advertise it."

"Why?"

"I've no idea," said Odalla. "I think he fears that he will lose his advantages if his skills are known. A future king who can See will have a bounty on his head. Kings are already powerful enemies. A Seer King will be especially despised."

"Is he… a good Seer?" said Ria, shock evident in her voice.

Odalla simply shrugged. "He opts to keep his visions secret. The science isn't exact. He fears the peasantry might assume he could promise them a year of successful crops, or a winter without disease, and revolt if he is incorrect in his interpretations." A soft, sad smile. "Even you appear to have a limited understanding of how these things work."

"I'm not a Seer," said Ria defensively. "I just want to know. I *deserve* to know. I'm marrying him."

Odalla stared at the sky and said nothing.

Ria retired to an iron-wrought table, but I remained at the railing, watching the clouds. Had I seen members of the Sky Kingdom in transit, and mistaken them for birds? Could I tell the difference between a bird and a winged man? If one came crashing to the earth, would I realize what was happening?

Princess Odalla straightened her shoulders and pointed to something in the distance. "There," she said. "That's a snowy owl. In the daylight. Do you see it there, in the tree?"

I squinted. The veranda overlooked the gardens, the elaborate hedges, and beyond that, the sea. A copse of trees swayed in the breeze just past the garden wall. Moss crawled up their trunks. I could only just make out a pale form nestled high in the branches. "I think so."

"A beautiful creature, and a poor omen. There is someone

among us who is less honest than we've been led to believe," said Princess Odalla.

"A traitor?" An uncomfortable shiver ran up my spine.

"Possibly. There are many options."

I thought of all the guests in the dining hall. Any one of them could be dishonest. In fact, that was probably the case for most of them. We royals were harshly scrutinized, and most of us were careful with our reputations. But nobles were almost expected to engage in debauchery and scandal, and they took to it with a flourish.

Almost everyone in that dining hall was only pretending to be respectable.

Did Odalla know that? Did she think something else was going on?

The rest of the day dragged on. None of the royals were at dinner, and little information had leaked from the war room. Ria and a pinched-faced Princess Odalla were the only two at the royal table.

The empty thrones loomed ominously.

As Ria poked despondently at her food with a fork, I overheard someone say, "They've identified the bodies."

I glanced to my left and spotted a young man with a crop of dark, curly hair staring contemplatively into the distance as he spoke.

His companion shrugged, turning so that I could just make out a green vest with a dragon embroidered upon it. The Baron of Rend, I thought, but I couldn't be sure. It had been years since he'd last visited our court in Olmstead. "Doesn't sound too difficult; only three of them."

Ria's gaze followed mine, then snapped back to her plate.

"All their messages were stolen," the curly haired man mused, leaning onto his elbows. "They *knew* something."

"Of course they did," huffed the Baron. "Why else were they killed?"

The curly haired man deflated. “Alright, well, *I* thought it was interesting.”

“War is never interesting,” said the Baron, shaking his head. “Just devastating.”

“Who says there will be a war?”

The Baron rolled drank deeply of his ale and rolled his eyes heavenward.

Dead messengers. Messages missing. What information did they have? Why steal it?

“It could be a fluke,” Ria suggested, staring wretchedly down at her baked fish. Even a dressing of butter and herbs could not whet her appetite; she picked at her food with the enthusiasm of a sickly animal. “Maybe it won’t happen again.”

I fought down a pang of worry.

“Maybe,” I said.

But when I returned to the servants’ quarters that evening, everyone was gathered before the fire, eagerly discussing the newest development.

“It’ll be here come morn,” said Helena, the most senior of the laundresses. One-eyed and astute, her dresses were always perfectly pressed, her collars starched, and her gaze unwavering. Sometimes, her stare grew so intense that I feared her remaining eye might pop free from its socket.

“Do you think we could have a tour?” asked Nella, a girl of only twelve who worked in the kitchens. She was sweet, but had a tendency to shout in the mornings before I was fully awake, and I couldn’t quite forgive her for it.

“Nay,” said Zellia, shaking her head. “It’ll be locked down tight.”

“What will?” I asked, joining the fray, alert now despite the way I’d practically dragged myself across the palace, bones heavy with exhaustion.

“The Sky Kingdom,” said Zellia, turning to me. “It’ll be here in the morning.”

"Oh," I said, baffled. "I didn't realize we could predict its whereabouts."

Laughter followed. Someone patted sympathetically me on the back.

"It's hardly random, my dear," said Helena, fixing her eye upon me.

"I-I didn't know," I protested. My face burned from humiliation.

"It's alright," said Prandi, one of the chefs, kindly. Her long, graying hair was pulled back into tight bun, revealing her ancient, weathered face and bright green eyes. I'd interacted with her very little since my arrival, but she'd never been anything less than kind. "But yes, it can be steered."

"Oh," I said, looking away. "That's—fascinating."

The night wore on. I didn't bother to go to bed like I really wanted to—the servants were too eager to speculate about what had happened, and I didn't want to miss anything. Some filtered off to the dormitory. Even the children's maid, an aging woman named Laney, drew up a chair to listen.

If the children's maid, always up before dawn, thought that it was important to hear the conversation, then I should probably stay.

"Maybe it was Nemonia," someone suggested. "They're probably eager to retaliate after we pushed them out of Blythewell."

"But then they would attack *us*," pointed out Helena. "Liridin is a sovereign nation."

"Does everyone know that?" I asked, prepared to be laughed at again.

"Round here, yes," said Helena. "Mostly. Not in Olmstead, apparently."

"Apparently not," I admitted, forcing down my self-consciousness. I needed information, and I might not get it if I stayed silent and demure. "We heard stories. We just… nobody knew they were true."

The fire crackled. Someone had put on another kettle. Now it vibrated fiercely, its whistle impending. A plate of slightly stale bread rolls, and garlic herb butter rested on the table. I'd already eaten my fill, but couldn't stop thinking of the flaky crust, the tang of garlic, and considered reaching for more.

"Strange," said Prandi, pulling her hair from its bun. Strands of silver swirled around her shoulders. "I wonder why."

"I think maybe nobody in Olmstead goes to Tocchia," I said, staring into the fire. Flames danced along the logs, licking the underside of the kettle. "It's—a difficult journey."

"You made it," Zellia pointed out.

Laney watched me silently, her pale blue eyes nearly silver in the firelight. Something about her unsettled me, and I looked away.

"I did. But I was traveling with a royal caravan. I imagine the circumstances might've been different if I took the pilgrimage in a small group."

"Your bard says he does it every year. Sometimes twice."

"Avens is hardier than people give him credit for," I said. And he was. For all his flash and laughter, he was quite prepared to make an arduous journey if it meant he could find a new audience, a new horizon.

Prandi gave a thoughtful nod. "I have no doubt of Avens' abilities."

"Nor should you," I said. I liked Prandi, but Avens was too good a friend not to defend.

Eventually, people retired to bed, leaving only the true conspiracy theorists behind. I knew I needed to sleep, but I was hungry for more than just rolls. I wanted information.

"There's conflict to the east," mumbled Malin, one of the kitchen assistants. He was an older man, tall and greying, with a tired, kindly face. Right now, his gaze was glued to the window, where a full moon hovered outside. "Always conflict to the East. I bet they're trying to finish off the Sky and Sea once and for all."

"Finish them off?" I lifted my head.

Someone laughed.

"None like them on the rest of the continent. There used to be other Sky Kingdoms. One for each realm. Most were destroyed over the years," said Helena, nodding to herself. She plucked a roll from the basket and began shredding the flaky crust. Little piles formed on the table.

"Destroyed?" I asked, watching the crumbs fall. "How does one destroy a Sky Kingdom?"

"War. Famine. Some of them were starved out. Others were overtaken. Rumor has it that some were stripped of their magic, became useless as boulders. Crashed down like boulders, too. Sky Kingdoms can't be ruled by anyone other than a destined heir. So if someone tries to invade, they just... end. Not immediately, no. But they drift off course. Crash into mountains. Drop into the sea." Malin shrugged. "Some say they convene over the seas now. That Liridin is the only one remaining near land, probably waiting for its heir."

A shiver ran down my spine, hitting every vertebra.

"A ship would've spotted it," huffed Helena. "If Sky Kingdoms were over the sea, we would know by now."

"Would we?" asked Malin, frowning down Helena's mess. "When they can cloak themselves in cloud and mist? How do we know that storms aren't passing Sky Islands?"

Helena scowled. "We just would. A storm doesn't come on like that."

Malin raised an eyebrow. "Ever been to sea?"

Helena gave a proud nod. "Aye. It's where I lost my eye."

"At sea?"

"Cannon hit the main mast. Got a splinter in my eye the size of a finger. Damn thing had to be removed." She shook her head bitterly. "The *pirates'* doctor had to do it for me."

"You were kidnapped by pirates?" I gasped, a thrill jolting through me.

Helena gave a hearty laugh. "Darling, I *was* a pirate. I mean, yes, they sure kidnapped me, but make no mistake, I was a pirate already."

"Oh," I said, forgetting all about the downed messengers. "How exciting!"

"Yeah," said Helena. "Sailed on *the Drowned Rat,* I did. Till she drowned, and we all fled like rats. Name was slightly prophetic." Her laughter boomed through the near-empty room. "It was actually pretty boring most of the time. Beautiful, but boring. Only time it was exciting was when we were on the chase." She grinned, showing yellowed teeth. "That was my favorite part. Stalking from port to port, gathering information on the whereabouts of certain cargo and," she leaned forward, voice dropping to a whisper, "plotting the best way to take it."

"That does sound exciting," I said, breath catching. I thought of the dozens of bodice-rippers I'd enjoyed featuring pirates and rogues, and hoped that Helena wouldn't read my mind.

"It's not what you think it is," she said, and winked.

"I'm sure it isn't," I said, a blush rising in my cheeks. I wanted to hide my face in my hands. "I could never."

Malin glanced between us and gave an exasperated sigh.

CHAPTER 22

There was no news. The atmosphere at the palace grew grim and tense. The royal family was nowhere in sight. The remaining nobles were granted permission to remain in the palace so that they didn't risk travel through a land on the brink of war.

Avens accompanied Ria and I on long walks through the gardens, chattering away in Prince Marius's absence. Privately, I wondered if this was a good idea. If Marius was incredibly jealous whenever Avens spoke to me, then how he would he react when he learned the bard had spent so much time with his betrothed?

But Prince Marius was locked away in the war room, not even surfacing for meals.

More representatives arrived. Some rode in great carriages that sloshed sea water across the lawn, others flew down from Liridin, which had anchored itself over the palace, casting us eternally in shadow. The glittering white bridge spiraled down from the rocky edge of the island. A court sorcerer created the illusion of trees around the base, so that no one could quite make it out without approaching. Soldiers made this next to impossible. The grounds were absolutely crawling with guards.

Today, Avens, Ria, and I were on our third lap around the gardens. I could just barely make out the conjured trees beyond the hedges and felt a wave of frustration. "Do you suppose," I wondered aloud, "that this is… an overreaction?"

Avens winced. Ria pursed her lips.

I knew it was a risky question. But the frustration beneath my skin was beginning to itch, and I could no longer stand it.

"Perhaps the phrase 'an abundance of caution' might be more appropriate," suggested Avens lightly. "And perhaps we might say that the caution is, indeed, abundant."

"Like pollen," said Ria ruefully. Come summer, she would be caught in the relentless grip of hay fever. Prince Marius would spend his honeymoon surrounded by discarded hankies, listening to an endless chain of sneezes.

"Or rabbits," said Avens, brows wrinkling as a pale hare ran past. "I wouldn't worry unless the Sky Kingdom is still anchored here next week."

"Is it true that this is the only one in the world?" I said. "The only Sky Kingdom, I mean?"

"Oh, yes," said Avens, brushing a fleck of dust from his jacket. "The others, well. They've been gone a long time, I think. They've certainly been lost from the common folklore." He hesitated, then examined our surroundings. Satisfied we were alone, he continued, "Do you remember that song I used to sing? About the maiden and the warrior who fell to their deaths?"

I nodded.

"There's a much older variant of that ballad. It was banned by King Gallaprinas of Nemonia over a century ago. It isn't actually about a couple going over a waterfall in a rowboat. It was about a couple fleeing the demise of the Sky Kingdom of Quile." He waggled his brows. "A great epic tragedy. Over fifty verses."

"Oh," I said, stunned. "Do you know the song?"

Avens grinned. "I might. But I couldn't sing it here. It's still banned."

"Why?" scoffed Ria. "Sounds like there isn't a good reason."

"There isn't anymore," said Avens. "But to sing it would cause quite a scandal. A pity, because it's quite a good song. Love, war, loathing, something about a ring, and of course, lots of awful, tragic, romantic deaths."

"A ring?" I asked, trying to keep my voice neutral, so that Avens wouldn't grow suspicious.

"Oh, *yes*. A powerful, enchanted ring that could fell kingdoms. I admit, it's a little funny. Seems out of place in a ballad about love and loss."

"Perhaps the writer simply liked rings," said Ria, shrugging her delicate shoulders.

"It's more than that," said Avens, chewing the inside of his cheek. His demeanor changed from carefree to stiff and worried. "When is the wedding again, Princess Valeria?"

"Ugh." Ria made a gagging sound. "This is the worst change in subject *ever*."

"I've forgotten, *and there are guards nearby*," hissed Avens.

I glanced to our left. The hedges were thick, and I could barely make out shining steel through a gap in the leaves. Avens was right.

"Fine," Ria grumbled. "It's in one month. Are you happy?"

"Quite, my dear," said Avens, bowing. "And would you perhaps like to discuss the song list? Of course, the Queen will have final say." He made a face. "But I'm quite happy to include any suggestions."

"Songs?" Ria sighed. "I… I'm afraid I don't know many songs suitable for a wedding. I'd demand The Prizefighter's Wife, but we all know that would be grounds for divorce."

"Or a civil war," I chimed in.

A laugh sounded through the hedges.

"*The Prizefighter's Wife is again in strife*," Avens sang softly, laughter seeping into his voice.

I rolled my eyes.

I SAW Prince Marius for the first time in a long while that evening. I slinked through the dark halls, hoping against hope that I'd be allowed inside the library when I arrived. I hadn't dared try since the messengers arrived, but I was restless tonight, and mentally prepared for rejection.

As usual, he stepped from the shadows, blending in perfectly despite his moonlit hair and pale skin.

I yelped and stumbled backward. "Gods!" I cried, pressing against a marble pillar. "What are you, a cat?"

"Something like that," said Prince Marius, so pleased with himself that he practically purred. "Are you on your way to the library?" There was something like hope in his voice as he looked me up and down.

"I might be," I said. Chin high, I continued down the hall.

"Oh, good," said Marius, following. "I've been dreadfully cooped up these last few days."

I bristled. "I'm sorry to hear that." After the way he'd treated me last week, I had absolutely no sympathy for him.

Why was he following me? I couldn't do anything to stop him, but Ria's anger was fresh in my mind. I would never earn back her trust if Prince Marius insisted on inserting himself into my life like this.

"I suppose sarcastic condolences are condolences nonetheless," sighed Prince Marius. "I shall accept them."

Since the hallways were poorly lit, I decided to indulge myself, and rolled my eyes. "How generous of you."

"Indeed. And I think you owe me a favor, since I've been so generous."

I fought the urge to groan aloud. "And just what is that?"

"It may come as no surprise to you that I need help with a few things. Things of... *a certain nature*. Can I count on you?"

"A certain *secretive* nature, I assume?"

"Yes," said Marius. We rounded a corner and found ourselves at the entrance to the library. As I'd feared, it was far emptier than usual, but its doors were still open, meaning I'd hopefully be allowed in.

"Fine," I snapped. "But we need to make it quick."

His eyebrow quirked. "Are the bodice-rippers calling to you?" A smirk tugged at the corner of his mouth.

I wanted to slap it off his face.

"What I do here is none of your business," I snapped. Telling off a prince was risky, but I was too tired, and too stressed, to apologize.

But when I looked at his face, I saw only stunned incredulity. "No one talks to me like that," he said, utterly delighted.

I had no energy for his nonsense. "Listen," I said, kneading my temples. "Your betrothed is very jealous, and I've no intention of upsetting her further. So I need you to—to rein it in a little bit. Alright?"

"Jealous," he repeated, abruptly serious. "Princess Valeria is *jealous*?" His voice echoed down the hall.

"Keep it down!" I hissed. "Yes, she's very jealous. Don't tell anyone I told you. Please," I added, because he was royal, and I should probably be more polite.

"I find that hard to believe," he said, waving to Jorg as we stepped inside the library. "I see her nearly every day."

"Have you ever talked to her?" I asked pointedly.

"We speak." Any leftover amusement fizzled away. He scowled down at the ground.

"What's her favorite animal?"

He only shrugged, the creases on his forehead deepening.

"What's her favorite color? Her favorite flower? Her worst nightmare? Do you know any of these things?"

"No," he admitted after a long moment.

We crossed the first floor and climbed a staircase. "That's the problem," I said.

"I don't know those things about you, either," he pointed out. "So she's no reason to be jealous, even if I've... admittedly failed to learn about her. I'm sure she couldn't tell me the same things about myself."

"It isn't too late to change that," I said, even as my heart clenched.

I didn't *want* Ria and Prince Marius to get to know each other better. I wanted them both to myself in different ways. Ria as the wonderful sister I'd always had, and Prince Marius... well, I could never have him, but I wanted him, regardless. By my side with entirely too many ruffles at his throat, rolling his eyes, making exaggerated gestures and snide comments, watching me with that strangely soft gaze...

All things I'd never have.

"I suppose not," he said. "Although I'm afraid I really can't afford to focus on that right now. I need some assistance, and I was hoping you would be willing to help."

"Fine," I said, abandoning all hope of a peaceful evening with a new book. Queen Tarra had ordered me to help him. Besides, I was more than a little curious what he might need.

We arrived on the third floor, before a line of shelves resting against the stone wall. Marius spent a few minutes scoping out the area, then said, "Don't tell anyone about this." Wearing an expression of intense concentration, he fumbled on the side of an old, scuffed bookcase.

There was a click. Then a grinding noise.

Marius straightened, grabbed at the edge of the shelf, and gave it a yank.

With a groan, the entire bookcase swung open like a door.

It *was* a door, I realized, astounded.

We had a few secret passages back in Olmstead, although ours were mostly alcoves hidden behind paintings and false openings, and only two tunnels. Nothing so sophisticated as this.

At least, not that I was aware of.

"It's through here," said Marius, gesturing. At my expression, he grinned, wide and smug. "What? You don't have anything like this in Olmstead?"

"No," I grumbled, stepping through the door.

A thousand scenarios ran through my head. This was some kind of test. Perhaps he'd lured me here to hurt me, or he was going to leave me here, stuck screaming behind the wall, or he'd take me back into the dungeons, and leave me there—

But instead, he followed me inside and pointed to a lever on the back of the door. "Use this if you need to leave," he said, showing me how to raise it just so, then click it into place. "Try to be discrete. Queen Tarra will have my ass if I let this secret out."

I gasped at his choice of words, then remembered that he was a prince, and hardly anyone cared. Many probably expected it of him. But if *I'd* used language like that, courtiers would have fainted. "I shan't say a word."

"Mm, I hope you don't mean that literally. Then I'd be bored." He let out a quiet laugh. "And I don't want that. So tell me. What should I ask Princess Valeria? Has she told you anything?"

"Well, you might start by complimenting her, I suppose," I said.

Prince Marius shut the door, and we were cast into darkness. I let out a choked little cry.

"I'd have brought a torch, but I assumed you'd come prepared. Or was I wrong about that?"

"It's hardly proper—Oh, it's not as if you can see me anyway," I huffed, reaching into my bodice, and freeing one of the stones tucked away there. By its soft aura, I was almost certain it was one that I'd enchanted to glow.

"Was that hidden where I think it was hidden?" Even the darkness couldn't conceal his amusement.

"Don't ask questions," I chided, grateful that he couldn't see my blush. "You're the one who led me into a dark passage." I smacked the rock against the wall, relieved when it illuminated instead of singing, exploding, or launching itself at the prince's head.

Now, I could just make out his face. "I suppose it *is* customary to issue a warning," he sighed, like he was the one inconvenienced. "Follow me, please."

I stuck close to him so that we might both be able to see. "I hope we're going somewhere with a torch. This isn't going to last forever."

"Yes, yes," he said, waving his hand dismissively. Rings glinted on his fingers.

In the dim light, I could just barely see the stone walls. There was only enough room for us to travel single file, but that didn't keep me from practically clinging to him. The walls pressed in on us as the passage continued, seemingly endless. My breath came in short pants.

Marius paused. "Alright?" There was an unfamiliar concern in his voice.

"I will be," I managed. "I'm not accustomed to such narrow hallways."

"Aren't the servants' hallways narrow?"

"Well, yes, but—I know where I'm going when I use them."

"Do you?" he mused. "I've always considered them something of a labyrinth. If it's any consolation, it's impossible to get lost here—it's a single hallway. And I truly think you'll like where we're going."

The toe of my boot caught on a loose stone, and I tumbled into his backside—solid and warm. Muscles shifted beneath his coat as he caught his balance. Hadn't King Hergarv claimed that Marius was sick? This wasn't the body of a sick person.

Startled gasps escaped us both.

"Are you alright?" Marius reached to steady me, but I'd already jumped away. After years of etiquette lessons, it felt like a crime to touch a man I wasn't married to. Especially when that someone was a *prince*.

I shivered and rubbed my arms. "Wherever we're going, I just hope we get there soon," I said, feeling rather like Ria. Was this what it was like to be surly all the time? I wasn't sure I liked it.

"We will," Marius assured me. Then, to distract me, he said, "Tell me, how did you meet the Princess? Were you always destined to guard her? How *did* that come about?"

No one had thoroughly questioned me so far. Not even Fallamor. I'd grown so complacent that I hadn't even bothered to coordinate a cover story with Ria. "That's... not something King Amonrew would wish me to share."

Which was true.

"Hmm," said Marius. "Olmstead's customs are so... *strange*." His tone was too smug. I was sure Ria had told him something. But what?

"No stranger than Tocchia's," I argued, feeling a swell of pride for my people and their ways, not so different from any other kingdom I'd visited.

"It must seem that way," Marius said with a chuckle.

And then we were at the end of the passage. I stood back while he swore and grasped at the lever, only faintly illuminated by the stone in my hand. There came a click. The door creaked open. Marius stepped inside. I followed, and found myself beneath a field of stars, shimmering against the night sky. Crystal orbs hovered in the air, drifting around the room like autumn leaves in a gentle breeze. A pale blue light emanated from them, as gentle as the stone in my hand.

The stone floor was streaked with gold and purple veins. The pillars were so pale and smooth that they looked like they were made of ice.

But it was the center of the room that stole the breath from my lungs. An altar, cut from gleaming black rock. Stars reflected on its surface, the constellations shifting with every movement of the orbs.

The ground beneath my feet hummed.

"What is this place?" I whispered, stunned. The walls were not made of brick or stone, but of volcanic rock. Moss crawled between crevices and dangled from the ceiling.

"The Star Room," said Prince Marius, beaming at me. "Obviously."

I stepped into the center of the room, staring up at the stars. Galaxies swirled. In the sea of glittering stars, constellations were nearly impossible to spy. The sky was not black but a deep purple. Over the altar, it faded to a midnight blue.

My breath caught in my throat.

"You've a cloak like this," I said suddenly, thinking of Marius's shimmering, dark cloak that he wore sometimes when the night was more than halfway over, and he wanted to melt into it.

Not that he needed a cloak to disappear into the shadows.

"Observant," said Marius, arching a brow. "But there's more. Come."

At the far end of the room was another passage, carved from rock and just as narrow as the first. The glowing orbs floated after us like sentries, their light just bright enough to keep me from tripping over my own feet.

I was endlessly grateful for them.

The passage was short, but Marius grabbed my hand, unabashed, and led me through.

CHAPTER 23

We emerged in a room lit by a chandelier whose crystals were so tiny that they were reminiscent of stars in the night sky. The ceiling was high and arched, the single window nearly twice the height of a human being. I could just make out the moon and the sea beyond.

Pillars of black and white streaked marble offset the flagged stone floor and glistening rock walls.

Were we in a cave? How had we gotten there? The passage from the library took an upward slant. If we began on the third floor, and only climbed upward, then there was no way that we could be in a cave.

And yet, here we were.

An elegantly carved desk sat in the corner. The bookcase beside it was stuffed full of books and papers. Two armchairs rested in the corner. A telescope was positioned near the window. Diagrams and illustrations were pinned to the walls, the pages overlapping and lopsided like they'd been pinned up by a madman.

I glanced at Marius and thought that maybe they had.

Crystals, rocks, daggers, corked vials, a cracked teacup, and an assortment of tiny potted plants filled the shelves along the opposite wall. My eye was immediately drawn to a silvery sphere the size of my hand. Opalescent, with undertones of sage and deep blue. Veins spiderwebbed across its polished surface like cracks in glass.

"Where are we?"

"Neither here nor there. This is the Seer's Room," said Marius, gesturing around us. "I'm the first person to have used it in decades. Nearly a century, in fact."

"Oh," I said, surprised. "Not even a court sorcerer?"

Marius shook his head. "They don't count. Only Seers of the Tocchian line." He sighed and dropped onto a stool near the window, where a telescope was set up. "Although there haven't been any of late."

How should I react? To say nothing would be callous, but a single *sorry* felt too cold and distant. "It must be a burden to be the first."

"Oh, hardly," he countered, leaning an elbow on the window's ledge. He always lounged in ways that made me think of a cat lying in a sunbeam, and this time was no different. His long limbs held a feline grace, his eyes a strange intensity. Far below us, the sea thrashed against rock, rhythmic and angry. "In fact, I'm quite glad of it. No one knows what to do with me, so they ignore my abilities altogether. If I'd been born when my family expected Seers, my upbringing would have focused solely on cultivating visions. As if it's so simple." Tension hardened his jaw, highlighted the angry arch of his eyebrows. The lace at his collar shifted, revealing the necklace, stark against his pale throat.

I knew little of Seers, except that most of them died when the local peasantry ran out of patience. They knew too much or too little, or their visions were irrelevant, perhaps poorly timed. In places like Winton, foresight was feared as much as war. Known Seers were executed quickly and mercilessly.

I thought of Queen Tarra's words, and knew she was right. A Seer King would find enemies everywhere he went.

"Does the public know?"

"Absolutely not." Marius shook his head, laughed to himself. "No, that would be… a perilous reveal."

"I understand." I clasped my hands together. "I won't say anything."

A loud groan of exasperation. His shoulders slumped, and he leveled a glare at me. "I assumed you'd keep my secret, but if you feel I *must* remind you for the sake of propriety, then I will. If word gets out, I will know exactly who to blame."

There was no malice in his voice, but the threat was clear. "I've had enough of the dungeons. You needn't worry."

"I actually was not worried," he assured me. "I wouldn't have brought you here if I thought you'd betray me, Arina. I'd not put either of us in that position."

Oh. I hadn't expected that. Warmth flooded my chest. He trusted me.

I thought of my own secrets, and the warmth faded.

"Why am I here, then?"

"Because I need to focus on a vision, and I need someone who can intensify the elements of the room."

"Intensify them?" I looked around, feeling foolish. This room was crafted for Seers. Of course the elements were aligned with their needs.

"Exactly that. I—I have a problem I need to solve, and it would be so much easier if I could conjure a vision rather than… relying on my own ingenuity. Which is admittedly lacking." A frustrated sigh. "As is my research."

"But you're in the library constantly."

"And yet, answers evade me."

I looked around the room. When I concentrated, I could feel the energy coming in pulses from the labradorite orb. I felt the heat from the stones, the intensity of the marble pillars. Could I do what he asked? I knew how to imbue a stone with power. Knew how to enhance its natural elements. But I understood best how to mount it in steel and enchant it into something far stronger.

"I can try," I said after a long pause. "I don't know if I really have the necessary skills."

"Excellent," said Marius, leaping to his feet as if he'd known my answer all along. "I only need a few minutes."

"Me, too," I said, walking to the shelf to examine the crystals on display there. "The lapis lazuli," I said, pointing to a blue stone with flecks of gold. "And the labradorite. I think you should use those."

"Very impressive," said Prince Marius, flitting past me. "I'd also like to suggest the moonstone."

"Yes, right," I agreed, feeling foolish. I'd not seen the pale, smooth stone tucked away between plants. I watched as he rifled through the bookshelf, emerging with a scroll. The edges were so torn as to appear frayed. "Is there anything I need to know before—"

"No," interrupted Marius. "Just don't touch me, and don't talk to me. If you do, the vision may end too quickly."

He gathered candles, and sachets of herbs, and a vial of something that looked like algae. With his thumb, he popped the cork. Then he grimaced, took a deep breath, and downed its contents.

I suppressed a gag as I watched the sludge slide into his open mouth.

Nostrils flared, eyes squeezed shut, he swallowed. "Eurgh," he said, wiping his mouth. "Fuck."

"What was that?"

"Mugwort. Chamomile. Yarrow. A few other things I can't disclose. They've been stewing in water from the sacred wells of Hildabar for the last, oh, hundred years or so," said Prince Marius, as if he'd merely taken a sip of wine instead drinking what looked like the contents of a swamp.

"Is that safe?"

"It's necessary." Prince Marius shrugged.

I knew not to drink from stagnant waters. Everything about this vial and its contents reeked of danger, but I kept my worries to myself. If Marius believed it was necessary to drink the vial's contents, then nothing I could say would stop him.

Instead, I helped him set up candles around the altar, careful to keep them away from anything flammable. I didn't want to risk starting a fire in a room without an easy exit.

When the candles were lit, and the stones arranged, Prince Marius approached the altar at the center of the room. "I'm going to lie here a while," he said, "and watch the stars. Just focus on enhancing whatever you can."

"I will," I promised, closing my eyes to block out the shimmering stars, bringing the energy of the room to the forefront.

Fabric shifted. Marius's shoes clicked against rock. I ignored it all, assuming he would call out if he needed me.

Without the canopy of stars overhead, my focus returned. No longer was I dazzled by the night sky. Now the energy of the room thrummed through my veins, in tune with my heartbeat. The essence of the marble helped me concentrate so that I could pick out the other elements in the room. The icy pillars exuded a strange calm. I latched onto it, trying to draw that tranquility to the forefront. I knew next to nothing about Sight, but imagined a vision would take a lot of focus. Racing thoughts would never allow for success.

A curious sensation emanated from the sky, a presence that slipped and drifted. Every time I thought I might grasp it, come to understand what it was, it disappeared like a puff of smoke. So I focused on the sphere of labradorite, where dreams and shuttered truths pushed and prodded. Weaving this with the calm from the pillars, I became almost too relaxed and reminded myself to prioritize my task. I could sleep later. Right now, my job was to help Prince Marius.

Beautiful, charming Marius, lying on a bed of hard, shining rock.

Then the thought changed to something else, and I only just stopped myself from gasping. *No, not now! Focus!*

But once pictured, the image of a naked Prince Marius would not leave. I imagined him writhing with pleasure, a blush spreading from his chest to his ears as he reached to pull me toward him...

I forced myself to breathe, to force my perverted thoughts from my mind as I exhaled.

I shouldn't be here. I wanted him too badly. It wasn't fair to Ria, it wasn't fair to me, and it certainly wasn't fair to Marius, who surely didn't want random maids lusting after him.

And now I couldn't even do the one thing he'd asked me to do. Whenever I tried, all the elements muddled into something with the energy of a vague dream. The kind where a presence lurked in the distance, biding its time, neither sinister nor well-intentioned.

Minutes passed. Tears burned at the corners of my eyes, and I wiped them away furiously. Eventually, I found the grounding sensation that radiated from the marble and let it travel from the soles of my feet to the top of my head. I drew in the quiet calm again, and tried to clear my mind, focusing only on the energy around me, pulling it to the surface. I felt like I was weaving a tapestry, grasping each thread, maneuvering them this way and that. Even the starlight became a lace of spider silk and silver.

And then there came a stirring, a soft grunt.

I lost my grip on everything and blinked back to reality.

Marius sat up slowly, gave a low hiss, and pinched the bridge of his nose.

With bated breath, I waited. Exhaustion settled in my bones. My head pounded, and I was dreadfully thirsty. I wanted nothing more than to crawl through the passage, and sleep in one of the armchairs at the library. I doubted I could've dragged myself back to the servants' quarters if I'd wanted to.

"Arina?" he mumbled, blinking at me with unfocused eyes. Had he fallen asleep?

"Yes, Your Highness?"

"Ugh," he said. "None of that. I don't want that." He frowned down at his knees, massaging his forehead. "It's always you. Why is it always you?"

I froze. "What do you mean?"

Marius rose unsteadily to his feet. I thought his legs might collapse like a newborn fawn's, but he braced himself against the altar and inhaled sharply. "I meant what I said. I always see you."

"I work closely with your betrothed," I reminded him, trying to keep my voice even. Should I be concerned? Should I go to him?

"That's not what I meant," he said. "I always *See* you, Arina."

Oh. The magnitude of his words hit me like a punch to the stomach. "What do you mean?"

What had he Seen? Did he know my secret? Did he suspect?

Another part of me jumped at the words. He'd *Seen* me. That meant I mattered in some way, that I was more than an insignificant maid.

"You're always a part of my visions," he said, finally pulling his hand from his face. "Always there in the background with me. I can't see anything I'm looking for because you're always there."

"Oh," I whispered. "Am I blocking you?"

"Something like that." A scowl. "It doesn't make sense," he said.

I didn't want to ask for any more information. I didn't want to know why I was in his visions. "What are you trying to See, if I may ask?"

"A path forward. A solution to the problem of… the ring."

"The ring," I repeated, thinking of the awful bone band, the empty prongs where a stone should be. But what about the fallen messengers? Didn't he want to pursue that, too? "I… I don't understand."

"You wouldn't," said Prince Marius. "It's a secret. A terrible one

I am bound to keep." He sat gingerly on the altar and watched me with something like regret.

I pondered this as I moved to sit on the stone floor. If it was truly a secret, then there was little I could do. I tapped my finger on my knee. Finally, I said, "What about the messengers?"

A scowl. "I'm afraid I've already tried for days. There's nothing, absolutely nothing that comes to me. I thought it might be best to change trajectory for the time being."

"Alright." I nodded, more to myself than to Marius. "How can I help?"

He gestured at the room around us. "This."

"There must be something more," I insisted, afraid that he'd soon realize my skills were subpar. Unless he had another use for me, he'd send me away. I didn't know if I could stand the rejection.

When he looked at me, it was with hunger. My face heated. Was I misinterpreting this?

"I'm afraid that's all I require," he said, and turned away.

That's it?! No, there must be something else for me to do. Anything. "I think—I think my presence might have ruined your visions. Shouldn't you ask someone else for help?"

"This was something of an experiment," Marius admitted, plucking a loose thread from his sleeve, and scowling at it. "I've Seen you before, even when you weren't here. I thought that might change if you accompanied me. Alas." His expression was one of regret, and… was that mischief? Was he *entertained* by all of this?

I adjusted my skirts around me. How would he react if I bared my legs? Let him catch a glimpse of more than an ankle or a wrist?

But those were lecherous thoughts that I wouldn't dare explore. Not so far from home, with few allies, and the weight of my lies on my back. "Why am I in your visions?" I asked, gritting my teeth in frustration. "It doesn't make sense."

Prince Marius shrugged miserably. "It doesn't. And yet."

"And yet," I echoed. I took a deep breath, fought against the panic welling in my heart. "What do you see?"

A long silence. He looked anywhere but my face. Finally, with a wobbly smile, he said, "You. Everywhere."

My pulse quickened. "And what am I doing?"

"That's just it. Nothing of import. You're sleeping, or eating, or riding. Just normal things." He raked his fingers through his hair, gave a frustrated sigh. "It took me a while to recognize you."

I froze. He knew about my hair. "What do you mean?"

"That first night, I thought you looked familiar. I couldn't place you. Then I realized where I'd seen your face." He plucked a loose thread from his sleeve. "Forgive my intrigue, but I've no idea why you're in my visions."

Hands balled into tense fists, I said, "I can't imagine why."

We sat in silence, looking anywhere but each other.

"May I be frank?" His voice cut through the silence, knife-sharp and determined.

I nodded, and tugged at the hem of my skirt. When he sounded like that, I was half-afraid of what he might say.

"I am far more attracted to you than I am the Princess."

I jerked to attention, agog.

"I did warn you I meant to be blunt," he said, a hint of mirth tilting the corners of his mouth. "Is it really so shocking?"

"I—" But words failed me. I could only gape at him.

"If you wish me to stop, tell me, and we'll never speak of it again."

I felt naked under the intensity of his gaze. How could eyes so icy have such fire in them? "I—I think I'd like an explanation," I choked.

Marius considered this. "Perhaps I could've been blunter," he said, faintly amused by my expression. "I fear that an inadequate explanation will leave you with the wrong impression."

I wanted to throttle him. For all that he beguiled me, he was sometimes too courtly, too theatrical. While he might've captivated an audience in a theater or the throne room, he had only succeeded in driving *me* halfway to madness. "Please explain," I ground out. My hands shook where they clutched at my skirts.

"I have been mystified and intrigued by you since the first day," said Prince Marius, squaring his shoulders, and meeting my eye with such intensity that I shivered. "I was surprised to learn of a stowaway. Even more so to discover that the stowaway was, in fact, a maid. I must admit that you caught my attention." He huffed a little laugh. "And kept it. Once I realized that I'd Seen you, I—I felt that I needed to know more. It became a game, a little mystery to solve." His eyes narrowed. "You intrigued me. And I despised it."

That was the reason I kept running into him. It felt like he was following me because he *was* following me. I didn't hate it as much as I would've expected to, even as a little shiver ran through me. "And now?"

He shook his head, gave a forlorn little smile. "Now I find that days without you are dull and dreary. I always want to be around you, even if it is 'improper.'" He scowled at the flagged stone floor. When he turned to me, his gaze had grown hot. "Everything that I want with you is improper."

My heart thundered in my chest. "I don't want to be your mistress," I said, but that was a lie. I would've given him anything he wanted if he kept looking at me like that—warm, devastated, unbearably fond.

"That is more than understandable," he said softly. "I won't mention it again." His grimace was brief, pained.

An ache settled in my breast. A terrible thrum, like the relentless drums of an encroaching army. The only man I'd ever wanted had just confessed his feelings for me, and I'd rejected him. A wave of grief overcame me, souring my stomach.

I couldn't do this to Ria. I couldn't do it to myself. Any affair we had would be just that—an affair. Sooner or later, it would end. Possibly in bloodshed.

But I wanted him. All of him. A visceral craving, a carnal desire to touch and be touched. I longed to see him smile, to see his mussed hair in the morning, to grasp his hand and know that at least for now, he was mine. I wanted to feel his heart beating against mine, feel his hand in my hair. I wanted to know more about his visions. I wanted to make him a sword that would strike true, a dagger that would turn flesh to ice as it penetrated. I wanted—

I wanted everything. I wanted the arguments, the passion, the adoration.

But I would never be his. I would be a secret, tucked away like poison in a cupboard.

"Wait," I said, chest heaving, hands shaking. "Wait. I—I don't know if I want that, either."

He regarded me silently, studying my face. Finally, he said, "You don't have to make any decisions right now. We can discuss this later."

I nodded, afraid to speak. If I said the wrong thing, the illusion would implode. Reality would settle around us like dust, and we'd go our separate ways. I couldn't bear the thought.

"Is there anything I should know?" he said, gently prodding.

"Aren't you the Seer?"

"That's not how it works," he scoffed, but I glimpsed the mirth in his eyes. "I've Seen almost nothing of you."

I was equal parts reassured and disappointed. A part of me wanted to hear that he'd Seen us together, that we might have some sort of future. Another knew that it was better not to consider this at all.

I threaded my fingers together. I wanted to tell him everything. That I wasn't who he thought I was. If we were to carry on, he should probably know.

But confessions were dangerous, and I hid my desires like pearls in an oyster's flesh. "What if I told you I had a secret?"

"Hypothetically speaking, I wouldn't be surprised." He looked me up and down, and shook his head, shoulders shaking in silent laughter. "I'd be far more surprised if you *told* me the secret without any prodding."

I glowered at him. "I can't do that."

"So there *is* a secret!" he said, lacing his fingers together beneath his chin, and beaming at me.

My glower turned into an outright glare. "I didn't say that."

"You didn't have to," he gloated.

Fine, he'd outsmarted me. But I'd never admit it. A question burned within my mind, and I feared I'd choke on its smoke if I didn't ask.

"I need to ask another question."

At my somber tone, he grew serious. "I'll do my best to answer."

I didn't ask the question I meant to. Instead, I blurted, "Why would someone try to kill the Princess? You must know."

He ran his fingers through his hair, loose today, and sighed. "I do know. And I cannot disclose it."

Fury cascaded over me. *Of course* he knew. *Of course* he couldn't tell me. How was I supposed to keep Ria safe when these damned royals kept every morsel of intelligence to themselves? Did they take me for a joke? Did they think I was only a pet?

But of course they did. I'd defended Ria once, and it was from a goblet of wine. I never trained with the guards—per Tocchian tradition, I wasn't allowed. Of course they thought I was weak, useless, primarily for show.

"Queen Tarra said you were ill. Is that true?" It felt almost cruel to ask, especially with such bite in my words, but I had to know. If he would dare proposition me, then he owed me this.

The question startled him. His eyes rounded, lips parted. His throat worked as he swallowed. "Yes."

"I suppose you can't tell me?"

Head in his hands, Marius inhaled deeply. When he looked up, he said, "I will. I shouldn't. But I don't wish to lie."

The depths of sorrow in his gaze caught me off guard. There was no more teasing, no more silent laughter. Only an aching grief.

I longed to comfort him. But I was afraid to touch him without permission, let alone draw nearer. "You don't have to—"

"No," he said, and there was that incredulous laughter again, spilling from him like marbles from an overturned pouch. "If I've the nerve to invite you to become my mistress, then I owe you an explanation."

I wanted to protest that I, too, had my secrets, but he shook his head as I opened my mouth, and continued.

"It's true. I was not projected to survive infancy, although I had a very determined nursemaid. My father has given her full credit for my continued survival. You may have met her. Her name is Laney. She watches my sister's children now."

I pictured the aging maid beside the fire and nodded. "I have."

"Good. Father says she's lucky to have kept her head, because she's the reason I'm spoilt." A quirk of the lips, and his tone sobered again. "I was slow to grow, but a quick study. While Gavin was outside learning to ride and fight, I stayed indoors with my tutors. Depending on the year, I didn't even do much studying. I was constantly ill. Weak constitution, underdeveloped lungs, that sort of thing. There were times when I could not leave my bed for weeks."

I studied him, taking in his sharp features, his lithe body. He was built like a swordsman as opposed to Gavin's boatwright, but he wasn't fragile looking. At six feet tall, he wasn't short, either. Other than his pale complexion, I'd never guess that he might have been ill.

"And then, my father's sorcerer found a solution," continued Marius. "And, well, I can't go into much detail, but I was no longer constantly ill. I learned to ride a horse, and to handle a blade, and everything else that my father feared I'd never be able to do." He ran a hand through his hair again, rings catching on the pale strands. "But there is always the possibility of relapse."

"Have you had any? Relapses, I mean."

Marius shook his head. "Not in a long while. Not since I was an adolescent."

"And this illness... Do they know what it is?"

"Of course they do," said Marius, sitting up a little straighter. "It is my birthright."

I waited for him to explain. When he didn't, I said, "Is it... hereditary?"

"Yes," he said, somber again. "It afflicts all Seers within my family. I am very lucky, in fact, that I am able to function at all. Many simply laid on the altar and recorded visions until their untimely deaths."

What a horrible fate. I shuddered. "How awful."

"Things are different now. No one expects me to do that," he said. He stood, walked over to me, and extended a hand. "I'm exhausted, and I suspect you are, too. Let's return to the library."

I reached for his hand, marveling at the warmth of it, the firmness of his grip.

I did not let go, and neither did he.

CHAPTER 24

I helped Marius in the Star Room again the next night. And the next. Our conversations were short, clipped. My head hadn't stopped spinning, and he was strangely quiet, almost reluctant to speak. Occasionally, our eyes would meet, our fingers would brush, and he would smile. Always the same smile—equal parts sad and affectionate.

What did he see in my eyes? Regret, confusion, desperation? All were accurate. It was torturous to have him so near and willing, and yet I was completely unable to act on my feelings. I couldn't—wouldn't—betray Ria. I'd skewer my own beating heart first.

I ached in his presence. Miserably, horribly. Was this love? The endless deprivation, the longing, the fleeting touches? Was this all I was destined for?

The heroines in my favorite books never suffered like this. If there was a period of separation, self-imposed or not, it ended quickly, often with the characters running away together.

But Marius could not leave behind the kingdom he would one day rule, and I could not leave Ria to grapple with my betrayal.

So I would continue to struggle with the ever-widening

wound in my chest, and he would go on to marry my sister, and we'd both suffer.

I would leave Tocchia after the wedding. I'd travel with Avens and carry my grief alongside my sword through the snowy pass. We'd have to part ways early so that my father wouldn't learn of his role in my disappearance. I doubted he would be grateful to Avens for returning me. Instead, he'd be furious that he hadn't been immediately notified of my whereabouts.

I hated to desert Ria during such a pivotal time in her life, but what choice did I have? If I stayed, I'd surely end up in her husband's bed. Even if I didn't, I'd be in constant agony, drowning in my own desire.

Nor could I risk having a child. I would not subject another human being to the same rejection and ridicule I'd suffered.

For all that I loved Ria, I knew that I would be lucky to be cast out. There was a very real possibility that she might have me killed for such deceit if she ever learned of it. She loved me, but her impulse control was poor, and her emotions ran high. I knew better than to trust her.

I had to leave.

The palace was as empty as my heart. Halls once filled with chatter now echoed with the sound of footsteps. Everyone kept their heads down as they went about their business. Aside from the nobles, who still rambled and laughed obnoxiously as they flashed about in their brightly colored clothes, but that was to be expected.

Liridin floated above, casting the land in shadow. For all that I'd once been fascinated by the island, I came to resent it. Whenever I looked out the north-facing windows, the Bridge of Glass shimmered in the sunlight, mocking me. No one was allowed up or down.

On my fourth evening in the Star Room, Prince Marius was especially tense. He waited for me by the door, foot tapping, arms crossed, hair mussed.

My shoulders sagged in relief. His usual energy had returned, and I felt strangely at ease. I hadn't known what to do with a grave, overly polite Prince Marius. Even Ria had noticed the change in his mood, and I was quite certain she made every effort not to pay any more attention to him than necessary.

"There you are!" he cried, spreading his arms wide. "I've been waiting exactly six minutes."

"I'm terribly sorry," I said, only half-certain he was joking.

"You ought to be. We've much to discuss," he said, whirling around and departing to the study beyond the Star Room.

Oh. My confidence waned. He *was* serious.

When I caught up to him, he thrust a leather pouch at me. At first, I thought it was a coin purse, but when I squeezed it, I felt the hard, smooth objects inside.

"Those are for you," said Marius. "Better quality stones than the ones you've been using. I've been told they ought to hold spells better."

I stared down at the pouch in my hands. The leather was soft, supple, tooled into a floral pattern. When I peered inside, stones of every color greeted me—red, brown, green, white, grey. Some were banded, others perfectly monochrome. All were smooth, and approximately the size of a hazelnut.

"I know you hunt for stones in the gardens," said Marius, head tilted, regarding me curiously as I examined his gift. "I thought this might be a little easier for you."

I actually enjoyed my walks around the garden, though Ria was exasperated each time I seized an appealing stone, stick, or acorn. "Thank you," I said, heart clenching.

These were expensive. Difficult for an amateur to procure, but less than desirable for a seasoned artificer. Nobody wanted to buy a blade with a chunk of river stone in the hilt when they could have a shiny jewel instead.

Though far from the nicest thing anyone had ever done for me, it was one of the few gifts that I'd ever received with my personal interests in mind. Once I became an adolescent, King Amonrew had absolutely no idea what to give to me, and while I was perfectly happy with dresses, horses, and access to the forge, it would've been nice to receive something a little more personal. A book, or a trip to the city, or another notebook for my designs. Even hair ribbons or blown glass figurines. Whenever Father was at a loss, he simply bought me more dresses.

But Prince Marius brought me rocks, and I was so grateful that my heart ached.

"On that note," he sighed, dropping onto the stool behind the telescope with such abandon that I worried he might fall right out the open window. "I do have to ask you something. Please don't consider it an affront."

I didn't like the weariness in his expression, the way his lips thinned. As gracefully as I could, I folded into one of the plush armchairs in the corner, and set the pouch on the floor beside me. My heart rabbited in my chest.

"What is it?" I said, trying and failing to remain cheerful.

He ran a hand through his hair, fingers catching on a knot. He tugged at it idly. "We've received communication from King Amonrew in Olmstead regarding his missing daughter, Princess Talina. I can't help but notice that you..." He paused, searching for right words. "...seem to have a few things in common with her."

I stared at him, eyes so wide that they nearly bugged from my head. "I-That's not true." I crossed my arms. "I am exactly who I say I am."

Marius sighed and got to his feet. He strode past me. At the end of the room, he turned on his heel to face me once more. "I am not accusing you of lying," he said, adjusting his cloak so that it hung elegantly over his shoulders, swishing behind him with every step. "But I need to know. I will not tell anyone else. I will not send you back to Olmstead. But I must know for certain. For reasons that are... deeply personal and perhaps slightly delusional."

Hair tousled, cloak trailing behind him, bruises beneath his wide eyes, he looked fevered and half-mad. A part of me longed to tell him the truth. Another part of me was frozen in fear.

"I won't let anything happen to you," he continued, gesturing with his hands. "I promise. I just need to—"

A surge of anger, hot and sharp, like a poker to my throat. "What do you mean, you won't let anything happen to me? You already let me get thrown into the dungeons!"

He stopped in his tracks as if transformed into stone. Slowly, he faced me, eyes squeezed shut, nose wrinkled. He blinked, revealing a redness in his eyes, a desperation in his face. "Arina, I —I… You're right. I failed you." He reached to massage the space between his eyebrows, kneading his fingers over frustrated wrinkles. "I failed you, and I'm so, so sorry. I had a plan to get you out, but my stepmother was faster. I—" He returned to his stool and slumped onto it, limp as an overcooked green bean. "I was so worried. Princess Valeria and I had a truly tremendous fight, and I went out with my knights to scour the city again. I was not the one to discover the culprit—that was Sir Henry, by the way, if you ever want to thank him—but I was..." he trailed off, threading his fingers together, staring straight ahead as he contemplated his next words. "Extraordinarily grateful that we had no further reason to keep you in the dungeons."

"Oh," I said, shocked. Prince Marius himself had gone out searching for evidence? Then why was he so angry after my release? If he cared so much, then he ought to have been relieved to see me. "I hadn't known… any of this. Thank you. For helping me."

"But you are right. All I have to offer is my sworn secrecy. I am far less powerful than my father, and I-I know it. I am not a fool. I know what becomes of men who defy him. I would not dare to think that he would show me much in the way of mercy. He might spare my life, but that's probably the extent of it." He scowled. "I was wrong to offer you my protection."

Pity and remorse throbbed beneath my skin like a wound. I knew all too well what it meant to be at the mercy of a king. A king who claimed to love me, and yet, longed to control me. My heart, my career, my entire life. I was nothing more than a bargaining chip. Those good intentions could be squashed under a heavy crown.

Ria was right. We were nothing but pawns on Father's war map. Any affection he felt for us was offset by the leverage we offered him.

"I'm sure that isn't true," I began, but Prince Marius shook his head. Something haunted and dark lingered in his gaze. A devil no words could exorcise.

For a long moment, we stared at each other. Then he smoothed his hands over the legs of his trousers, stood, and said, "Well, you didn't tell me anything, so I shall have nothing to report. Just be aware that there may be scrutiny upon you."

I might be in more trouble than I thought. "Did they ask you to report back?"

Blond hair flew as he shook his head vigorously. "No. But I wanted to be the first to know. I thought damage control might be necessary. That if I knew—" Fists clenched at his sides. "If I knew, I might be able to either help you continue to hide your identity, or help you come clean, if you were, in fact, Princess Talina."

My throat tightened. "So if I were Princess Talina, you would have helped me?" My name tasted strange on my tongue after so many months. Like the first bite of a fresh apple after a long winter of preserves and dried fruits.

"To the best of my ability," said Marius. "Provided I had no reason to believe you committed treason. Which I don't," he added quickly.

"That's very sweet of you," I began, standing. How strange it felt to call the prince sweet! As if he'd ever been anything other than loud and brash and determined. But over the last few days,

I'd seen his softer side, the gentle core hidden beneath spiky outer layers. "But I don't need protecting."

He rolled his eyes. "I believe you've so far needed protection from my own father, a bear, and the stairs, dearest. Don't lie to me."

Dearest. My heart stuttered. No one had ever called me that before. I liked the sound of it. I wanted to hear it again. "I think *you* needed protection from the bear," I argued. The corners of my mouth ticked upward.

"I think we'll have to agree to disagree," he hummed, feigning offense and turning his back. But when he glanced at me over his shoulder, he was grinning like a fool.

The rest of the evening was spent much the same as the others, with Marius lying haphazardly on the altar, foot twitching off and on, like something kept startling him.

When at last he sat up, his eyes were red, his shoulders slumped. For one awful moment, I thought he might have been crying. But his eyes cleared when he blinked, and he seemed pleased to see me, lighting up like he'd forgotten I was right there the entire time.

"Any luck?"

"No," he sighed. "I can't—there's a block. I'm not entirely sure I'll ever find an answer."

"Perhaps tomorrow," I suggested. I wasn't entirely sure which visions he sought—ones of the downed messengers, or of the ring?

"Unfortunately, I am wanted in the Sky Kingdom tomorrow, although I am not entirely certain I will go."

"The Sky Kingdom?" I asked, just managing to keep my voice from becoming a squeal. Would he tell me all about it if he went? Then I realized how I'd miss him if he left, and deflated. "How long will you be gone?"

"Two weeks," he said through gritted teeth. "That is, if I am allowed to go at all."

"Why wouldn't you?"

Marius massaged his temple. "King Hergarv fears I am unfit for the journey. As though I am still a sickly child."

"Oh," I said, surprised. It made sense that King Hergarv would take precautions with his heir, but I hadn't anticipated that Marius would be excluded from such an important diplomatic event. "Have you been ill?"

"Not at all," said Marius, tapping his chest. "Perfectly healthy. Apparently, I'm clear to navigate Halliway Pass, but not to spend a few hours climbing a bridge."

"That is... strange," I agreed. Then again, he'd had a rather impressive army accompany him to Olmstead. If he suddenly fell ill, there were plenty of people willing and able to assist him. The spiral bridge, on the other hand, had no neighboring villages, no places to stop and rest. If Marius became incapacitated, there would be nowhere for him to go. I understood King Hergarv's precautions, even if I agreed that they were unnecessary.

"Visiting Liridin won't benefit the land," he grumbled. "I'm sure that's the excuse he'll use."

"Will Princess Valeria accompany you?"

Marius shook his head. "I sincerely doubt it. The Sky Kingdom is discerning, especially during times like these."

"Well," I said, pulling my cloak tightly around me, so that it hugged my body. "I shall miss you."

He looked at me with familiar warmth in his eyes and smiled. "I shall miss you, too. We shall see if this comes to anything. If I'm forced to stay, then I think I should like to resume as usual tomorrow."

"Agreed," I said, starting toward the door. He followed me with something like hesitation. When I noticed, I asked, "What's wrong?"

But he only shrugged, and said, "It's nothing to worry about."

So we started down the dark passageway, hand in hand like always.

CHAPTER 25

The next morning, I was relieved to spot Marius at breakfast. He was pale-faced and exhausted, foot tapping in annoyance. But he was present, whole, not a distant dot upon the white spiraling bridge, as I'd feared. I had no claim to him, but two weeks' separation felt unbearably long after so many days spent together.

I forced my expression to remain neutral. Standing behind Ria as I usually did, I surveyed the room for any sign of danger and did not wave to him like I really wanted to.

Both Gavin and King Amonrew were suspiciously absent, along with a number of guards. Princess Odalla sat beside Queen Tarra. Neither of them addressed each other.

Not for the first time, I wondered when King Amonrew had remarried. Marius was only a year older than Ria, but he treated the Queen as a peer rather than an actual parent.

Marius and Ria exchanged only cursory greetings and ignored each other completely in favor of their breakfasts of bacon, toasted bread, preserves, and ale.

Eventually, Queen Tarra made her way to the front of the table. A deep blue dress with golden accents and a high neckline clung tightly to her body. Her hair was coiled high upon her head, holding her crown in place.

Within seconds, the atmosphere in the room changed from casual to tense. Everyone had noticed the King's absence, and Marius's presence. "People of Tocchia, and esteemed guests," began Queen Tarra, arms spread wide in greeting.

All eyes were upon her. Forks dropped. Silence fell over the room.

"As you may know, today is the day King Amonrew and a few chosen companions ascend the Bridge of Glass to Liridin. This is the first in a series of visits meant to determine the identity of the assassin or assassins still on the loose. Court will continue as usual until their return. If there is any news, you will be informed."

"Are you in charge, then?" called a man dressed from head to toe in a beaded grey suit.

"Yes," said Queen Tarra through gritted teeth. "Any other questions?"

"Why's he here?" asked someone else, pointing to Marius.

Any mortification he must have felt did not show on his face. "I'm here to assist with any needs that might arise. Including those of investigations," he said, voice lowering to a growl. "You certainly wouldn't want to impede by asking silly questions, would you?"

"No, I wouldn't," the noble agreed, returning hastily to his breakfast.

Apprehension returned to the palace. Ria, frustrated by everyone's dour mood, retired to her chambers immediately after dinner, citing a headache.

With free time on my hands for the first time in days, I decided to spend an evening curled up in my favorite armchair at the library, hopefully with a good book in hand. I hadn't even made it downstairs before I was intercepted by Prince Marius, slinking from the shadows like a wolf in moonlit woods.

"How do you do that?" I demanded, crossing my arms. "It isn't even dark yet." I'd have to remember to retrieve my tracking pebble from its place on my dresser; I was quite sick of him sneaking up on me.

"It's a talent," said Marius, flitting to my side as though he belonged there. As naturally as he might step into place beside Ria. "May I accompany you?"

"I'm only going to the library," I said, starting forward again.

"I've seen you few other places," he said, biting his lower lip as though this bothered him.

"There are only so many places I *can* go," I reminded him. "Speaking of which, I'm very glad to see you."

"I'll admit, I'm rather bitter that I was forced to remain behind," he said, tucking a strand of hair behind his ear. His shoulder brushed against mine, quick and playful. "All the same, I'd hate to leave for long. It is good to see you."

As we walked, his good cheer faded. A frown appeared, then deepened. At his sides, his hands twitched. We'd nearly reached the library when he said, "You've nowhere to practice your magic, do you?"

I startled, stopped. "I-Well, no. No, not really."

He tapped his foot. "That seems unfair."

"I-I don't know that I agree," I said. "I'm just a servant. Besides, you're the one who mentioned the forge."

Something about that seemed to bother him, but he pursed his lips and said nothing else.

In the library, we went our separate ways. I broke from my routine, and read about the history of Tocchia, which seemed more important than the sequel to the romance novel I'd finished last night, which detailed the relationship between a maiden and the fearsome dragon she was sacrificed to (and seduced by). Though I badly wanted to know how the rest of the story went, I wouldn't be caught dead reading something like that in front of Marius. I was sure he'd poke fun at me.

The history books revealed little in the way of answers. I searched for any mentions of Marius's cursed ring and found none. Instead, I found stories of great battles. Many featured tales of the Red Man, a fearsome warrior who appeared at the apex of combat, when things felt the most hopeless. He was painted crimson (presumably with blood) and fought naked, with only shield, sword, and boots to protect him. Singlehandedly, he felled armies. When the Red Man appeared, foes knew to flee—the fight was already lost.

But the Red Man hadn't been seen in nearly three hundred years, and Tocchia lost her reputation as a formidable adversary.

I skimmed the great prophecies of Marius's ancestors: predictions of death and creation, murders and marriages, war and peace. All were at least a hundred years old, and so far as I could tell, not applicable to the current circumstances.

Was this all that would remain of Marius after his death? Just a long list of prophecies, a mention of his reign, and a single line about his demise?

How unbearably depressing. I would hate to end up as nothing more than a moss-covered tombstone and a dry paragraph in a history book.

Midnight approached, and I was thoroughly depressed. My fingers ached from turning pages. A litany of dead royals (and their names and birthdates) flashed through my mind, their often gruesome fates described with the passion of a merchant's inventory list.

I could not stop envisioning wars that ended with villages burned to the ground, fields of fallen soldiers whose corpses rotted in the sun, royals dead in their thrones, anointed in blood.

According to one the books I'd flipped through, the old gods had died, and mysteriously reappeared centuries later, vengeful and angry, demanding their temples be restored. I'd not seen a single temple in Tocchia thus far, but I learned that they dotted the lands, that the locals believed they demanded a sacrifice of blood. Most villages slit the throat of a goat or pig beneath the full moon. Some preferred human sacrifices.

The kingdom I imagined now was fertile with blood and bone, so different from the insulated palace I'd experienced. Even nearby Dranning was a mystery to me, glimpsed only from southern-facing balconies and windows.

"What's so important about the ring?" I demanded when Marius and I were alone in the Star Room. I was too anxious, too exhausted to try and contain my curiosity any longer.

An expression of measured surprise. His tongue darted out to wet his lips.

I could not help but imagine his tongue in other places, and squeezed my thighs together, so that I might quash such thoughts into oblivion.

"Well," he said, adjusting one of the jeweled rings on his hand. "It's cursed, for one thing."

"But why are you so determined to break it? Can't you just lock it away, and try not to think about it?"

Marius sat on the altar and put his head in his hands. "It's cursed. I can hardly ignore it." He rubbed at his eyes and fixed his exhausted gaze upon me. "And it must be passed on."

When he looked at me, it was with fiery determination, a hint of possessiveness that sent heat flaring in my belly. His face expressed what words could not; longing, desire.

In that moment, I wanted to offer myself up. A willing tribute. A sacrifice. A vow and a lie all at once.

"What do you mean?" I asked, taking a step forward, half-ready to comfort him even though I knew better. If I touched him, we would not finish this conversation. The tension between us thrummed beneath my skin, reflected in his tortured gaze.

If I touched him, it would all be over. Everything I'd built and balanced so delicately would come crashing down. I was drawn to him like a moth to a flame, and I'd burn all too gladly in exchange for one glorious moment together.

"It must go to my betrothed," he said at last, tearing his gaze away from me like it physically pained him. Fingertips dragged down his face, leaving pink streaks behind. "And I would not wish it upon anyone."

A heartbeat passed. His words stung. A reminder to both of us that he was marrying Ria, not me. I should care about the ring not for his sake, but for my sister's.

"I see now," I said, drawing my cloak tight around my shoulders.

"There must be a way to avoid it," Marius said, voice tight. "I just… I don't know how."

"We'll find a way," I said, somber and frozen through with trepidation. Ria would not suffer the ring. I'd make certain of it.

"You don't understand," he murmured. "This is… Centuries of pain, all contained in one single piece of jewelry." He shook his head. "The old gods were merciless."

"The old gods?" What did they have to do with this? I thought of the stories I'd read. The demands they made. The atrocities committed in their names.

Rubbing his jaw with the back of his hand, Marius said, "I lied to you, when I said I didn't whose bone was used to make the ring."

I frowned. "You did?"

"I was not yet certain if I could trust you." His shrug was apologetic, almost guilty.

Biting down irritation, I said, "Fine. Then whose bone is it?"

"A priestess named Guin Pellin. She was, according to the legends, the first to open the gates of the catacombs, and release the gods after their imprisonment by Ratsun Callick centuries earlier. I assume you're familiar with the story?"

I gawked at him. I knew little of the northern gods, and only vaguely recalled the tale of Ratsun Callick. Once considered the king of the gods, he wreaked havoc wherever he went. Charming, fierce, and wily, he tricked and smited everyone who crossed his path. When his siblings banded together to stop him, he imprisoned them in a catacomb, where they were forced to survive on bones and earth.

Not until tonight had I realized they were released. The story, I'd always thought, was meant to explain the disappearance of the gods. A reflection of collective feelings of abandonment as times and fortunes changed.

I'd never considered that there might be any truth to it.

"Yes," I managed. "I've heard it before."

"Good." Prince Marius nodded to himself, satisfied with my answer. "Of course, no one has seen or heard from *any* god in centuries, so the legend is impossible to confirm. But according to the stories, they devoured Guin Pellin body and soul, right in front of the gates, and created the ring to bind the kingdoms together. This is all very much a secret," he added, plucking a loose thread from his sleeve. "If you speak a word to anyone, I will not be able to defend you." His shoulders sagged. "Though it would kill me."

"Then why tell me?" I fumed, hands on my hips, blood rushing in my ears.

"Because you deserve to know," said Prince Marius. "Because I don't want to keep secrets anymore." His left leg bounced up and down with ferocity.

"Why not?"

"Don't make me say it, Arina."

I let out a groan of frustration. "Say what? I don't understand."

"The ring is my inheritance. I must pass it on to a member of the royal family in Olmstead, or Tocchia will fall. And in one hundred years, my descendants will pass the ring to the royal family in Nemonia. It is the will of the gods." He looked up at me with wet eyes. "That is why I had to have Princess Valeria. It is hardly some misplaced passion or possessiveness. It is a matter of keeping my kingdom intact."

My knees went weak. "What are you trying to say?"

"I think you know," said Prince Marius, his voice pained.

"I really don't," I managed, voice breaking.

This was all a ruse. It had to be a ruse.

And if any of this was true, why did Father want to break off the engagement?

"This can't continue," said Marius. "The ring provides entirely too much leverage. Do you know what happens when it isn't passed on?" He didn't wait for me to respond. "Food rots. Weather turns foul. The land withers. War and rebellion are inevitable." He tapped his fingers against his thigh. "That is what King Amonrew would have done to us if we hadn't fought back."

A frozen mist filled my chest, shot into my veins until I felt as if I'd turned to ice.

Father didn't need to go to war with Tocchia. He only needed to prevent the ring being passed on. If Tocchia fell, trade routes would open. Father could claim the land easily, including its fertile fields, generous mineral deposits, and sea routes.

"But why?" It wasn't impossible for me to comprehend Father's cruelty—I'd seen it enough—but I didn't understand the reasoning behind it. Why ruin a centuries-long alliance?

Marius tipped his head back and let out a hollow laugh. "Power. Control. If Tocchia is weak, she is easy to take."

"Why haven't I ever heard of this?" I demanded, watching his face for any sign of a lie.

A slow sneer spread across his face. Something dark and feral that threatened to reach out and *ruin*. "Because this is information that can only be passed between royals. It's part of the curse."

I scrutinized his expression. He was too smug, too calm. Something was wrong. I was missing something. "Then why are you telling me?"

"Ah," said Marius, grinning a grin that reminded me of a shark's. "That's not the question. The question is; *how* am I telling you?"

I pondered over the words. *How? How* was he telling me? *Here in the Star Room beneath a twinkling sky, using his full mouth to form the words.* But that wasn't the answer he wanted, was it?

My stomach plummeted as I realized.

"Ah," said Marius, noting the change in my expression. An eyebrow raised. "Mull on that, Princess Talina." He climbed elegantly to his feet, strode past me, and out the door.

CHAPTER 26

Prince Marius had tricked me.

I spent hours pacing back and forth in the Star Room, failing to quell my panic.

He knew who I was. Didn't even give me a chance to dispute his claims. Just let them fall at my feet before leaving abandoning me.

Marius said he'd protect me, but I couldn't bring myself to believe him. Not after that exit. Anger radiated from him, and I couldn't even be angry. I'd lied about everything, just when we finally started to trust each other.

I needed to leave. But the second I set foot outside the room, I'd be arrested. Tried for treason. Probably executed. Any feelings Marius might've had for me were null and void.

I was a liar, and I'd die a liar's death. There was the possibility I could be extradited to Olmstead, but I held little hope. It would take too long for word to reach King Amonrew. Even if I somehow made it to the palace pigeon coop, or paid a messenger with my meager savings, it would take days for my letter to reach the king. I didn't have that kind of time. It didn't matter if I was a princess. Tocchia would think that Ria brought me with her to steal their secrets—to study the layout of the palace, or the movements of the guards. If Tocchia was anything like Olmstead, they'd rather go to war than let a potential spy go free.

Even if I convinced them of my identity, there was a real possibility they'd leave me to rot in the dungeons.

I'd recognized the danger I was in and failed to remove myself from it. Instead, I'd convinced myself that things were going to be fine, that I could afford to wait and see.

Now, I'd doomed not only myself, but potentially Valeria and Avens. Ria probably wouldn't be outright killed, but Avens was just a bard. A good one, but not valued highly enough to be spared.

Guilt tore through me, crawled along my bones and through my guts like a fleet of maggots chewing through rotten flesh. Bile worked its way up my throat.

I needed to leave. Tonight. I couldn't wait for Avens. I couldn't tell Valeria. I needed to slip out of the palace while I still could. There was a possibility—however slim—that Prince Marius hadn't said anything yet, that I might be able to escape if I was quick enough. I'd grab my money, my sword, some food, clothes, and make my way out of Tocchia.

But I'd be too slow on foot. I needed a horse, and there was no way I could afford one on my pitiful servant's wage. Stealing a horse would only add to my charges if I were caught.

I wouldn't be, if the horse I stole was fast enough.

Fuck. I paced between rooms until my feet ached. Even then, I couldn't stop. I was terrified to leave. Terrified not to. Even if Marius had a change of heart, if he came back and forgave me, I couldn't rely on him.

Would Tocchia grant me mercy if I chose to stay and confess?

I thought of all the criminals Father had executed over the years. The ones who begged for forgiveness as they went before the axman. The ones who'd stolen a piece of jewelry, or expensive cutlery, or overheard a pertinent piece of information. The ones who had families waiting for them.

There would be no mercy for me. I'd broken the laws, and I'd have to run, or face the consequences.

I stood before the door, inhaling and exhaling frantically. Tears burned their way down my face like streams of acid. I reached for the handle, then retracted my hand as if stung. I sank down to the floor and wrapped my arms around my knees.

Prince Marius found me there, a puddle of fabric and despair.

"You're still here," he said, stepping into the Star Room, boots clicking against stone. His voice was barely a murmur—a low rumble in the silence.

"Yes," I mumbled, afraid to look at him.

He knelt beside me. I scooted away on instinct, afraid of a hand closing around my wrist, or catching in my hair. The guards were rough when they brought me to the dungeons, and I didn't expect much in the way of compassion from the man who'd tricked me.

"Why?"

I shrugged. "There's nowhere to go."

"Don't you have a bed?"

I stared at him, bewildered. "I—You think I'm a traitor. I can't just *go to bed*."

His jaw clenched. The gravity of my plight must have dawned on him, because his gaze swept over me, cool and critical. "At what point did I say you were a traitor?"

"You said that you think I'm—I'm Princess Talina," I said. "That means you think I'm a traitor." I couldn't believe we were having this conversation. That I had to spell out my sins for him.

"And how exactly would Princess Talina have betrayed us?" There was no malice in his voice, only genuine curiosity. I wanted to slap him until his nostrils flared like a bull's. I wanted to *see* his wrath and face it, not cower beneath this facade of kindness.

"By lying about her identity."

"I'm not *quite* certain that's a crime, my lady." That wasn't my title, but I liked the sound of it on his lips. He sat across from me, careless of the dirty floor, and his impeccable wine-red trousers.

"False pretenses," I reminded him.

"Less than ideal," he admitted, stretching one leg until he poked my knee with the toe of his shoe. "But hardly a death sentence."

"I'm quite certain this makes me a traitor."

"It would if you planned to betray us," he said. "Which I have no proof of."

"I don't," I said quietly. "Plan to betray you, I mean. But when you tell them—"

"Tell who?" he snapped. "I was hardly planning to expose you. I already promised to do everything in my power to protect you. I wouldn't just—just hurt you." He dragged his long fingers through his hair, which was rather greasier than usual. Dark circles formed beneath his eyes, and his cheeks were sunken.

When had he become so gaunt? Why hadn't I noticed it sooner?

"I-I know I made a mistake," I began, the words bursting free with a sob. "I couldn't let her go with her kidnapper, and there was nobody to watch out for her, and I-I put myself and Valeria in danger, and—"

Marius watched me. He started to reach for my hand, then hesitated. His hand fell back into his lap. "Valeria is your sister."

"Yes."

His brow furrowed. He refused to meet my eye, instead examining the floor like he was searching for something in the cracks between stones. "Under the circumstances, I couldn't blame you. I-I know how that looked."

"It isn't about how it looked!" I spat, furious. "*That* was coercion! You destroyed my home and stole my sister away! It looked bad because it *was* bad!"

"And what was I supposed to do? Let the kingdom fall to ruin while King Amonrew laughed from his throne? I had to do something!" cried Marius, looking directly at me now, a tortured despair in his strange, pale eyes. "I didn't know what else to do."

I laced my fingers together, squeezed. The tension and pressure eased the agony building in my chest. "I know you didn't have much choice," I said, forcing myself to breathe. "But that doesn't change the fact that people were hurt. That Ria and I were pushed into positions we never should have been in."

"I know," said Marius, placing his head in his hands. "I know, I know. I thought that this was better than outright war. That fewer people would be killed. My father wanted to storm the castle and take it for ourselves! I thought—I hoped we could negotiate. That it wasn't too late. Death was inevitable, but I wanted to minimize the bloodshed." Slender fingers buried in his hair. The jewels in his rings peeked through. He met my eye and lowered his shaking hands into his lap. "I can't say enough that I'm sorry. I never wanted to be in this position, and I never wanted to hurt anyone. This was the best compromise we could come up with."

I wanted to believe him. Certainly, I pitied him. Longed to console him even as I wanted to chastise him. A thousand different replies circled round and round in my mind, like vultures over carrion. In the end, I said, "I understand why you did it."

"That doesn't make it right."

"My father was wrong," I said, and winced. These were words of treason. No matter how I wanted to trust Marius, the reality was that I *shouldn't*. I knew better. These rules had been drilled into me over the course of my life. You don't speak ill of the king, and you don't give people information about the king's whereabouts, movements, or motives. "I don't approve of what you did. But I understand why you did it."

Marius nodded.

"That doesn't change the fact that I'm in danger," I said.

"My lips are sealed," said Marius. The stone at his neck shifted as he leaned against the wall.

"Why do you wear that?"

Marius reached for the pendant. "This? This is the reason I survived childhood. I've been instructed to never remove it."

"So it's enchanted?"

"I suppose so," he said, fingertips gliding along the stone's polished surface. "Though I've no idea what its exact function is."

"Have you ever removed it?"

He shook his head. "I wouldn't dare."

"That's probably good," I said, leaning back against the wall, suddenly exhausted. All the adrenaline had drained from my body, and left me limp, tired, doll-like. I could lay here, on the stone floor, and sleep until dawn.

My eyelids drooped. The silence between us was comforting. My earlier despair was a descent into depths so vast, so incredible that I could not quite recall what had and hadn't happened. Already, my memories were blurry.

"I didn't mean to scare you," said Marius. "I didn't think about —well, I didn't think about anything, really. I was hurt that you lied to me, and I shouldn't have left under those circumstances."

"Thank you," I mumbled, drawing my cloak around me. "I just need a few minutes, and then I'll leave, I swear."

"Take all the time you need," said Marius gently. "Do you want me to escort you?"

I didn't respond. Nor did I remember falling asleep. I woke briefly when he tucked his cloak around my shoulders, fell back asleep when he murmured, "It's alright, it's just me."

CHAPTER 27

I lurched back to consciousness with a crick in my neck. My legs were freezing, but my entire right side was deliciously warm.

And slightly damp. I blinked my eyes open, and saw mussed blond hair pressed against my shoulder.

Stars glittered overhead. Pale lights streaked across the ceiling —aqua blue, seafoam green, deep purple. The Northern Lights.

Fuck. I was still in the Star Room. Marius's face was buried in my shoulder. From his position, it looked as if he'd sat a respectable distance away, then fallen asleep and tipped over until he planted against me. His body was at an odd angle, legs splayed out to the side. When he woke, he was sure to be sore.

Was it morning? Was I late for work? Would the false sky above reflect the time of day? The only windows were down the hall, in the study.

I shook Marius's shoulder. "Wake up," I pleaded, relieved when he opened his eyes.

"What? What?" He shot up, glancing wildly around the room.

"We fell asleep," I hissed, unable to keep the panic from my voice.

"Oh," he said, blinking heavily, pawing blond hair from his face. "So we did."

"I have to work!" I snapped, hoping he'd grasp the gravity of the situation. Princes and princesses could sleep in, but maids could lose their jobs for doing the same. And if I lost my job, there was a good chance I'd be cast out of the city, and we'd never see each other again.

His jaw stretched in a yawn. "Is it morning?"

I swallowed down a frustrated groan, and said, "I've no idea!"

He was on his feet and down the hall before I'd even managed to stand. My leg had fallen asleep, and I limped on pins and needles. My charmed hairpin was loose, threatening to fall to the floor—I quickly adjusted it.

"Good news!" he called. The words echoed down the long hallway. "It's still dark."

Knees weak with relief, I sank back to the floor. "Thank goodness."

"I didn't mean to fall asleep," he said, emerging from the study. "I'm sorry."

"It's alright," I said, thinking of the way he'd felt pressed up against me, mourning that I didn't have a chance to enjoy it. "I should go."

He nodded. His features were still soft from sleep, and his hair was mashed flat on one side. My fingers itched to caress him, to feel the planes of his face beneath my hand, to pull those wayward strands back into place.

Not for me. Never for me.

Still, I lingered there.

He looked at me and uttered a little laugh. "Go on," he said, gesturing for the door. "Unless you'd like me to come with you?"

A thousand times yes. And yet, I couldn't seem to speak the words. Nor could I walk away. Longing burned in my heart, hot and pulsing.

To say nothing of *other* places.

I don't know who moved first, if I lunged for him, or if he reached for me. All I knew was that suddenly I was crushed against him, my hands in his hair, his arms around me, squeezing tight. Our mouths clashed, and my lips parted in a gasp. I moaned as our tongues met, as his fingers tangled in my hair, rings tugging at the strands.

I melted against him, clutching at the back of his shirt for purchase. He hissed as my nails dragged over his spine. "Talina," he mumbled, pulling free for a single breath, and then we were devouring each other, a mess of clutching hands and heat and mouths.

The wall met my back, and Marius pressed me against it, his hand dipping lower. When it reached my hip, he pulled me against him. I moaned, loud enough to make the stars overhead blush. He responded by nipping at my lip.

Normally, I hated that, but there was no blood, no real pain. A thrill ran through me. I kissed him with fervor, and bit him back, teasing a surprised gasp from him. He pulled away, wiped at his mouth, now red and swollen, and grinned at me. "I didn't expect *that*."

"You should adjust your expectations," I panted, tracing my fingers along his shoulder blades, admiring the firm muscle there.

"Clearly," he said, an impish tilt to his lips.

Heat pooled in my stomach, traveled to the apex of my thighs. I wanted him. Wanted that darkness, that strange intensity that lurked within him. I wanted all of it, and I wanted it directed at me—his uncouth mouth, his decorated hands, even his filthy, cursed ring. Illness, weakness—it didn't matter. In that moment, I forgot even his impending marriage to my sister. It was just the two of us, tangled together beneath the Northern Lights, hearts beating frantically, bodies flush. His arousal pressed into my core, insistent even as he paused to gasp, "Ah, sorry—"

"Don't be." My hand slipped between us, grasping his length through the cloth. A loud, startled moan escaped him. The kiss turned frantic as I pulled my hand free, tried to climb into his arms and wrap my legs around him. My hands found his shoulders, taut and strong. Sick or not, he'd trained often with a blade, and I felt the evidence of that as his muscles shifted. He scrambled to hoist me up, gripping my thighs, then my buttocks. One hand snaked beneath my skirts, squeezing at the flesh there, pausing at the hem of my knickers.

I nibbled on his lip. Fingers clenched around me. Slipped beneath the lace, and climbed until they brushed against my molten core and the wetness there. He made a sound halfway between a purr and a laugh, and I ground against him, gasping when his finger slipped between folds, traveling high, rubbing a circle exactly where I wanted him to.

The sound that escaped me was nearly a squeal, and he drew back, pressing kisses to my jaw, and down my throat. "How do you want to do this?" he murmured, breath hot against my skin. "Is this—"

"How do you want me?" I demanded, impatient. My breaths came in harsh little gasps as I writhed against his fingers. Sparks gathered at the base of my stomach and shot upwards like a hail of arrows.

There are far too many clothes between us, I thought, but I was too distracted by his mouth and hands to do much about it. If I backed away to yank at his shirt, he'd stop, even if for a moment, and I didn't want that.

"Any ways. All ways," he said, lips dragging over the most delicate parts of my throat. I could not suppress a shudder and a gasp as he sucked a bruise against my neck, slow and sensual. I clenched my legs around him, tangled my hand in his long, blond hair, and tugged just hard enough to get his attention.

"No marks," I choked, even though I didn't want him to stop. His mouth was unbearably warm against the sensitive skin of my neck, just below my ear. "I can't—"

"Yes, of course, I'm sorry—"

"Don't be," I hissed as his finger breached my core, delving deep inside, crooking in a way that made me writhe against him. Heat shot through me, puddling between my legs. "Just fuck me."

"Are you sure?"

"Yes," I cried, throwing my head back with too much excitement—my skull cracked against the wall, and I yelped in pain.

I was immediately set on my feet, then wrapped in Marius's warm embrace. "Are you alright?" Without waiting for an answer, he began parting my hair, searching for blood or bruising.

"I'm fine, it's alright," I panted, even as the bruise throbbed in time with my most intimate parts.

"That sounded like it hurt," he said, pressing a kiss to the top of my head. "Are you sure?"

"Absolutely," I said, rising on my toes to place my lips against his, terrified he'd change his mind now that I'd managed to injure myself, afraid that one smack of my head would bring him back to that drab reality where Ria was his future bride, and I was just her lowly servant. "Let's go."

"If you're certain," he said, gaze caught somewhere between wary and ravenous.

"More than ever," I said, clasping his hand in mine, dragging the pad of my finger over his wrist, eliciting a shiver and a bright-eyed glance.

With the fever of the moment diminished, I realized very quickly that there was nowhere comfortable to lie with him. But that didn't much matter when Marius's lips met mine. One hand caressed my lower back. The other cupped my breast, cradling the weight of it in his palm. A thumb dragged over my nipple, and I couldn't help the way I gasped, clutched at him, intensifying the kiss until I thought I'd fuse to him.

With a chuckle, Marius started walking us in the direction of the altar, the hard lines of his body pressing against mine. When I saw where we were going, I broke free, and said, "Not there."

"Why not?" he asked, eyes half-lidded, head cocked in curiosity.

"Isn't it sacred?"

"Ah." An eyebrow lifted. "Not in the sense that you're thinking. For this lifetime, it's mine to use as I please. Visions, death, sex." He shot me a playful smirk.

"People have died on it," I said, resolve weakening. I wanted him *now*, and if the altar was the best option, well... Maybe it would be worth it. Maybe Marius would find it empowering. A way of reclaiming a place of death and gloom for himself. But I didn't like it.

"It's been cleaned," he added, as if reading my thoughts. His hand stilled on my hip, rested there, a reminder and a promise all at once.

"That's hardly reassuring."

"Fine," he groaned, taking a step back to better survey the room. I immediately missed his touch. "You're right. Where do you propose—"

I kissed him again. "Anywhere," I mumbled into his lips, and he gave a curt nod before gently extricating himself from my embrace. At once, his cloak was spread across the floor, and I was scooped off my feet, laughing and kicking as he deposited me onto the fabric. The stone beneath me was hard and cold, the cloak a weak barrier. But I didn't mind, pleased with the way his gaze raked over me, hungry and wanting.

"You said anywhere," he reminded me, a teasing grin on his kiss-swollen lips. He crouched before me, and my heart flipped.

"I did," I admitted, and then he was climbing up over me, his grin wide and cocksure. Large hands pushed my shoulders to the floor, and I went willingly, eager for the press of his body against mine.

As he hovered over me, I grasped the fabric of his shirt, far finer than anything I'd touched in months. I ripped it free from his trousers and simpered when his eyebrows raised. He surged to meet me, fumbling with the buttons of my blouse. I batted his hands away. "I can do it faster."

"Fine," he huffed, rolling his eyes and rising up again, so that I was acutely aware of the way he straddled me. His long legs flexed beneath pants molded to his form as he leaned back, away from me. Then he tugged his shirt over his head, and my fingers stuttered on my blouse. Like I'd suspected, he was all lean muscle and hard abdominals, his shoulders surprisingly broad. Nestled securely between his collarbones, the pendant heaved with each breath.

"Oh," I said, and he flipped his hair back, preened as my gaze roved hungrily over him. Gods, I hadn't realized he was so well-built. Slender, but with defined pectorals, biceps, shoulders. No wonder he could lift me with ease. "That's, um..."

"Like what you see?" he asked, a mischievous glint in his eye. His long blond hair swept across his collarbones as he leaned forward, bracketing me with his arms and legs. "Have I rendered you speechless?"

"Um, yes," I said, trying and failing to find words, eager though I was to prove him wrong.

A frown tugged at the corners of his kiss-swollen lips. "Are you sure you're alright? I think you hit your head pretty hard."

"I'm fine," I grumbled. "Stop asking."

"If you say so."

"I do," I said, grinning devilishly at him as the final button of my blouse popped free. Marius was only too happy to help divest me of it, pulling the fabric free with unbridled glee.

And then I was in nothing but my skirts and chemise, with Marius's hands already sliding under the fabric, reaching to skate across my ribs, to cup my breasts. I lunged for him, pulling him down on top of me with a growl that shocked even me.

His eyebrows raised, but I didn't give him a chance to speak. I found the bulge at the front of his pants and pressed my palm against it, held it there, waiting for his reaction. A tease, a question all at once.

His hand caught my wrist. When he spoke, his voice was a rumble, hazy and wrecked. "I don't think we're quite there yet."

"What do you mean?" I asked, taking in his flushed face, blown pupils, parted lips.

When he moved, it was with the grace and speed of a panther. Suddenly, my skirts were up around my waist. My knickers were torn free and launched somewhere into the abyss of stars, and then he was leering up at me from between my legs, a self-satisfied glint in his eye. One hand trailed up and down my thigh, his fingertips burning like hot coals. "May I?"

"Oh," I said, startled indeed. I'd used the bath yesterday evening, and things ought to be clean enough, but I was hyper aware that I hadn't washed today. It was only one day's neglect, but I couldn't squash down a coil of worry. "I haven't—"

His hand stilled on my leg, grip loosening. "Haven't what? We don't have to do anything you're uncomfortable with."

"Haven't washed," I managed, pushing through my embarrassment.

A startled little laugh escaped him. "I can *assure* you that's hardly a problem."

"Well, it's just—it's gross." I crossed my arms over my breasts, giggled as he made an exaggerated face.

"I don't know if you've noticed, but I am wildly attracted to you and would very much like to fuck you." His grin turned lecherous. "I'd like to taste you, Your Highness. May I?"

After a speech like that, I didn't want to say no. "Yes," I squeaked.

"Tell me if you want me to stop," he said, and then his head disappeared beneath my skirts. And though I wasn't wearing half a dozen layers like Ria always did, there was enough fabric to completely obscure Marius. I wouldn't be able to watch, to see what he was doing. A little thrill ran through me.

Hands gripped my hips. One captured my thigh, and pushed it gently to the side, so my legs were parted wide. Everything beneath my skirts was on full display. I forced myself to relax. Arousal drowned out my nerves as Marius made a sound of approval.

I felt a hot breath at my labia and shuddered. Then came a soft, experimental lick that sent sparks flickering up my spine. Another press of his tongue, firmer, more confident. A brush of his lip just below the bundle of nerves at my center. I fought the urge to squirm, to moan.

And then his tongue lapped against my most sensitive point, swirling and hot. I groaned then, loud and wanton. His answering moan vibrated through me. A pulse of pleasure accompanied it, and then I was lost in the sensation. The drag of his tongue, his lips, the building heat.

A finger slipped inside of me, crooking just so, and I gasped, shivered. Marius paused. I caught sight of the top of his blond head rising above my skirts, and said, "Wait, don't stop!"

An answering chuckle. "Whatever you wish, my princess." And he was on me again, sucking at that most exquisite spot, two fingers massaging inside of me.

I breathed heavily, trying not to give into the rapidly approaching crescendo, the building intensity. Then I realized there was no reason not to. Marius wanted this. Marius wanted to put his mouth on me and drive me to that final point, that cresting euphoria, and my first instinct was to fight it? Perhaps he *had* driven me mad.

"I think I'm going to—"

"I'd like nothing more," he said, the words muffled by my body.

His mouth was like a flame against me, and I was molten steel. I pulsed, fingers clenching, thighs squeezing, and Marius swirled his tongue with a fury, fueling wave after wave of my orgasm, until I was nothing but a trembling, panting mess. He emerged from my skirts and swiped the back of his hand across his mouth, then came to embrace me. He kissed me hard, claiming my mouth. I whimpered as I tasted myself on his lips, then grappled for him, finding purchase on his magnificently carved shoulders.

His breath came in soft pants between brushes of our tongues and lips.

"Good?" he asked, and I nodded against him, lightheaded and weak-kneed.

"I think you broke me."

"Mm," he said, stroking my hair, peppering kisses along my neck, my collarbone. "I hope not. I had so many exciting plans."

"Plans?"

"Indeed," he said, lifting my chemise to expose my belly, my ribs, my breasts. "I was quite proud of them."

"Seems a shame to waste them," I said, breath escaping in a rush as he brought his mouth to my breast, kissing my nipple, then sucking it gently between his teeth. I quivered. The sensation shot straight to my still-throbbing core.

Marius lifted his head, and said, "It does, doesn't it? Do you still want me to fuck you?"

"Yes, please," I said, reaching for the ties at his trousers, where his cock bulged, eager and ready. I wanted to taste it, feel it in my hand, firm and steady. Even without seeing it, I knew the size was impressive. It more than filled my hand, would probably burn when it breached me, but I craved it, anyway.

Fingers trailing lightly down the front of my blouse, he asked, "Do you plan to keep your clothes on?"

I shook my head, and started to work my way out of my chemise, my skirts. By the time I kicked off my boots and stockings, he was fully nude, proud cock on display, the V of his hips pointing at it like an arrow. I bit down a laugh.

"What?" he demanded, hands on his hips, a playful tilt to his lips.

"I—It just looks like an arrow," I said, gesturing.

He glanced down at himself, and then back at me. His eyes rolled heavenward. "Mature."

"For what it's worth, it's absolutely pointing the right direction," I said, and he cackled at that.

"I've got something else pointing in the right direction," he said, coming to embrace me. "With startling accuracy, really."

I started to giggle, then gasped at the sensation of his skin against mine, the feel of his broad chest, his firm hands, the velvet-smoothness of his cock as it brushed across me.

I wanted to melt all over again. Legs still shaking, I rose up on tiptoe to kiss him. My hands came to a rest behind his neck, while his wrapped around my waist, skimming the small of my back.

In this silent moment, I felt a strange sense of vulnerability. I released it without fanfare, aware that I was, at least for now, safe in Marius's arms. No one would interrupt us, and dawn was still a few hours away.

For now, I'd drink down this moment, memorizing every detail, relishing everything that I could.

Because this might not happen again.

Before I had time to worry, Marius drew back, arms loosening around my waist. "Cloak?" he asked, jerking his chin in the direction of our makeshift bed, and I nodded, all too eager to lie down with him again.

"Sorry I don't have anything more comfortable," he said, lowering himself gracefully to the floor. "I didn't consider all the angles."

"This is fine," I said, and it was. My first sexual encounter happened in a stable, and subsequent ones weren't much better. As concerned as I was about appearing virginal and graceful, I had to be careful indulging the occasional dalliance. Which meant that I mostly fucked servants, and the occasional bard (not Avens, obviously), mostly in the kitchens or the stables. At least the Star Room was fully indoors, and nothing smelled of shit. "Thanks for sacrificing your cloak."

"Think nothing of it," he said, reaching for me as I came to join him, guiding me onto his lap. I draped my arms over his shoulders and stared into his icy eyes, crinkled with fondness. "I'll have it cleaned, and it will be a nice reminder of this."

My heart stuttered at the thought of him wearing this cloak again. At the thought of what it might mean. Did he want some memory of me to carry with him long after his marriage to Ria? Or would he wear it simply because he liked me?

"Or maybe I won't have it cleaned, and it will smell of you," he said, considering. "I think I'd like that the most."

"People will notice if you've stains on your cloak," I pointed out, trying to keep the laughter from my voice.

Nuzzling his nose to my forehead, he chuckled. "Then I invite them to speculate."

I adjusted myself in his lap, moving so that my leg nudged against his cock, which gave an excited twitch. I laughed, reached to wrap my hand around it.

Marius froze beneath me, let out a soft exhale as I began stroking, admiring the fullness of him. "Have you had this hiding in your trousers the entire time?" I teased, nipping at his lip.

"No, I swapped it for a larger model this morning," he said, and rolled his eyes. "Of course I've always had it hidden away. Much the way you've been concealing your magnificent hips," he said, gathering my buttocks into his hands, and giving a squeeze. "I believe that's the nature of clothes."

I flicked my thumb over the head of his cock and delighted in the fire that lit in his eyes, the way he met me in a kiss that left me positively steaming, warm and pliant against him.

But I wanted more. Wanted to feel that searing length inside of me. Wanted to feel him above and below me, surrounded by his firm thighs, strong hands.

I slipped from his lap, hands falling away from him. I came to a rest on my back and shoved my feet beneath his calf.

An eyebrow raised. "Oh?"

I let my legs fall open. At once, he was upon me, pressing a kiss to the pulse point of my throat. Hands roved up and down along my sides, pausing to brush over my breasts, the peaks of my nipples.

"At the risk of redundancy, I really must insist that you're beautiful," he murmured, his breath ghosting over the shell of my ear.

"You've never told me that before," I told him, wrapping my legs around the backs of his thighs.

"No, but I'm certain plenty have."

"Yes, but they weren't..." I struggled to find the words. Faces whirled through my mind, an endless parade of half-forgotten admirers and lovers, all of whom I'd found lacking in some way. "They weren't the people I wanted to hear it from."

Marius lifted onto his elbows to look me in the eye, gaze softening into something warm, reverent. "I'm going to assume that statement doesn't apply to me."

"No," I said, running my hands over his shoulder blades, the bumps of his spine. "You're the only one I've ever wanted to tell me that."

"Then let me say it again," he said, voice a rumble in his chest. "You are breathtakingly, wonderfully beautiful, and I am incredibly happy to be here with you."

My eyes slid shut. Lucky. I was lucky to be here, with this man I'd grown so unbearably fond of, in this secret room that he trusted me enough to share. "Marius," I began, but he nibbled at my ear, and all my words were lost in a moan.

We stayed like that a long moment, shifting against each other, panting, and then I could stand it no more, and reached again for him. "I'm ready if you are," I told him, and he bent to kiss me fiercely. His hips aligned with mine. I parted my thighs to allow him entrance, breath hitching when he bumped against me, the head of his cock hot and blunt.

"Are you sure?" he said, head tilted to the side, the faintest hint of worry visible through his usual brash confidence.

"Yes," I said, reaching down to grasp his member, and guide him between my legs.

"Alright, then," he said, regarding me with a mixture of shock and approval. "Alright."

And finally, finally he pushed into me. I bit my lip, pulled him closer, lost in a haze of pressure and pleasure.

He was big. I knew that already. For all that he was rumored to be sickly and weak, he was incredibly well-endowed. Maybe I should have expected this—he was too proud, too arrogant to have been anything else.

Within a few moments, he was fully inside of me. The stretch shifted from uncomfortable to incredible as he began to thrust, cautiously at first, circling his hips. When I moved my hips to meet him, he leaned down to kiss me, gathered my wrists in his hand, and held them above my head. Hips snapping with newfound energy, he drove into me, and I matched his rhythm so that we moved in tandem, frantic and feverish. His mouth devoured mine, and I gasped against him, pushing up, trying to fuse us into one. Intensity built in my core, muscles tightening, heat flooding.

In that moment, I was his. Completely and utterly his, and I wanted nothing more than to stay that way, claimed and debauched, melded at the hips with Marius hovering above me, bringing me closer to the clouds with every kiss, every thrust.

I scrabbled to free my wrists. When he released me, I pulled him closer, moaning and shaking. I came with a sound that was more a sob than anything else, spasming around his cock.

He made a frantic noise and increased his speed. "Talina," he said, my name like a prayer on his lips. When he came, it was with a low groan that reverberated across the room, a stutter of his hips. I groaned, too, still not fully recovered, and ran my fingertips down his spine.

Our lip met in an open-mouthed kiss, punctuated by gasping laughter. There was an impossible fondness in his gaze, and I wanted to melt beneath it.

He collapsed beside me, laid his head against my arm. I wriggled closer to him, basking in his warmth like a snake fresh from hibernation, soaking in the first rays of springtime sunlight.

"I've thought about it a lot," he said, after a long moment, in which I nearly fell asleep. "More than just that, I mean. All of it."

I blinked my eyes open. The Northern Lights twisted and stretched above us. Blue and teal and green, they danced together in an exquisite, ever-changing tapestry. "Have you?"

"You might be surprised," he said, watching me with a mixture of affection and curiosity. The tips of his fingers trailed across my sternum, down my arm, coming to a rest at my wrist. Our hands laced together.

Desire and dread flooded me. I didn't want to talk about this. Not yet. I wasn't ready for reality to come crashing down around me.

I was a mistress. To my sister's future husband, of all people.

At the same time, I wanted to know exactly what he'd thought about. If there was any hope for us. If there might be some tiny glimmer of hope in the far away future, ready to taunt and tantalize.

"I think I have to get back to work," I said, worried I might offend him, but afraid I'd start crying if I spent any more time with my thoughts.

"Alas," said Marius, arm and leg tightening around me. "I feared as much."

"I'm sorry," I said, and I was. Even with Marius's cloak providing the only cushioning between our bodies and the floor, I was more comfortable than I'd ever been, halfway to sleep.

"This *is* one of the things I considered," he said, and rolled away from me. "There's no need to be sorry."

We dressed quickly, and in silence. "The servants might talk," I said. My hands shook. Nerves flooded me as I imagined everyone gossiping over breakfast, stealing glances at me, giggling amongst each other. "I'm going to be very late returning."

"Yes," said Marius evenly. "We'll… need to be more careful in the future. Well, that is, if you want to do this again."

Did I? My stomach twisted into knots. Sour bile rose in my throat. "I do," I told him, because that was the truth of the matter. I hated to betray Ria. I hated the way that I longed for Marius. But I already yearned to be in his arms again, safe in his embrace, laughing at his antics, the subject of his adoration, however fleeting. "But I should go. I'll see you later?"

"You couldn't get rid of me," Marius promised, as if he understood the underlying question. He kissed me on the cheek. "I'll see you soon."

I practically ran back to my bed. My cheek was on fire where his lips had brushed it. My hair and clothes were in absolute disarray, but no one woke as I slipped into bed. With any luck, they'd just assume I just got in late.

CHAPTER 28

The teasing was relentless.

Everyone mocked my midnight tryst, and the way I woke up that morning—sputtering, fully dressed, hair in tangles.

"Who did *you* see last night?" they asked, gawking and cackling, as if the subject of my romance was the most entertainment they'd had in years.

"Good lay, was it?" asked Zellia, winking at me as she made her way to the kitchens, a basket of linens in hand. "You were gone almost all night."

"Again and again and again, eh?" said Dana, one of the laundresses. Rumor had it that she was at least two hundred years old and nowhere near to dying. Wrinkles deep as pits lined her face, and what remained of her hair was whiter than snow. Her grin revealed pale gums. "Must've been a good time. Look at your hair!"

I washed hurriedly, yanking a brush through the snarls in my curls.

"No hope for that!" Dana called gleefully as she went to spoon pottage into her bowl.

"It will be fine!" I shouted back. The bristles of the brush caught in a particularly furious knot, and one of them pulled loose, sticking out of the tangle like a single tooth. I let out a scream of frustration and collapsed onto my cot. I was running late. I was exhausted and sore. Though the memory of last night made my pulse pound, I had half a million chores to complete, and Ria was going to be late to breakfast because of me, and—

Dana took pity on me and pulled the bristle from my hair, her gnarled hands surprisingly dexterous.

Prince Marius intercepted me in the hall after lunch, drifting from the shadows with a specter's ease. I was only too easily coaxed into an empty room, eager to see him again even after a brief separation. We kissed until we were desperate and panting, and were halfway out of our clothes when a sound came from outside the door.

Marius drew me into the shadows, but the moment was ruined. The voices of servants echoed just down the hall. We dressed hastily, afraid of being caught. That didn't stop him from kissing me fervently as I approached the door, clothes wrinkled.

I saw him later that night, but only briefly. As usual, he visited me in the library, heartbreakingly beautiful among the torchlit shelves. But he wore an expression of barely contained irritation over his usual excitement. My stomach flipped at the sight of it. "King Hergarv demands an audience with me this evening," he groused. "I'm afraid I won't be available tonight."

Disappointment weighed heavily in my chest, but I steeled myself. If I continued seeing Marius, this would be my reality. I would always, always come second to his other duties. In time, I would come second to my own sister, a thought that I pushed to the back of my mind and buried, like a broken and mottled corpse.

"Then I'll see you tomorrow," I said, smiling with false cheer. A sense of abandonment took root in my breast and quickly flowered into a thorny tangle that pierced my heart with each ragged beat.

"I shall miss you," he said, fingers brushing lightly over the back of my hand. With one final glance, he was gone again.

The next day, I was brought before Queen Tarra. Shaking in my boots, I followed the guards to her tearoom, hoping I looked demure, instead of like someone on the verge of throwing up. But Queen Tarra greeted me without fanfare, and once again ordered me to take my pick of cakes and tea. I ate nervously, and only to appease her. Eventually, she sighed, folded her hands in her lap, and ordered the guards from the room. When it was just the two of us, she said, "I've noticed you spending a lot of time with Prince Marius."

I nodded hesitantly. The cakes sat in my stomach like something rotten and foul. "Yes, your Highness. You asked me to assist him."

Her eyebrows raised, lips forming a quiet chuckle. "Yes, indeed," she said. "But might I suggest you try to be a bit subtler?"

My entire face burned. "I—Your Highness—"

"I don't much care what the two of you get up to," said Queen Tarra, indifferent to my suffering. "But do try to halt the rumor mill. Princess Valeria is pathetic enough without learning that her maid is intimate with her betrothed."

"I—"

"I'd also suggest a trip to the apothecary. It pays to be responsible, and you don't want to birth a bastard," said Queen Tarra, taking a sip of her tea. "I must say, I'm rather surprised. Marius isn't what I'd call a romantic, but he seems rather enamored with you. What is it, do you think?"

I tried not to shy away from her scrutiny. "Truthfully, I don't know," I began. When she laughed, I realized that she wasn't expecting an answer. If I gave one, it wouldn't be taken seriously.

"Well, it certainly isn't your mettle," she said. She paused to stir more sugar into her tea, and tasted it carefully, mulling over the taste. She must have found it unsatisfactory, because she reached for more sugar. I watched the granules slip from the spoon, spilling into her cup like flakes of falling snow. "But whatever it is, I'm sure it won't last long. He isn't known for long term romantic connections."

If I blushed any harder, I'd surely burst into flames. Had she brought me here to humiliate me? "Thank you, Your Highness."

"Don't thank me yet," Queen Tarra said. Dollops of cream swirled in her tea. She stirred until they dissolved, silver spoon clicking against the rim of the cup. "I brought you here to warn you. I don't like to see women hurt by fickle men. And I know you value your position as Princess Valeria's maid. I want you to know that I think Prince Marius is not worth the effort, although I'm quite certain you'll ignore me."

I gawked at her, open-mouthed. Was Marius's reputation of no consideration to her? "I—Thank you for your honesty, Your Highness. But how am I to continue assisting him if I decline his, um, romantic advances?"

"I should've forbidden such advances when I spoke to you weeks ago," sighed Queen Tarra. A dainty hand lifted a green frosted pastry to her lips. When she took a bite, its interior crumbled free, spilling onto the pristine tablecloth. "*Both* of you. Alas, it's a bit late for that. Just remember: Prince Marius is not marrying you. At some point, this *will* become a problem."

I left the room reeling. The cakes in my stomach had turned to sawdust.

"THE QUEEN HAS NOTICED," I told Prince Marius. We had just stumbled through the door of the Star Room, and my hand was still warm from his grasp.

"Bollocks," he grumbled. "I ought to have known."

"How does she know?" I pressed, trailing after him into the study, where he frowned at the shelf of bottles as though they'd personally offended him.

"She has her ways," he said. "Spies, mostly, though I've been advised that the court sorceresses are quite handy with their scrying glasses."

"Wait," I said, horrified. "You mean the sorceresses watched us have sex?"

"I'd assume so." He shrugged. "If she knows."

"The servants knew I'd seen someone," I said, pacing around the room. "Perhaps she connected the rumors?"

"Perhaps," mused Marius. After selecting a bottle from the shelf, he turned it over in his hand, as though ensuring its quality. "Though I doubt it. She has her ways."

I chewed my lip. *My reputation will be ruined,* I thought. When my identity was eventually revealed, word would get out. I'd fucked Prince Marius. I could no longer claim I was virginal. My value was sullied. Father would be disappointed, if not outright furious.

I envisioned months spent locked away in my rooms, my only entertainment the rising and falling of the sun. Eventually, I'd be married off to some doddering old fool, the only sort of person who would agree to marry me.

This was a mistake. I shouldn't have done this.

"Talina?" Marius set the vial down on the desk, and approached me, lines of worry carved into his forehead.

Oh. I hadn't realized my face was wet. "I'm fine," I said, even as a sob broke free.

"Yes, clearly," said Marius, pulling me close to him, wrapping his firm arms around me. I buried my face in his shoulder and smelled woodsmoke, pine, and something softer, like cinnamon. "All fine and dandy here. Tell me, my lady, what ails you?"

I was definitely going to ruin his shirt with my tears, but he seemed unconcerned as he pressed his face into my hair, holding me as though I were something delicate, precious. "I'm going to be in so much trouble," I managed to whisper. "This will get out, and I will be punished, and—"

"Punished by whom?" Marius said, rubbing circles on my back. "No one here will particularly care. Not about the sex, anyway."

"Queen Tarra will. And King Amonrew," I said, biting down a moan of despair. "Trust me, it will go horribly for me."

This gave him pause. His hand slowed its circles, and his embrace loosened. "Do you think it's likely he'll find out?"

"He will," I said. "Eventually, when this is all over, word will reach him, and when he finds he can't marry me off like he planned..." I swallowed hard. "And that's if your family doesn't think I'm a spy."

"I will not allow that," said Marius, hugging me once more. "You are here, under my protection, and I will not allow your father to take you away and imprison you. Even if word gets out. As for my family, that's, well, admittedly trickier." He deflated against me. "But I'm not going to let anyone hurt you."

"That might be enough to start a war," I said, my words muffled against his chest. My heart felt heavy as an anvil. It threatened to drag me down to the floor.

"I'm not sure if you've noticed, but I took that risk once before. What makes you think I wouldn't do it again?"

"I'd hoped you'd developed some common sense in the interim," I grumbled, wiping tears from my eyes.

I was rewarded with a smirk. "Here," said Marius, steering me toward one of the armchairs. "Let's sit down."

I fell into the armchair with the grace of a maiden mid-faint. Marius knelt beside me, looking for all intents and purposes like he might be posing for a portrait. But when he gazed up at me, his icy eyes soft and gentle, I was reminded that this moment was between us, and only us, nosy sorceresses be damned.

"Do you want to stop?" said Marius. "We—we do not have to do this. If I've ever made you feel like you couldn't say no, then please understand that wasn't my intent. I only want to do this if you do. I will not retaliate, or punish you, at any point should you change your mind."

The pain in his gaze pierced me through like the tip of a spear. I did not want to stop. I also didn't want to hurt anyone, least of all Ria.

But ending our newfound relationship right now *would* hurt me, and it would certainly hurt Marius.

Agony rippled through me, and I sobbed into my hands. "No," I said. "No, I don't."

A hand touched my knee. "Neither do I. But I think perhaps some discussions are in order before we carry on."

I peered at him between my fingers and had to avert my gaze. I'd wounded him with my tears. I could already sense his change of heart, his hesitation. I'd been assessed and found lacking. "It's alright if you change your mind," I mumbled.

A quiet laugh. "I'm not quite sure you heard me," he said. "I just told you I didn't want to stop."

"Yes, I know," I whined. "But—"

"Have I ever kept my opinion from you?"

I frowned. "Probably."

He frowned too, as if he'd just realized that his phrasing was poor. "Alright, well, I've never kept anything of import from you. You're quite right, I haven't actually subjected you to every opinion that has ever crossed my mind. Because if I had, you would've known my feelings toward you a long time ago."

Curiosity piqued, I said, "How long?"

A faint blush colored his cheeks. "Months," he said. "Since before the bear, if I'm perfectly honest."

Oh. I'd thought him a phenomenal idiot back then. (A part of me was convinced that he still might be.) "Truly? So long?"

His hand found mine. "Easily. I was impressed by your entrance, if I'm perfectly honest. And my curiosity could not be quenched." He swallowed, Adam's apple bobbing. "At the time, I wondered why a maid would feel so compelled to follow her employer. It makes sense now."

I nodded. My tears were tacky on my face, and I wiped them away.

"Then I spotted you and your crystal in the woods, and I-I told myself that I panicked when the bear arrived because I needed to earn favor with my betrothed, but really, I desperately did not want to see you harmed." He scowled down at the ground. "Seeing you for the first time felt like a brush with fate, and I was unnerved. Even before I recognized you as the girl from—admittedly—my dullest visions." The corners of his lips turned into a weak smile.

A twist of reverence and guilt. For all that I wanted to melt beneath his words, I could not return the sentiment. "I thought you were foul," I mumbled, ashamed. "Beautiful and foul and I couldn't look away."

"I hope part of your opinion has changed," he said, eyes crinkling as his lips raised into a ghost of a smile.

"It has," I acknowledged. "I think you're beautiful and *ridiculous* now."

He threw his head back and laughed throatily. "I can't say I've ever aspired to be anything else." His face shined with roguish delight. "Truly, I'm flattered."

"You could do better," I said, tugging gently on his hands, drawing him closer. "You could have Valeria."

"I'm not sure if you've noticed," said Prince Marius softly, his face inches from mine. "But I don't want anyone but you."

I kissed him then, sweet and gentle. He cupped my face in his hands, drew back to gaze at me so serenely that I had to look away, a blush rising on my face.

I pulled the pin from my hair, inhaled sharply, and waited for Marius to react.

"Oh," he said, glancing from the pin to my hair, and back again. "More surprises, I see." His voice softened. "It's red."

Afraid to speak, I nodded.

"I like it," he murmured, stepping forward to kiss me again, his slender fingers tangling in my hair, caressing the strands like they were made of gold, like he couldn't get enough of them.

I spoke between kisses. "You never Saw it before? My hair, I mean."

Marius grinned against my lips. "That's what threw me off course, initially. I knew your face. Without the hair, you were harder to recognize."

"That was the point," I said, sighing against him. "Not to be noticed."

"A tragedy," Marius hummed. "But a necessity. I understand."

We ended up on the floor of the study, this time still fully dressed. My blouse was open, skirts rucked up around my waist. His pants were halfway down his legs. My knickers were the only piece of clothing to disappear, once again tossed by the wayside.

At this rate, I'd have no underwear left. A part of me suspected that was the point, but I was too absorbed in the moment to do any chastising.

Grinning wickedly, Marius climbed over me. My hand fumbled along his thigh, then stroked his cock up and down. For the briefest moment, his eyes slid shut. I couldn't help the self-satisfied smirk that painted my lips. Then he caught my eye, and his mouth lowered to my breast, tongue flicking over my nipple. I gasped, and he closed his lips, sucking and swirling. Eyes closed, I tried to keep stroking him, but quickly lost the rhythm when his free hand sneaked between my thighs and slipped into the folds hidden there. Clever fingers found my most sensitive place with ease, circled experimentally. I let out a gasp, and his gaze flickered to meet mine. "Don't stop," I pleaded, and he didn't. The pads of his fingers danced a pattern around the bundle of nerves between my thighs. He trailed kisses from one breast to the other, lavishing my chest with attention, moving to the most delicate area of my neck—open-mouthed, careful not to leave a bruise.

I shuddered through an orgasm, stroking him clumsily, determined to keep him fully hard if nothing else. He groaned against my throat. The reverberation nearly sent my eyes rolling back in my head.

When I was at last drained and sated, he drew back, kissed me fully on the mouth with such devotion that I began to tremble. How was it possible to feel so wonderful in his embrace, safe and whole?

Would he become bored? Should I insist on something else?

But I was boneless and scraped raw, and when he shifted his hips, I parted my legs, grasped at my skirts. He could tell me if he wanted to do things differently. Right now, I wanted nothing more than this slow pace, this gentle discovery.

When he entered me, it was with a hiss of breath. My hips rose to meet his and he paused when I gave a choked-off moan. His thrusts were slow, measured. I grabbed his shoulders, and pulled him toward me until our lips met.

"My lady," he said, looking down at me with such fondness that I felt I might cry. "My beautiful lady."

"Marius," I mumbled, dragging my nails over his pectoral, just catching the edge of his nipple. "I-I—"

But I couldn't say the things I wanted to say. What could I tell him that he didn't already know? He was beautiful, strong, witty, kind—and staring at me with affection and lust in a way that made my throat ache, my most intimate parts throb.

I was nearly certain that I loved him. That I would break if we were parted. I wanted nothing more than to be his in every way that mattered. I'd wear his cursed ring if it bound me to him, if it meant it was his embrace I could dissolve into at the end of the day. If his lips could claim mine, and I could share his bed, his goblet, his room full of twinkling stars.

In the future, I'd ride his cock, or demand he take me from behind. Find ways to make our encounters less intimate. But right now, I desperately wanted the fantasy, so I kissed him and rolled my hips, devouring his every gasp and benediction.

Heat and ecstasy built in my abdomen, and I clutched Marius

harder, insisting that he must go faster. He was only too happy to oblige me, pulling back with a mischievous grin, and driving back into me as if he intended to fuck me straight through the floor.

Under other circumstances, it might have hurt, but I only tightened my legs and matched his rhythm. It would be remiss to call our pace violent, but it was certainly enthusiastic and unguarded, and he very quickly pounded me into a climax that left me boneless and exhausted.

And while I shuddered and moaned through the aftershocks, he chased his pleasure, and came with an open-mouthed gasp, head thrown back, sweat glistening on his bared throat. The sight of his ecstasy made me want to start all over again. There was no way a single round could possibly satiate me.

But our time together was limited, and my visits to the Star Room held a purpose outside of intimacy.

Marius pulled free and tucked himself back into his pants. With a great thud and an exaggerated groan, he laid beside me, languid. My face pressed into his shoulder, breathing in the scent of him. I traced lazy patterns on his chest, and his hand found mine, pulled it close to his heart, and rested there. The thump of his heart was slow, steady, strangely reassuring.

I could've fallen asleep there, relaxed and reassured by his solid warmth, but eventually he winced, squeezed my hand, and said, "We, um, probably should work tonight."

I sat up. "Fine," I grumbled, replacing my hairpin, and fumbling for the buttons on my blouse.

"You haven't changed your buttons," he said, watching my hands.

"No," I sighed. "I've been rather busy lately."

"What are they for, again?"

I pointed to the top button. "Anxiety." My fingers moved to the fifth button. "This one is a smoke bomb."

"Very handy, yes," said Marius with an approving nod. "Highly necessary."

I rolled my eyes. "And this one is to force open stubborn locks," I finished, gesturing to the final button.

"*Any* stubborn lock," he repeated. An eyebrow quirked. "Have you tested it?"

Oh no. I probably shouldn't have admitted that. He surely suspected that my reasons for creating it were nefarious, untoward.

"No," I admitted nervously.

"Would you like to?"

"Oh," I said, nearly sagging in relief. He hadn't accused me of robbing the palace. *Good*. "Certainly."

"Excellent, because I've a particularly pesky lock, and the court magicians have no interest in assisting me with quite literally any of my problems." He leapt to his feet, and offered me a hand. I took it, and started to follow him out the door, then realized I had no idea where my knickers were. Certainly not anywhere they ought to be.

But it was too late. He was already halfway down the passage, and I could only just keep up with him. "Marius!" I hissed as the door slammed behind me, plunging us into darkness. "Slow down!"

Oh," he said, and his footsteps stopped. "Of course. I'm sorry."

I crashed into his back, and he steadied me, sturdy hands catching me by the waist. Even in the pitch blackness, he somehow knew exactly where I was. "No pebbles today?"

I shook my head, then remembered he couldn't see me. "I forgot to grab one."

"No matter," he said. "I ought to have come prepared. I'm afraid I've gotten rather lazy. Or spoiled, perhaps." His hand found mine, and our fingers interlaced.

"Spoiled," I teased, and bumped against him with my shoulder.

"Fine, fine, I agree."

CHAPTER 29

I expected him to let go of my hand when we reached the library, but he his grip remained firm, so we slinked along together, keeping behind the tall shelves until we reached the entrance.

There, Marius finally dropped my hand and donned his hood. "I'm sorry," he said. "I can't subject you to the humiliation, let alone the frankly terrible courtly gossip."

I gave him a light shove, right between the shoulder blades. "Walk ahead," I said. "I'll follow at a distance."

"Good idea," he said, and took off like an arrow shot from a bow.

At first, I scrambled to keep up, but he slowed as soon as we were away from the more populated parts of the palace, where servants finished their nighttime tasks, and courtiers wandered. I didn't dare speak or stray too close to him.

For a long time, I was unsure of our destination. I probably should have asked earlier, but I'd been swept up in his enthusiasm. To call out now would risk ruining my cover. We were alone in the halls, but anyone could be lurking around the corner.

Along with any pesky, scrying sorceresses. How could anyone keep a secret in this place?

I knew next to nothing of scrying, or of court magicians and their ways. In Olmstead, we had only a few, and their jobs were to neutralize the weather, to ensure a bountiful harvest, and to protect the castle in an emergency. I'd overhead enough to be under the impression that even sorcerers were rarely Seers. No one had ever told me that spying through a scrying glass was an option. Not outside of fairytales, anyway.

Had people watched me my entire life, unbeknownst to me? How many perverted old sorcerers had watched me undress? More importantly, had anyone seen me jump into the supply wagon?

Had King Amonrew known the entire time?

A chill sucked the heat from my bones. Was he only biding his time?

No. No, that was impossible. He was too brash, too angry to allow something like this to transpire. Queen Tarra must have located the best scryers on the continent, and employed them here, in Tocchia. Not every kingdom had access to these resources, I was sure of it.

Momentarily satisfied, I trailed Marius up a flight of stairs, and down a long hallway. Here, he paused, gesturing for me to join him, so I did, walking quickly until I was at his side. "Stay close," he said. "These are my quarters."

Oh. This was a privilege I hadn't expected. One that I'd silently resigned to Ria. Marius and I would have the Star Room, but I'd never lie in his bed. It was too risky, too disrespectful.

A thrill darted through my heart.

Guards were posted at the end of the hallway. If they saw me, they didn't react. Their arms remained crossed, their weapons at their sides, gazes unwavering. In the light of the sconces, they might as well have been statues. "They won't say anything," Marius assured me, voice low. "They practice discretion."

Back at Castle Ackervail, the guards would've immediately reported any personal guests to my father. But things were different for princes, I supposed, fighting down bitter resentment.

I gave a hesitant nod and followed Marius through a heavy door bearing a carving of a heron. Candles flickered to life when we stepped inside.

"Here," he said, leading me past the entryway, where paintings hung alongside elaborately crafted swords, still and dusty as a museum display. We passed the washing room and the bedroom (where we did *not* stop to make love again as I'd very much hoped we might) and made our way into a grand study. Half workshop and half library, it was as exquisite as something conceived in a dream. The bookshelves were carefully carved and painted a sage green. Potted plants filled the empty spaces, their vines trailing, leaves vibrant and shiny. A desk sat in the corner, equipped with a set of drawers, and wide enough to comfortably seat two. Ink pots crowded around a jewel encrusted vase holding pens and quills. Pages and trinkets were scattered about the surface; I fought the urge to dig through them and find the perfect objects to enchant.

Beneath the window was a work bench. Marius's tools, beakers, and ingredients were neatly arranged, catching the moonlight so that they nearly glowed.

It was chaotic. It was beautiful. I stood transfixed, mouth open in wonder, and Marius sidled up to me. "Knew you'd like it," he said.

For once, he wasn't gloating, merely pleased.

"It's... phenomenal," I managed. "I didn't know this was here."

"Yes, well, people aren't generally permitted in my quarters," he said, striding to the desk, where he opened a drawer that squeaked and stuttered. While he rummaged about, I explored the rest of the study, examining scrolls of paper, the worn titles of books.

"I have to make a concentrated effort not to live as a hermit, it's true," he said, approaching me from behind. "Left to my own devices, I could entertain myself for weeks in here. Lucky if I'm ever ill again, I suppose."

He gestured around the room with his free hand. The other held a box just small enough to balance on his palm. Perfectly cube shaped, its corners were sharp as daggers. Nicks and scratches marred the wood. A single, rusted lock sat at its center, the keyhole reminiscent of a skull.

Immediately, I had my doubts. "What is that?"

"Well, it's a box, and I can't seem to open it," he huffed. "The lock is eroded, and the key won't work. I think it's related to the ring, but I'm honestly not sure."

I stared at it, unnerved by its energy. While it didn't frighten me in the same way as the ring, it felt somehow resentful, unwelcoming. "I think we should reconsider," I said. "Marius, it's—It doesn't feel right."

He frowned, first at me, then at the box. "I need to know what's in there," he said, more to himself than to me.

"No, you don't," I told him, growing worried. Maybe I'd underestimated the box's influence over him. "Not yet. Why don't you set that down, and we can talk?"

His lip twitched. With great reluctance, he returned it to the drawer and faced me. "I have to get rid of this ring," he said, scrubbing a hand down his face. "If this box is tied to the ring, then I must know what's inside."

I plopped down on the work bench. I should have worried about dirtying my skirts, but at that moment, I was back at the forge, watching Cranz scowl over a particularly stubborn enchantment, sweating and swearing. I knew how to work through magical problems. At least, in theory. "Let's start at the beginning. Let's ignore the box for the moment. If the ring came from the gods, then how does one get rid of it?"

He sat beside me and buried his face in his hands. "I don't know. I can't bear to pass it on. Nor can I bear to see our lands destroyed and our people killed. But the history of this ring—it's brutal, bloody. Hundreds of years of wars and betrayals, famines, forced marriages. Besides…." His voice lowered in hesitation, and his hands fell to his lap. "I'm not entirely convinced the ring is the work of the gods."

Shock rippled through me. Perhaps I shouldn't have been surprised. After all, I'd only recently learned of the ring and its origin. But to claim that the gods were credited for another's work was very bold indeed. "Oh."

"Of course, it's difficult to ascertain, as no one wants to aid my search. Everyone suspects I'm up to something, and they're right. But they aren't grasping its importance," Marius scoffed, twisting one of the rings on his finger. "I know I ought to be more focused on Liridin, and I am trying, but this… No one understands how important this is."

"I disagree," I said, even though I suspected I hadn't fully grasped the enormity of his statement. "I do."

His answering smile was remorseful. "I'm sorry I dragged you into this. I know you didn't ask to become involved in something so… scandalous."

Marius was nothing if not a walking scandal—he loved who he pleased and what he pleased, fought for his people, sought to destroy the very thing that kept him enslaved in a system that would destroy him right back. But I admired that about him—his tenacity, his eager, unashamed ways. Hardly becoming of a king, but a prince—a prince need not conform to those world-weary views just yet.

And I hoped he never did. Hoped he stayed just as fiery and ridiculous as always.

"What do you think is inside the box?" I asked, instead of assuring him that I loved chasing rumors and sneaking about with him. I did. But I didn't want him to know it yet. Unlike Marius, I *was* ashamed. I'd broken so many rules. Rules that I'd grown up with and never challenged until I came to Tocchia. A part of me wasn't ready for this, while another part relished these newfound moments. Sometimes, in my darkest moments, I wondered what my father would say when he found out. If he found out.

I didn't want to know.

"I'm not sure," he said. "It was last in possession of my father, obviously, and he never tried to open it. Before that, it belonged to Duke Harledon Mair of Luminden. According to the legends, he was the last person to attempt to destroy the ring." Marius winced. "If you're curious, he was wildly unsuccessful."

I frowned. The name was familiar. But where did I know it from?

Then I remembered. A long-forgotten lecture back in Olmstead. I was perhaps eleven or twelve years old, baking half to death in the summer heat and watching a fly buzz around the classroom. My tutor was probably the same age that I was now, twenty-two or twenty-three, overeager and primped to the extreme. Valeria sat beside me and repeatedly kicked me in the shin to keep me from drowsing. If I was caught sleeping again, we'd both be punished.

That was the day we learned what happened to traitors of the gods. With perhaps too much excitement, the tutor told us the story of Harledon Mair, who claimed the gods had *not* created all that was before us, and argued they didn't exist at all. For his defiance, he was confronted by Tynd, the god of creation. At his side was his magical sword, Goffir. In a fit of terror, Mair fled, ascending the highest tower of his estate, and clinging to its turrets. A furious Tynd summoned a great rainstorm that flooded the fields and drowned the crops, but failed to dislodge Mair. So Tynd invoked a great burst of wind, strong enough to send Mair tumbling free. He dropped six stories down to the sodden earth, and only just survived. Though he pleaded for his life and swore fealty, lightning struck down, and Mair was incinerated where he stood.

That afternoon's lesson left my father furious. His children were not to be told the ways of gods. Specifically, we were not to be taught to fear or pledge our loyalty to them. The gods, he argued, were not real, and neither was the story of Mair. While it was important to appease the masses, and to pretend to believe, *actually* believing would compromise our integrity, leave us open to manipulation.

I never saw the tutor again after that.

"I remember the story," I said. "Mair was smote, wasn't he?"

With a shrug, Marius said, "Supposedly. It's all legend now. Difficult to say what really happened."

"What do you think happened?"

"I think he was nearly successful in destroying the ring and was killed for it. Not by a god, as such, but a member of the royal family. Possibly someone who stood to benefit from the ring. Or thought they would, anyway."

"Have *you* ever tried to destroy the ring?"

Marius dragged his fingers through his hair. His face and neck flushed. "I may have allegedly—according to Gavin—downed an entire bottle of wine by myself and launched the ring out a window. There was a manhunt afterwards, but it wasn't recovered. Interestingly, it was on my bedside table when I woke, and no one admitted to placing it there." He sighed. "And I *may*—allegedly—have smashed it with a hammer a time or two. It's always right back on my bedside table by morning, whole and hale, like nothing ever happened."

I shuddered. "That's horrifying."

I couldn't stop thinking of Mair's demise. Was the box related to the ring?

Only one way to find out. I took one breath, then another, and said, "Get the box."

Marius jerked to attention. His stare was baffled and elated at once. "Are you certain?"

"Not at all." I squared my shoulders. "Let's open it."

"I've no intention of forcing you—"

I spoke through gritted teeth. "Marius. Get the box."

He leapt to his feet and lowered into a deep, sweeping bow. "As you wish, my lady."

I couldn't help but giggle. "Now what would your stepmother think of that?"

"She learned a long time ago that her disapproval won't change me." He winked and departed in a rush of maroon coattails.

When he returned, the box rested in his palm, balanced there with unnatural ease. I tapped the button on my blouse. "I hope this works."

Marius's forehead wrinkled. "Why wouldn't it?"

"I'm not a professional," I reminded him. I hated to shatter his favorable impression of me, but Cranz would never forgive me for mismarketing my skillset.

"Regardless," said Marius, waving his hand. "It's worth a try."

I nodded. "Ready?"

"If you are." He waved a tiny bronze key and inserted it into the lock.

There was no clicking sound, only a loud grinding.

I closed my eyes and touched the button on my blouse. Focused on the energy emanating from it—perceptive and impartial. Then my attention shifted to the box, which radiated a sinister desperation.

Opening it now felt criminal, forbidden, but I wanted to help Marius. To see if there was any connection to the ring he was so eager to be rid of.

Screwing my eyes shut, I willed the box to open.

At first, I met resistance. I fought against it, but it was like slamming into a wall of solid steel. The longer I struggled, the weaker I became.

The lock did not give.

I began to panic. I'd claimed this would work. I'd accidentally lied to Marius, and I was going to look like an idiot, and—

The box clicked open.

Marius leapt back. One hand flew out in front of me as if to protect me from some nefarious trap that might spring forth.

"Oh," he whispered, hand lowering. "It worked."

"It did," I said, bewildered.

We shared a glance, then stepped closer. "Let me," said Marius, reaching for the lid.

I smacked his hand away. "I'll not be caught with your corpse if this thing turns out to be cursed."

"And I couldn't bear to live with yours," he snapped.

"Well, ideally you'd bury me in a day or two. I'm sure you've the means."

He crossed his arms. "I won't live without you. I'm afraid I'd have to crawl into the grave with you, dearest, and it would be quite the spectacle. If you won't spare my feelings, *at least* spare my reputation."

I scowled at him. Surely, he had more composure than that.

Surely, he wasn't in love with me.

Deep down, I wasn't so confident.

"Fine, fine," I agreed, waving my hand dismissively. "Your reputation may live another day."

"Oh, goody."

In the end, I used a stick to pry the box open. Marius grumbled a bit, but I was adamant that I wouldn't be blamed for his death if things went awry.

The lid lifted, revealing nothing but a pile of dust the size of my fist.

"What the hell?" Marius breathed. Snatching the stick from my hand, he poked carefully at the mound. "This is… ash. Only ash."

I watched carefully, half-expecting to see something hidden there—a scroll of paper, a vial, a rock, a key—*anything*.

There was nothing but dust.

"Fuck," Marius hissed, swirling the stick frantically now, so that some ash rose into the air and dissipated. "Fuck. There's got to be—Is this really just ash?"

"I think so," I said. "Marius, I'm so sorry. I know you were hoping—"

"It's quite alright." He met my gaze with a strained smile. "I was hopeful, but I knew that it might be a failure."

"Still," I said. "I'm sorry."

"Don't be," he said, closing the lid, and starting toward me. "That's one mystery solved, at least. Thank you for the sacrifice of your button."

The button was still securely attached to my blouse. But it was just a button now. The enchantment that resided in it only moments ago was gone, depleted.

And even though this was a difficult charm to master and I'd spent hours of spare time building up the spell, imbuing the button with magic over a series of weeks, I was quite pleased that it worked. I couldn't help the way my cheeks lifted into a smile. "You're welcome."

CHAPTER 30

The next few days passed much the same. I met Marius in the evenings, and we tried to summon visions. Sometimes we scrutinized the ring or the box, but we found nothing.

The wedding loomed, only two weeks away. King Hergarv returned with his Tocchian advisors, tired and disheartened. There was no sign of Toral and Halin. Marius and I made frantic love nearly every night. Although I was exhausted, dragging so badly that even Ria noticed, I felt rejuvenated. Gone were the days when I languished around Olmstead with only a dull husband and the occasional new shipment of dresses to look forward to. Running about the palace with Marius gave me renewed purpose, and I was eager to indulge.

I visited the apothecary and began taking a single sip of potion nightly. The servants jested and laughed, but no one dared suggest that it was Prince Marius's child I hoped to prevent, so I took their jokes with ease.

The news broke one morning over breakfast.

Once everyone was seated, King Hergarv rose from his great chair and cleared his throat. Instantly, all eyes were on him. Even the servants stopped in their tracks. "Good morning, everyone. It is our greatest..." He paused, mustache twitching as he sought his next words. "...*honor* to announce that King Amonrew of Olmstead will be joining us for the union between my son, Marius, and his betrothed, Princess Valeria."

I kept my face impassive, careful not to let anyone believe that I had reason to fear, but Ria's shoulders tightened. Beside her, Prince Marius choked on a sip of wine.

"We are delighted to welcome them to our court," continued King Hergarv, sounding anything but. He glared at Marius, who was still coughing, and gestured to a guard, who thumped him on the back. This seemed to fix the problem, and Marius sat up, red-faced.

Ria glowered at him.

Did she know? Marius probably didn't, but had Ria kept this a secret? Occasionally, she received letters from home, and I was allowed to pore over them like textbooks, eager to glean any piece of Olmstead from them. Our brothers were fine—bored, but fine. Father was angry, overwhelmed by shifting trade routes and shady wine sellers. In a completely uncharacteristic display of diplomacy, even Queen Elberia inquired as to Ria's welfare.

But I'd seen no hint of an impending visit in those letters.

The rest of the day passed in chaos. The guest rooms had to be prepared, and quickly. My father and brothers were only a week out at this point, probably nearly halfway down the pass.

Unfathomable. Dread crept up my spine.

Avens sought me out, frantic. "Miss Arina!" he whispered, whisking me into a room empty of everything but a desk and bookshelves. I had just dropped off the laundry and was mercifully empty-handed. I'd hate to be accused of absconding with Princess Odalla's linens. "You need to leave!"

I tried to smile. I felt like my face cracked in half. "I can't. Where could I go?"

"I've enough coin for a room in the city," insisted Avens. Today, he wore a pale blue doublet that washed out his freckled complexion. "Listen, you can hide there for a few nights. After the wedding, we'll leave. Get a head start toward Olmstead, eh?" His twitching eye betrayed his angst, ruined his most dashing grin that he always threw at the patrons of taverns and royal courts (and now, apparently, *me*).

"I can't go," I mumbled, staring at the ground. I noted with detachment that it was in desperate need of a good sweeping. Dust and dirt gathered in the cracks between stones like a grout of filth.

"Why not?" he demanded. "Princess Talina, do not, I repeat, do not ask me to witness your execution. You are one of my oldest friends, and I won't abide by it. Let me help you."

"I can't," I said, forcing myself to meet his eye. "If I leave now—"

"Valeria will be fine!" he howled, throwing his arms up. "It's *you* I'm worried about. If the Tocchians finds out who you are—"

The door swung open behind us. Avens and I both gasped, leaping away from each other.

Marius sauntered through the door, like it was completely normal for a prince to spend time in what I now realized was probably a scribe's office.

"*Tocchia* is already aware," Marius said, straightening his cloak around his shoulders. He didn't make eye contact with either one of us. "Or, well, part of it is."

Avens took a protective step toward me. "Look, we can work something out—"

"We don't *need* to work anything out," said Marius, with pained patience. "Listen, it's not—" He massaged his temple with ringed fingers and frowned. "May I talk to Princess Talina alone, please?"

I was shocked at his civility. The last few times he'd seen me with Avens, he looked ready to punch a wall.

"I don't think that's a good idea," said Avens firmly, chest puffing out.

Something in Marius's eyes flashed. But when he spoke, his tone was calm, civil. "Listen, I'm not going to hurt anyone, I promise. I would *also* very much like to find a solution to this dilemma."

Avens glanced between us, appalled. "You didn't," he said to me, wide-eyed and disbelieving.

I winced. "I might have."

Marius, for his part, kept his usually expressive face flat. "She definitely did."

Avens took a slow, measured breath. "Right, then," he said. "Seems I'm not needed here. Come find me if you change your mind," he said. With a nod and a twitch, he was off, through the heavy wooden door and down the hall.

"Avens!" I cried, starting after him, but he was already gone, flashing around the corner.

Marius stood behind me, wearing a pained expression. "Sorry," he said. "I shouldn't have—"

My chest heaved with anger. "You're right! You shouldn't have! He was just trying to help!"

"Yes, and I actually do appreciate that," said Marius, face softening. "If worst came to worst, I know he wouldn't abandon you."

"It's a flaw," I sighed, and leaned my hip against a desk piled high with papers. "What do you want?"

"Mostly, I wanted to know if you were alright. Then I saw you go into a room with the bard, and I—well, I wanted to know why."

Wait. Was he jealous? Had he truly not realized? "Yes, well, I'd follow Avens anywhere. We're old friends and he's not interested, if you know what I mean."

"Um, yes," said Marius, glancing down at the ground. "I realize that. Listen, I'm sorry, I ought to have just asked you about it later."

"You should have." I glared at him. "I need to get back to work."

Marius gave a stiff nod. "I'll see you tonight?"

"Yes," I said. A part of me was angry enough to consider not showing up, but I knew I'd regret it later, when our interactions were even more limited.

"Alright, then," he said, lips twitching in a grim imitation of a smile. "I look forward to it."

I left, eager to return to work. But the day dragged on. I fretted after Avens. Conjured fantasy after fantasy of all the ways my father's arrival could go wrong. He might see me as I tried to hide. Might wage war for my custody. Might abandon me to Tocchia's whims as punishment for leaving him.

Now matter how badly he wanted to, Marius might not be able to protect me. I thought of the dungeons and a tremble reached all the way to my bones.

Maybe it would be better to run away with Avens. Perhaps I still could. Marius might help us, if reluctantly.

I spent the day fighting back tears, reeling from possibility to possibility as I gathered laundry and emptied chamber pots and prepared the guest rooms. Which rooms would belong to my brothers? Which was King Amonrew's? If I sprayed their favorite perfumes on the pillows, or placed a vase of my favorite pink peonies on the bureau, would they know that I'd been there?

That evening, I helped Ria prepare for bed. "Did you know?" I asked, selecting a nightgown from her wardrobe. "That they were coming?"

She shook her head. "No. It was a shock to me, too." When she looked at me, her eyes were wet. "What will you do?"

I shrugged. "I don't know. Avens thinks I should hide out in the city for a few days."

Ria nodded. "I could arrange the coin for you."

My heart thundered in my chest. Words formed on my tongue and grew stale there. Finally, I managed to say, "Should I—should I simply... tell everyone?"

At Ria's expression, I knew I'd made a mistake. "No!" she hissed. "Have you gone mad? Tocchia will think you're a spy!"

I slumped onto the bed. "You're right," I said. "You're right. But what if I pledged my loyalty? Do you think they'd accept me then?"

Ria ducked behind her changing screen, nightgown in hand. "If they did, you probably wouldn't like the terms."

"Good point." I fell back onto the bedspread and kicked my feet off the floor. "But they already knew I was from Olmstead. Why would it matter if I just lied a little about who I was?"

"They have more authority over a servant," Ria explained. "A princess? Under these circumstances? They'll want you punished. Exiled, at absolute best."

Exiled. The word carved itself into my heart one stinging letter at a time. I hadn't been in Tocchia long, but I hated to be banished. My stomach turned into a mess of knots. I'd miss the sea, the fields, the mountain view, even Liridin as it drifted through the sky and cast its massive shadow. "I don't want that, either."

"Yes, well, that would probably be the best outcome for you," said Ria, ever the realist.

"So you think I should hide?"

Ria's head popped out from behind the screen. "Yes. That's *exactly* what I think you should do."

~

TWO NIGHTS LATER, I found Marius pacing before the altar. Back and forth like a caged beast, teeth gritted.

The nighttime air was hot and swampy, even in the Star Room, which was always chillier than the rest of the castle. (Probably because it wasn't *actually* in the castle. Marius refused to confirm or deny its location, but I had my suspicions.)

"Princess Talina," he greeted, spinning to face me.

Our last meeting had gone as I expected. Marius was tense, I was exhausted, and we spent the entire night trying to amplify his visions. I suspected he must have been successful, because he looked haunted when he sat up, and quietly asked me to leave. I was too tired to do anything other than oblige, though I hated to abandon him. We had mere days left together. Afterward. I'd be in hiding, and he'd be wedded to my sister, and then what? Would we still see each other?

It was unfathomable to think that I'd never feel his embrace again. I could not bear to part from him. If we ended things, it would surely devastate me.

But what else could we do?

"Prince Marius," I replied, lifting my chin, smiling politely.

Something in his expression eased. "I've missed you," he said. But he did not come to embrace me. "I would like to talk. About something rather serious. Care to join me in the study?"

"Must we be serious?" I quipped, stepping up to him, hoping to crack his facade.

A grimace strained his face. "I'm afraid so, my lady. Would you follow me?"

Dread built in my stomach like foul rot. I took his hand, and joined him in the study, where he continued to pace. I sat in a chair, hoping he might follow my lead, but he was lost in his worry, stalking from one end of the room to the next.

"I have a proposition," he said, glancing toward me, then out the window. "It is… completely and utterly mad. Dare I say kingdom-shattering." He twisted the ring on his index finger. "But I would be remiss not to suggest it."

My jaw dropped. I hurried to close it, to keep from gaping like a fool. *Kingdom-shattering?* What insanity had he concocted? "Don't keep me in suspense," I said, adjusting my skirts, praying that he wouldn't say anything traitorous. Nothing that could land us in worse trouble than we were already in. I waited with bated breath for him to parse out the words.

His hands clenched and unclenched. He glanced again to the window, as if half-tempted to leap from it, and then turned back to me. The long line of his body was silhouetted by moonlight. Beneath his cloak, I could barely make out his lithe form. "I… am under the impression," he began, taking deep breaths between words. "That you are, definitely, absolutely of royal blood. Am I correct in that?"

Oh. Oh no. "There are rumors," I said, letting my gaze drift to the wall. Shame flooded me like poison. "That I am not King Amonrew's daughter."

A muscle twitched in his jaw. "And your mother?"

"She was a northern islander. Desmink." I shifted uncomfortably. "They do things differently there, but she was a princess, if that's what you mean."

"So it's uncertain," said Marius. He was halfway to madness—eyes too bright, movements too sharp, jaw constantly tightening so that the muscles in his neck corded out. He paced the length of the room.

"My father has always insisted that I am of his blood. I don't think he would have defended me if he doubted my mother's loyalty," I said. "It's just—my hair—"

Marius nodded. "I'm familiar with the rumors. They're the reason my father decided I was to marry Princess Valeria. But if you have royal blood... If you're certain..."

"Yes," I said, nodding. I wanted to smooth the lines from his face, but I was afraid to distract him. Whatever he had to say, I wanted to hear it. "As far as I know."

"Then it doesn't really matter if there's a public dispute," said Marius, turning a corner, and facing me once more. His brow was furrowed, his mouth tight. "In theory, if you wanted to—" He inhaled. And inhaled again. And again, until I feared that his lungs would burst. Then he coughed, blinked rapidly. "I'm sorry," he said, falling into the chair opposite me. "I'm afraid I've lost my mettle."

"It's alright," I told him, too confused to say anything else. An idea picked at the edges of my mind like a crow at a carcass, but I couldn't quite grasp it.

"We could..." He coughed, sat up. Caught my eye. He burned

with a feverish intensity. "*We* could marry. If you wanted. It would be the scandal of the ages, but, well, no one could really contest it. I'd pass on my inheritance to a member of the Olmsteadian royal family, as intended. Of course, you'd have to keep the ring until we figured out what to do with it, although I'm told it's rather more pleasant once it's found its new owner. But I wouldn't blame you at all—Gods, I'm babbling. I mean, you probably aren't shocked, this is by far the worst proposal—actually, *second* worst proposal—"

The buzzing in my ears drowned him out. My heart sprinted in my chest. A mixture of panic and frantic joy gripped me. I had not dared to think that Marius might consider me as a real possibility. I thought I'd be nothing more than the occasional dalliance, hidden away in the night, neatly tucked away by morning. Valeria was the reasonable choice. Anyone would choose her over me.

If I agreed to marry Marius, all my disguises would fall away. No longer would I have to weave a web of lies. I could just be Talina, for the first time in my life. Not a suspected bastard, or a struggling artificer, or a maid.

But a crown was a hat like all the others, and I'd have to wrap my identity around it. If I went home to Olmstead, I'd likely marry into a lower station. If I married Marius, I'd one day be queen. I could wake up beside him, curl around him at night, sit beside him in the library, walk with him in the gardens, travel to new realms...

...and bear the burden of the ring, the war that brewed on the horizon, and hundreds of other royal duties, which I'd always been glad to avoid.

Marius had stopped talking. His eyes were glued to my face.

Shock numbed me, made me clumsy and weak. I breathed out, in. I should say something. Questions swept about my skull like clams caught in a tide, but none of them made it to my mouth.

"Listen," said Marius, now panicked. "We don't have to—"

"Wait," I said, holding out my hand. "Wait. I-I have questions."

"Oh," he said, looking down at the floor. "Questions. Yes. I can handle questions."

In an effort to quell his panic, I stretched out my leg and placed the toe of my boot over his. "I'm not saying no," I promised. "But won't the King be angry?"

Marius scratched the back of his neck and frowned as he considered this. "I think there will be more than one angry king," he said. "But my father can't protest too much. The ring would be passed on, according to tradition." He nodded, more to himself than to me. "Ultimately, it would be allowed."

I wasn't quite ready to trust him, but he had a better idea than I did about what was acceptable in Tocchia. "What about Valeria?"

He swallowed, gave a miserable shrug. "I don't know. I imagine she has other prospects."

"She does," I said, thinking of all the princes and counts and dukes who had inquired to her over the years. "But that doesn't mean she won't be hurt."

"I am not even entirely sure she likes me," said Marius softly. "I think she tolerates me. But I fear she would grow to despise me." He crossed his long legs at the ankles and stared out the window. "We never connected like I'd hoped we might. I would like for her to be happy. And I would like that for myself as well, if I'm perfectly honest. But you're right. I don't want to hurt her. If our marriage were broken off, I imagine she would be compensated for her time, although I understand that won't change her feelings on the matter."

No, I imagined it wouldn't. I sighed, head hanging. Was there no way for both of us to be happy?

"My father will be furious," I said, raising my head at last. Marius's eyes were red. A muscle in his jaw shivered.

"I can't imagine it would change his plans drastically. One daughter would still marry a prince. Valeria may yet, as well. Just not *this* prince." He gestured to himself.

"There's nothing I want more," I said finally. "But we should plan this carefully."

"Yes, of course," he said. "We've only a few days before our cover is blown, but I'm sure we can work this out." He grinned at me, but his eyes were wet. "So does that mean...?"

I thought I'd be happier to accept his proposal. Elated, even. But tears sprang to my eyes, too, as I stood on wobbly legs and deposited myself into his lap like bad news. "Yes," I said, draping my arms around him. "I want to marry you."

"Good," said Marius, relaxing for the first time. His arms wrapped around me, pulled me close. I buried my face in his shoulder and inhaled the scent there. Pine, and something musty, like old books. Even through his clothes, I felt the beating of his heart, strong and sure. "I-I want to marry you, too. I could say more, but I should probably shut up, shouldn't I?"

"Yes," I growled, only half-playful. I drew back to glare at him. "We can talk more later. Right now, I'd rather you kissed me."

"Oh, gladly," he said, leaning in until his lips were only inches from mine. Wet droplets sparkled on his long lashes, left tracks of his high cheekbones. Even in tears, he was exquisite, closer to an artist's rendition than a flesh and blood human being. "My lady. My love. My—"

I closed the gap and devoured his words. Our kiss was salty, punctuated by the occasional wet laugh. Neither one of could stop crying, or giggling, and I was thrilled to be in his arms, knowing I was wanted, I was chosen, I was safe. If everything worked out, I'd have no fear of losing him, or of a life spent on the run.

But it was too early to celebrate. If only I could convince my foolish, fragile heart.

"I'VE A PLAN," said Marius, the next day. The Northern Lights flickered and wove above us, stretching and bending like a musician's fingers. "It's admittedly a little risky, but I think it could work."

I tore my gaze from the ceiling to his face. We'd only just made our way into the Star Room, and I was still tired, not yet energized by any of our usual midnight activities. "Risky?"

"Well, admittedly, this entire endeavor is risky," he shrugged. "I don't believe we'll be punished—I've checked the laws, and so long as my father and stepmother don't break them, we should be fine—but our reputations will be marred. If Father is spectacularly upset, I may be forced to forfeit my claim to the throne to Gavin, which is honestly no great loss. I think I should be a little aimless, but I wouldn't be disowned, exactly. I'm sure I could find something to do with myself, and you—you've no real interest in ruling? I've never heard you mention it."

"It wasn't an option before," I reminded him. "But no. Not really. I've always thought it seemed dull. And like a great responsibility." I mulled over his words. *Not disowned.* Did that mean we would be ousted from the palace? Perhaps to another estate?

Or thrown to the wide world like a handful of ashes?

"Good enough. I wanted to be sure," said Marius. "I don't think we could be exiled, or anything so serious." He sighed and plopped down on the altar like an old man collapsing after a long day in the fields. "I plan to speak to my father the night prior to King Amonrew's arrival. I will inform him of the situation. It will be an ordeal, of course, but—" He inhaled sharply. "—that will be that."

"Should I come with you?" I asked, following him to the altar. He made no move to stop me, and scooted over to make room, so I sat gingerly. It was exactly as uncomfortable as it looked, and I wondered how he could lie here so long, on this literal stone slab, like a sacrifice waiting for death.

"Do you want to?" he asked, turning to look at me. Pale lashes framed wide, wild eyes.

"If you think it would help."

"I think it would help *me*," he said, nodding. But his lips pressed into a thin line, and I saw his worry even before the little wrinkle appeared between his eyebrows.

"Then I'll go with you," I said, before he could reconsider. My hand found his, and our fingers laced together.

"Good," he said, kissing me softly. "I'd be glad to have you."

CHAPTER 31

The palace was ablaze with energy. It was the day before King Amonrew's arrival, and servants flitted around like flies, tidying corners, setting up last minute rooms, preparing endless feasts.

All day long, my hands shook. There were a million ways this could go wrong, and I was wholly unprepared for every single one of them. I could not even look Ria in the eye.

For all that I loved her fiercely, I also desperately loved Marius. Watching them eat their breakfasts side by side, I feared that there was no way I could keep both of them.

Last night, both Ria and Avens pleaded with me to hide in the city. I shook my head each time, stubbornly determined to stay until Marius met with King Hergarv. Neither could understand it. Ria cried. Avens swore to stand by until the last possible moment, ready and willing to skip the wedding and run, should I change my mind.

Inspired by their fears, I packed the essentials, prepared to flee if things went badly. I hid the bag under my bed and hoped no one looked at it too closely.

I was faint with anxiety. It would be too easy to lose my footing, or to drop something irreplaceable, so I clung to even the feather duster with white knuckles and watched every step like a dancer in a competition. By the end of the day, I was exhausted, depleted by panic.

After dinner, I followed Ria up to her rooms. Tension built in my shoulders, my chest. I knew even before she spoke what she would say. Regret writhed within me like a beast caught in a bear-trap, desperate to escape.

I dug through her wardrobe in search of a nightgown, my hands trembling with such force that I nearly tore the fabric as I ripped the dress free from its hook.

"Talina," Ria said, her voice tight. She pulled the dress from my hands, and laid it on her bedspread, then turned to face me. For the first time, I noticed that her lips were bitten and raw. "Please. Just go with Avens. He can make sure you're safe."

"I'll decide at midnight," I told her, the same line I'd repeated all week. "I promise."

"I'm afraid for you," she said, chewing on her lip, eyes meeting mine. Unshed tears shined there, and I shifted guiltily.

"I know," I said. "I just—I can't decide."

"What decision is there?" Ria groaned, pulling the pins loose from her hair so that it tumbled around her shoulders. "You need to go. Go be happy. Free. Away from this place."

"I don't hate it here," I reminded her, but she only shook her head.

"You should. It's full of miserable people. A miserable king, a miserable queen, a miserable future husband..."

"What about Princess Odalla? And Prince Gavin?" I'd seen Ria interact with Gavin plenty, especially at meals, where he told jokes that left most of us unaffected. But Ria stifled her laughter and lowered her gaze. If they weren't friends, they were at least friend*ly*.

"Oh, they're all right, I suppose. But you shouldn't stay here. It isn't worth the risk, Talina." Her hands grasped mine. "Please."

"I'll think about it," I promised, and left for the night, my knees so weak that I nearly collapsed outside her door.

On shaking legs, I waited for Marius in the library. Two hours before midnight, he said. Later than I usually met him, but that was all right. If it meant that our plan had even the slightest chance of working…

But he didn't appear. I fought the urge to search the library, to scour between shelves until I found some trace of him.

Only grim determination kept me from panicking. I sat primly, pretending to read. There was no way I could focus right now. Not when the words blurred before my eyes, and my pounding heart drowned out my thoughts.

It was nearly midnight when Fallamor found me. He strode between shelves, long braid draped over his shoulder. In the oppressive summer heat, he wore breeches, a flowing shirt, and little else. While Marius always slinked around in a hooded cloak after dark, Fallamor looked like he belonged on a beach.

I was surprised to see him. As far as I knew, he'd left to convene with his people and hadn't yet returned.

When he spotted me, he hurried over. There was a strange urgency to his normally unflappable demeanor. "Miss Arina," he said, voice low, eyes flashing. "Come with me. Quickly, please."

I leapt to my feet as though spring-loaded. "What is it? What's happened?"

"Keep your voice down," he whispered. "And nothing yet."

"Then why follow you? I promised Mar-*someone* that I would meet him here," I said.

"*Someone* is in a spot of trouble," said Fallamor, reaching for my hand. "I think it's best if you aren't easily accessible."

Reluctantly, I followed Fallamor downstairs, out the library door, and across the hall. We dipped into the alcove beside a staircase, where he searched along the stone wall, pressing and prodding at individual bricks until a *click!* sounded. There came a faint grinding, and then a rectangle of wall sprang out, roughly the size of a coffin. I yelped and jumped away, then realized it was only a door. Another hidden passageway.

Unfazed, Fallamor yanked on the door until it swung open on ancient, creaking hinges, revealing a long, cavernous hallway.

"In here," he said, gesturing. "Quickly."

"It's dark," I protested, but strong hands shoved me into the shadows. I shrieked. Fallamor pushed his way in behind me, and the door closed. My old fear of attack or imprisonment flared to life, and I fought down panic. I trusted Fallamor, even if I was afraid of being trapped in a tight, dark passage.

"It's alright," he said. His voice echoed in the tunnel, which was black as a void. "I promise. Listen, we're just going to hide in here for a little bit, all right? Marius knows where to find us."

I shivered like a wet dog. "What's going on? Why won't you tell me anything?"

"Because I don't know anything!" he snarled. I recoiled. He'd never spoked to me like that before. Gone was his familiar gentle mockery, his even-keel tone. Right now, he sounded one inconvenience away from punching something. *Hopefully not me,* I thought, and took a step away from him. "I only arrived last night. Marius more or less confessed that he'd gone completely mad, and then he asked me to look after you if he was intercepted. Which he was," Fallamor grumbled.

My stomach dropped. "Intercepted? How?"

"I don't know," Fallamor groaned. "All I know is that he was summoned to meet with the king earlier than scheduled, and he never reappeared."

"What does that mean?"

"Could mean anything. He might be taking tea. He might be having a lovely meeting with his father. Or he could be in the dungeons. I was sent to remove *you* from danger, not him."

The dungeons. Gods, how could we be so stupid? How could Marius have believed his father would listen to us? And I'd fallen for it all!

"Shit," I said. Tears poured down my face. "Shit, shit, shit."

"It doesn't have to mean anything," said Fallamor gently. "Come on, follow me. If we take this passage, there's a nice little hidden room. We can go there, alright?"

"Alright," I whined. Using the wall to guide me, I trailed after him. I tripped twice on the uneven floor but managed to keep my balance. *Probably a good thing,* I surmised. I didn't want to know what sorts of creatures populated this passage, and I certainly didn't want to find out firsthand. When we reached the end of the tunnel, Fallamor pulled a lever, and another door opened.

The room revealed might've been cozy if it weren't so dusty. An artificial moon hovered in the air, illuminating two armchairs, a cabinet of weapons (two swords and a rather brutal-looking mace), and a table with an ancient set of Troop. Carved from wood, it was halfway to rotten. If I scraped my fingernails over the pieces, they would surely disintegrate.

"Guess no one has used this in a little while," Fallamor said, patting one of the armchairs. Dust flew.

I glanced around. "Whose room was this? How do you know about it?"

"Centuries ago, this was Princess Prella's room." He shrugged. "And I only know about it because Marius showed me."

I exhaled. Maybe Fallamor *had* brought me here to imprison me, but I had no real reason to distrust him. I sat in one of the dusty chairs, and a cloud erupted around me. By the time I left this place, I'd be grey as a ghost. "Thank you," I said.

My sword was stowed carefully under my bed, but I wore a knife strapped to my thigh. Marius warned me that it might be considered an act of aggression if I brought a weapon to our meeting with the king, so I begrudgingly left it behind, and reached instead for my thigh sheath. I'd not be left defenseless in an emergency.

The knife was pinched between my leg and the chair, but I

made no move to adjust it. What use was a secret weapon if it wasn't a secret?

"You're welcome," said Fallamor, sighing. He flopped into a chair as though he hadn't seen the layers of grime. The chair screeched, wood and nails threatening to pull free, and Fallamor tensed as if expecting it to collapse. When that didn't happen, he looked me in the eye, and said, "Marius tells me you're Princess Talina. Is that true?"

The blood drained from my face. I forced myself to whisper, "Yes."

"I see," he murmured, gaze growing distant. "What a foolish endeavor," he said, almost to himself. When he spoke again, it was with uncharacteristic severity. "Marius also told me he wants to marry you."

I was too exhausted to do anything other than nod. "I know. It's mad."

"It *is* mad," said Fallamor, rubbing at his temples. The chair squealed in time with his movements, and he scowled. "But life is short. If you find someone you want to spend your life with, you should certainly try." His smile was strained. "But it's harder when certain expectations are in place."

"I know," I groaned, leaning my head back. "All of this was probably a mistake."

"Don't lose hope," said Fallamor, though I sensed he only said this for my benefit. Something about his expression told me that he didn't really believe the words coming from his mouth. "If this is what Marius wants, then I'm going to trust that it's what's best for him. And you. Even if I'm, well, skeptical."

"Thank you," I said. "I was surprised to learn that he was serious, but I suppose I shouldn't have. He has no qualms chasing what he wants." I couldn't keep the note of pride from my voice. Somehow, Marius wanted me back.

Fallamor rolled his eyes. "Princess Talina, I regret to inform you that the only reason he spent so much time with Princess

Valeria was because he was absolutely enamored with you, and had no idea what else to do."

A blush came to my cheeks. "I thought he hoped to change Valeria's mind about him."

Shrugging, Fallamor said, "Maybe initially. But he's woefully transparent. You should've seen the way he looked for you every time he entered a room." A pause. "He told me about the visions. The boring ones, he calls them."

My face flushed. "How long have you known?"

"About as long as I've known you're a princess. So about an hour," he quipped.

I squirmed uncomfortably. I had nothing to say to that. No apology seemed quite adequate. I'd lied to everyone, and it would take time to earn back trust. If I was given the opportunity at all.

We lapsed into silence. Fallamor was not the chattiest companion on the best of days, and I was too worried about Marius to hold a conversation. More than once, Fallamor tried to distract me, but I couldn't let go of the mental image of Marius sitting on a frozen floor, hunched in the darkness.

There were no windows in our little sanctuary. I flashed back to my time in the dungeon, in the oppressive dark and cold, with no window and no escape—

I must've gone pale, because Fallamor took one look at me, and demanded, "What's wrong?"

I twisted my hands in my lap. "It reminds me of the dungeons."

"Why? Because it's dark?"

"Because I'm trapped," I said, voice small.

So Fallamor showed me how to leave the room, revealing a lever hidden behind a shelf. It turned with a deafening screech, but I felt relieved as the door inched open. I could manage a few levers, and a dark passage. I wasn't a prisoner here.

Not yet, anyway.

As soon as I'd proven I could wrench the rusty lever on my own, Fallamor said, "I should see what's going on. I'll be back soon. Stay here, alright? Promise me. I won't leave you any longer than necessary."

"I promise," I said, even though I had no intention of staying any longer than I had to. If the room grew too oppressive, I'd flee in an instant, even if I still wasn't entirely sure what I was hiding from. The wrath of King Hergarv? Nosy onlookers? "Hurry back."

"I promise," echoed Fallamor. The passageway ground shut behind him.

I sat in tense silence. Minutes dragged past. The room seemed to grow smaller and smaller until I finally closed my eyes and drew my knees to my chest.

Fallamor would not betray me. Marius trusted him.

But Marius was in trouble. Something was wrong. I felt it in my bones, reverberating like a siren's cry.

An hour passed, perhaps longer. Then came the telltale grinding.

I pulled my knife from its sheath. I'd not be caught off guard. I'd examined the cabinet of weapons near the door and found no way to open it without breaking the glass. If I needed to, I wouldn't hesitate, but I didn't want to ruin an antique cabinet without good cause.

Footsteps echoed down the hall. My ears strained, but I only detected one set of footsteps. *Good.*

The lever squealed, and the stone door creaked open. Fallamor appeared. Blood streaked from his eyebrow to his hairline, and his braid was disheveled.

"It's fine," he said quickly, gesturing at the open door behind him. "I fell in the hallway. There's no fighting. Not yet, anyway."

I slipped behind the chair and stowed my knife where Fallamor couldn't see beneath my skirts.

"Going to stab me, were you?"

"I wasn't taking chances," I said primly, smoothing my skirts. "What's going on?"

"Another messenger fell from the sky," said Fallamor. He

rubbed at his forehead as if trying to clear away the faint lines there. "Everyone has been summoned to the War Room. Except me, apparently." His lips thinned into a line. "It appears news of my arrival has not yet reached the king."

"Oh," I said, throat tightening in trepidation. There was no way for Marius and I to run our proposition past King Hergarv now. Father would arrive tomorrow, and he would see me, and—

I couldn't speak. I gasped like someone on the verge of drowning, and I couldn't stop.

"Princess Talina," said Fallamor, stepping closer. Warm hands settled on my shoulders. "It's all right. Here, breathe with me: inhale, hold, hold, alright, now exhale nice and slow…"

I followed his instructions as best I could, but I was lightheaded and terrified. Fallamor guided me to a chair, where I sat with my head lowered, trying to regain control of myself. "I have to flee," I said, when my breaths had evened out, and my pulse had slowed. "King Amonrew—"

It was Fallamor's turn to pale. "I've an idea about that," he said. "But you probably won't like it."

"Tell me," I begged, and he did.

He was right. I didn't like it.

CHAPTER 32

Marius, Fallamor, Toral, and I crowded into the Star Room with only hours to spare before dawn.

Pain knocked at my temples. Exhaustion ate away at my peripherals. Marius's hand was cold in mine, but his firm grip was grounding.

The Northern Lights shifted above us. The globes of light, drifting lazily, brightened as they sensed us.

Toral gasped aloud, his dark eyes flitting from the shimmering stars to the aquamarine pillars. "I had no idea this room existed."

"Well, it's a secret," said Marius, turning in a circle as he gestured broadly around us. "So don't tell anyone."

Fallamor, too, was mesmerized, stunned by the ceiling, the lights, the gemstones. "I'd heard of this place," he said. "But I never envisioned it like this."

"You've heard of it?" said Toral, eyebrows leaping in surprise.

"From Marius," said Fallamor. He raised one shoulder up and down. "Hardly anything scandalous."

"I feel left out," Toral pouted.

"Don't," said Fallamor. "He was incoherently drunk when he

told me. Afterward, I had to drag his ass to bed, and he threw up on my shoes."

I bit back a laugh.

"Thanks for reminding me," Marius said, rolling his eyes. "Sorry about your shoes."

"Gods." Toral spun to face Marius and I, still hand in hand. "Are you two sure you want to do this?"

"Yes," I said, glancing quickly at Marius.

"Yes," he echoed. He gave my hand an affectionate squeeze and returned my gaze with such fondness that the most strained parts of me finally start to relax.

"And you're sure you can grant us clemency if King Amonrew retaliates?"

Marius nodded. "I doubt he would dare alienate his allies over this, but yes, I can. Besides," he shrugged. "If two witnesses sign the contract, the marriage is legally binding, and they can't dissent it."

I was a bit short of breath at that. *Legally binding. Contract.* Gods, this was real.

Fallamor looked unconvinced but remained silent.

"Then by all means," said Toral. His great wings flexed and caught the air as he walked. Starlight glittered on their glossy surface. "Let's begin."

Prince Marius produced the familiar box from his pocket. Its energy practically pulsed throughout the room. He set it on the altar and turned to me. "You're sure you want to do this?"

I nodded. Though my heart threatened to beat free of my chest, I knew I would regret it if we didn't try. The whole thing was wildly impulsive, but neither Toral nor Fallamor tried to talk us out of it. Both seemed to understand that there was more at stake here than a torrid love affair. Regardless, they appeared to care for Marius a great deal, and I was grateful that they were so willing to help us commit what would surely become the scandal of the century.

"Gods," said Fallamor, stepping closer, neck craning to get a better look at the box. "I never expected that the ring would feel so… angry."

"It's always like that," said Marius, scratching the back of his neck. "And it will be until it's passed on."

"I'm eager to see if that changes," said Toral, wings folding neatly behind him as he leaned in to examine the box. "Will you be alright if it doesn't?" he asked me.

"I think so," I said, though I wasn't so certain. "I'll have to be."

"Every piece of literature I could get my hands on says that this won't be the case," Marius assured me. "I'd never hand it off to you if I weren't sure."

"I wouldn't accept it if I didn't trust you," I said, giving him a solemn little smile. Right, maybe that was a lie. I'd accept nearly *anything* if I thought it might earn us a little more time together, a few extra minutes before reality set in.

"So," said Fallamor to Toral, "am I reading the vows, or are you?"

My chest tightened. Vows. *My* wedding vows, exchanged in a dusty maid's uniform. Not what I'd wanted or expected, but there was no time. This was the best way to ensure that I wouldn't be imprisoned for espionage or worse, that Marius wouldn't be denied permission to marry me.

"By all means," said Toral, nodding to Fallamor. "You've officiated more weddings. You go ahead."

"Alright," said Fallamor, turning to face us. His braid hung lank over his shoulder. After brushing pieces of hair behind his ear, he straightened his shoulders, and said, "Are you ready?"

"Yes!" I said, voice barely above a whisper.

Marius looked to me. The light caught his cheekbones, illuminated the planes of his face like the ghostly subject of a painting. "I'm ready if you are," he said, dipping his chin, meeting my gaze with such warmth that my chest tightened.

I tried to smile, but my lip trembled with nerves. "Of course

I'm ready," I said, as firmly as I could. Shivering be damned, I clung to his arm.

That seemed to satisfy him. He pulled his hand from mine, wrapped his arm around my waist, and pulled me close.

"Fine," said Fallamor, briefly closing his eyes, as though mentally preparing to indulge our nonsense. "Then do you, Prince Marius Mentis Harel of Tocchia, take Princess Talina den Grauten of Olmstead as your beloved wife, to honor and respect, until the end of your days, or until one of you gets frustrated and shoves the other one out a window?"

A little laugh burst out of me. Marius caught Fallamor's eye, shook his head, gave a long-suffering sigh, and said, "I do."

"Are the window clauses customary?" I asked.

"No, but they are necessary," said Toral with a mischievous glint in his eye. "Trust me. I've known Marius long enough."

"I'd never shove you out a window," said Marius quickly, grasping my hand firmly in his. "I should've disputed—"

Fallamor flipped his braid over his shoulder and narrowed his eyes. "Do you want to be married or not?"

"Yes," I said, instantly at attention.

"Then I'd like to continue, please. Do you, Princess Talina, take Prince Marius as your beloved husband, to honor and respect and possibly shove out a window, until the end of your days?"

"Yes," I said, a little breathless. "I do."

"And do you accept the burden of this ring, to keep in the custody of the den Grauten family for the next hundred years?"

Blood roared in my ears. This was what I was really afraid of. That ring, furious and reeking of death, eternally encircling my finger. This would be no token from the man I loved, but a curse. One that I was determined to bear. Even if Marius assured me that it wouldn't stay like that, I would never be able to forget the way that it felt now, sullen and repugnant.

"I do," I whispered.

"Excellent," said Fallamor, waving a hand. "You may kiss, and all of that."

"*Not* all of that," amended Toral with a knowing smirk. It cut through his sharp features, added a roguish charm to his dour exterior.

"I wouldn't invite you two to watch, anyway," said Marius, turning to me. Though outwardly at ease, a muscle twitched in his jaw, and he carried tension in his shoulders.

But his eyes held a brilliant warmth and affection, a fathomless desire that sent heat flaring in my belly.

I rose up on my tiptoes, closed my eyes, and kissed him. Full on the mouth, but brief. I ached when we parted.

"Now for the hard part," said Toral. From his pocket, he produced a simple dagger. No jewels encrusted the hilt, only a simple carving of leaves and thorns.

Marius nodded, swallowed hard, and opened the box.

I choked down my anxiety like a foul elixir and held out my hand.

"Ready?" said Toral, looking first at Marius, then at me.

"Never better," said Marius, words wavering in a way that suggested he had definitely been better. With the resolve of a soldier off to battle, he held out his arm.

Toral took his hand. For the first time, I noticed the dark stains in the box's lining. A shiver darted down my spine.

The tip of the dagger drove into Marius's fingertip. He winced. Blood dribbled free, pooling in the center of the ring's empty prongs.

Toral released his arm. Marius dabbed at the wound with one of the many kerchiefs he'd taken to carrying around. I went to examine the extent of the damage, but Toral shook his head at me. "Your turn, Princess."

Aflame with apprehension, I extended my arm. The dagger, tipped red with Marius's blood, pricked the pad of my finger, and drew a slit. Blood welled in the cut.

"Sorry," said Toral. "I know it hurts." He squeezed my finger. Blood dripped free, falling like rain, where it mingled with Marius's. A wayward droplet stained the bone band and joined the splatters on the blue lining.

My breath caught in my throat. Not because of the pain, which was nothing substantial, but because of the way our mixed blood began to *move*. At first, I thought it was merely congealing. Then it gained the consistency of gelatin. Still red and gleaming, it wriggled and writhed like a sentient creature, and then slowly formed a sphere. In horrified fascination, I watched as the lumps smoothed over. The blood hardened into something solid and jewel-like.

I stared, fascinated by the ruby-red stone that now rested in the center of the ring. Even the band shifted, its color paling into something reminiscent of silver. For the first time, I noticed the delicate carvings along the outside of the band—a pattern of leaves and flowers.

Even its terrible aura had faded into something nearly undetectable. Its pulse weakened.

It was beautiful and deadly and suddenly I was far, far less opposed to wearing it.

At my side, Marius was tense. He'd tried to push a kerchief at me, but I was so distracted by the changing ring that I hardly noticed. I was only dimly aware that he'd grabbed my hand and started applying pressure to the cut. His grip softened, nearly lapsed, as he, too, was drawn in by the spectacle before us.

Someone, either Fallamor or Toral, let out a gasp.

"Fuck," said Marius in a choked voice.

"It's magnificent," I said, unable to tear my gaze away. "How does *that* work? Who made this? Is there any record of the spell?" I was afraid to touch it but couldn't tear my eyes away.

"It's a shame you were never in a guild," said Marius, sighing. "Absolute cruelty."

I ignored him. I was lucky that Father let me anywhere near

the forge, let alone allowed me to study under Cranz. Perhaps, one day, I might be able to do more than just enchant pebbles in my spare time, but I wasn't confident enough to do more than hope. Even with my new husband beside me, I couldn't fully grasp the concept of freedom. I was still trapped in my father's iron grip, twisting and screaming.

Fallamor shot me a confused glance, but neither of us bothered to explain.

Toral cleared his throat. "You still have to transfer the ring, Marius."

"Oh, yes," said Marius, straightening his spine, and stepping forward. "Well, this is rather less hideous than I expected, actually. It's almost pretty." With a trembling hand, he grasped the box, and slowly, gently extricated the ring from its slot. In his fingers, it looked nearly dainty, like something crafted by an artisan rather than vengeful gods.

Flashing a brittle grin, Marius slipped the ring onto my finger.

I expected to feel something. A flare of devastation. A rumble of anger. But there was nothing, just the odd sensation of polished bone against my skin.

Marius withdrew his hand cautiously, as if afraid that the ring would combust. But nothing happened.

I examined my finger, turning my hand this way and that. Stars reflected in the scarlet sphere and shined upon the band so that it nearly glowed.

"It's surprisingly nice," said Toral, watching me. The stars glimmered in his dark eyes, too, like a vision of the night sky.

Fallamor pursed his lips.

"I think it worked," said Marius. Disbelief lingered in his voice.

The ring glittered on my finger, solid evidence of our union, our devotion. "It did."

Toral produced a slip of paper. A marriage certificate, I realized, squinting. A scribe's neat handwriting filled the page, save for a few blank spaces where the four of us signed our names. I was half-giddy as I wrote my name beside Marius's.

"Great," said Fallamor. "Now remember, don't blame any of this on us."

Any joy I felt was quickly stamped out by reality.

Ria would soon find out I betrayed her. The King and Queen would learn that we had deceived them. No matter what I told myself, I was wholly unprepared for the consequences.

"I would never," said Marius, crossing his arms. "Thank you, eternally, for bearing witness to our union."

"And now kindly fuck off," Toral joked.

Marius pretended to consider this, and said, "Yes, actually. I would like one night with my wife, so if you don't mind—"

"Fine, fine," said Toral, turning toward the door. He stalked forward with the determination of a king. For the first time, I saw the weight of his role in his posture, his movements. Acting as regent must have exhausted him, but he carried himself with the air of a ruler. *Back to the war room,* I thought, and wondered why he even bothered with our little ceremony when his people were being struck down like clay pigeons. "I can see myself out."

"Wait for me," called Fallamor, trailing after him with all the urgency of someone taking an evening stroll through the gardens.

When they were gone, I turned to grin at Marius. Jumped into his willing arms, and pressed my lips to his neck, his jaw, his perfect lips. "We did it," I gasped, overwhelmed by a sudden swell of emotion. "We actually did it."

"We did," he agreed, kissing me back fiercely. A hand roamed down my back. "I was afraid—"

"Me, too," I said, loosing a tiny squeak when his hand found my right hip, and grabbed it playfully. "I thought it would go wrong, somehow."

"But it didn't," he said, his grasp moving from my backside to my hand, where the ring rested. "It worked. They can't argue against that. I was so afraid they wouldn't allow us to marry, but now it doesn't matter. We did it ourselves."

"No," I agreed, breathless. "The ring transformed. That means that it accepted us, right?" I really was King Amonrew's daughter. My fears of illegitimacy fled, leaving me giddy with relief.

"Right," he said, drawing me into another kiss, this one so slow and sensual that I couldn't help but soften against him. Heat enveloped me and raced to my core.

"Is now a bad time to mention that I love you?" I mumbled, face hot, heart pounding.

"Not at all," he said, holding me close, blue eyes alight with an adoration so deep that I thought I might fall in, and drown there. "In fact, I'd argue that it's the perfect—"

A distant clang.

Marius paused, head tilted toward the door. His embrace loosened.

There came the sound of footsteps charging down the passageway.

"Shit," said Marius, catching me by the arm, leading me behind the altar. "Get down."

"Surely it's just Toral and Fallamor?"

"I don't like the sound of it," Marius insisted. The lines of his body drew taut with tension as he watched the door. His hand pushed against my shoulder, and I finally ducked down beside him. Knife unsheathed, I waited.

A shout. A cacophony of footsteps, like a herd of frightened cattle.

The lever wrenched. The door flew open with a *bang!* and Valeria burst through it, her eyes wild, hair untamed, a livid twist to her lips.

Fallamor and Toral crashed into the Star Room behind her.

"Oh," I whispered, stomach flipping.

Something in Marius's expression shifted. In it, I saw a hint of regret, a smidge of embarrassment, but mostly, raw determination.

"Valeria," he said, rising from his position behind the altar. He stepped toward her, spine straight, pointed chin jutting out proudly. If he was remorseful, I saw no indication. "Welcome."

Ria was panting, her face so pale that even her lips were white. "I knew it," she hissed, looking right at me, still crouched behind the altar, knife in hand. "I fucking knew it."

Panic overcame me, forceful as a riptide. "Ria," I said. My knife clattered to the floor.

"Don't you dare," Ria growled, stalking toward me, teeth bared like a wild animal. "Don't you dare."

The ring slipped to my knuckle, suddenly loose around my finger. I didn't dare adjust it for fear of drawing her gaze. Would've torn it from my finger and flung it across the room if I thought it would soothe Ria's rage.

But the sight of the ring would only deepen the wound.

Marius stepped between us. "Valeria," he said, calm and businesslike, as if he were negotiating the price of wheat. "I hoped to have a conversation with you over breakfast."

"Breakfast?" Ria repeated. "As if we were discussing the weather?" Her glare returned to me. "What the fuck have you done, Talina? Is *he* the reason you won't leave?"

I flinched. My mouth opened, but I couldn't find the words.

"Yes," said Marius evenly, crossing his arms over his chest. "I asked her not to."

Fallamor and Toral stood behind Valeria, their faces stony, their shoulders squared. I wondered how many weapons they had hidden in their clothes (and if they'd dare draw them).

I wondered how many Ria had. If she'd thought to bring one at all.

"Perhaps this is not a conversation that should wait for breakfast," said Marius, spinning on his heel, gesturing to the tight corridor that led to the study. "Please, Princess Valeria, if you'd just follow me—"

The ring slipped again; I had to clench my fist to stop it from falling to the floor. Ria caught the movement. Saw the glint of silver.

For the tiniest fraction of a second, she did not react. Then her lips pulled back into a sneer. "What the *fuck* is that?"

Marius fought to keep his face neutral. A muscle in his jaw ticked, and his eyelids fluttered. "That… is a ring. I—Look, Valeria, we should really sit down—"

I thought of the massive window in the study and shook my head. Not a safe place for an altercation. It was too easy to imagine someone falling—or being pushed—from it.

Marius wasn't looking at me, but Fallamor saw my reaction, and gently suggested, "Perhaps an evening in the great hall would be for the best."

"The great hall," Ria repeated, a dangerous edge to her voice. "So that everyone will know? I don't think so."

"Then at least the library," said Marius, clapping his hands together like he'd found the perfect solution. "I can ask the staff to vacate. It will be far more private."

"No." Valeria crossed her arms. A slippered foot tapped a frenzied beat against the floor. "No. You owe me an explanation, and you owe me my privacy. Tell me, right now, what the fuck you've done. Is she pregnant? Is that the problem?"

Marius glanced at me. Worry twisted his expression, like the thought hadn't even occurred to him. I quickly shook my head.

Valeria hissed through her teeth. "So you're not pregnant? Just a whore then? Just like our mother?"

A dagger to the gut would've hurt less. My eyes went wide. I felt the burn of tears, and willed them away. I could cry later. This moment was not about me or my feelings—not really. It was about the way I'd taken everything Ria was entitled to, and stomped on it. "Yes," I mumbled. "But I'm not a whore."

Desperate thoughts swirled through my head. I'd ruined my relationship with Ria. There was nothing I could say or do to earn her forgiveness. I could implore her every day, and she'd only scowl upon me.

I deserved every minute of her ire.

"Gods, you're pathetic," she snapped, throwing her hands in the air. "You're both pathetic. What the hell is that on your finger? Are you going to tell me you're married now?"

"Valeria, please calm down—" Marius started, moving toward her.

That was the wrong thing to say.

"You *are*!" she shrieked, stepping towards me. Both Fallamor and Toral followed after her, ready to intervene. "What the fuck, Talina? Were you going to tell me?"

"Yes," I said. Tears streamed down my face like twin waterfalls. "Yes, of course I was going to tell you! Ria, please—"

She scoffed, stalking past Marius to stand before me. He followed and caught her by the shoulder. "Don't," he said, voice low and gravelly.

"Don't tell me what to do with traitors!" Valeria snarled, whipping to face him. "You—you went so low! Seducing my own sister!"

"It wasn't like that," I protested, but my voice fell upon deaf ears. Valeria's ire was purely focused on Marius now, her glare sharp enough to lacerate.

"What did you offer her?" she demanded, turning to me, hands on her hips. "Money? Asylum? Your undying *love*?" She spat the last word like a mouthful of tar.

"All of the above," said Marius, arms crossed, scowl marring his face. "Because she *has* my undying love, and everything that comes with it."

Her answering screech was feral. "And *me*? What was wrong with me?"

"Nothing," said Marius, taking care to lower his arms and

speak gently, as if to a frightened child. My heart stuttered, equal parts charmed and alarmed by his tone, and all the ways Ria could react to it. "There is nothing wrong with you. I simply... don't love you."

"Please," I said, wiping the tears from my eyes. I caught a glimpse of the ring. Its silvery sheen had faded. The band had returned to old, yellowed bone. What was happening? "Ria, I—"

She glared at me. Agony and despair lurked beyond her anger. "Did you think about me at all when you did this? I've endured so much, and you've just thrown it all away! You absolute fucking bitch!"

Ria dove at me, tears and spit flying. My hands flew up to block her, but she slammed into me with such force that we crashed to the floor. I glimpsed the knife I'd dropped earlier, glinting in the starlight, but didn't dare reach for it. Ria might eventually forgive me for stealing her husband, but she would never let it go if I brandished a blade at her.

With a roar not unlike that of a bear, she tore at my hair. I tried to shove her off, but it was no good. In her fury, she was nothing but claws. Spittle landed on my cheek, hot and stinking of wine. A hand fisted in my dress. Fabric ripped—the sound split the room.

Shouts echoed around us. Someone tried to grab Ria, and she fought them off, screaming and writhing. A foot connected with my ankle. Pain erupted, and I tried to roll out from under her, but she howled and grappled for something behind me.

I heard rather than saw the knife as it plunged into me. A terrible squelch, followed by a lance of agony. I yelped and fought in earnest even as blood spread across my blouse. I caught Ria by the back of her gown and used the last of my strength to flip her over. Her back slammed against the floor. A loud grunt sliced through the high-pitched wheeze coming from somewhere behind me.

And then she was on her feet, a screaming flurry of hands and arms.

I looked up and saw Marius grappling with her. Marius, whose eyes were locked on me, on the blood blooming across my abdomen. He'd managed to pin Ria's arms to her sides, but she knew enough self-defense to maneuver her way out. Within seconds, she'd torn free of his grip.

Toral shouted something. I couldn't hear it over the ringing in my ears. Fallamor lunged.

Silver flashed in Ria's hand as the knife drove through Marius's ruffled collar and into the meat of his throat. A startled cry escaped him. He stumbled backward, hands flying to his neck.

A great cracking sound echoed through the room.

Fallamor tackled Ria to the ground, where she gasped and writhed beneath him. The knife skittered across the floor. He was quick to retrieve it.

For two horrible heartbeats, I waited for the blood to spray from Marius's wound.

But when he lowered his hands, I saw no telltale crimson stains—just the shattered pieces of the stone at his throat.

CHAPTER 33

"Fuck," Marius said, staring at his hands, then at his torn shirt, still littered with shards of stone. "Fuck."

"Marius," I cried. Shock thrummed through me. I tried to stand, and found that my legs were weak, shaking.

"Talina," he said, holding out a hand to stop me. "Stay there. Stay right there, alright? Everything is going to be—"

But he choked on his words. Gave a violent, full-bodied shudder, and then a confused blink. He swallowed. Tried again. "Everything—"

A violent cough. A strangled gurgle. Without warning, he dropped to his knees. Toral darted from Fallamor, still struggling with Ria, to kneel beside him. "Marius! What's wrong?"

Marius shuddered again, crashed onto the palms of his hands. "I—"

Vomit splashed against the floor. He stared down at it in dismay and groaned, arms and legs twitching.

"Shit," said Toral, with none of his usual sophistication. "Hey, hey, look at me—"

"My wife is bleeding out," said Marius through clenched teeth. "Please—"

He convulsed, hard enough that I feared he'd collapse into his own vomit.

"Did you poison him?" Fallamor demanded, twisting Ria's arm with such force that her entire torso lifted from the floor.

"N-no!" Ria whimpered. With great effort, I lifted my head, and saw that she, too, watched Marius in horror. "I swear!"

"Lies," sneered Fallamor, twisting harder. Ria cried out.

"Stop!" I said, but my voice was too weak. I felt the heat of my blood as it blossomed beneath my hands and knew without looking that my injury was serious. "You're hurting her!"

Marius dropped to the ground. A sound like the cry of a dying beast echoed across the room, high and anguished. He thrashed and shook, twisting this way and that as if trying to shed his own skin.

A red stain spread across his coat. Marius's back swelled like he'd suddenly developed a hump. The fabric stretched around it, drawing tighter as the bulge grew from the size of a fist to a sack of grain.

Toral ripped the dagger from his pocket—the same one he'd used to prick our fingers only a few minutes ago.

I sat up, and managed to prop myself against the altar. "Marius?"

His answering groan was low and guttural—I doubted he'd even heard me.

Marius twitching on the stone floor. At his side, Toral inhaled sharply, braced himself, and thrust the blade into Marius's spine.

"No!" I shouted. But I was too late.

There came a ripping sound. The back of the coat split open in a gush of scarlet and gore. Something red and flimsy spilled out, shining with blood. I blinked, but I couldn't make out what it was. Marius's exposed organs? That seemed impossible. But what else could it be?

"What the fuck?" said Fallamor, mouth agape.

Even Ria stopped struggling. Her arms fell limp at her sides as she let out a shocked gasp.

The pile of organs on Marius's back began to shift, slithering like snakes. One extended into something long and wet, and slapped against his back like a spare limb.

My scream nearly unhinged my jaw as it ripped from my lungs and up my throat, tearing into the world raw and forceful.

Toral snarled, and sliced the remainder of Marius's coat open.

I crawled over to them, one hand clamped to my belly. My blood was slippery against the marble floor. Exhausted, I dropped from my hand to my elbow.

The grotesque mass on Marius's back spasmed—like something with a heartbeat.

No sound escaped him. Had he fallen unconscious? I prayed that he had, that he wasn't awake to suffer through this.

"Is he dying?" I whispered, stalling to a halt mere paces away. My vision swam. I forced myself to stay conscious, to keep focused on the scene before me.

"No," growled Toral. His gaze flitted to my injury. "You're hurt."

"Yes," I said. Every breath I took was shallower than the last. "I think it's probably bad."

"Fuck," said Toral. His gaze lingered on Marius and his twitching organs, then moved to me. "I need you to lay on your back. Can you do that for me?"

"Listen to him, Talina," said Ria, her voice frantic, hoarse. I barely registered her words.

I didn't lay on my back. I just collapsed against the stone floor.

The mass at Marius's back shuddered again. A long, spider-like limb pulled free, and flopped against his spine, leaving behind a streak of blood and slime.

Then it unfurled like a roll of parchment, fanning out pale and green. The image of a half-moon was burned into it.

Fallamor's gasp cut the silence. "That's impossible."

I'd gone completely limp. Toral struggled to flip me over. The wound at my side pulsed and throbbed like its own entity.

"It's not impossible," he said grimly, heaving me onto my side, so that I had a better view of my fallen husband. "Just unlikely."

Another spider leg fell from Marius's back and began to slowly unravel.

It reminded me of a moth's wing, I thought, as Toral ripped the sleeve from his shirt. How funny. Was Marius a moth the entire time?

Everything was turning red. I blinked. My hand lay in front of my face. The ring was loose around my finger. The ruby-red sphere was gone, replaced by a smear of blood.

How strange, I thought, as the room faded around me. *How very strange.*

I WOKE in fits and bursts. Once, to Toral's frantic's face. The stars shimmered above him. I fell into that endless darkness and was gone.

I thought I heard Marius, his voice low and pleading, but when I blinked, it was only Valeria, whimpering and frightened. My throat ached. Voices rumbled in the distance like thunder. My vision went dark like a storm at sea, but not before I glimpsed a stone wall, and sheets white as stars.

Marius's snarling voice roused me. "Then stab me and be done with it!" I imagined the way he might throw his arms into the air, the way his sleeves would billow with the motion.

Stop inciting violence! I wanted to tell him. But I was already drifting down into darkness, and I didn't have the fortitude to fight against it.

When I woke properly, it was to my brother, Rowan, slumped in a chair, snoring lightly, his neck at an angle that couldn't be comfortable. Two or three days' beard growth scoured his jaw, and he smelled of sour whisky and sweat.

I wrinkled my nose. "Rowan?"

He jumped with such force that the chair scooted back and smacked against the wall. "Talina! You're awake!"

I wasn't entirely sure of that but didn't have the energy to contradict him. "Where 'm I?"

The room was just barely large enough for one bed, a cart loaded with potions and supplies, and two rickety chairs. Sunlight slipped between the drawn curtains, so bright that I had to look away.

"You're in the healer's ward," said Rowan. "Hold on a minute, I need to get help." With a final, worried glance in my direction, he slipped out the door.

I laid there thinking that this must be what a fish felt like in those moments before death—too weak to flop anymore, dry and parched like a wrung-out sheet, lying on the beach with an eye pointed toward the sun, unable to look away.

Outside my room, footsteps raced. The door opened. In peered a face I only faintly recognized—Iana the healer, I realized with a jolt—and my father, ruddy-faced and angry.

I tried to shrink away from him but couldn't coordinate my limbs. All my strength leaked away.

The door opened again, and Rowan squeezed inside, wringing his hands.

"Talina," said my father, approaching my bedside. His gait was slow and stiff. Tears glistened at the corners of his eyes. "Talina, I have never been so angry in my life." He sank into Rowan's empty chair while Iana bustled around me, first pressing a finger to my pulse, then pulling back the blankets to check my abdomen, covered by a great wad of bandages. *How odd.* "And I'm so glad you're awake."

Some of my fear trickled away. "I'm so sorry," I said, tearing up, too. "I made so many mistakes."

"I know," he said, leaning forward, wrapping his enormous arms around me in an awkward, crushing hug. "I know."

"Where's Ria?"

He shushed me. "Don't worry about her right now. She's fine."

"Where'd she go?" I slurred, on the verge of hysterical. I needed to see her. Needed actual proof that no one had harmed her.

"She's *fine*," he growled. "She's getting ready for her wedding."

"To Marius?!" I cried, sitting up. That was a mistake. My stomach ached horribly. I felt as if I'd been stabbed.

Which I had been, I realized. Memories came flooding back. Valeria screaming. The knife in my stomach. A flash of silver at Marius's throat. The entrails seeping from his back.

I began to weep, loud and unrepentant. Exhaustion crashed over me, and I couldn't think, couldn't calm down. All I could do was cry. I was in agony, with a skull full of cotton instead of brains, and Marius was injured, and...

"She's marrying Prince Gavin," said Rowan, hurrying to push me back onto the bed. His face hovered over mine, but he wasn't looking at me.

"Right," I mumbled between sobs. "I already married Marius. But—"

Father scowled. "That wasn't legally binding."

What? "No," I said, struggling to remember. "We signed a form. There were witnesses."

Satisfied that I wasn't going to sit up again, Rowan took a step back, skirting deftly around the healer to stand guard by the door.

"You acted without the approval of the court," said Father. Disdain flooded his voice, even as he fought to keep his expression guarded. "Two foreign representatives don't count."

Fallamor was a prince, but I wasn't sure if that meant much to my father.

Iana busied herself arranging bottles on the cart, looking like she'd rather be anywhere else. I couldn't blame her. I didn't want to be here, either.

"Where's Marius?"

"Never coming within a mile of you again," snapped Father, leaning back in his chair. It creaked beneath his weight.

Numbness spread from my stomach to the tips of my fingers.

"*Father*," said Rowan forcefully from his place by the door.

"He died?" I asked, searching Father's face for answers.

"No!" Rowan cried, shoulders taut, rage flashing in his eyes. "No, he's not dead. Father, this is just cruel. Don't do this to her."

"Do what?" I asked. My head throbbed. My eyes burned. My stomach felt strange, like the bandages had been wrapped to tightly around my waist.

Iana plucked a vial from the cart, uncorked it, and handed it to me. "Drink this," she said. When she looked at me, it was with sympathy. I wanted to flinch away from it.

"What is it?"

"It will dull the pain," she said, dipping her chin deeply enough to assure me that it would help in more way than one way.

I lifted the vial to my lips and drained it in one gulp. The liquid burned all the way down.

"Do not upset my patient," Iana told my father sternly. With a final nod to me, she disappeared from my bedside, and out the door, empty vial in hand.

Rowan glowered.

"Is Marius dead?" I asked again.

"No," said Father, closing his eyes. His beard trembled. "But he is no longer eligible for the throne. You are not to see him again."

"But I married him."

"That marriage was a sham, Talina. The ring didn't even accept it."

"Because I'm not royal," I said, nodding. The movement made my head ache. My brain rolled in my skull like a loose stone.

My mother had cheated after all. I expected to feel upset, but a strange sort of acceptance rolled over me, not unlike the lapping of waves against the shore on a still morning.

What would happen to me now? Would Father still claim me? Would I have anywhere to go but my mother's land? Could I stay in Tocchia?

"Because Marius isn't the prince of Tocchia," Rowan interrupted.

My jaw dropped. "That's preposterous."

"It should've been," said Father, shaking his head. "Can't believe they let something like that happen."

Wait, what? A thousand possibilities flashed through my mind, each more ridiculous than the last.

"Marius is the lost heir of Liridin," Rowan informed me, grim-faced.

I remembered the spider's leg protruding from Marius's back, and the way it unrolled like a banner. That was a wing, I realized. A soaking wet, bloody moth's wing.

Marius hadn't died. Hadn't somehow ejected his own organs out of his back. He'd just... grown wings.

I must have gone mad. Nobody just grew wings out of nowhere. That was impossible.

The room began to blur. A strange sort of calm settled over me, but I fought against it. I couldn't sleep until I knew what happened to Marius. Why he wasn't here with me right now, at my bedside, when he claimed to have loved me?

"The lost heir?" I breathed. "But he's the prince of Tocchia. How did that happen?"

Rowan started to answer me, but Father interrupted. "It's not important. Right now, I want you to rest, and stop worrying. We're due to return to Olmstead as soon as you're well enough to travel."

My eyelids were heavy. I wanted to protest, but the bed was soft enough that I felt like I'd been sucked into it.

Father continued talking, but I was lost to the world, dissolving like poison in a goblet.

CHAPTER 34

Three days passed with no word from Marius. Neither Toral nor Fallamor came to visit me. Not even Zellia, who I'd hoped might take pity on me. My only companions were Iana, Rowan, and my father. Occasionally, Rowan tried to slip me pieces of information, but Father outright forbade reports of Marius. As the days passed, and my condition improved, I grew fretful.

I'd *married* Marius. Loved him, longed for him, worried for him. How unbearably cruel to keep this from me. My resentment festered into something hostile and insurmountable, thorny and reeking of rot. It radiated from me, until I began to feel like the ring itself, baleful and ominous, borderline hateful.

My thoughts had serrated edges and deep shadows. My smile became a knife. Something verging on madness bubbled deep within me.

There is nothing worse than a long recovery, I decided. I had far too much time to muse on everything that brought me to this point. The healer gave me plenty of potions that left me fuzzy and lightheaded, eager to fall into the arms of unconsciousness, where no one had abandoned me or attacked me or stolen my husband away without explanation. But those fleeting hours of awareness devoured me like maggots at a wound, and they did not even have the decency to clear away the decay that built within.

On the third day, I lay propped up on pillows. The stone wall beside me was illuminated by sunlight, and I spent most of the morning mentally tracing the grooves in the rock, imagining them as some sort of long road. Eventually, this devolved into a full-fledged daydream about a group of travelers traveling along said road. Thus far, they crossed a raging river (a crack in the wall), traversed a great forest (a particularly textured rock), and fought off a gaggle of bandits (several smaller stones all clustered together).

By mid-afternoon, I was drowsing. Father would not visit for another few hours, and I hoped to while away the time unconscious.

The door swung open. I anticipated the healer, and hoped desperately for Marius, but it was Queen Tarra who stepped over the threshold, trailed by a gaggle of guards. Elegant as always, she wore her hair piled upon her head, held in place by combs glittering with sapphires. The hem of her emerald green skirt dragged across the floor.

Standing before the window, cast in afternoon light, she was absolutely stunning.

I sat up, torn between fear and awe and something else. Sentiment, perhaps? This might very well be one of the last times I saw her; certainly, the last time I would have the privilege of interacting with her.

"Princess Talina," she said, settling into the chair at my bedside. Guards flocked to her side. One waited at the foot of my bed, while the other blocked the door.

"Your Highness," I said, biting back tears. It wouldn't do to cry in front of the queen, although I really, really wanted to.

"I had my suspicions," said Queen Tarra. A fledgling smile

played at her lips. "You were just a bit too familiar with Princess Valeria. Not uncomfortable enough when you spoke to me."

I blinked in surprise, and she laughed.

"Oh, you were uncomfortable, but not in the way that servants are. Especially new ones. I admit, I was curious to see when you would admit your identity." An eyebrow quirked. "I'm not surprised Marius was the first to confirm it."

I squirmed beneath the bedsheet. Her gaze was unreadable. Was I to be punished? Or had she come to gloat at my incompetence?

I wouldn't blame her. I deserved it.

"He told me that you knew about the ring," said Queen Tarra. "Which all but confirmed my suspicions." She sighed. "I'm sorry things turned out the way they did." Golden, dangling earrings caught the light. I watched them instead of her face, hoping that she couldn't see the way my sorrow crushed me into nothing more than a shivering pile of dust.

"Thank you for your kindness," I said, my voice barely above a whisper.

"It is always regrettable when love ends," she said, voice gentle as the breeze coming through my window.

My stomach clenched. Queen Tarra adjusted one of her combs and looked me in the eye. "I've been told that you are woefully uninformed. I've taken it upon myself to ensure that you do not leave Tocchia with the wrong impression. First and foremost, I find it pertinent to inform you that the marriage between yourself and Prince Marius was legally binding under Tocchian law, despite what you may have been told. The problem here is that—" she swallowed, and a muscle in her throat quivered "—Marius is not, and was never, the Crown Prince of Tocchia. The legitimacy of your marriage must be determined now by Liridin, and their laws on such matters are complex. There is a possibility that your father will not be able to keep you away from Marius much longer, but that remains to be seen."

I struggled to comprehend what she was saying. "He's alive? He's alright?"

"Yes," said Queen Tarra. "But he isn't here anymore." Her lips parted to allow a deep inhale before she continued, "He did not go willingly. I'm sure you're familiar with his tenacity. His departure was... something to behold." She shook her head, as if trying to brush away the memory image of Marius, of his fury and anguish. I could imagine it now—the tilt of his chin, the tension in his muscles, fury in his eyes. The way he would have stalked forward, hair swinging behind him, hands clenched into fists, footsteps quick and sure. "Specifically, he did not want to leave you behind. I am fairly certain the entire palace heard *that* argument."

My poor heart could not take much more. "Why did he go?" I demanded. "If he didn't want to leave me, then he should've stayed."

Queen Tarra's laugh echoed throughout the tiny room, shrill and incredulous. I shrank beneath it, shoulders hunching. "My dear. The Sky Kingdom has waited a long time for their heir. If you think they are willing to wait any longer over a marriage whose validity they would surely challenge, you're very ignorant indeed."

"So they forced him to leave?"

"I'd like to say he went willingly," said Queen Tarra. "But that would be an exaggeration. He was more or less hauled away."

The thought of Marius being dragged out of the palace by guards was too much for me. Hot tears welled in my eyes, slid down my cheeks. "Did they hurt him?"

"I doubt it," said Queen Tarra. "He is still under the protection of Tocchia, at least for the time being. To do so would be a diplomatic insult, and cause for retribution."

I nodded. Tried to sort my feelings, and found them a jumble of half-formed thoughts and rose-tinted memories, all clawing to the forefront of my mind, competing for attention. "Your Highness?"

"Yes, Lady Talina?"

"Did you know he was Liridin's lost heir?"

This time, her answering laugh was booming, nearly deafening. I cringed away from it, fought the urge to cover my ears and hum until the sound died away.

"No," she gasped, dabbing at her cheeks with an embroidered kerchief. "No, and neither did my husband. We thought he was Hergarv's flesh and blood, not some changeling swapped by a desperate midwife." Again, that awful laugh. It burrowed under my skin and burned there. I wanted to rip it loose. "No, the Sky Kingdom would never have allowed him to stay here, under our care, if they had known." She shook her head.

Something slotted into place. My fingers fisted in the sheets. *This* was the reason the ring had reverted back to its original state. It wasn't because of me. It was because Marius had no claim to the Tocchian throne, even if he wasn't aware of it.

An unbearable gloom festered within me. Marius lost everything he knew and loved, quite possibly overnight. The family he grew up with was not his own. The kingdom he was destined to inherit belonged to someone else. The marriage he was willing to fight for was being challenged on a technicality. All of this to end up forced from the home he'd expected to keep throughout the rest of his days.

I couldn't imagine the devastation, the confusion.

"Do you know what happened?" I asked her, bracing for her horrible laugh.

But it never came.

"I suppose I may as well tell you." She brushed a strand of hair from her face. The motion sent her golden earrings spinning. "Word has already gotten out, and there are better sources than myself, but I've spoken King Amonrew, and I can see that he's committed to keeping you as blind as possible. Very well.

"Twenty-five years ago, Liridin was at war from within. The people were starving, unhappy, and King Ilea took no notice.

Queen Rimsa was pregnant at the time. She went into an early labor when the castle was stormed." A flippant wave of the hand. "I'm not shocked—I'm sure the experience was terribly traumatic. At any rate, the castle was sacked at the hands of angry peasants. King Ilea laid in hiding for many years. The people elected a new official, a man named Harus Damius, and when he earned their ire, Ilea emerged, and convinced the people to take him back."

"Did it work?" I couldn't imagine that it had, but why else would anyone in Liridin care about Marius's identity?

Queen Tarra shrugged. The motion was graceful, practiced. I was nearly as in awe of her shoulders as I was her story. "Eventually. People were slow to accept him, even after he killed Damius, and reclaimed his throne. Shortly after that, it was revealed that King Ilea's only heir was missing. Until then, it was widely assumed he was in hiding with his father. Ilea lived just long enough to regain favor among his subjects. When he perished, there was a mad hunt for the missing child." She sighed. "He was right here all along. Sitting beside us, eating our food, caring for our people, living as one of us."

"How did he get here?"

"The midwife." Tarra scowled. "Laney Mill. She confessed to all of it. As I mentioned earlier, Queen Rimsa went into an early labor. In an effort to keep her out of sight, the guards brought her into the dungeons, and that was where Marius was born." She shuddered. "I cannot imagine her terror and discomfort. The birth was not an easy one, and she died there, on the dungeon floor. Miss Mill took the infant, and ran."

I pictured Laney Mill, elderly and stern-faced. No wings graced her back. It would have been impossible to fly to safety. "How did she escape?"

Tarra hummed. "After the siege, she had no choice but to stow away in the back of a cart. I imagine she was well hidden. Better hidden than you were, at any rate."

I ignored the jab. "And she brought him here?"

"She took a position as a maid in the castle, shortly before the death of Queen Galira. The midwife was unavailable when Queen Galira delivered her child. Miss Mill stepped in. Both mother and child died that night. Mill claimed the dead baby as her own and replaced him with the living one."

"Why would she do that?" I frowned. As my injury improved, I felt more myself, finally able to think clearly. But none of this made sense. "Didn't Marius have wings already?"

"She went to great lengths to hide them. A court sorcerer agreed to help her keep the child's identity hidden for as long as possible. And she never gave him up. Not really. She graduated from midwife to nursemaid to nanny. It was through her efforts that Marius's true nature remained hidden." Queen Tarra sighed. "We thought Marius was simply sickly. We didn't realize that he was reacting to an endless barrage of spells. When the sorcerer suggested the talisman, it was like a beacon of hope. A chance for Marius to see adulthood."

"But the talisman just kept his wings hidden," I finished, recalling the stories Marius had told me. The way he suddenly stopped being ill. The talisman must've been gentler, but no less powerful than the spells that he'd been subjected to.

"Apparently, yes," said Queen Tarra. "I suppose she thought he'd have a better life if he grew up here, raised as a prince, rather than return to Liridin. They would've skewered him on sight."

I sometimes forgot the inherent danger of royalty. For all the power that kings and queens wielded, for all the ways they could punish and torment their subjects, they had to remember that their subjects could and would do the same to them. A thousand terrible rulers had died at the hands of their people, and many more would follow. If Marius had grown up in the Sky Kingdom, he would've been in incredible peril. Even if the midwife had raised him herself in Tocchia, she would've never been able to stray far from magic casters. Eventually, the danger might fade, and Marius's wings wouldn't draw so much attention, but that wasn't something I expected a loving parental figure to chance.

"I think she loved him rather dearly and thought this was his best chance at survival." The Queen shook her head in disgust. "Obviously, this kind of deception cannot be tolerated, and Miss Mill will face charges."

Obviously, I thought. The word rang hollow. How terrible that the woman Marius joked had raised him was probably going to die for the crime of having saved his life. But I understood how royal bloodlines were valued, how carefully heirs were conceived and raised. This kind of lie would not go unpunished, whatever the intent may be.

"How terrible," I said, staring down at my rumpled sheets, the outline of my legs and feet.

"I know," said Queen Tarra, contrite. "I can only imagine the position she was in. She and Marius would be killed on sight if the Sky Kingdom learned of a woman with a winged infant. It's something of a miracle that we only just now discovered the truth."

"What about the sorcerer? Will he be punished, too?"

Queen Tarra's lip curled. "He's been dead for five years. No, I'm afraid the gods have already judged him." She sighed, and examined her flawlessly buffed fingernails, searching for imperfections that didn't exist. "King Hergarv is in awful shock. He and the sorcerer were quite close for years, and he had no idea."

Of course no one told him. Why would King Hergarv expect the sorcerer to confess to something like this? But I bit my tongue. "That does sound appalling," I lied.

"It is, isn't it? But we are a court of lies and deceit, after all. Neither you nor Marius was who you claimed to be." She clucked her tongue. "Ordinarily, you would've been punished for this, but given the circumstances, and the potential for war with both Liridin *and* Olmstead, we've elected to grant you amnesty."

"Your Highness," I breathed, eyes going wide. "*Thank you.*"

She regarded me thoughtfully. "I think of Marius as my son. I will not see him harmed. Do not give me a reason to hurt you. Is that clear?"

"Yes, Your Highness." I could barely believe it. No trial. No fight for my life. Just clemency.

"Now," she said, rising from her chair. "Do rest and recover, and I'll see you at the wedding."

She disappeared in a flurry of skirts. The guards followed, armor clanging as they went.

CHAPTER 35

Ria was radiant. Dressed in a blue gown with silver embellishments, she positively glittered down the aisle. Banners of lilac and gray were hung about the garden. Tiny ornaments sparkled in the trees. The crests of both Olmstead and Tocchia were on full display, bracketing opposite ends of an altar absolutely overflowing with red roses. The court sorcerers ensured a sunny day, and I blinked furiously, unaccustomed to the bright light after more than a week of confinement.

This was my second venture outside in two days, and I was properly upright, seated in a chair, bulky bandages hidden beneath my dress. I sat beside the rest of my family, who were solemn and sullen as Ria passed us, sparkling in the sunlight.

I wanted to tell her that she was exquisite. That Prince Gavin would be lucky to have her. That I wished her nothing but unfettered joy when I saw the way she caught his eye and beamed. This was the sort of elation that Marius could never have brought her.

(Because he was outspoken and absurd and *mine*. I felt that claim, all the way to my bones. I was his, and he was mine, and we would be together, one way or another.)

But I couldn't say any of this, because I'd been forbidden from stepping within five paces of Valeria, and she was ordered not to talk to me under any circumstances.

That hurt worse than the stab wound. I desperately wanted to tell that I forgave her. That I understood I'd stolen her betrothed—her birthright—out from under her without even an apology. I would've understood if she'd stabbed me a second time.

I didn't regret a single moment with Marius. But I regretted the pain I caused Ria. The rift I'd created between us.

During the vows, tears formed in my eyes. They ran down my face for the rest of the ceremony. Truly, I was happy for Valeria. Excited for the life ahead of her. Another part of me could not stop thinking of the vows Marius and I had exchanged, so brief and perfunctory, brought about by necessity. I nearly sobbed when Ria and Gavin's blood pooled together within the ring.

For a few minutes, I wore that ring and dared to hope. Now it was in its rightful place on Valeria's finger, and I was alone, torn away from the man I thought I'd spend the rest of my life with. While I hoped for a reunion, I didn't dare anticipate one. Didn't let myself think about it for longer than a second or two, pushing the thought down before it could crush me.

There was a very real possibility I'd never see Marius again. That my father wouldn't let him near me. That I'd spend the rest of my days locked in my room.

I'd lost much of my value, after all. My injury was so severe that I was unlikely to bear a child in the future. And though I hadn't particularly wanted one, the diagnosis left me shaken. I hadn't expected to have the choice taken from me.

And my prospects with it.

Even Marius might not want me anymore. We'd hardly discussed family planning, but as a future king, he would be expected to produce an heir. Perhaps several.

I couldn't bear to think of it, so I tried to focus on the ceremony.

When Ria kissed Gavin, it was just a brief peck on the lips, but her grin betrayed her exuberance. I wondered if she'd been fucking Gavin the entire time I'd been with Marius.

I hoped not. The hypocrisy would eat away at me.

Fallamor found me afterwards, when the reception was underway. Couples swayed to the music. Others milled about the gardens, or sat, still eating. A plate rested in my lap, holding a tiny piece of cake. I'd not eaten a bite, too wary of the many eyes on me. It seemed everyone wanted to crane their neck for a glimpse of the wounded idiot who'd tried to marry Prince Marius in secret and failed.

As self-conscious as I was of my sallow skin and limp hair, I couldn't be upset with them. In their shoes, I'd have done the same.

"Princess Talina," Fallamor hissed, voice just as panicked as it had been that fateful night in the Star Room. "Fuck, are you alright? They wouldn't let me see you."

I looked into his wide, frantic eyes, and believed him. "I'm going to make a full recovery," I said, gesturing down at myself. "I'm sorry. For everything."

"What are you talking about?" he demanded. In his formal attire, he was every inch a prince of the sea. Silky blue fabric clung to him. Lace frothed like sea foam at his collar, his sleeves. Long, dark hair fell in waves down his back. A wreath of pearls and tiny starfish rested atop his head. "No, no. I should be apologizing. I watched you nearly die, and I-I did nothing."

"You restrained Valeria," I reminded him. "I appreciate it."

"She didn't *need* to be restrained," Fallamor groaned, tugging at a lock of his hair with so much force that I thought he might tear it out. "She was completely hysterical, watching you bleed out. Screamed at me to either help you, or let her up, so she could."

That warmed some small, frozen part of me. "It's alright. Listen, it was really chaotic. I appreciate your help."

He shook his head. "Marius was furious, and he was right to be."

Marius. I fixated on that name. For the first time in days, I found the strength to sit up straight. "Have you seen him? Is he all right?"

"He's… fine," said Fallamor, tilting his gaze skyward, then back to me. "A force to be reckoned with, as always. Angry beyond belief. He's not allowed to leave Liridin until after the coronation." He lowered his voice until it was just above a whisper, "He went on a rampage. Tried to break out of the palace. Had to be contained because he doesn't really know how to use the wings yet. I guess they thought he'd try to fly away."

"I can only imagine," I said, flinching at the mental image of Marius halfway out a window, determined to learn to fly in the way of baby birds, ignoring the guards tugging at his legs. "Are you in contact with him?"

Fallamor shook his head. "Not right now. Halin's been updating me, but he isn't here today."

Maybe, when I was well enough, I'd climb the Bridge of Glass and track down Marius myself. The palace was cast in Liridin's shadow, but not a single winged person was present for today's festivities. Their absence was impossible to overlook, and I shot more than one dirty look at the veil of mist high above.

I wouldn't get the chance to find Marius. I was too weak to walk up the bridge. Even if I somehow managed, Father would fight to have me brought back to Olmstead. I refused to bring war to Marius's doorstep.

Several glasses of wine later, I caught Valeria's eye and waved at her.

She waved back, hesitant and uncertain. Even the slightest acknowledgment eased the tension in my shoulders.

~

THOUGH I FOUGHT AND STRUGGLED, I was dragged from the palace, deposited weeping and thrashing into a carriage. From the tiny, latticed window, I watched the city fade behind me until the palace was a tiny pinprick atop a hill. The sea beyond it was white capped, and angry. Gulls circled in the sky, bright against the oncoming storm clouds.

Rowan held my hand, and napped intermittently. After a long while, I joined him.

Liridin was visible the longest. Through its veil of trees and mist, I could barely make out a distant tower, spiking into the clouds.

And then that, too, was gone, obscured by the clouds.

A sea of tall, green grasses surrounded us, swaying in the breeze. Beyond, the mountains awaited, craggy and forested, their peaks dusted with snow. The forest around us thickened, and I closed my eyes, drifting into darkness.

ACKNOWLEDGMENTS

A thousand thanks to my beta readers, my family, and friends.

ABOUT THE AUTHOR

Cressida Hawthorne lives near the Rocky Mountains. She has a Bachelor of the Arts in English, and loves stationery, reading, and sleeping.

www.ingramcontent.com/pod-product-compliance
Lightning Source LLC
Chambersburg PA
CBHW021954140825
30840CB00002B/42
9798349515194